Hal winced at Andrea's suggestion. Teaching her how to please a man would be like placing a loaded weapon in the hands of a martial arts expert. Too much overkill.

"Hal?" Andrea prompted. "Well?"

"Oh, what the hell. Since you're determined to experiment on somebody's body, it may as well be mine. Just go easy on the broken arm and tender ribs."

Andrea stretched out beside him. "Now then, Love Doctor, how *does* a woman go about turning a man on?"

"I've never been a clinical study before . . ."

"Good," she said, her forefinger tracing figure eights on his bare chest. "I like being your first at *something.*"

Hal threw her a wary glance. "You thinking of writing a sex manual?"

"Sure. I'm good at how-to. Remember how I tackled that plumbing leak under the sink?" She leaned over and whispered in his ear. "So . . . how do I excite a man?"

"You're doing a pretty good job already. Just remember the steps you followed with your plumbing."

Andrea burst out laughing. "Good sex is like good plumbing? Next I suppose you'll tell me that my hand is like a pipe wrench."

"Could be," Hal said. But he forgot to breathe when Andrea's thick, wavy hair cascaded across his chest and her lips skimmed his ribs. Impulsively, he reached out to return the pleasure of her touch . . .

ROMANCE FROM FERN MICHAELS

DEAR EMILY   (0-8217-4952-8, $5.99)

WISH LIST   (0-8217-5228-6, $6.99)

AND IN HARDCOVER:

VEGAS RICH   (1-57566-057-1, $25.00)

CRIMSON MOON

Carol Finch

Zebra Books
Kensington Publishing Corp.
http://www.zebrabooks.com

ZEBRA BOOKS are published by

Kensington Publishing Corp.
850 Third Avenue
New York, NY 10022

First Printing: March, 1997
10 9 8 7 6 5 4 3 2 1

Printed in the United States of America

This book is dedicated to my husband, Ed, and our children, Jill, Christie, Kurt, Jon, and Jeff, with much love.

One

A lily-livered, yellow-bellied, insecure cowboy who's afraid to take orders from a woman?

Hal Griffin fumed, remembering the long string of uncomplimentary remarks Andrea Fletcher had spewed into his answering machine. Well, they would see who was the biggest coward when he and Miss High-and-Mighty Fletcher were face-to-face.

Standing six-feet-three-inches in his stocking feet, weighing in at a solid two hundred and twenty pounds, Hal Griffin could look pretty damned intimidating. Smart-mouthed Andrea Fletcher would be cowering and apologizing all over herself—or else he wouldn't accept the job she had asked him to do. *Demanded* was more like it!

With a skill honed by driving from one side of the continent to the other—and back—a hundred times, Hal negotiated the narrow road that veered around the wooded hills southwest of Kanima Springs. The headlights of his extended cab pickup flared against the patched segment of guard railing. This, Hal speculated, had to be the scene of a previous auto accident. Somebody must have taken the short way down the cliff into the rock and timber ravines below. The thought prompted Hal to ease his booted foot off the accelerator.

The drive from Hal's home at Chulosa Ranch to

Fletcher Ranch was taking longer than he anticipated, but Hal had used the time wisely. He had formulated and rehearsed exactly what he intended to say to Andrea Fletcher.

Her most recent message on his answering machine had lit a fire under him. Irritated by that nuisance of a female who had been leaving him insulting messages all week, Hal had impulsively stalked to the barn to load his best two cow ponies in the stock trailer and zoomed off—much to his older brother's amusement.

There was just so much badgering a professional rodeo cowboy could tolerate. Hal had reached the end of his patience with the switchblade-tongued Andrea Fletcher!

He could visualize Little Miss Priss Fletcher—scraggly black hair, buck teeth, and a hooked nose large enough to hang his Stetson on. The word *ugly* probably wouldn't do that woman's looks—or disposition—justice.

There were three reasons why Hal had decided to round up Miss Priss's cattle. He wanted to get her off his *back* and his *answering machine*. Thirdly, his older brother, Nash, had gotten tangled up with that bombshell of a physical therapist and left Hal feeling like a fifth wheel at Chulosa Ranch.

Watching his tough, sensible older brother go mushy over Crista Delaney had been enough to curdle his stomach. He had left the ranch before he got sick . . .

Hal automatically reduced his speed when he encountered another winding curve.

All he wanted to do was concentrate on gearing up for the National Rodeo Finals in Las Vegas . . .

Just as soon as I deal with that nagging Fletcher woman and round up her livestock, Hal reminded himself sourly.

The fact that Hal was actually bending to that female's

will went against his grain. These days, Hal Griffin rarely gave a woman her way, unless it was to his advantage. He had learned at the tender age of twenty that half the women in this world were devious, cunning liars who were only interested in what a man had in his wallet.

The other half only wanted what he had in his pants.

That business about meaningful relationships and lasting commitments was a crock of crap that women dreamed up to their advantage. Hal Griffin was wise to the wiles of women, and Andrea Fletcher was about to discover just how cold, harsh, and candid he could be!

Hal had learned—the hard way—that love was an illusion and women weren't worth all that emotion. Twelve years ago, Hal had vowed never to involve his heart in his relationships with women. When he felt like getting laid he made double-damned certain the women who came and went from his bed understood—and practiced—the rules in Hal's Handbook.

And speaking of rules, Hal planned to lay down the law to Miss Priss Fletcher! If she wanted his cooperation and his expertise, then she could damned well show some respect!

"Damn that lily-livered, yellow-bellied, insecure cowboy!" Andrea Fletcher fumed as she stamped toward the supply room in the barn.

Angrily, she jerked open the cabinet doors, searching for the plumbing thingamabobs her father kept in case of emergencies.

"Refuses to take orders from a woman? The wimp!" Andrea scowled as she rummaged through the cabinet in search of a plastic sink pipe trap. Still grumbling, she scooped up a can of pipe joint compound and tucked the sink trap under her arm. Wheeling around, she made a beeline for the house.

Andrea had gone on cursing Hal Griffin long after she had spewed her latest message into his answering machine. He had become the target for all her aggravation—her scapegoat. And why not? The cocky creep hired himself out—in between rodeos—to other ranchers in need. Except to female ranchers. Andrea desperately needed help and Hal refused to cooperate!

To compound her frustration, Andrea had hurried through the kitchen on her way to her brother's high school football game and had found the floor flooded with water. That wasn't Hal Griffin's fault, but had he been here, rounding up the scattered cattle, he might have been able to lend a hand.

"Oh, right," Andrea smirked. "Like, Hal Almighty Griffin would stoop to replacing sink pipe traps. That hot-shot rodeo star probably thinks he's too good for menial chores."

Still muttering, Andrea opened the "How-To" manual that had belonged to her father. She peeled off her shirt and scrunched under the kitchen sink, then sputtered and hissed when globs of corroded sediment slapped her in the face.

"Damned plumbing . . . and damn Hal Almighty Griffin, too!" she added as she wrestled with the wrench—and pipe joints that refused to budge.

Why can't one thing go right these days? Andrea asked herself, squirming to find a comfortable position in the cramped space. The world was crowding in on her like the sides of this narrow cabinet. She was near the end of her tether. Anger, frustration, and grief battled to dominate her emotions. She wanted—needed—to get away from the mountain of responsibility at the ranch, to watch Jason play football, to forget her woes for a couple of hours. Instead, she was squirming under this blankety-blank sink, spewing oaths at a hot-dog rodeo cowboy who refused to help round up her cattle so she could get out of the financial scrape she was in.

"Face it, Fletcher," Andrea said to herself as she nudged the pipe wrench into place, then gave a mighty heave. "The only one you can depend on in this world is yourself. Men are virtually worthless. They're nuisances you have to tolerate but don't have to like. Did you really expect Hal Almighty Griffin to be any different?"

Andrea braced her booted feet on the wet floor, put muscle behind the pipe wrench, and cursed the plumbing—and Hal Griffin, once more for good measure.

The pickup's high-beam headlights spotlighted the arched gateway, indicating that Hal had reached his destination. In the darkness, two stone pillars rose like twin sentinels. Hal veered onto the gravel road lined with cedar trees. Grumbling about the Lord's miscalculation when He created women, he drove half a mile before he spotted the bunkhouse-style home on a ridge overlooking the horseshoe bend of Fire River.

Hal caught his breath as he cruised toward the spacious house and numerous outbuildings. Until now, he thought Chulosa Ranch, which sat upstream, boasted the most panoramic view of the river. But Fletcher Ranch rivaled Chulosa's breathtaking beauty with its rolling hills and winding river bed. Crimson moonlight shimmered across the river, making the water burn like liquid fire.

This truly was a spectacular sight. Too bad this impressive ranch belonged to a smart-mouthed female who harassed men via the answering machine.

Hal killed the engine and left the two horses stamping restlessly in the stock trailer. No doubt Popeye and Bowlegs were anxious to climb down. The highly-prized horses had spent as many hours on the nation's highways as Hal, traveling from one nameless rodeo and state fair to another, remaining in one place for only a few days at a time. Hal had no complaints about his grasshopper lifestyle. Traveling cured that restlessness that nagged at him.

Striding past the old, beat-up Ford pickup in the driveway, Hal approached the front porch. He broke stride when a feminine shriek erupted from the side door, then switched directions when he heard a "clank," followed by another yelp.

Frowning curiously, Hal strode across the elevated wooden deck to investigate.

"Thank goodness you finally got here," came a now-familiar voice. "Get in here and help me!"

Hal opened the door, unsure of what to expect . . . and froze in his tracks. A female body—partially concealed by the cabinet beneath the kitchen sink—was sprawled on the floor. The woman's scuffed cowboy boots were braced against the tiled floor covered with a layer of water. Long, shapely legs, wrapped in faded blue jeans, protruded from the cabinet.

Hal scrutinized the lower portion of Andrea Fletcher's body as she wriggled and squirmed into another awkward position. The shapely body didn't fit the image Hal had conjured up during his evening drive. Of course, he had yet to see the top portion or her face. The cabinet blocked his view.

"Hand me the other pipe wrench, Jason," Andrea demanded irritably. "The collar joint on this new trap pipe won't screw in properly. Damned, confounded thing! I've been wrestling with this for over an hour."

Hal wished the hell she would lie still. The twisting and arching of her well-shaped hips brought to mind the bump-and-grind associated with mating games.

When Andrea's grimy hand emerged from beneath the sink, Hal picked up the wrench and slapped it into her palm. Amused, he watched her squirm sideways. Her boot heel slid on the brick tile, causing her hip to slam against the corner of the cabinet. She yelped, assuring Hal that the little lady was losing the battle. Working on faulty pipes obviously wasn't Andrea Fletcher's forte, but Hal had to give her credit for tackling the task, even if she was lousy at it.

The razor-sharp retorts Hal had rehearsed during his evening drive deserted him as he watched Andrea dig in her boot heels—literally—and strain to loosen the faulty sink trap. Her body suddenly went rigid, her shapely derriere rising as she put all her strength behind her pipe wrench.

"Damn . . . it . . . to . . . hell!" she hissed in frustration.

"Want some help?" Hal asked as he squatted down on his haunches.

He wasn't sure, but it sounded as if Andrea had conked her head against the pipe. He supposed he shouldn't have deliberately startled her, but the sound of her snippy voice on his answering machine still echoed in his ears. He owed Andrea Fletcher one, Hal told himself self-righteously. If the dull thunk under the sink was anything to go by, he'd just received a measure of satisfaction.

And then Hal paid for his spiteful revenge tenfold.

When Andrea wiggled out from under the sink, her pipe wrench clutched in her fist like a lethal weapon, Hal's midnight-black eyes popped. Although she wasn't naked from the waist up, she was the next thing to it. The damp sports bra clung to her full breasts like a coat of paint. Though he had no intention of actually *liking* this fire-breathing female, she did have two redeeming features between her waist and her chin.

Andrea's bare shoulders were smeared with goo, but Hal hardly noticed. His gaze dropped to the pebbled peaks that teased him through the wet, white fabric. When he pried his gaze away, he found himself staring into the most unique eyes he'd ever seen. They were an extraordinary shade of orchid, surrounded by a fan of long, sooty lashes. Hal was vaguely aware of Andrea's hostile expression as his gaze shifted to the mane of wavy auburn hair drawn back in a ponytail.

Hal had encountered some beautiful women in his time, but Andrea Fletcher was one of Mother Nature's truly breathtaking creations.

There was nothing more appealing to a down-to-earth man like Hal Griffin than a woman who didn't try to conceal her flaws with synthetic wizardry. Far as Hal could tell, Andrea had no flaws to conceal.

Hal Griffin, the undisputed Cynic of Kanima Springs, Oklahoma, found himself face-to-face with the woman he disliked, sight unseen—and now he couldn't take his eyes off her. Damnation—why couldn't Andrea Fletcher have had the decency to look as repulsive as he had imagined?

Before Hal realized what he'd done, his hand skimmed Andrea's cheek to wipe away the grimy smudge. She recoiled and raised her wrench, prepared to pound him flat if he dared to make another move toward her.

"I thought you were Jason," she hissed.

"As you can plainly see, I'm not."

Self-consciously, Andrea grabbed the soiled flannel shirt she had been lying on while working beneath the sink. Her attempt to cover her breasts brought Hal's attention back to her chest. Watching him cautiously, Andrea scooted a safe distance away—the wrench raised defensively.

Generally speaking, Hal Griffin did not bring out the wariness in women. They usually flocked to him—uninvited—especially those glossy, rodeo-groupie types who followed cowboys back to motels. Andrea, however, continued to stare at him as if he were a serial rapist—and the pipe wrench was her only protection.

Hal decided to defuse the situation before that steel wrench put a permanent dent in his skull. "Take it easy, honey. I'm not going to hurt you. I'm Hal Griffin."

"I know who you are," Andrea muttered as she thrust her arm into her shirtsleeve. "I've seen your picture in *ProRodeo Sports News* plenty of times."

"Then stop looking at me as if I'm about to molest you. It's hardly my style."

Andrea didn't appear to be reassured. She remained in the corner, wedged between the wall and a cabinet.

Hal sighed impatiently and extended his hand. "Gimme the wrench, Fletcher. I'll fix your sink, even it wasn't part of the original job description."

She eyed him uncertainly. "I've heard of tooth fairies, but a plumbing fairy?"

"Rodeo cowboys are nobody's idea of fairies, lady," he said indignantly. "But I've done my time with leaky pipes, automotive breakdowns, and bad electrical connections. I've had to become a jack-of-all-trades to survive."

Those intriguing orchid-colored eyes roamed over him for a contemplative moment. The sassy female he had met over the phone wasn't as bold and self-assured when Hal was squatting down in her kitchen. For the life of him, Hal couldn't figure out why Andrea was so wary and mistrusting.

That was usually *his* role.

When Andrea didn't offer him the pipe wrench, Hal sprawled on the floor, then thrust his head under the sink. He knew no other way to reassure Andrea that he wasn't going to attack.

"You put the pipe collar on upside down," he reported. "Hand me the wrench . . . and grab a flashlight, will you, Fletcher?"

Hal extended his hand, relieved when cold steel dropped into his fingertips. Progress, he thought. At least Andrea hadn't whacked him in the most sensitive part of his anatomy.

A beam of light flared against the white plastic pipes above Hal's head. He glanced sideways when Andrea crawled under the cabinet with him to shine light on the problem.

"I'm no good at this sort of thing," she mumbled. "It's my first time."

"It shows." Hal fastened the wrench around the plastic collar, giving the tool a careful twist to keep from stripping the threads. Ever so slowly the collar came loose from the dangling trap. Hal scooted sideways, just in case the grimy water that had splattered on Andrea's face landed on his head. She shifted, careful not to let their bodies touch.

"I suppose I should apologize," she murmured.

Hal unscrewed the lopsided collar. "For what? For being a lousy plumber?"

"For calling you those awful names over the phone. I was . . . upset . . ."

"I never take orders from women if I can avoid it. I made you the exception."

"Why?"

"Because you ticked me off and I decided to drive down to see if you had the nerve to say those things to my face . . . Move the light over here."

Andrea did as he requested. "So, are you going to gather the cattle . . . or aren't you . . . ?"

When Andrea's voice faltered, Hal glanced at the bewitching face so close to his own. She swallowed audibly and then stared at the pipes above them. Her drastic mood swings baffled Hal. Pretty but peculiar, he decided as he turned his attention back to the plumbing.

Hal gave the plastic collar one last twist and it dropped into his hand. "I'll round up your cattle," he promised as he squirmed into a more comfortable position.

Her shoulders sagged in relief. "Thanks." She hesitated and then added, "I tried to do it myself and didn't have much luck. I've lived through two hellish weeks, but I shouldn't have taken my frustration out on you."

Hal didn't ask her to elaborate. He wasn't about to get involved. He would fix the leaky sink, gather the stray cattle, and hightail it to the next rodeo on the suicide circuit. Cut, dried, and simple. Beginning and end of story.

"Do you have any pipe joint compound?" Hal asked as he threaded the collar into proper position.

"Ready and waiting." Andrea squeezed the gooey substance onto her fingertips and then smeared it on the threads.

Hal stared at the young woman who didn't bat an eye at wrestling with leaky pipes or dirtying her fingers with adhesive. He noticed Andrea didn't fuss over her nails, either. Her hands didn't boast those glued-on acrylic nails coated with blood-red polish. She was natural, from the top of her auburn head to the toes of her boots.

Dismissing that thought, Hal threaded the collar onto the pipe—good and tight. "Turn on the faucet. Let's see if you have any leaks—"

"What the heck's going on here?" came a booming male voice that sent Andrea wiggling out from under the sink in nothing flat.

Hal contorted his bulky body to survey the pair of dusty leather boots and jean-clad legs that came into view.

"We're fixing the sink," Andrea announced as she grabbed the faucet. "How did the game go, Jason? I'm sorry I couldn't make it. Unexpected plumbing problems."

"Who's that?" Jason Fletcher demanded to know.

"Hal Griffin," Andrea announced.

Hal saw the dusty boots stagger back two paces. "Hal Griffin is fixing our sink?" he croaked. *"The* Hal Griffin? Wow!"

Hal was pleased to be receiving some measure of respect at Fletcher Ranch. Assured there were no more leaks, he slithered from the cabinet to appraise the athletic build of the teenager. Hal noticed the family resemblance immediately. The kid had the same shiny auburn hair, the same expression around the eyes and mouth. They were two peas from the same pod, he decided.

"Hal Griffin, this is my brother Jason," Andrea said hurriedly.

"I c-can't believe you r-really came," Jason stuttered, owl-eyed. "I'm sure Andi told you how much trouble we've had since Dad—"

"No, I haven't," she cut in quickly.

Hal glanced at Andrea and then frowned. He had no idea what was going on at Fletcher Ranch since Andrea hadn't volunteered any information. She was too busy steering clear of him, as if he were highly contagious.

Although Hal didn't see the headlights reflect off the kitchen window, he *did* hear the crunch of gravel that indicated another vehicle had arrived. Raucous laughter erupted, followed by the sound of shattering glass. A male voice boomed in the darkness, spouting crude obscenities.

A carload of obnoxious teenagers had arrived, Hal guessed. Obviously, the latest arrivals didn't hold Jason Fletcher in high regard—his name was attached to every foul, offensive oath.

To Hal's astonishment, Andrea barreled through the door like a one-woman army. Hal fell into step behind her, certain she was heading for more trouble than she could handle.

Jason charged after his crusading sister. "Andi, don't!"

When the driver of the old, souped-up car hurled a lead pipe through the back window of Jason's pickup, Andrea muttered her own curses. Head bowed and fists clenched, she stormed toward the carload of drunken hoodlums.

Hal grabbed Andrea by the nape of her flannel shirt, towing her to his side. "Steady, wildcat," he warned. "You're asking for trouble if you pick up the gauntlet."

"I can take care of myself," she insisted, flicking an angry glance at Jason's broken pickup window.

"Hiding behind your sister's skirts again, dickhead?" Garbage Mouth sneered at Jason.

Hal quickly assessed the situation. The four drunken teenagers had taken their dislike for Jason out on his truck, trying to start a fight. Hal figured he was the only one here who could put a stop to this without worrying about repercussions. After all, he would be gone in a couple of days. In the meantime, he was going to make a lasting impression on these sleazebags.

When Tony Braden hurled another insulting remark at Andrea, she girded herself for battle.

Hal clamped hold of her arm before Andrea stormed off. "Let me handle these creeps."

"It's not your problem, Griffin," Andrea snapped, glaring at the foul-mouthed driver. "That thug insulted me and my brother, not you."

Bobby Leonard stuck his head out the back seat window and jeered at Andrea. "Planning to get laid tonight, hot pants?"

"Probably a lousy lay, if you're kin to your prick of a brother," one of the other boys chimed in.

Howling with laughter, the boys tossed their empty longnecks in the gravel. Glass shattered everywhere.

Her body rigid with fury, Andrea shot past Hal. In one long stride Hal cut her off at the pass, then promptly deposited her beside her brother.

It was apparent these creeps weren't leaving until they had provoked a fight.

A menacing gleam in his eyes, Hal approached the sniggering teenagers.

"Who the hell are you?" Tony Braden slurred out.

Hal halted beside the car door and stared into each smirking face. "I'm your worst nightmare, punks."

Hal thrust out his leg, kicking the side mirror off the car.

"Hey, motherfu—" Tony Braden's breath lodged in his throat when Hal's hand shot through the open window. His fist clenched around Tony's neck, Hal jerked the toilet-mouthed teenager through the window and slammed his head against metal.

While Tony shrieked and cursed, Hal leaned down, his harsh words sizzling in the darkness. "If I ever catch you and your friends around here again, I won't stop with a bump on your thick skull. I'll beat the shit out of you. Do you understand me, punk?"

"Screw you, cowboy," Bobby Leonard snarled from the back seat.

The cocky teenager lost his nerve when Hal whipped open the door, grabbed him by his long, greasy locks, and jerked him from the car. Shrieking, Bobby wormed loose and dived back into the car. Before Hal could plunge in after him, Tony shifted gears and laid rubber.

Four middle fingers saluted Hal before beer-bottle missiles crashed against his stock trailer, causing the two horses inside to bolt sideways. Lewd curses filled the air as the hoodlums sped down the path and disappeared from sight.

Hal strode toward the trailer to calm the horses. He couldn't risk having the best cow ponies on the professional rodeo circuit injured before National Finals. These well-trained horses had carried him—and dozens of other cowboys—to success in the arena. Popeye and Bowlegs were galloping gold mines to the Griffin Brothers. Indeed, they had become prestigious members of the Griffin rodeo family.

Before Hal could latch the trailer door, Andrea was beside him, volunteering to help. To Hal's shocked surprise, he saw tears glistening in her eyes.

This courageous female who had been prepared to take on a carload of creeps had reduced herself to tears? The woman was a walking contradiction!

One moment Andrea had been raking Hal over hot coals on the answering machine, then she was shrinking away as if he were about to attack her. A few minutes later she ignored personal danger to protect her younger brother. And now she was in *tears?*

Talk about your emotional land mine, Hal thought, shaking his head in astonishment.

Very soon, he was going to sit Andrea down and demand to know what the hell was going on around this three-ring circus of a ranch. He wasn't going to get involved, of course, but he wouldn't mind being briefed on the facts.

"Be careful," Hal cautioned when Andrea made a grab for the horses' lead ropes. "These are high-spirited animals and they've already been startled."

Andrea paid him no heed. She stepped into the trailer to coax Bowlegs to the ground.

"Watch him," Hal warned. "Bowlegs hates loading and unloading. When he's ready to climb down—"

Bowlegs was ready sooner than anticipated. Holding true to form, the roan gelding spun himself around and clattered from the trailer like a discharging bullet, knocking Andrea into the metal rails. Hal leaped out of the way, his hand darting out to retrieve the trailing rope.

At Hal's request Nash Griffin had given this young roan gelding a crash course in rodeo training. Bowlegs had been on the circuit for a few weeks, but he was showing great promise and lightning-quick speed. Now, if only Hal could teach him to step down from trailers instead of bailing out!

Hurriedly, Hal tethered Bowlegs to the side of the trailer and then hopped inside to see Andrea cradling her left arm against her ribs. "You okay, Fletcher?"

Andrea nodded mutely. In the dim light Hal could see tears dribbling down her cheeks. Unsure of what to do about this puzzling enigma of a female, Hal turned his back on her and tapped Popeye on the rump. "Get out, Pops," he instructed the veteran cow pony. "Show that rookie how it's supposed to be done. Bowlegs is a slow learner."

With dignity and style, Popeye backed down from the trailer, as he had done a thousand times. Then the horse patiently waited to be led to a stall for his evening rations of grain and hay. Unlike the jittery Bowlegs, Popeye liked routine and behaved admirably.

Hal heard a muffled sniff inside the trailer. His probing gaze settled on the shapely silhouette. Feisty and spirited though Andrea Fletcher proved to be, she refused to meet Hal's stare. Still favoring the arm Bowlegs had unintentionally slammed into the metal railing, she stepped to the ground.

"Are you sure you're okay?" Hal asked as Andrea quickly turned away.

"I'm fine."

He heard her muffle another sniff. The woman had the kind of fierce pride that wouldn't quit. She was hurting, but she didn't want him to know it.

"You can stable the horses in our barn," Andrea offered, leading the way. "Jason will see to it that your livestock has plenty of hay and grain."

"I brought my own feed."

When Andrea spun abruptly to face him, Hal pulled up short. Fascinated, he stared at the misty tears that made her eyes sparkle.

"While you're at Fletcher Ranch, you and your horses will be well fed and well accommodated. It's the least I could do while you're gathering our cattle." Turning on her heels, Andrea motioned for Hal to follow her toward the old wooden barn that boasted a fresh coat of ranch-red paint with white trim.

Although Hal wasn't the kind of man who followed a woman anywhere—not after his first disastrous encounter with love—he broke Rule Number One by obediently following where Andrea Fletcher led . . .

Two

Andrea felt as unstable as Hal probably thought she was. Compared to that tough, ruggedly handsome rodeo dynamo, *she* was the wimp! But damn it, she had been holding onto her emotions by a thin thread for two weeks. She hadn't allowed herself the luxury of falling to pieces—she didn't have the time. There was too much to be done, too many responsibilities mounting up.

All Andrea held near and dear had been snatched away from her—or was about to be. She and her seventeen-year-old brother faced the threat of losing the ranch that had been in their family for generations.

Each time Andrea had encountered stumbling blocks on the ranch, she had placed another call to Hal's answering machine, letting him know—in precise terms—what she thought of his chauvinistic tendencies and lack of respect for women.

Andrea winced inwardly, remembering all the names she'd called that cowboy. God, she had really been on a roll!

Truth be known, Andrea hadn't expected that brawny hunk to show up at all. When he suddenly appeared in the kitchen, she couldn't believe her eyes! She had confronted more than six feet of rugged, dynamic male, wrapped in snug-fitting jeans that clung to muscular hips and horseman's thighs. A gold and silver rodeo trophy belt buckle was strapped around his waist and a black Stetson—with an encircling rattlesnake band—was pulled down low on his forehead, partially concealing a thick crop of raven hair.

Eyes as black and shiny as Oklahoma oil had zeroed in on Andrea. The unexpected impact of the man—and his sudden arrival—caused her to react the way she always did when a man startled her.

The unforgettable trauma she'd experienced during her first year of college had leaped at her like a living nightmare. Preservation instinct put the pipe wrench in her fist—and kept it there.

Damnation—Hal Griffin probably thought she belonged in a loony bin. Andrea's barely restrained emotions were whipping up and down like a runaway roller coaster, and Hal had been trapped in the backlash.

And then those hoodlums had arrived to fling their filthy remarks and damage personal property, reminding Andrea of the four young men from her tormented past. Flashbacks had caused her to strike out at the carload of creeps. But Hal Griffin had taken command of the situation, and now Andrea found herself indebted to that hard-edged cowboy.

Four years ago, she had vowed to avoid men, and she had kept her record clean . . . until she was forced to seek help from the devilishly attractive rodeo star. Hal Griffin had turned out to be more dynamic in person than he was in the pictures she'd seen in the newspapers and magazines. He was appealing, yet intimidating. Not at all the kind of man a leery woman wanted underfoot—unless it was absolutely necessary.

Under the circumstances, Hal Griffin was *very* necessary.

Massaging her throbbing arm, Andrea stepped inside the barn to hear Jason chattering incessantly, awestruck by the famed rodeo star. The boy had visions of trying his hand on the rodeo circuit, but Andrea, who was now her brother's sole guardian, had other plans for him.

When Jason completed his senior year in high school he would be college bound. That was what Robert and Maggie Fletcher had wanted for their son and daughter. Tragic circumstances had prevented Andrea from completing her education, but Jason would have his degree. That was the pact Andrea had made with herself two weeks ago.

No matter what, she would hold this ranch together, too—somehow. It was what her parents would have wanted and expected. The Fletchers may give out occasionally, but they never gave up—or at least that had been the family motto until Robert Fletcher . . .

A wild rush of grief swamped Andrea. She could feel emotion churning inside her, threatening to burst loose and embarrass her. Andrea had refused to break down completely, but she could feel herself tripping along the brink of self-control.

She swiped at her unwanted tears. She had to find a private place to fall apart—away from Jason and this invincible man who would probably ridicule her for bawling like an abandoned child. When the first sob wracked her body, causing pain to pound through her injured arm, Andrea wheeled around and dashed from the barn. She knew Hal would think she was half-crazy—if he didn't already, but if she didn't allow herself time for a good, hard cry, she would never return to normal.

Andrea headed for the tack room at a dead run.

* * *

Hal glanced over his shoulder when Andrea fled from the barn as if pursued by the hounds of hell. Although Jason was still rattling on nonstop about the imagined thrills of life on the rodeo circuit, Hal's gaze—and thoughts—were focused on the blur being swallowed up by the darkness.

Hal was thoroughly disgusted with himself for being so attuned to that female. Why the hell did he care what was bothering Andrea Fletcher? Why was he wondering why she had recoiled in the kitchen, expecting him to assault her? What woman in her right mind would hop into a trailer with two startled horses? And why in the world had she tried to take on that carload of drunken teenagers?

"How did you get started on the circuit?" Jason quizzed as he shut Bowlegs in the stall. "I'd love to rodeo. I've had plenty of practical experience on the ranch. But where do you learn the fine points of bronc riding and calf roping?"

Hal shook his head at Jason's youthful enthusiasm. The kid made him feel ancient. This young, athletic-looking teenager had stars in his eyes—and rocks in his head—if he thought rodeo was all glitz and glamour. What it was, was rough, unpredictable, and challenging.

Hal had ridden the suicide circuit for years on end, living in fleabag motels and surviving on junk food. He was still nursing cracked ribs—compliments of a wild bronc at some nameless rodeo in Texas. He'd felt the strain the moment he'd snaked out his arm to grab that foul-mouthed punk in the back seat of the car. Hal thought his wounds had healed—but not quite.

No, Jason Fletcher didn't have a clue about how gru-

eling life on the circuit could be. It was a dangerous profession—a man could grow old before his time during
one of those eternal eight-second rides on the back of a
devil bronc or monster bull.

There were times when Hal swore he was crazy for
putting himself through it all, but rodeo had become his
way of life. He was good at what he did, and saw no
reason to change professions, as long as his body could
withstand the abuse.

"The best way to learn the finer points of rodeo is by
attending camps like the ones my brother and I give in
the spring and fall. I'll put your name on the list if you
really want to give it a try," Hal offered as he strode toward
the barn door.

If nothing else, rodeo camp would cure Jason of his
fantasies. Reality hit damned hard when a man got bucked
off and landed on his ass in the dirt. It wouldn't take long
to determine how serious this kid was.

"Really? Wow!" Jason said excitedly. But then his
smile evaporated and his shoulders sagged. "We can't afford camp right now. Andi probably wouldn't let me go,
even if we could. She's become so protective lately that
she practically smothers me."

Hal recalled how Andrea had leaped to Jason's defense
earlier. No self-respecting teenage boy wanted his sister
doing battle for him.

Ambling outside, Hal scanned the shadows, wondering
where Andrea was. "I'll talk to your sister about letting
you come to camp next month."

"It wouldn't do any good," Jason mumbled. "Since Dad
died, Andi pinches every penny. She even sold her good
pickup and uses Dad's old farm truck so we'll have the

funds to pay funeral costs and living expenses. Andi would consider rodeo camp an extravagance."

Jason kicked at the tuft of grass beneath his feet. "All of a sudden Andi has visions of me becoming a rocket scientist or something. She's been trying to discourage me from playing college football because I might get hurt. And since those assholes from school started pestering me, Andi is worse than a mother hen. It's downright embarrassing the way she tries to protect me at the first sign of trouble."

"Let's start with that," Hal suggested as he led the way to Jason's truck to clean up the broken glass. "What have those creeps got against you?"

Jason opened the door of the truck, then sank down to gather shards of glass that had fallen on the seat. "It's because of Brenda, I guess."

"Brenda?" Hal smirked. He should've known there was a female involved.

"That's my new girlfriend," Jason explained. "A couple of weeks ago, Tony Braden started hitting on Brenda. When I saw him trying to put the make on her I told him to back off. He started pushing and shoving me around. I busted his lip and blackened his eye. Since then, Tony and his thugs have been following me around, trying to pick a fight."

"Your pal Tony obviously likes four-to-one odds," Hal commented.

Jason nodded his dark head as he gathered the glass. "Tonight was the first time those punks went as far as breaking windows and insulting Andi. Usually it's just drive-by wisecracks and obscene phone calls. It must have been the booze," he speculated. "They were waiting for me after tonight's football game at Hochukbi. I got lucky and threw a couple of touchdown passes. Tony can't stand to see me in the limelight. I guess he thinks my success makes him look even worse to Brenda."

"This girlfriend of yours," Hal said as he plucked up slivers of glass, "does she encourage fighting between you and Tony?"

Jason glanced up, startled. "No way! She detests the way Tony has been behaving. He's been trying to get her to go out with him since school started this year. It took me six months to work up the nerve to ask her out, and now I have to deal with that thug."

Hal smiled past his customary cynicism, remembering those difficult years of male rivals and dating rituals. He'd almost forgotten the innocence of youth.

"I suppose Brenda just happens to be the best-looking girl in school," Hal surmised.

Jason grinned broadly. "Kinda like my sister when she was in high school. Guys stumbled all over themselves to follow Andi through doors. They said she had a sexy walk."

Hal was sorry to say he had noticed the subtly alluring way Andrea's hips moved when she walked. The most frustrating thing was that it wasn't premeditated. It was natural—just like the rest of her. She had class, style, and the kind of sex appeal that drew a man's interest, even against his will.

"I guess what happened to Andi must be happening to Brenda," Jason said philosophically.

Hal jerked up his head. "What happened to your sister?"

"She must have gotten soured on men after they followed her around for so many years." Jason shrugged his broad shoulders and gathered more glass. "When Andi came home that first summer from college, she wouldn't have anything to do with men. You know, real standoffish. Dad used to say the boys were wearing out the floorboards of our deck, prowling around Andrea—and getting nowhere.

"Now she rarely smiles, refuses invitations for dates, and devotes herself to the ranch. She takes everything seriously these days."

Hal would dearly like to know what had caused Andrea to become so defensive. That scene with the wrench in the kitchen hinted at secrets that even Jason wasn't privy to. Something drastic must have happened, he decided.

Jason sighed deeply as he draped his arms over the steering wheel. A mist of unshed tears clouded his blue eyes while he stared through the windshield. "This has been one helluva year," he confided quietly.

Hal was beginning to feel like Dear Abby. Who would have thought this kid would want to pour his heart out to a beat-up, worn-out cynic of a cowboy? He didn't think he looked or behaved like anybody's compassionate confidant, but Jason seemed anxious to spill his soul. Hal settled himself more comfortably on the seat and listened, hoping to gain insight.

"Mom died in a car wreck about three months ago," Jason murmured shakily. "She was on her way home from the bank where she worked. According to the police report, she lost control on the rain-slickened road and . . ." His voice cracked. It was a moment before he could continue. "Mom went through the railing and plunged into the ravine."

Hal grimaced. He remembered seeing the patched guardrail—and speculating that someone had taken a fatal dive off the cliff. Sure enough, somebody had.

"It nearly killed Dad," Jason said brokenly. "He and Mom had been married twenty-seven years. They were inseparable, the very best of friends. Mom had stayed home with us until the year before Andi started college. Dad even drove into Hochukbi three days a week to meet Mom for lunch. If I ever get married, I hope I have what my parents shared."

Hal couldn't imagine that kind of devotion. His own father had been a rounder who ran off with another woman leaving his wife and brother-in-law to raise Hal and Nash. What Jason claimed about his parents sounded like a fairy tale to Hal.

Jason blinked back the tears and plunged on. "When Mom died, Andi insisted on quitting vet school—"

"Vet school?" Hal interrupted. "How old is your sister?" He had guessed her to be twenty-one—barely. Much too young for a jaded cowboy who was growing old before his time.

"She'll be twenty-five day after tomorrow," Jason informed him. "Dad wouldn't hear of Andi quitting school and coming back to help out at the ranch. He said Mom had taken the extra job in town to pay college expenses and ranch loans, and that Andi wasn't going to let Mom down. But when Dad died two weeks ago . . ."

When Jason broke down and cried, Hal felt oddly inadequate. He watched the boy's thick chest heave in an attempt to regain his composure.

From the sound of things, the Fletcher offspring had too much responsibility and grief bearing down on them. Hal regretted his harsh response to Andrea over the phone the first time she called to ask for his help. He had been injured and up to his ears in his own problems at the time. He had come down hard on Andrea, and she had retaliated.

Hal liked to think he would have been more accommodating if he had known the details of Andrea's problems, but she hadn't told him anything. She was too proud and stubborn. Hal had discovered that within minutes of making her acquaintance.

"Dad never missed one of my football games," Jason mumbled as he dabbed at his eyes with his shirtsleeve. "Even before I was starting quarterback he was always there. So was Mom. Even Andi came to the games when she could get away from college for the weekend. But two weeks ago—"

Hal kept his mouth shut and watched Jason lose all vestige of self-control. It was several minutes before the youngster resumed speaking in a quivering voice.

"Two weeks ago Dad didn't show up for the game. When I got home at midnight his truck was here, but he was nowhere to be found." Jason paused again, struggling with his emotions. "Saturday morning, I found him at the bottom of the cliff, facedown in Fire River."

Hal stifled a groan. The Fletchers had taken two devastating blows in less than four months. No wonder Andrea seemed so unstable. She and Jason had had their legs knocked out from under them.

"Everybody says Dad was so lost without Mom that he decided to end it all. But how could he leave us like that?" Jason's tormented gaze swung to Hal. "How could he do that when he must have known Andi would have to drop out of vet school to manage the ranch and find a way to pay the loans? Dad was the one who said Andi should stay in school, and yet he was the reason she had to quit. She only had one year of internship to go!"

Now Hal understood the full weight of the burdens on Andrea Fletcher. She had lost both parents and then been forced to take over the ranch and pay its outstanding loans. Not to mention riding herd over her seventeen-year-old brother, Hal added silently. Andrea and Jason had to feel as if the world had come crashing down on them. To complicate matters, Andrea hadn't been able to gather the cattle to pay off her loans.

Why didn't she put the place up for sale and cut her losses . . . ?

Even as Hal considered that alternative, he knew why Andrea was battling to keep the ranch. He and Nash had busted their butts to keep themselves afloat at Chulosa Ranch when financial tidal waves threatened to drown them. Until recently, they had been footing the medical bills for their best friend's rehabilitation. The rodeo accident that had crippled Levi Cooper, and put him in a wheelchair, had left the Griffin brothers with staggering expenses.

Hal had hustled two—sometimes three—rodeos a week. For extra cash, he hired himself out to ranchers. Nash had managed the ranch and trained horses for eager clients while Hal and Choctaw Jim were traveling the circuit. The mount money received from other cowboys during competition had contributed to the cash flow.

Hal and Nash had scratched and clawed, refusing to give up Chulosa, refusing to let Levi quit his physical therapy sessions. Yes, Hal understood what motivated Andrea, because he had been there himself.

"Now Andi has to sell calves to make payments or we'll lose our home," Jason murmured. "I offered to miss a couple of weeks of school to help round up cattle, but she wouldn't hear of it. She swears I'll get my high school degree—or else. If I miss any school, Andi says I have to be flat on my back in bed. Otherwise, I'm there before the tardy bell rings.

"But every time Andi gets some of our cattle penned in, they break loose and scatter to the four corners of the ranch. Some of them have camped out in the underbrush and trees along Fire River. Getting those crazy Brahmas out of the brush has been nearly impossible. That's why Andi called you. Amos Harden said you accomplished the nearly impossible for him last year when his cattle spooked and stampeded to kingdom come."

Hal well remembered the job with Amos. He'd had to rent a helicopter to scout the area and drive the spooked cattle from the thickets. Using skills he had perfected in military service, he had driven those crazy cattle three miles by helicopter before he could straddle a horse and herd them into a portable corral.

"Since tomorrow is Saturday, I can help with round-up," Jason offered as he eased off the seat, toting a paper cup filled with broken glass. "I guess I better get to bed before Andi starts nagging me about getting enough sleep to keep up with my studies, football practice, and farm chores."

Jason glanced back as Hal climbed down from the truck with a paper sack full of glass. "You can stay in Dad's room."

"I'll drive home and come back in the morning," Hal insisted.

"Andi won't hear of it. She doesn't like me to drive back and forth on these winding roads more than necessary, especially after Mom's accident. She won't want you to make the drive, either." Jason managed his first grin in a half hour. "I don't recommend arguing with Andi. It's usually a waste of breath."

"Your sister is a regular army drill sergeant, is she?" Hal smirked.

"These days she's hell on wheels," Jason confirmed. "Tough as a boot, too. I've broken down several times since Dad died, but not Andi. She won't let things get to her, no matter how bad it gets."

That's what Jason thought, but Hal knew better. He had seen the shiny tears Andrea valiantly fought to control. Maybe Jason didn't know Andrea was hurting, but Hal could tell she was standing on the crumbling edge. Her erratic behavior indicated she was close to losing her cool—if she hadn't already.

In fact, Hal suspected that somewhere on this ranch there was a woman who was pouring out her frustration and grief privately, refusing to let anyone know the full extent of her pain.

And speaking of pain, Andrea's left arm probably needed medical attention. She wouldn't have been cradling it against her ribs if she hadn't sustained a fierce blow when Bowlegs rammed into her.

After Jason strode into the house, Hal ambled around the side of the barn. Andrea had to be out here somewhere, raging at life's injustice, paradoxically pulling herself apart and trying to hold herself together.

Andrea was thoroughly ashamed of herself. She had spent the past half-hour in the corner of the tack room, curled up and crying her eyes out. Two weeks of keeping her chin up and her emotions down had taken its toll. Once she started crying, she cradled her injured arm against her belly and doubled over, heaving soul-wrenching sobs.

This may have been the perfect therapy to relieve pent-up

tension and misery, but Andrea was humiliated to find herself reduced to such a pathetic state. She had spent four years assuring herself that she wasn't like the majority of her gender—flighty, emotional creatures who spilled tears over little or nothing.

Damn it, through sheer will and determination she had fought her way out of—and back from—a traumatic ordeal at college. She had immersed herself in her studies, intent on becoming the best damned veterinarian—male or female—in these United States. One more year and she would have been out on her own, providing services for ranchers in the area where she had grown up. She had intended to be close at hand to care for her parents, after they had made so many personal sacrifices to pay her way through vet school.

And then disaster struck—not once but twice. When Andrea had received Jason's distressing call, she immediately dropped out of school and moved home. To add to her torment, she had pored over her father's financial files, discovering just how far he had gone into debt to pay her exorbitant fees.

Robert Fletcher had refused to let Andrea apply for government loans to meet the expenses. He had wanted his daughter to begin her career free from the debts most young vets faced. Yet, when Robert had flung himself off the rock ledge that overlooked the river, he had defeated his purpose.

How could her father have done such a thing, knowing what it would do to Andrea and Jason? Had he been fighting a deep depression after losing his wife? Had he put up a bold front for his children? And why hadn't Andrea been able to foresee this disaster? Because she was trying to recover from the loss of her mother and had been wrapped up in her own world and her own heartache.

Andrea drew a shaky breath and wailed aloud. Her father couldn't have taken his life and left his children to flounder. This had to be an awful nightmare. Any minute now, she was going to wake up and find her world exactly as she wanted it.

God, what terrible sin had she committed to deserve this?

Even during those weeks when her father had seemed to be on some mysterious crusade, noticeably preoccupied, Andrea hadn't realized he was showing symptoms of depression. If she had just paid more attention, if she had encouraged her father to confide in her, she might have been able to help him overcome his grief. Obviously, he had withdrawn into himself, privately making plans to end his misery.

Too bad Andrea hadn't decided to become a psychiatrist instead of a vet. Maybe she would have recognized her father's mental condition in time. Instead, she had returned home to make his funeral arrangements . . .

The thought had her wailing again, and not as quietly as she preferred. Andrea muttered curses at herself when Hal Griffin materialized at the door.

Great! This was all she needed—to be found blubbering. This cowboy had to think she was the wackiest female west of Fire River. She was proving to this hard-as-nails cynic that women were the incompetent pansies he believed them to be.

"Fletcher, I want to talk to you," Hal announced as he zigzagged around the saddles toward Andrea's secluded corner.

She bit back her tears, battling for composure. "Your

room is the first one on the left at the head of the stairs. You have a private bathroom. I'll serve breakfast at six-thirty," she told him in the most businesslike tone she could muster.

"That's not what I came in here to find out."

Andrea was afraid he was going to say that, but she wanted to dodge the issue until she had herself in hand. "I already put clean sheets on the bed, in case that's what bothering you."

Hal squatted down in front of her, his grin evident in the scant light. "You're as much of a hard ass as I am, Fletcher, I'll give you that. But there's no need for this. Your brother told me what's been going on around here. Jason needed to get a load off his chest. Obviously you do, too, or you wouldn't be holed up in here, flooding the tack room with tears."

Andrea groaned inwardly. She had let her brother down. While she was trying to carry the load, Jason had turned to a total stranger for support. Well, she wasn't about to make that mistake. Hal Griffin had agreed—reluctantly—to track down her missing livestock, but he was nobody's idea of a compassionate shoulder to cry on. She didn't want or need his sympathy. She needed no man. Men always had hidden agendas when it came to women, and Andrea would never allow herself to forget that.

"Wanna talk about it?" Hal prodded.

Andrea thrust out her chin. "No."

"You plan to cry until you're dehydrated?"

"Why should you care one way or the other? You're getting the going rate," she flung back.

When Hal reached out to draw her to her feet, Andrea instinctively shrank deeper into her corner. He frowned curiously when she cursed under her breath. Old habits died hard, didn't they? Hal didn't look as if he were about to attack her, and yet she avoided his touch.

"Why do you do that?" he asked after a moment.

"Do what?"

"Avoid me. Does it have something to do with your freshman year of college?"

"Good grief, Jason really did spill his guts during your male bonding session, didn't he?"

Or at least what little Jason knew about the situation, Andrea amended. No one knew the graphic details of the incident that had turned her against men. No one ever would, either. It was personal and private and Andrea refused to discuss it with anyone.

"Jason also told me all about Brenda and the hoodlums harassing him. He thinks Brenda is tired of being chased, just like you are.

"He's also having trouble dealing with so much tragedy," Hal went on to say. "The difference is that he chooses to cope with his grief by discussing it. You, on the other hand, crawl into corners and bleed in private. If it helps, I'm sorry I was so terse with you on the phone. If you had explained the situation—"

"You didn't give me much of a chance," she reminded him bitterly. "I had to listen to how some woman was ruining your big brother's life and coming between old friends. I also caught an earful about how you wouldn't take a job for a bossy, nagging woman, even if your life depended on it."

Hal grimaced. "Like I said, I was having a bad day."

"You weren't the only one, cowboy," Andrea muttered. "I had just finished totaling the cost of two funerals, the bank loan for cattle, and the payments for vet school. Dad had drained all his savings to keep our heads above water.

And unless I can sell the weaning calves by Monday morning, the bank will foreclose and I'll lose this ranch. This place has to be Jason's inheritance when he finishes college."

"What about *your* inheritance?" Hal quizzed her.

"I'll have the satisfaction of knowing I held it all together. It will be enough," Andrea assured him nobly.

"I told you I'd gather your cattle, so you don't have to worry about that."

"We will gather the cattle," she corrected him.

His thick brows flattened over glittering, black-diamond eyes. "Now hold on, Fletcher—"

"No, *you* hold on, Griffin. I'm not letting you do this job by yourself. I know my way around this ranch and, though I can't rope and ride as well as you, I intend to do my part. I have a vested interest in this round-up."

"I don't want to have to take care of you. If I wind up in the middle of a wild chase or stampede, I need to protect myself without worrying about you." he told her candidly.

His sharp tone brought Andrea to her feet when little else could have. Hal bounded up, standing toe-to-toe and eye-to-eye. "You don't have to take care of me—I can take care of myself!" she all but yelled.

"So you've told me. I'm still wondering which one of us you're trying to convince. And let me add that you need your head examined for thinking you could have taken on those four hoodlums. By the way, you're welcome—for lending a hand."

"You're getting no thanks from me for interfering in something that was none of your business," she flung back, wondering why she felt so blasted defensive. All this emotion was causing her to be ultrasensitive to everything he said and did.

"I'm making your problems my business because you can't handle them," Hal said bluntly. "Even if you had had a loaded shotgun this evening, you would have had trouble with those punks. Women usually do."

That really did it! Andrea wanted to claw that smirking smile off his handsome face and pluck those black eyes from their sockets. She struck out in angry impulse and found both of her arms pinned between her and the powerful expanse of Hal's chest. Andrea automatically battled for freedom, though it put excessive strain on her throbbing arm.

"Let me go!" she sputtered.

"Not until you calm down."

"I won't calm down until you let go!" she shouted.

"Fletcher . . ." His voice softened considerably. "Just relax, will you? I'm not going to hurt you."

For some unexplainable reason Andrea found herself relaxing in the confines of Hal's arms without feeling threatened. He wasn't crushing her to him or exerting his superior strength. He was simply defining the boundaries in which she could move. Surprisingly, Andrea took comfort from his presence, oddly lured by the tantalizing scent of this man who had ventured closer than she allowed other men to come. But could she trust him to be this close? She doubted it. Hal Griffin—even though she found comfort in his strength—was all man, every solid, muscled inch of him.

Andrea tilted her head back to survey the angular lines of Hal's bronzed face. "What are you expecting from me, Griffin?"

"A truce," Hal requested. "A simple truce. I'm not too keen on women and you obviously have little use for men. According to the message my brother relayed to me, you don't intend to seduce me and you plan to pay my wages in cold, hard cash."

Andrea felt a blush working its way up her neck to stain her cheeks. She had popped off to Nash Griffin over the phone earlier in the week and he had conveyed her comments to Hal—verbatim.

"I came down here to do this job, expecting no fringe benefits," he told her frankly. "Those were the original terms. No hanky-panky. That was the deal then and that's the deal now, Fletcher. Do you agree to your own terms or don't you?"

"Yes," she declared without hesitation.

"Good."

"Are you going to let me go now?"

He looked down at her and smiled wryly. "Nope, not until you're convinced that if I reach out to touch you at some point in the future it's not because I have ulterior motives."

"Are you always this straightforward, Griffin?" Andrea inquired.

"Generally. It saves time and trouble."

"Good, then let me be just as candid. I'm not interested in anything except a business relationship with you. I've sworn off men indefinitely."

"Then we have swearing in common," he retorted with a teasing smile.

"Then we can be friends and business acquaintances for the duration of your stay," Andrea decreed, though her voice wobbled a bit from the startling effects of being held in such strong but surprisingly gentle arms.

"Agreed."

"Now let me go," Andrea repeated.

Hal did as she requested. Andrea breathed easier when

she was allowed to put some distance between herself and this brawny cowboy. She hadn't wanted—or expected—to enjoy the feel of her body pressed familiarly to his, but she did.

That worried her. This wasn't the right time—or the right man. This handsome rodeo superstar could have his pick of females—they fawned all over him. He didn't want or need an emotional cripple like her. Besides, Hal wouldn't be around very long. He was a here-today-gone-tomorrow kind of man. That was the good news—and the bad. Andrea wasn't sure she actually trusted him not to take advantage if he had the chance. But to Hal's credit, he had twice proved he wouldn't pounce on her the way—

Andrea halted the forbidden thoughts and then glanced back to see Hal striding toward his truck to retrieve his duffel. "Lock the door on your way in the house," she requested as she ambled onto the deck.

"Sure thing, boss lady. I'll even mop the kitchen floor before I turn in."

Andrea pivoted, squinting into the shadows. When Hal moseyed toward her, she noticed the lopsided smile that tugged at his lips. *"Boss lady?* That sounds like a big concession, considering what you said to me on the phone."

When Hal stepped onto the wooden deck Andrea reflexively retreated into her own space.

"It *is* a concession. I am capable of making one on occasion and I expect you to make one of your own."

Andrea's brows knitted in wary consternation. "I thought we just made a deal."

"We did," Hal replied as he reached around her shoulder to open the door. "I would appreciate it if you would stop acting like a skittish colt when I come near you. I told you I'm not after your body, boss lady."

Andrea surged through the door. "I am sorry," she murmured. "But I don't know you well enough to trust you." *And you won't be around long enough to gain my trust,* she added silently.

"What did he do to you?" he asked out of the blue.

Andrea halted abruptly, her back as rigid as a steel fence post. She refused to meet Hal's curious stare, but his penetrating ebony eyes missed nothing. Eagle eyes, she found herself thinking. "My past is none of your business. Your job is to round up cattle. My lovelife—"

"Or lack thereof?" he inserted wickedly.

Andrea didn't dignify the question. "Sleep tight. I'll see you in the morning."

"Sleep as *up*tight as *you* are?" Hal chuckled as she walked away. "Thanks, but no thanks. I wouldn't be surprised to learn that you sleep standing up. And no, I do not plan to sneak into your room to find out for sure. You don't have to bother locking me out. I'm not the big bad wolf. That *used* to be my brother," he added with a grin. "Now Nash is as gentle and tame as a golden retriever. If that isn't proof of what a woman can do to one of the most invincible cowboys I've ever known, then I don't know what is. You'll never catch me fetching and heeling."

Even though she and Hal had called a truce, she doubted his ornery nature would prevent him from running off at the mouth. Judging by that long string of remarks, he was accustomed to having the last word.

Andrea grabbed the mop from the closet and thrust it at Hal—he'd offered, after all. He reflexively accepted the mop, realizing, too late, that mopping ranked right up there with fetching and heeling.

The faintest hint of a smile pursed Andrea's lips when

Hal muttered under his breath. She had managed to have the last word without opening her mouth—and he knew it.

On her way through the dining room Andrea heard Hal shove the deadbolt into place. The mop plopped against the floor, gliding back and forth to clean up the plumbing leak.

Andrea chuckled for the first time in two weeks.

Three

Hal woke up in the king-size bed, staring at the ceiling, trying to remember where the hell he was. Because of his extensive travels on the rodeo circuit it always took a moment to orient himself.

The smell of bacon and coffee floated through the room that had once belonged to Andrea's parents. Hal stretched leisurely, grimacing when the tug of ligaments around his tender ribs reminded him that he still wasn't in top form. But then, he mused, roping and riding with injuries had become a way of life. He had learned to overlook the pain.

He wondered how Andrea Fletcher was coping with her pain this morning.

As Hal donned his jeans, his thoughts drifted back to the previous night. When he'd heard Andrea's heart-wrenching sobs coming from the darkened tack room something squeezed around the region where his heart had once been. Truth was, Hal felt sorry for Andrea Fletcher. She was bearing a heavy burden on her proud shoulders. One emotional blow after another had sent her reeling.

According to Jason, something had happened during Andrea's freshman year at college that had spoiled her cheerful, carefree perspectives on life. Date rape? Gang rape? Hal wondered as he fastened himself into his shirt.

Was that why the jeering of drunken teenagers had set Andrea off last night? Had the incident unearthed unpleasant memories? Considering her volatile reactions to him and to the carload of hoodlums, he knew she was carrying excessive emotional baggage. He found himself wanting to draw Andrea from her self-imposed shell, to reassure her that all men weren't like the bastard who had shattered her innocent dreams . . .

Geezus! What the hell was he thinking! He was the most unlikely candidate to restore a woman's faith in men. He had been preaching the evils of women to his besotted brother for weeks. Helping Andrea recover would be like the blind stumbling over the blind!

Hal stuffed his stocking feet in his boots, then headed for the stairs. He had called a truce with Andrea—in order to get the job done. He was not going to sit here analyzing her! Even though he found himself physically attracted to that standoffish female, he was going to resist temptation. Besides, he had made a pact with Andrea: there would be no hanky-panky at Fletcher Ranch. If Hal Griffin was nothing else, he was a man of his word.

The phone rang just as he reached the bottom of the staircase. When he ambled into the kitchen, Andrea was pulling a tray of bacon from the microwave. The cordless phone was wedged between her left ear and shoulder. Hal noticed that she was still favoring her left arm, but it was the abrupt tone of her voice that drew his attention.

"I don't have time, Tuff," Andrea muttered into the phone.

Hal heard the muffled sound of a male voice responding to her comment.

"No." Her reply was decisive. The single, uncompromising syllable indicated Andrea had gotten very good at saying no—and meaning it. "If you drop by, chances are I won't be here. You're wasting your time and mine."

"Tuff," whoever he was, was still pleading his cause when Andrea replaced the receiver in its cradle. When she turned around, Hal was propped leisurely against the door-jamb, studying her astutely.

"Who's Tuff?" he inquired.

Andrea poured a cup of steaming coffee. "Do you like it black or doctored, Griffin?"

"Black. Who's Tuff?" he persisted.

Andrea handed him the coffee and then spun toward the stove to crack eggs into the skillet. "A high school boyfriend who doesn't seem to have anything better to do than look up old, uninterested girlfriends. Just because I'm back in town, I have the misfortune of being the new flavor of the month."

Hal smiled to himself as he cautiously sipped his coffee. He was making progress. Last night Andrea's reflexive response had been: None of your business. Now, she had opened her shell—just enough to let him peek in.

"How do you like your eggs, Griffin?"

"Sunny side up, just like my women," he popped off, and then wished he hadn't. Andrea glowered at him.

"Don't start with me. I just got through listening to Tuff tell me I was badly in need of his special brand of fun-and-games According to him, staring up at a sky full of stars while lying on my back will cure whatever ails me. Tuff seems to have forgotten why I refused to go out on more than three dates with him in high school."

"Because he had as many arms as an octopus and was horny as hell?" Hal speculated.

"Are you an authority on those subjects?" she tossed back with rapid-fire speed.

Hal nearly dropped his coffee cup when Andrea glanced over her shoulder and grinned wryly at him. Sunlight reflected off those hypnotic orchid eyes, blinding him. God, she was devastating when she broke loose with a smile. Hal was beginning to wish Andrea was as young as he first thought she was. He couldn't afford to be thinking the kind of erotic thoughts that sneaked up on him when he let his guard down.

No fooling around with the boss lady, Hal told himself fiercely. Andrea is off limits and don't you forget it.

Hal shrugged a broad shoulder and sipped his coffee. "I was a kid once," he answered belatedly.

"Hard to imagine."

"Horny comes with high school territory. Overcoming the rioting male hormones is a phase a man has to work his way through."

"How old does a man have to be before he figures out that a woman prefers to be a friend, companion, and equal partner and not just a sexual conquest?"

Hal swallowed a gulp of coffee when he realized Andrea's teasing banter had become a quest for information. She was still smiling, but the expression in her eyes indicated she really wanted to know. Too bad he didn't have a good answer.

Hell, all these years Hal had believed a *woman* was out to take whatever she could from a man—financial security or a fast roll in the sack. But Andrea was an altogether different kind of female. She didn't trust men any more than Hal trusted women. She had also been out of circulation so long that she didn't understand men.

"You're a lot of help," she grumbled when he declined to answer. "And here I thought I might make use of our truce by delving into the mysterious male mind."

"Why? So you can handle your younger brother competently? Or so you can avoid the prospective male admirers who have heard you're back in town?"

"Both."

Hal set his cup aside and strode over to butter the bread that popped from the toaster. "I don't think you need to worry about your brother turning into one of the Tuffs of the world. Jason has a good head on his shoulders when it comes to females. He seems to have respect for and protective instincts toward Brenda whoever-she-is. Jason said it took him months to work up the nerve to ask her out. I doubt he's going to blow his big chance with the girl of his dreams by wrestling her down on the seat of his pickup to do the horizontal two-step."

When Andrea blushed, Hal couldn't resist a grin. "Sorry, honey, I don't beat around bushes—unless I'm flushing contrary cattle from underbrush. I prefer to tell it like it is."

"So I've noticed."

"As for Jason's protective instincts, he probably told you why Tony Braden has been badgering him."

"Actually we've had so many other problems since I got home that Jason never went into detail. All I know is that he got into a scuffle with the bad boy of Hochukbi and Tony Braden turned vindictive."

"Knowing that kind of punk mentality, Tony will probably spread it around school that Jason's big sister was screwing around with me. After last night's incident, he'll probably try to retaliate any way he can."

"Damn," Andrea fumed as she flipped grease on Hal's sunny-side eggs. "Why do guys do that? I had to put up with gossip from jilted high school boyfriends years ago. Do I have to go through that again?"

"If you can't beat the rumors, play them to your advantage," Hal suggested.

Frowning, Andrea scooped the eggs onto the plate. "And how, great wizard, am I supposed to do that?"

"Next time Tuff calls, tell him you're seeing someone on a regular basis."

"Like who?"

"Me," Hal volunteered generously.

Andrea smirked. "That would only verify what Tony is probably saying. Besides that, I don't expect you to run interference for me. Getting you to work for a woman is already beyond the call of duty. I don't want to push my luck."

"It was just a thought," Hal said with a shrug. "Who knows? I might prefer protecting one woman to outrunning rodeo groupies who want to tie me down with my own pigging string."

Andrea stared at Hal for a long moment. "I can't figure you out, Griffin," she said, mentally retreating.

"Then we're a matched pair, Fletch. I can't figure you out, either."

For some reason, Andrea didn't seem capable of standing beside him for very long. It made him wonder if he had morning breath or something.

Andrea bent at the waist to check the biscuits in the oven, unintentionally granting Hal an unhindered view of her shapely bottom in trim-fitting jeans. He wasn't sure what annoyed him most—the fact that she wasn't trying to invite his interest, or that he was vividly aware of her when he didn't want to be.

Hal munched on the crispy bacon—cooked just the way he liked it—then nearly choked when Andrea rose to full stature and let loose with a whistle that could have raised the dead. "Jason! If you aren't down here in one minute, Griffin will have devoured all the bacon!"

"On my way, sis!" her brother called from upstairs.

"Next time you do that, I'd appreciate advance warning," Hal chuckled, tapping his ringing ear. "Where'd you learn to do that?"

Andrea's expression sobered in the space of a heartbeat. "Dad taught me. He did it every morning while Mom was fixing breakfast."

Hal had the good sense to eat his bacon in silence. For a few minutes he and Andrea had enjoyed the kind of casual camaraderie Hal wasn't accustomed to sharing with women. But the instant Andrea was reminded of her bitter losses—and the resulting responsibility—the sparkle in her eyes died and she withdrew into herself.

Jason's arrival distracted Andrea from her glum thoughts, Hal noted. The kid took the steps two at a time, tucking his shirt inside his jeans as he approached the kitchen.

Jason was right about his sister, Hal concluded. Andrea had taken the responsibility of caring for her brother very seriously. In a motherly tone she questioned Jason about his studies, his upcoming football schedule, and lectured him on the importance of treating Brenda Warner with respect.

When Jason rolled his eyes in exasperation, Hal swallowed a grin and kept his mouth shut. Andrea was definitely treating Jason like a child. If that pleading glance was any indication, Jason was silently begging Hal to come to his defense. When the time was right, Hal would point out to Andrea the importance of cutting Jason a little slack.

Damn, and he had vowed not to get involved! In the space of a day he had made the Fletchers' problems his own. Now, if only he could treat Andrea like the sister he never had, things would work out fine. Unfortunately, he had become too aware of her as a woman. When he'd held her in his arms last night . . .

"Let's get to work," Hal insisted the instant he polished off the last slice of bacon. "There's no sense wasting daylight when we have cattle to round up." *No sense thinking unproductive thoughts, either,* he added silently.

Mounted on Bowlegs, Hal trailed behind Andrea, who rode a high-stepping black quarter horse. Despite Andrea's objections—and she'd had plenty—Jason had accepted Hal's offer to ride Popeye. The boy was still beaming in delight over the fact that he was straddling the Pro Rodeo Roping Horse of the Year. Andrea, of course, insisted the Fletchers would feel beholden if Popeye was injured while rounding up their cattle. It wasn't until Hal sarcastically offered to sign Popeye's medical release form that Andrea backed off—begrudgingly.

In all his thirty-two years, Hal had never met a female so bound and determined to refuse his generosity. Most women leaped at his offers, though he doled them out sparingly. But then, Hal reminded himself again, Andrea Fletcher wasn't "most women" Damn, if she got any more independent she'd have to dress in the American flag!

"I had this herd of cattle penned up three days ago," Andrea reported, gesturing toward the broken corral in the pasture beside Fire River. "By the time I drove back with the truck and stock trailer, the cattle had knocked down the fence and scattered in all directions."

Hal frowned as he surveyed the hilly terrain to the west

and the thick canopy of trees to the east. "Do you usually have trouble with cougars or coyotes spooking your herds?"

"Occasionally," Jason spoke up. "We sighted a cougar crouched in a clump of trees last year, but I haven't seen one lately. The pack of coyotes that hunt by the river usually stick to their caves and don't give us much problem."

Hal reminded himself that *Hochukbi* was the Choctaw word for cavern. This area had been aptly named by his forefathers, he decided as he scanned the bluffs, noting the deep crevices in the rocks.

"There's part of our herd," Andrea indicated. "If we can drive them from the underbrush while Jason repairs the corral, one of us can ride back to bring the stock trailer."

"I'd rather help Hal," Jason quickly volunteered. "After all, I'm riding the best cow pony in the country."

Andrea threw her brother a meaningful glance. "I'm aware of that. But I don't intend to put Popeye in any situation that might leave him with a broken leg or gored flank."

Jason tried to object. "But Hal said—"

"Follow the boss lady's orders," Hal interrupted. "If *I* have to, so do *you*, kid."

Leaving Jason to his grumbling, Hal urged Bowlegs into a trot to keep pace with Andrea's long-legged horse.

"How old did you say Jason was?" Hal asked as he eased alongside Andrea.

"Seventeen."

"When do you plan to treat him like he's seventeen? When he's forty?"

Andrea's head snapped up, her long ponytail curling around her neck like a mink stole. "Is this one of those male things I don't understand?"

"Yep," Hal confirmed. "Your brother needs his own

space and your respect, not your mothering. Boys struggling to become men don't like to be coddled."

"I was trying to save wear and tear on your prize horse," Andrea said defensively.

Hal switched topics as fast as a good cutting horse changed direction. "Jason wants to come to the rodeo camp Nash and I are putting on next month."

"No, we can't afford it."

"I plan to waive the fee for Jason."

"The answer is still no. He's going to college to continue his education, not playing football or joining the rodeo team. Two rodeo dynamos in Kanima County are plenty. I doubt Jason will ever be as good as you and your brother are."

"Come on, Fletch, give the kid a break," Hal persisted. "Just because you won't let yourself have any fun doesn't mean Jason can't enjoy life."

Andrea's chin went airborne and her eyes flashed. "I like to have as much fun as the next person."

"Could've fooled me," Hal smirked caustically.

"Well, pardon me, but I have a lot of responsibility at the moment." Andrea scowled at him. "And furthermore, I think rodeo is unnecessarily dangerous to man and horse."

"What the hell do you think *this* is?" Hal countered, gesturing toward the cattle. "We could both be gored by a crazed bull or thrown from the saddle and trampled."

"This is business, a way of life," Andrea contended "Rodeo is an entertainment. It's like going to a movie."

"Like going to a mo—" Hal's words trailed off into an offended gasp. "Let me remind you of something, Fletcher. My *entertaining* skills are going to get your business back on its feet. And you can get the hell out of my way right now. I can handle this job by myself. In fact, I'd damned well prefer to work alone!"

With that, Hal gouged Bowlegs in the flank, sending the cow pony off in a gallop.

All those skills that usually impressed women didn't amount to a hill of beans where Andrea Fletcher was concerned. Not that Hal cared to impress that snippy female. She wanted quick results, did she? Fine and dandy. Hal would do—in a half hour—what would probably take High and Mighty Fletcher two hours to accomplish.

Entertainment? He fumed silently, and then asked himself why he was so damned sensitive to what Andrea-the-man-hater had to say.

Hal didn't have time to ponder that question. He had cattle to round up for his lady boss—his first and last lady boss, he promised himself. In two days—three at the most—he'd be outta here. And he wasn't coming back, either. Andrea Fletcher wasn't his problem. He would take the money and shake the dust from Fletcher Ranch off his boots.

Entertainment? Hell! She'd eat those words before he was through!

Andrea bit back a mischievous smile when Hal thundered off, his rugged face set in an outraged scowl. She swore a devilish imp had perched on her shoulder, provoking her to prick Hal's male pride. She knew she had insulted and belittled his profession, but he had it coming. His catty comments about her inability to let her hair down and have fun provoked her to retaliate.

It hurt to discover Hal considered her a fuddy-duddy. She had become surprisingly comfortable in his presence.

He didn't ply her with constant come-ons and smoldering glances. In fact, he had nicknamed her "Fletch" and treated her more like a sister than a prospective girlfriend. For some reason, that disappointed her.

Tossing the ridiculous thought aside, Andrea put her mount into a trot to circle the underbrush. She intended to block the cattle's retreat, in case the herd tried to charge off in the wrong direction.

In silent admiration Andrea watched Hal put his cow pony through the rigorous paces of circling, doubling back, and then chasing down contrary calves. There was no question as to Hal's exceptional skills. What had taken Andrea hours to accomplish earlier in the week he had managed to do in a matter of minutes. He had put half the herd in motion, cut off three cantankerous ringleaders that headed toward the river, and then flushed out several cows from their sanctuary in the trees.

When a stray calf bolted and veered toward a clump of cottonwoods, Hal and his horse moved in synchronized rhythm. Before the calf could plunge into the thicket, the loop of Hal's lariat settled neatly around the runaway's neck. Despite the calf's bellowing, he led it back to the herd like a puppy on a leash. Once the calf was moving in the right direction, Hal and Bowlegs eased alongside the animal. With experienced skill, Hal leaned away from his horse to loosen the noose, setting the calf free.

When he glanced in Andrea's direction, she tried to look nonchalant. Her dismissal put another scowl on Hal's face. Good, she thought, let him wonder what it would take to impress her. Served that cocky cowboy right for putting on a performance for her benefit.

The man already had Jason's undying admiration, Andrea reminded herself. He didn't need hers. As it was,

Jason had hurriedly nailed the fallen fence rails in place and was studying Hal's every move, as if the rodeo dynamo was a riding textbook. The boy idolized Hal Griffin, who also appeared to carry more clout with Jason than his own sister did. That rankled.

Nothing like being upstaged by a dadblasted hot-shot rodeo cowboy, Andrea thought sourly.

While she kept the partial herd moving toward the corral, Hal made sure the cantankerous rebels didn't pose more problems. Jason swung into the saddle to funnel the herd into single file. Without further mishap, the cattle were penned up, awaiting transport to the stockyards in Keota Flats.

Andrea sincerely hoped this first sale would appease the loan officer at National Bank in Hochukbi. Tom Gilmore had been calling every two days, reminding her that interest was past due on her father's loans.

Although Tom had apologized for adding to her woes, he kept insisting that he was running a bank, not a charity. It made Andrea wonder if the man had the slightest regard for his present—and previous—employees. Apparently not. Andrea's mother had worked for Tom for six years before her traffic fatality. He had to know the unexpected expenses had drained the Fletchers' cash flow. Obviously, Tom Gilmore didn't care. He simply wanted his money—now.

With Hal's help, Andrea would soon have all the weaning-age calves separated from the herd and sold at market price. Surely the presentation of the first cattle check would reassure Tom Gilmore that Andrea intended to honor the debt.

"Do you want me to ride back to the house and bring the trailer?" Jason asked his sister.

"I'll take care of it," Hal volunteered as he halted beside Andrea. He stretched out his hand, requesting the keys to the truck. "After all, I want to earn every cent of my wages. Wouldn't want to be caught hanging around the corral, twiddling my thumbs."

Andrea dropped the key in his callused palm without making physical contact. "Can you find your way back, via the gravel road?"

Hal's onyx eyes glittered. "I think I can handle it, boss lady. Do you think you can keep this herd penned up until I get back?"

"That depends on how well Jason patched the broken corral fence."

"I hammered enough spikes into the planks to set off a metal detector," Jason spoke up. "I *can* handle a hammer, sis."

Andrea noted Jason's resentful tone. Her gaze darted to Hal, who was looking much too smug for her taste.

"Told ya," Hal murmured. "Give him a little credit, honey."

"I'm not your honey," Andrea gritted out.

"You're right. You're more like a bee with its stinger poised and ready to strike. Lighten up on the kid and give me a break, Miss Attila."

Andrea glared at Hal. Not to be outdone, he glared back, then hightailed it toward the house. When he was out of earshot, Andrea glanced apologetically at her brother.

"I'm sorry if I came off sounding critical of you, Jase. I didn't mean to."

"Yeah, well, I'm not the same little boy you left behind when you went off to college."

Having made his point, Jason's gaze drifted to the veteran cowboy as he disappeared over the hill. "He's really something, isn't he, Andi? He's so good at handling a horse—he makes it look downright easy."

Andrea squirmed in her saddle. "Hal Griffin is something else, all right," she admitted reluctantly. "He told me you wanted to attend his rodeo camp. You know we can't spare money for that, don't you? And I don't want to take his charity. We'll be lucky if we can afford to hold this ranch together. When the cattle are sold, I'll have to find an outside job to pay the bills until we get back on our feet."

Jason's head dropped and he nodded somberly.

"Dad was in heavy financial debt, though he didn't say a word about it," Andrea murmured, staring into the distance, fighting tears. "That's partly because of me. He footed the bill for vet school so I wouldn't have to start my practice in debt. Without Mom's paycheck coming in, things deteriorated quickly."

"Maybe I should cancel my date with Brenda tonight," Jason mused aloud. "I was going to take her to a movie in Keota Flats."

"No, you're definitely going out," Andrea insisted, remembering what Hal had said about allowing Jason to have fun. "I'll see to it that you have spending money. Dad always said that if we were willing to help with the ranch chores he would provide cash for entertainment. You've been earning wages around here for years, and I don't want you to stop living."

Jason was silent for a moment. He sat in the saddle, stroking Popeye's muscular neck, a faraway look in his eyes. "Why do you think Dad did it, sis?" Jason asked quietly. "Do you think it might have had something to do with that scuffle he got into with Tom Gilmore?"

Andrea stared blankly at her brother. "What scuffle are you talking about?"

"I guess Dad didn't want to worry you while you were away at school. It was kind of embarrassing, after all."

"What the devil do you mean?" Andrea demanded impatiently.

"It was all over town."

"I haven't been in town long enough to hear the latest gossip," she reminded her brother.

"Dad was none too pleased when the bank demanded the interest payments so soon after Mom died. He didn't think much of Gilmore. Three days before Dad . . ." Jason paused momentarily and then forged ahead. "Dad went to the bank to talk to Gilmore about getting a loan extension. Nobody knows what was said in that conference, but Dad shoved Gilmore across his desk and put a knot on his head. Gilmore called Sheriff Featherstone and threatened to press charges if Dad came near him again."

Andrea groaned. Her father had obviously been in a state of depression and lashed out at the man he held personally accountable for his financial woes. She had caught herself thinking the same thing lately. No wonder Gilmore wouldn't cut the Fletchers much slack. Robert Fletcher had allowed his temper to get the better of him, and Tom Gilmore hadn't forgotten it.

"Did Dad say anything else about his conflict with Gilmore?

"Very little, except that if he had known what a creep Gilmore was, he wouldn't have let Mom work for him all those years. Later, I wondered if Gilmore had told Dad he was going to foreclose if he didn't make the interest payment. Dad was about to lose everything he had spent his life acquiring. He'd been moody and distracted the last two months, and he didn't confide in me very often. But I knew something was eating away at him."

Maggie Fletcher's death had torn Robert apart, Andrea speculated. In her opinion, her father hadn't been the same since he laid his beloved wife to rest. Andrea had hoped her father would recover after a reasonable amount of time. Instead, Robert Fletcher had taken the easy way out . . . and left her to pick up the pieces . . .

Andrea glanced up when she heard the pounding of hooves and saw Hal racing down the slope. Now what? she asked herself. She was beginning to think Murphy's Law applied at Fletcher Ranch. Damn! If things could possibly go wrong, they would!

Four

Hal swore foully as he raced toward the cattle corral beside the river. He had returned to the house to find Andrea's stock trailer tires slashed. Someone had also taken a baseball bat—or similar object—to his own horse trailer. It looked as though Tony Braden and his pals had returned. The sorry bastards.

"What's wrong?" Andrea questioned when Hal skidded his horse to a halt in front of her.

"We'll have to move the cattle down the road to reach the house. Somebody slit your trailer tires."

"It must have been Tony," Jason growled. "I'll beat the living shit out of him this time."

"Jason, watch your mouth," Andrea scolded. "I won't have you expelled from school because of that hoodlum."

"Then I'll beat the *tar* out of him *after* school hours," Jason vowed vindictively.

"You're not going to fight him at all," Andrea insisted. "If Tony was responsible, I'll take the matter up with his parents."

"Tony doesn't have anyone who cares about him. That's part of his problem. His dad is serving time in prison and his mother is rarely sober long enough to notice what Tony does."

Hal glanced toward the gravel road that formed the

western boundary to the pasture. "Do you have much traffic on this road?"

"Not usually," Andrea replied. "It hits a dead end at Possum Bend on the river, leaving only a dirt path and gate that borders on Amos Harden's property."

"There's been more traffic than usual this fall," Jason contradicted his sister. "Maybe it's hunters and fishermen, but I've seen several cars and trucks coming from this direction when I'm driving home from football practice."

Andrea frowned curiously. "What have you got in mind, Griffin?"

"It would be easier to trail the herd up the road, using bar ditches and fences, than herd them along the river and drive them through the three pasture gates between here and the house."

Andrea nodded. "The only trouble spot is that stretch of fence on Amos's side of the road. He hasn't had time to repair it after he moved his cattle to another pasture. I'll ride ahead and patch the fence as best I can before you and Jason drive the herd in my direction."

"Are you sure you don't want me to gather the strays we left beside the river first?" Hal questioned. "They'll be easier to move as a large group."

"The cattle we left behind are the most troublesome," Andrea informed him. "We'll round them up later. The young calves we have penned up should bring enough money to get Tom Gilmore off my back."

Hal swiveled in the saddle to stare at the twenty head of Brahma cows and calves that had escaped the round-up. They were scattered in the underbrush that lined the river. If he was boss, they wouldn't be left until another day.

But he wasn't the boss.

"They're your cattle, Fletch, but nothing good ever

comes from leaving the wildest members of a herd until last. We'll have to contend with twenty troublemakers."

Intense orchid eyes zeroed in on Hal. "If I don't have a check in Gilmore's hand Monday morning he'll foreclose. He might anyway. I don't want to risk losing this ranch because of twenty contrary cattle, when the others are penned and ready to move."

Hal cast the cantankerous strays one last glance. "You ought to consider selling those renegades to a rodeo stock company. They definitely have the right mentality—hardheaded, half crazy, and all mean disposition."

Andrea wasn't listening, Hal noted when he swiveled around in the saddle. She had already trotted off to open the pasture gate. The saddlebag of tools and the roll of wire Jason had carried behind him were now in Andrea's possession. She was on her way to patch the downed fence.

When she disappeared over the hill, Hal unlatched the corral gate. The herd trotted into the bar ditches, pausing to graze on chest-high Johnsongrass.

"Let them take their own sweet time," Hal instructed Jason. "They'll be more cooperative if we nudge them along while they graze instead of letting them run hell-for-leather."

Jason nodded, then reined toward the opposite bar ditch. Slowly but surely, Hal and his young protégé herded the cattle along the road.

A sense of impending doom settled in Hal's bones when he noticed the cloud of dust billowing over the gravel road. He could see Andrea working feverishly in the distance, trying to patch the fence so the cattle couldn't veer into Amos Harden's pasture.

When the old-model car topped the hill at high speed, Jason scowled. "That bastard."

The roar of bad mufflers and the swirl of dust startled the cattle. The herd bolted into a dead run, heading for the only escape route in sight—the patch of broken fence.

"Get out of the way!" Hal bellowed at the top of his lungs.

Even as he shouted to Andrea to dash to safety, he knew that damnfool, stubborn female wasn't about to let the cattle into Amos's pasture, not if she could help it. She stood squarely in the section of sagging fence and let loose with her famous loud whistle.

It was a waste of her breath. The roar of the approaching car and bawling of the cattle drowned her out. The terrified herd plunged into the bar ditch and stampeded toward Andrea. She managed to divert a few of the timid-hearted cows, but she was no match for ten wild-eyed steers and a fifteen-hundred pound bull that had set their sights on the plush pasture behind her.

Heart pounding, Hal gouged Bowlegs in the ribs and took off at full speed. He shot across the road, colliding with cattle, glaring at the driver of the car. He wanted to grab Tony and slap that cocky smirk off his face, but necessity demanded that he divert the frightened herd before Andrea was trampled.

Hal heard Andrea scream when she was sideswiped by the charging cattle. Cursing the air purple, he saw her go down in the tall grass. First chance he got, Hal was going to take Tony Braden apart with his bare hands for scaring the cattle and putting Andrea in harm's way.

"Andi!" Jason shrieked when he saw his sister disappear from sight. Spewing his own curses, Jason headed for the ditch to avoid the speeding car.

"Fuck off, Fletcher," Bobby Leonard jeered as the car blazed over the hill.

Hal was long past hurling spiteful expletives at the teenagers. His primary concern was getting to Andrea and rerouting the cattle that had yet to make it through the break in the fence. The fact that Andrea wasn't still screaming worried the hell out of Hal. She was sprawled somewhere in the grass, and he was afraid Bowlegs would trample her before sighting her.

"Fletch!" Hal yelled as he raced alongside the spooked cattle. "You okay?"

Andrea didn't reply. All he could hear was the alarmed cattle bawling as Hal forced the herd back to the road.

And then Hal saw Andrea lying facedown in the Johnsongrass. Wheeling around, he motioned to Jason to keep the herd moving toward the house.

"Is sis okay?" Jason questioned worriedly.

"I'm not sure yet." Hal swung to the ground and knelt. "Fletch? Can you hear me?" When Andrea didn't respond, he gently eased her onto her back.

Hal and his brother had been on hand a hundred times when cowboys were injured in the rodeo arena. Most of them usually managed to find their feet and walk away, Hal reassured himself. But then he remembered the tragic incident that had left Levi Cooper in a wheelchair. The man who had been like Hal and Nash's adopted brother had permanently lost the use of his legs . . .

The bleak thought tormented Hal as he stared into Andrea's pale face. He noticed the discolored knot swelling on her forehead, just above her hairline. She must have caught at least one hoof—probably more. He ran his hand along her right arm, checking for breaks. Methodically, he followed the same procedure on her abdomen and legs.

He breathed a sigh of relief when he had assured himself that Andrea was still in one piece—more or less.

What bothered Hal most was that he'd had to remind himself that he was giving a physical examination, not caressing those soft feminine contours concealed beneath baggy flannel. He cursed the man in him for making note of each curve as his hands drifted over Andrea. This wasn't the time—or the place!

A few moments later, a dull groan came from Andrea's lips. Her long, sooty lashes fluttered up. Hal wondered how many of him she was seeing. Her dazed gaze refused to focus directly on him.

"That was one of the stupidest stunts I've ever seen anybody pull," Hal growled, his concern turning into anger. "And believe me, I've seen a lot of stupid stunts in my time. Who the hell do you think you are, superwoman?"

Andrea grimaced at his booming voice and instinctively nestled in his encircling arms. "How many head of cattle ended up in Amos's pasture?" she wheezed.

"A dozen," Hal snapped at her. "You ought to know, since their hoofprints are all over your back. Can you move your legs?"

Disoriented, Andrea glanced down her torso and then drew her left leg upward. She flinched uncomfortably. "It still works, sort of."

"What about the right one?" Hal demanded as he cradled her against his chest.

Andrea bent her right knee. "Sore but functioning," she reported.

"Next question: Who are you?"

A faint smile pursed her lips. "Um . . . superwoman?"

Hal muttered under his breath. Being trampled sure hadn't knocked all the sass out of her. *He* was worried about her and *she* was cracking jokes. That was a switch. Damn, just what he needed—a death-defying, daredevil, boss-lady to drive him nuts!

"Let's try standing up and see how that works." Slowly, Hal came to his feet, drawing Andrea up beside him. She staggered and winced as her bones and muscles complained. When she grabbed at Hal's shoulder for additional support, he scooped her up in his arms, feeling his own mending ribs object to carrying extra weight. Nonetheless, he toted Andrea to her horse.

"When we get home, we're going to check you from stem to stern for bruises and sprains," Hal announced.

"I'm fine," Andrea insisted as he situated her on the saddle.

"Right. You're in splendid shape," he snorted sardonically. "You have a knot the size of an ostrich egg on your head and hoofprints on your back to prove it."

Andrea tentatively touched the bump on her noggin. "I must have butted heads with the bull."

"Hard to tell which one has the harder head," Hal remarked as he led her mount through the ditch. When Andrea attempted to grab the reins, Hal glowered at her. "Now what?"

"I'll round up the cattle in Amos's pasture and bring them home," Andrea volunteered, playing tug-of-war for control of her reins.

Hal grabbed the black gelding by the bridle and threw Andrea his most menacing glare. *"I'll* round up the rest of the cattle and *I'll* have your butt if you don't do what I tell you."

Andrea scowled down at him. "I thought we agreed that I was boss around here."

"You just got demoted. Anybody dumb enough to pose

as a human blockade against stampeding cattle hasn't got enough sense to hold the title of boss." Hal slapped the gelding on the rump, sending the horse on its way before Andrea could voice further objections.

"Women," Hal muttered as he stalked toward Bowlegs. No, he silently amended, *woman*. He had never encountered such a headstrong, determined woman, and he preferred not to run across another one in this lifetime. Though he begrudgingly admired Andrea's spunk and determination, she could be a real pain in the ass.

Hal stuffed his booted foot in the stirrup and swung onto Bowlegs' back. His gaze—like a magnet—followed Andrea over the hill and out of sight. Too bad that woman wasn't as easily put out of mind. He could only hope that when Andrea's livestock had been converted into cash to pay principal and interest on outstanding loans, she would let herself relax. Then he could stop worrying about her.

The sooner those cattle were hauled to Keota Flats the better, Hal decided as he trotted after the escapees that grazed in Amos's pasture. He was going to send an SOS to Nash and Uncle Jim. Hopefully, Nash could tear himself away from Crista Delaney long enough to lend a hand. These days, he was so distracted by that curly-headed physical therapist that he couldn't function properly.

Hal couldn't fathom being so obsessed by a woman. Even the one time he had foolishly fancied himself in love, he hadn't felt that possessive. He had only been outraged by Jenna Randall's betrayal—so much so that since then he had avoided lengthy relationships that might demand more than he would allow himself to give again . . .

Hal disregarded his meandering thoughts. Andrea was in a race against time and she needed all the help she could get. Hal would make sure she got it.

* * *

Blinking away the pain in her skull, Andrea trotted her horse toward the cattle pens beside the gargantuan old barn. She noted that her brother had succeeded in corralling the herd and had begun to sort the weaning calves from the cows.

Her fuzzy gaze drifted back to the aging wooden barn where she and Jason had played hide-and-seek and king of the mountain in the spacious hayloft. Before their time, Robert Fletcher and his brother, who had died in adolescence, had chased each other around the grain bins and stalls . . .

Andrea stared across the sloping pasture that stretched toward Shotgun Ridge and the river beyond. Giving up this ranch was inconceivable to her. Her roots were here, wrapped in hundreds of fond memories. Even when she was away at college, she had known she would come back one day. She *couldn't* sell her home, her heritage. It would be like selling a part of her own soul.

Tony Braden and his infuriating pranks weren't going to stop her from making the loan payment, either, Andrea promised herself. She was hauling the cattle to the stockyards if it was the last thing she did!

Andrea dismounted to help her brother separate the remaining calves. She and Jason had performed this task a hundred times, but always with their parents working alongside them. Maggie Fletcher had never complained about pitching in for round-ups. She had loved and enjoyed this ranch as much as Robert had.

"Doesn't feel quite right, does it?" Jason murmured as he closed the gate on the calves.

"No, it doesn't." Andrea squeezed her eyes shut, willing

her pounding headache to go away and grant her peace. "I could almost hear Dad's instructions while we were sorting cattle."

Jason propped his forearms on the fence rail and stared at the milling cattle. "I can't quite forgive Dad for what he did. I miss him . . . and Mom."

"Me, too." Her voice cracked as she fought for control. Andrea had allowed herself the luxury of falling to pieces the previous night. She'd had her cry. She couldn't afford another one until the cattle had been hauled off and the first payment had been delivered to the bank.

Thanks to Tony and his hoodlums, Andrea was fighting the clock. If the cattle weren't unloaded at the stockyards in Keota Flats by one o'clock this afternoon, the livestock wouldn't be allowed in the auction. The calves would bring a good price from feed lot owners who purchased cattle to fatten for sale to meat packers. All Andrea had to do was transport the cattle to auction—on four slashed tires.

Her thoughts trailed off when she saw the runaway cattle trotting obediently down the path to the barn. Hal was behind the herd, reining Bowlegs from one side to the other to discourage the livestock from reversing direction. The sight of him on horseback sent an unexpected tingle of pleasure through her. She shook herself from her admiring daze and hurried over to open the gate to the empty pen.

"Can you get the calves separated and locked in the loading chute without my help?" Hal questioned as he brought his horse to a halt beside Andrea.

Andrea surveyed Hal's tousled hair. From all indications he had been on a fast-paced chase through Amos's pasture. And then the thought of Hal cradling her in his powerful arms, after she'd been knocked down, assailed her. Strange, she didn't feel threatened by this particular man, intimidating though he most certainly could be. And yet, he could easily overpower her the same way—

Andrea squelched the forbidden memories from her nightmarish past. No, Hal Griffin wasn't like that, she reminded herself. He would never hurt or abuse her.

And anyway, Hal didn't find her physically appealing. If he had, he would have taken advantage last night in the tack room. But he hadn't. Instead, he had called a truce and assured her that he didn't expect sexual perks for doing his job.

"Are you still groggy, Fletch?" Hal questioned when Andrea continued to stare up at him.

She snapped to attention, her face flaming at the very idea of offering sexual favors to Hal Griffin. Where had that come from? Lord, the blow must have scrambled her brain!

"I'm just fine," Andrea assured him.

"You'd say that if you had one foot in the grave," he grumbled at her.

Andrea tilted her chin a notch higher. "Jase and I can sort the cattle if you need to leave."

"I'm not leaving until this job is completed," Hal informed her curtly. "But I am going to take time to call my uncle and brother and have them bring our livestock trailer down here to haul these cattle."

"No. Absolutely not!" Andrea objected. "I do not intend to be beholden to anyone besides you. I can barely afford you as it is."

"I won't charge extra for calling in my brother." Hal hitched his thumb toward the slashed trailer tires. "Nash and Choctaw Jim can be here before I can jack up the trailer, remove the rims, and drive to town to buy new tires. Besides, our trailer has a larger capacity. We can get the cattle to Keota Flats in two loads. It'll take four loads with your trailer. We don't have time for that."

Andrea let out her breath when Hal reined toward the house to use the phone. And *he* called *her* stubborn? Hal Griffin was accustomed to doing things his own way, and he wasn't worth a damn at taking no for an answer.

"Gawd," Jason gasped from behind her. "Does this mean I get to meet Nash Griffin, too? Imagine, *two* world champion rodeo stars right here on our ranch. Boy, would I love to—"

Andrea cut him off quickly. "Forget it, Jase. No rodeo camp. I want you to concentrate on college."

"I haven't even finished high school yet," he grumbled.

"You'll need to concentrate on that, too." Andrea gestured toward the cattle waiting to be separated. "You're welcome to steer-wrestle as many calves to the ground as you like, just so you get them in the loading chute."

"Damn, sis, you're no fun at all," Jason mumbled.

Andrea snapped her mouth shut before she loosed another sarcastic rejoinder. Hal had said something to that effect, she remembered. Well, maybe she was too pushy and overprotective to enjoy herself these days. But life couldn't—and wouldn't—be any fun at all if she had to sell Fletcher Ranch!

When the blaring phone interrupted what was fast becoming a steamy embrace, Nash Griffin reluctantly withdrew from his greatest temptation—and most precious treasure. He had originally intended to help himself to a few kisses to tide him over until evening, but one thing had led to another on the living room sofa at Chulosa Ranch. Nash had been savoring his dessert—Crista Delaney à la mode—while Bernie Bryant was preparing lunch.

Groping for the phone on the end table, Nash gathered Crista close. "Hello?"

While Crista tormented him with whispering kisses down the side of his neck, Nash tried to concentrate on the phone call.

"Nash? Are you okay? Your voice sounds funny."

"Crista is here for lunch," Nash said hoarsely.

"Sounds like you're *having* her for lunch," Hal scoffed.

Nash frowned at his brother's snide tone. "Are you still in the same grouchy mood you were in last night? And where the hell are you anyway?"

"At Fletcher ranch. I could use some help—if you can pry yourself loose," he said sarcastically. "Some teenage hoodlums slashed Andrea's trailer tires. The cattle have to be at the stockyards by one o'clock to make today's sale. I don't have time to hunt all over creation for replacement tires. Can you and Choctaw Jim haul these cattle to town?"

Nash checked his watch. "How long does it take to drive to Fletcher Ranch?"

"Thirty-five minutes on winding, two-lane roads. The cattle will be ready and waiting. You'll be doing this out of the kindness of your heart," Hal added hastily.

"I will?"

"You will," Hal confirmed. "The boss lady is short on time and money."

"The *boss lady?*" Nash laughed at the very thought of his cynical brother calling any woman *boss lady.* "Since when did you care if a woman found herself in trouble?

I thought you tore off last night to tell Andrea Fletcher where she could go and what she could do with herself when she got there."

"Knock it off, Nash," Hal scowled into the phone. "I can play Good Samaritan if I feel like it. The lady and her kid brother have fallen on hard times."

"And you're suddenly so sympathetic that you're taking on charity cases?" Nash snickered. "Gawd, I don't believe what I'm hearing."

"Shut up and bring the stock trailer," Hal growled. "We're on a tight time schedule."

The line went dead and Nash frowned at the dial tone.

"Can I come along?" Crista asked as she eased off the couch.

"Lady, don't ever think I'll let you out of my sight again, unless I absolutely have no choice." Nash hooked his arm around Crista's trim waist. "It's going to take me a while to forget how close I came to losing you—permanently."

Crista reached up on tiptoe to press one last kiss to Nash's lips. "I'll tell Bernie to put lunch on the back burner while you track down your uncle."

Nash watched Crista walk away, his smoldering gaze flowing from the long, curly, blond hair that trailed down her back to the shapely curve of her hips. Nash wondered if he should break the news to Hal that Crista had accepted his marriage proposal. Considering the foul mood Hal was in, Nash wasn't sure he should risk making the announcement. Since Hal didn't believe in love, and didn't trust women in general, he wouldn't be thrilled at the prospect of acquiring a sister-in-law.

Nash grabbed his hat and strode out the front door. It was mighty interesting that his brother was bending over backward to accommodate the very woman he had intended to rip to shreds with his rapier tongue. Could it be that the jaded Hal Griffin had met his match? Nash couldn't wait to meet the female who had left tongue-lashing messages on the answering machine and had somehow managed to persuade Hal to join her crusade to save her ranch.

This should be real interesting, Nash thought as he and his uncle hitched the stock trailer to the four-wheel-drive pickup.

Hal slammed down the phone and then reversed direction. His next order of business was to haul Andrea into the house and give her a thorough going-over. He suspected she was going to be stiff and sore the minute she allowed herself to sit down.

What Andrea needed was a warm, relaxing bath to soothe her aches and pains, but getting her to agree to that would be worse than pulling teeth. She was still running high on adrenaline, not to mention the aftereffects of her close call.

"Fletch, you're officially off duty," Hal announced as he strode toward the corral. "Nash and Choctaw Jim are on their way. Go soak in the tub."

"I'm fi—"

"You are *not* fine," he bit off. "Your forehead is turning purple and you're still favoring your left arm. Stop trying to hide the fact that you're hurt."

When Hal halted beside Andrea, she regarded him with an annoyed frown. He didn't give a damn how irritated she was with his high-handed demands. This was a *coup d'état.* He was taking command of the field, and she would just have to deal with it.

"I'll fix lunch while—"

"Jason can fix lunch," Hal interrupted. "We'll have sandwiches. Go soak your head, Fletcher."

"Remind me to remind you who's running the show around here, as soon as the cattle are on their way to the stockyards and I've had the bath you're hell-bent on me having," Andrea huffed. "I don't like domineering men who—"

When her voice trailed off and she wobbled unsteadily on her boot heels, Hal offered a supporting arm. "Hold down the fort until I get back, Jason," he called on his way to the house.

"Right, boss."

Woozy though she was, Andrea flashed her brother a glare that branded him a traitor. "I don't like being treated like a child," she hissed as Hal shepherded her onto the deck.

"And I don't like women swooning at my feet," he countered as he shoveled her through the kitchen door. "Until I've given you a clean bill of health, you're going to take it easy. And if you don't like it that's just too damned bad!"

Five

Without wasting a moment, Hal had unfastened the sleeve of her flannel shirt to examine her left arm. "Geezus, Fletch!" he hooted. "Your elbow is swollen up like a football."

"One of the cows must have stepped on it," Andrea murmured. "It wasn't quite so swollen this morning."

"I thought you were studying to be a vet," he muttered at her.

She frowned quizzically. "What's that got to do with anything?"

"You ought to know that muscles and joints need medical attention when they get banged up." God, listen to him! He had toughed it out in the rodeo arena for years, so who was he to lecture her?

Andrea avoided his piercing stare. "I had things to do this morning besides sit around whining about an injured arm."

Hal cupped her chin in his hand, forcing her to meet his unblinking gaze. When he peered into her eyes, he felt his resolve deteriorating. If ever a woman needed to be kissed and held and assured that everything would be all right, it was Andrea Fletcher. And if ever a man needed to kiss a woman who'd scared the pants off him when she tried to stop a stampede—single-handed—it was Hal Griffin.

Truth be told, he had wanted to test his reaction to Andrea last night, but he had settled for holding her in his arms in the tack room.

Just a simple kiss, Hal told himself. Just an experimental touch of lips. What could it possibly hurt? It would serve to assure this cautious lady that he wasn't like the mysterious man from her past who had made her so mistrusting.

When Andrea looked at him uncertainly, Hal felt himself lured ever closer. His gaze dropped to her soft, lush mouth and he groaned inwardly at the fierce throb of desire that assaulted him. Almighty damn, you'd think he was starving to death for a taste of this woman. What the hell was wrong with him?

"Griffin?" His name was a wary question.

"Don't panic," Hal murmured, his voice a little on the raspy side. He tilted his head slightly, lowering it inch by inch, watching Andrea watch him like a skittish colt. "I just want to kiss you."

"Why?"

Now that was a first, Hal thought. No woman had ever asked him *why*. Leave it to Andrea Fletcher.

"Why? To make it better, of course," he replied, smiling as he erased the small space between them.

"It isn't my mouth that's injured," she said, her voice an octave higher than usual.

When Andrea tried to step back apace, Hal's arm slid around her waist, encircling without restraining her. Ever so gently, he pressed his lips to the purple knot on her hairline. Hal marveled at the satisfaction he derived in doing the *chasing* for a change. Until now, he hadn't realized how tired he'd grown of aggressive women. Andrea wasn't the least bit aggressive. She had to be tamed, wooed, and reassured before a man could win her trust or affection.

"Does your head feel better?" Hal smiled to himself when he heard her breath catch, felt her pulse hammering against his chest.

"No," she said a little too breathlessly.

Hal lifted her left arm. His lips and tongue glided over her swollen elbow. "Does this help?"

Andrea's lips parted, as if she intended to reply—and then couldn't trust herself to speak. She simply stared at him.

"What about this . . . ?"

His lips slanted over hers in the slightest breath of a kiss. Hal, unaccustomed to proceeding at a snail's pace in romantic encounters, discovered he'd been deprived of simple but satisfying pleasures. He wasn't just kissing Andrea as an obligatory preliminary to intimacy, he was *tasting* her, *experiencing* her.

The instant Hal got up close and personal, Andrea instinctively retreated. But when he didn't threaten to devour her, she relaxed against him, letting him hold her. With her supple body molded to his, he could feel each and every response.

Hal's right arm slowly contracted, pressing her closer. His left hand glided behind her neck, tilting her auburn head back to accept a deeper, more intense kind of kiss. What had initially begun as an experiment began to become desire. Heat coursed through his body as he coaxed Andrea's lips apart to explore the moist recesses awaiting him. When her tongue tentatively mated with his, Hal felt his knees soften like cooked macaroni.

Everything about this cautious female intrigued him, lured him against his will. It felt natural to have her in his arms, as if she were something he'd been missing and had unexpectedly found. When her feminine scent wrapped itself around his senses he absorbed her, savored her.

Hal muffled a groan. He felt like Prince Charming who had been carrying around a glass slipper, searching for his mysterious Cinderella. He had indulged himself by kissing one woman after another for years, and pow! He had found his lips pressed to a dewy-soft mouth that seemed to have his name engraved on it.

Where had this woman been all his life? And why the hell had he bothered kissing other females when, with one touch of Andrea's lips, he detected the drastic difference—all the way to the soles of his feet?

God, he could've gotten drunk on the taste of her, could have stood in the kitchen for hours sampling such tantalizing delights.

A distant yelp tapped at Hal's fuzzy senses. From the sound of things, Jason had his hands full separating the last of the jittery calves. Reluctantly, Hal raised his head, his gaze focused on Andrea's stunned expression. She seemed as bewildered as he was.

"I thought you said no hanky-panky," she bleated. Her shaking hand lifted to her mouth, as if to wipe away the lingering sensations of his kiss.

"Things change, Fletcher," he told her huskily. "The original rules no longer apply."

Andrea wobbled back two paces, bracing her hip against the kitchen counter. "Nothing's changed," she insisted, stubborn as ever.

"Hasn't it?" Hal challenged. "Next, I suppose you're going to tell me you didn't kiss me back."

Her chin went airborne. "I suffered a blow to the head. I barely know what I'm doing."

One thick black brow elevated in contradiction. "Don't kid yourself, Fletch. That's the last thing I'd expect from a woman like you. You can defy many of the difficulties you encounter, but don't deny this. I gave up trying five minutes ago. Something just happened between us."

"It damned sure did," Andrea insisted. "You just stepped over the line when I was beginning to think I could trust you."

"You can," he affirmed.

"Trust you to do what? Take advantage while I'm weak and wounded?"

When Jason cursed loudly, Andrea automatically pivoted toward the door to lend a hand. Hal caught her good arm before she whizzed by. "Go take a bath," he ordered, noting her defensive reaction when he grabbed at her too abruptly. Again he wondered what had happened in the past that made her so jumpy.

When Andrea tried to worm loose Hal hauled her up against him—firmly but gently. "Do you want to be kissed again, Fletch?" he breathed on her flushed cheeks.

"No."

"Then go take a bath. Those are your only two options."

"You can go to hell, Griffin," she snapped.

"Why? Because I kissed you and you liked it?"

"I most certainly did not," she sputtered defensively.

This woman could teach stubborn to a mule, Hal decided. "Go take your bath," he repeated as he turned Andrea around and gave her a nudge in the right direction. "My brother will be here in thirty minutes."

"I wish I would have hired *him* in the first place," Andrea sniped as she wobbled away. "Nash probably wouldn't cause me as much trouble as you do."

Hal watched her disappear around the corner. An odd

mixture of amusement and annoyance pelted him. He had ridden broncs and bulls that weren't nearly as hostile and contrary as Andrea. And for sure and certain, he had always steered clear of complicated women. Yet, here he was, determined to dredge up all her secrets, to understand her.

Before Hal left Fletcher Ranch, he intended to find out why Andrea had become so standoffish. Unpleasant memories seemed to loom between them. Even if Andrea refused to accept the fact that sparks flew when they kissed she *was* going to discuss her troubled past. She might not thank him for it now, but she definitely needed to hurdle the obstacle that stifled her relationships with men.

Wheeling around, Hal ambled out the door to help Jason. By the time he reached the corral, Jason had latched the gate behind the last calf. He was breathing hard, an indication that he'd done some fancy footwork to avoid being run down by contrary cattle.

Hal had been breathing heavily himself—thanks to Andrea.

"Damned cow," Jason muttered, gesturing toward the oversize Simmental that darted around the corral, looking for an escape route. "She ran me up the fence when I cut her calf from the herd."

"But you got the job done," Hal noted. "Nobody said it would be easy, not when Tony Braden managed to spook the herd before you started working with them."

Hal motioned for Jason to follow him. "We'll jack up the stock trailer while we're waiting for Nash. You can drive to town and buy new tires." Hal grabbed the heavy-duty jack from the bed of his truck and then positioned it beneath the trailer frame.

"Hal?"

"Yeah?"

Jason took the tire tool in hand to loosen the lug nuts. "Do you mind if I ask you something?"

"Fire away," Hal offered as he jacked up the trailer.

"How do you make a girl like you?" he asked self-consciously. "I mean *really* like you?"

Hal halted in mid-task and glanced at Jason. "Are we discussing Brenda Warner?"

Jason nodded, his attention focused on the tire tool in his hand. "You know how some of the guys in high school carry on. Always keeping score and stuff. But that's not what I want. I've waited a long time for Brenda. I don't want to blow my chance with her."

Jason's comment put a wry smile on Hal's lips. He found himself thinking the same thing about Andrea—reluctant though he was to admit it. "She's pretty special, huh?"

"Yeah," Jason murmured, setting the lug nuts aside. "We have a date tonight—if I can manage to get to the movie in Keota Flats without Tony sabotaging my truck. It's our first official date, so how am I going to make sure there'll be lots of other ones?"

Hal was feeling like Dear Abby again. Having lost his father, Jason was looking to him for advice. Cynical as he had been about women, he wasn't sure he was the one Jason should be consulting.

That would be the other *Griffin brother,* Hal mused. Nash had so many stars in his eyes these days that he was too blind to place one foot in front of the other. After a five-year abstinence Nash had gone crazy over Crista Delaney.

When Hal didn't respond immediately, Jason went to

work on the second slashed tire. "Sorry, Hal. Just forget I asked. This isn't your problem. You're here to round up cattle."

True, that's how it had started, Hal agreed silently, but he'd had difficulty remaining detached. He would've had to have a heart of solid granite not to care what happened to Jason and Andrea.

Nash had been right when he claimed Hal had inadvertently managed to adopt the Fletchers. Unfortunately, Hal was scheduled to ride in another rodeo the following weekend—if he hoped to remain at the top of the standings. He may not be around to resolve all the difficulties Andrea and Jason faced, but he would do what he could while he had the chance.

"I don't consider myself an expert on women," Hal said as he removed the slashed tire. "But I imagine Brenda wants a little respect and consideration from you. Treat her special. Hold doors open, ask her opinions, listen to what she says—the whole nine yards. And don't try to put the make on her, first buck out of the chute."

Jason's face flamed when Hal grinned devilishly at him. "I wasn't planning to. The truth is, I haven't dated all that much. With school activities, sports, and helping Dad at the ranch, there hasn't been much spare time. I don't want to come off looking like a *dork* to Brenda, though."

Hal appraised the muscular, good-looking teenager. Jason Fletcher wasn't a dork, never would be. He was a nice kid who needed his parents' guidance. But fate had intervened cruelly, leaving Andrea and Jason with overwhelming responsibility.

"You'll be fine. Just follow natural instinct—within reason," Hal qualified. "If Brenda doesn't like you the way you are, then she isn't worth the effort. If you think she's tired of being hit on, then make it easy for her to relax and enjoy being around you."

"In other words, keep my hands in my pockets and my mouth fastened around the straw of a Coke," Jason paraphrased.

"Something like that." Hal chuckled. "If Brenda is as skittish as your—" Hal halted in mid-sentence and went back to his chore. "Give the young lady some time and space. She needs to know you're interested, but let her set the pace. It won't make you a wimp. From what I've heard, sensitive, accommodating men are all the rage these days."

"Even on the rodeo circuit?" Jason questioned.

"That's a whole other world," Hal said. "Hopping from one rodeo to the next doesn't lend itself to the kind of meaningful relationships we're discussing."

Jason grinned. "I'll bet you've had your share of women."

Hal shifted awkwardly. That was one topic he refused to discus with Jason, especially now that he found himself attracted to Andrea—even if nothing could ever come of it.

"Is there a service station in Hochukbi that sells tires?" Hal asked, leaping to another subject like a kangaroo.

"One of Dad's friends owns a station where we do business."

"Good. Have the new tires put on these rims."

Jason glanced toward the house. "We can't afford—"

"Charge the tires to me. I'll take care of it Monday," Hal interrupted.

"Andi won't like that."

"I'll deal with your sister. You get the tires replaced," Hal ordered. "And if you happen across Tony Braden, turn the other cheek, kid. We'll contend with the juvenile gangsters in due time."

Jason was ready to drive off when the clatter of an approaching vehicle caught his attention. Hal glanced up to see Nash behind the wheel of his shiny new truck, Crista Delaney nestled beside him. Choctaw Jim was riding shotgun.

Hal noted the anticipation glittering in Jason's blue eyes as he pivoted to greet the new arrivals. Strange, Hal thought. He never considered himself or Nash celebrities. Obviously Jason saw things differently. You'd have thought Joe Montana or Michael Jordan had arrived on the scene.

He made the quick introductions before sending Jason off on his errand. While Nash backed the pickup and trailer to the loading chute, Hal appraised the attractive woman who had come into his brother's life. Nash and Crista looked so content and satisfied it was nauseating. If that curly-haired blonde didn't treat Nash right, she would damn well answer to Hal!

Shoving the thought aside, Hal grabbed the cattle prod from the back of the truck and strode toward the pen. With veteran cowboys on hand, loading cattle was mere child's play.

Nash pivoted to get instructions from Hal, but the sight of the woman who appeared on the wooden deck stopped Nash in his tracks. "Is that Andrea Fletcher?"

Hal glanced over his shoulder and nearly fell off his boot heels. Andrea's long auburn hair cascaded over her shoulders like a cape rippling in the wind. Sunlight danced in the thick mass like banked flames. It was the first time she had let her hair down, and the effect was absolutely enthralling.

"Damn, little brother, I can see why you're feeling uncharacteristically charitable."

"The woman needs a keeper," Hal grumbled. "She injured her arm trying to unload Bowlegs, and then she tried to stop a stampede by herself. She probably needed a trip to the emergency room after she got trampled and cracked her head, but she refused to go."

"She sounds like someone else I know," Crista inserted, grinning impishly. "As I recall, I once wanted to transport you to the hospital to have your ribs X-rayed. You, of course, refused. So why are you criticizing Andrea?"

Hal scowled and looked away, only to find his uncle staring at him with twinkling black eyes. "What's your problem?"

Choctaw Jim shrugged as he appraised Andrea. "I don't have one. But then, I don't have your boss lady, now do I?"

That infuriatingly wise and mysterious smile Jim Pryce wore so well had Hal scowling again. He hated it when his uncle did that. Hal wasn't sure he cared to know what Choctaw Jim was thinking. Thankfully, Jim, who had a philosophical quote for every situation, kept his trap shut—for once.

"Andrea Fletcher," Hal announced, hitching his thumb toward her. "This is Uncle Jim, my brother Nash, and—"

"My fiancée, Crista Delaney," Nash finished as he curled a possessive arm around Crista.

"Glad to meet you," Andrea said cordially.

When she smiled at the new arrivals, Hal studied her discreetly. Gone was the wariness. Obviously, the little lady saw no threat here. She could relax and be herself when she wasn't in a one-on-one situation with a man.

Hal suddenly remembered the advice he had given Jason. *Don't push. Let the lady set her own pace.* He hadn't exactly done that with Andrea, now had he?

"I really appreciate your help," Andrea told Nash. "We've had unexpected complications."

"So Hal told us. I'm sorry about your difficulties."

Andrea nodded, purposely avoiding eye contact with Hal. "I'll pay you for your time and expenses—"

Nash flung up his hand to forestall her. "Forget it," he insisted. "We'll get this load of cattle to the stockyards and be back to pick up the rest. No charge."

"But, I couldn't possibly—"

"Don't argue with my brother," Hal cut in. "If you want your livestock at the auction on time, you'll stop objecting and let Nash hit the road."

Andrea spared Hal a brief glance—noticeably brief.

When she retreated to the house, Nash frowned pensively. "Is she allergic to you, little brother? I don't recall your having that effect on women before."

"Fiancée?" Hal questioned, mentally scrambling to switch topics.

Nash dropped the sensitive subject and focused on Crista. "I proposed to Curly and she said yes."

"When's the fatal day?" Hal smirked.

"Next month."

Hal stared at Crista for a long moment. "Rushing things a bit, aren't we?"

Nash smiled wryly at his brother. "I don't know, are *you?* Is that why Andrea couldn't look you in the eye?"

It didn't take a genius to realize Nash had noticed Andrea's standoffish attitude toward Hal. The kiss in the kitchen must have been playing hell with her conscience. Hal was back to square one with that wary female.

"Andrea needs her cattle check in hand today," Hal said abruptly. "Tell the secretary at the business office that I'll be there to collect for Andrea when the auction is over."

He glanced up at the bank of gray clouds piling high on the southeastern horizon. "We may be in for some rough weather, so you better get going."

Nash nodded his dark head as he slid into the cab of the truck. "If the meteorologist's forecast is correct, we may be in for a long stretch of wet weather. Hurricane Amy hit landfall on the Texas coast and is headed in our direction."

That wasn't the kind of news Hal wanted to hear. From the sound of things, he would be rounding up the next herd of cattle in a cloudburst. That should be fun.

When the threesome drove off, Hal glanced toward the house. He decided to follow the advice he had offered Jason. He was going to give his leery boss lady the space she seemed to need.

Well damn, he thought as he strode off to unsaddle the horses. He was turning into one of those ultra-modern, sensitive males who were attentive to a woman's needs. Better not let his brother know that. After the lectures Hal had delivered to Nash about Crista's probable ulterior motives, Nash would razz Hal until hell wouldn't have it.

Andrea breathed a huge sigh of relief when the cattle were transported to market and Hal volunteered to drive to Keota Flats to collect the cheek. She hadn't coped well with the kiss in the kitchen. During her bath she had played the scene over a half dozen times in her mind, disgruntled by her explosive reaction.

At the first touch of Hal's lips, Andrea knew she was out of her league. Heavens, she hadn't allowed a man close in four years, and then she had been dealing with boys, not men. Hal Griffin was certainly no boy and he probably sensed how inexperienced and self-conscious she had been with him. Despite her awkwardness, Hal had made her feel luring sensations for the first time. He had melted emotions that had been frozen inside her for years.

The innocence and anticipation of youth had been stripped away from Andrea that terrible night during her freshman year of college. To her, Hal Griffin—all well-honed muscle and brawn—posed a dangerous threat. He could overpower her if he had the inclination. And yet, he hadn't thrown himself at her. He had been tender and gentle and Andrea wanted to trust him, wanted to enjoy her responses to him. But it was damned hard to shake what had become a self-preservation reflex.

Andrea knew perfectly well that a celebrity like Hal could have any woman he wanted, as intimately as he wanted. So why would he waste time on a woman whose first impulse was to break and run when a man ventured too close?

Was it pity for her situation that had caused him to become amazingly gentle? Probably, Andrea decided. Hal knew of the difficulty and tragedy in her life.

Truth be known, the *kiss* had probably been meant to be therapeutic, not romantic. And anyway, Hal would be back on the rodeo circuit in a few days and Andrea would be left to salvage her ranch. He would drive off without looking back, she told herself realistically. She didn't dare let herself get attached to a tumbleweed like Hal Griffin. He could break her heart if she let him.

Knowing the kind of life he led, he was probably the love-'em-and-leave-'em type who never took women seriously. Early on, Hal made it clear that he had no faith in women and no need for long-term relationships. If he felt anything at all, it was the usual male lust.

Andrea gave herself a mental shake when she found herself staring through the window, anticipating Hal's return. *Rule Number One,* she told herself sensibly: *Don't start looking for a man who won't be around long enough to get attached to. Rule Number Two: This is strictly business, despite that earthshaking kiss.* It was probably just a mercy kissing to Hal, a sympathetic gesture that meant nothing to him.

When Andrea heard Jason bounding down the staircase like a jackrabbit, she automatically strode into the kitchen to prepare supper.

"Don't bother, sis. I've decided to take Brenda out for a burger and fries before the movie."

Andrea raised her eyebrows when she got a close look at her brother. He was spruced up in recently pressed jeans, polished boots, and a colorful western shirt. A whiff of cologne greeted her halfway across the room.

"My, my, you do clean up well," she complimented teasingly. "And dinner before the movie? Is that your customary procedure?"

Jason broke into a wide grin. "Brenda Warner is somebody special, and this is our first official date. I thought I'd do it up right."

"Be sure you treat her with respect," Andrea lectured sternly.

"So I've already been told."

Andrea blinked in surprise. "By whom?"

"Hal told me the same thing."

"He did?"

Jason nodded affirmatively. "Dad always said that before you step into unfamiliar territory, you should consult an expert. I figured Hal has been around enough to know what girls like and what they don't."

Andrea couldn't argue with that! Hal Griffin had probably forgotten more about romance than she had learned, especially after she had put her lovelife on hold for four years.

Before Andrea could quiz Jason on the other pearls of wisdom Hal might have dropped, the approach of a vehicle caught her attention. She found herself tingling in anticipation—and not because of the sizable paycheck she expected to receive when Hal returned. The damnable truth was that she was anxious to have him back—for a few minutes at least, while Jason was there as a buffer.

When Hal strode through the door, his Stetson tilted low on his forehead, Andrea's heart flip-flopped in her chest. Did the man have to be so cursed handsome?

"Your check, boss lady," Hal said with a flair. "Now that Phase One has been completed you can breathe easier."

Andrea smiled gratefully, careful not to make contact with his fingertips as she retrieved the check.

Hal frowned at her behavior before he turned his attention to Jason. "You don't believe in giving girls much of a chance, do you, kid?"

A pleased grin spread across Jason's face. "I have to meet Brenda's parents tonight."

"Throw in a few 'yes, ma'ams' and 'no, sirs', but don't get carried away or they'll know you're faking it," Hal advised. "When they ask about your future aspirations, don't tell them you have dreams of being a rodeo cowboy." He shot Andrea a pointed glance. "Some people don't find the profession particularly impressive, just *entertaining.*"

Jason noted the exchange of glances between his sister and Hal. "What am I supposed to tell Brenda's parents? That I don't know what the heck I want to be yet?"

"Just rattle off two or three respectable professions and you'll do fine," Hal coached.

When Jason walked out the door, Andrea immediately began puttering around the kitchen, preparing steaks for the grill. She was all too aware that Hal was lurking behind her.

"Nervous?" he inquired, propping himself against the wall to monitor her activities.

"Why should I be?"

"We're all alone," he reminded her. "No telling what a big brute like me might do, you know. Can't be too careful, can you, Fletch?"

Andrea ignored his comment. "I expect you'll want to go home after I feed you. We can wait until Monday afternoon to gather the rest of the cattle."

"Trying to get rid of me?"

"Yes—no—"

His dark brow elevated in amusement. "Well, which is it?"

Andrea set the meat seasoning aside and spun to face him. "I hired you to do a job for me. I don't intend to interfere with your social life. It's Saturday night. Go do whatever you usually do, with whoever you usually do it with."

"I'm usually at a rodeo, trying to keep my seat on a wild bronc for eight seconds," he informed her.

"Then hanging around here, when you're accustomed to all that excitement, would bore you to death."

Andrea shifted her attention to the window when she heard the crunch of gravel in the driveway. After Tony Braden's vicious prank she had come to expect trouble. To her relief Charles Seever unfolded his bulky frame from the low-slung sports car. Tuff—as he had been nicknamed in high school—hiked up his cream-colored breeches that had slipped beneath his rounded belly as he headed toward the deck. He had warned Andrea that he was coming to see her and, much to her dismay, he was true to his word.

"Who's the new arrival?" Hal questioned. "The Pillsbury Doughboy?"

Andrea stifled a grin. The years had definitely added unnecessary pounds to Tuff's physique. In his trendy jacket and slacks, he did look like Pillsbury's mascot. "It's Tuff," Andrea informed him.

"Want me to make myself scarce?"

"Because of Tuff?" Andrea chuckled. "I told you, he's just somebody I dated a long time ago. I have no intention of rekindling a flame that never existed in the first place."

"On your part, maybe," Hal contended as he studied Tuff. "Obviously *he* has other ideas."

Tuff halted abruptly when he saw the towering figure looming behind Andrea. "I thought we had plans for tonight."

"*You* may have. *I* made it clear you were wasting your time."

Hal reached around Andrea's shoulder, deliberately brushing his arm against hers as he offered his hand to Tuff. "Hal Griffin," he introduced himself.

"The rodeo star?" Tuft's full jowls dropped open as his gaze leaped back and forth between Hal and Andrea.

"He's gathering cattle for me," Andrea said before Tuff got the wrong idea and spread gossip around town.

Behind her, Hal smiled as his gaze moved caressingly over Andrea's shapely derriere, staking his claim. "We were just getting ready to have supper . . . etcetera . . ."

Andrea held her tongue, but she itched to shake Hal for planting seeds for the gossip she hoped to avoid.

"Well, nice to meet you, Hal. Good luck on the rodeo circuit."

When Tuff lumbered off, Andrea rounded on the suddenly innocent-looking Hal. "Now it will be all over town that you and I have something going. That will verify what Tony is probably saying," she muttered sourly.

"At least it will keep unwanted boyfriends off your deck," he reminded her with a grin.

"Right, and after you leave, the rumors will claim I'm sitting out here, pining away after you tossed me aside and rode off into the sunset. Thanks a lot, Griffin."

Flinging Hal a condescending glance, Andrea scooped up the plate of T-bone steaks and stalked onto the deck. Curse the man, she thought as she plunked the steaks onto the grill. She'd like to roast that ornery rascal over hot coals, burning his hide evenly on both sides!

Six

Hal grinned in amusement, his intense gaze fixed on the gliding motion of Andrea's hips. She did indeed have a walk to die for. Too bad the little lady had been so soured on men. She had the kind of body and natural sensuality that could more than satisfy some lucky man.

Unfortunately, before that could happen, Andrea would have to lighten up considerably. Hal intended to resolve that problem, starting now. He had picked up a few supplies of his own for their evening meal.

Reaching into his brown paper sack, he retrieved the fixings for margaritas. After rummaging through the cabinets he located the blender. While Andrea was cooking the steaks, he mixed the only drink he had learned to prepare.

With a margarita glass in each hand, Hal shouldered his way through the door—and met Andrea's wary frown.

"What's that?" she questioned as she closed the grill lid. Smoke rolled around her like a gray cloud.

Hal thrust the glass at her. "It's a margarita. We're celebrating."

"Celebrating what?" she asked suspiciously.

"The sale of your first cattle herd and your upcoming birthday," Hal announced.

Andrea stared dubiously at the drink. "Are you trying to get me drunk, Griffin?"

"No, I'm trying to get you to loosen up. Making the first part of your loan payment and turning twenty-five are monumental occasions. You need to kick back and enjoy yourself."

Hesitantly, Andrea took a small sip. The expression on her face indicated the margarita suited her. Hal felt an odd sense of satisfaction in knowing he had done *something* she approved of.

"It's very good," she admitted. "I've never had a margarita before."

Hal sank into the lawn chair to nurse his drink and admire the panoramic view of Fire River. He felt astonishingly content here, watching Andrea grill the steaks. Watching *her* mostly, he amended.

A frown plowed Hal's brow when Andrea set her glass aside. She had polished off her first margarita like a dry-throated camel. Hal promptly retrieved her glass and went inside the house to refill it. When he handed Andrea the drink she eyed him warily—again.

"Are you sure you aren't trying to drown my defenses?"

"I just want you to loosen up. What's the harm in that?"

Andrea's fingertip skimmed the salt around the rim of her glass. "The harm is that I'm not altogether sure I can trust you—you being a man and all. Since I'm not accustomed to drinking, what's going to happen if I start getting silly? And what's Jason going to think when I have to prop myself against a wall to wait up for him?"

"I doubt Jason would want you to wait up for him."

"I want to make sure he arrives home safely," Andrea

defended, then sipped on her second margarita. "He's all I have left."

"I understand your need to protect what's left of your family, but Jason needs growing room."

"Maybe he does, but I want him to know I'll always be there for him."

Hal admitted defeat and sipped his drink. He knew exactly where Andrea was coming from, because he and Nash had made all sorts of concessions when Levi Cooper's rodeo accident landed him in a wheelchair. The brothers had devoted themselves to providing and caring for Dogger—as he had been nicknamed. Nash had all but stopped living to provide for Dogger while Hal hauled the rodeo horses around the circuit and entered as many competitive events as he could manage, in order to provide extra income.

Yet, there were times when Hal had let off steam. Andrea hadn't learned the knack of coping with pent-up pressure. He vowed to teach this fiercely determined and devoted female to learn to relax before it got the best of her. If he could nudge one smile from her lips he would have accomplished his mission for the evening.

"Steaks are done," Andrea announced.

Hal picked up her half-empty glass and followed her into the kitchen. He wasn't sure, but it seemed there was less tension in her shoulders, a more relaxed air about her. Progress, Hal noted with a smile. The margaritas were beginning to soften Andrea's rigid edges.

While she retrieved the baked potatoes from the oven, Hal set the table, asking himself when was the last time he'd shared a woman's company like this. It had been so long that he couldn't remember if he ever had. He had gone from the grueling rodeo circuit and a broken wedding engagement to the armed services and then back to the circuit. During that time there had been no casual meals, only an occasional sexual encounter. No frills, very little conversation, just quick-paced sex and fast getaways.

And then along came Andrea Fletcher to redefine the boundaries of his relationships with women . . .

Hal nearly dropped his drink when he glanced up to see Andrea grinning at him. Grinning! The effect was even more transforming than the demure smile of greeting she had bestowed on Hal's family. When she laughed softly, every bone in his body seemed to dissolve.

"What's so funny, Fletcher?" he quizzed.

Andrea set an ear of corn on his plate. "You are. I never pictured you as the domestic type. A rodeo cowboy like you looks out of place setting tables. No arena, no cheering fans in the grandstands."

"I *am* out of my element," Hal admitted as he pulled out the chair for her. "I'm used to fast food—to go. Sitting down to a meal with my family once a month—maybe."

A rumble of thunder broke the silence. Andrea reached for her drink, then stared at the window. "I hope Jason takes those winding curves with caution."

"I'm sure he's as aware of what can happen as you are," Hal insisted. "Besides, he has the girl of his dreams with him. I doubt he'll take unnecessary risks."

Nodding, Andrea slumped in her chair. "I'm worse than a mother hen, aren't I?"

"Yep," Hal confirmed as he cut a slice of steak. When he popped the chunk of meat in his mouth, his taste buds went wild. "Lord, this is good. Practically melts in my mouth."

Andrea smiled at the compliment and took another sip

of her margarita. They ate in companionable silence, until she mentioned rounding up cattle.

Hal flung up his hand. "We're celebrating, remember?"

"Right." Andrea grinned impishly as she plucked up her empty glass. "I'm supposed to get rip-roaring drunk and dance on the table."

Hal reached behind him to grab the blender, refilling her glass to the brim. "You don't have to go to extremes to prove you can loosen up." He winked at Andrea. "Besides, if you two-step on the table you might break the dishes. That would be hard to explain to Jason."

"I really think he likes this girl," Andrea murmured between sips. "First love, I suspect. Have you ever been in love?"

"I thought I was once," he admitted begrudgingly.

"What happened?"

"None of your business, Fletcher."

Regarding him curiously, she eased back in her chair. "Don't wanna talk about it?"

"Nope."

"Why not? Too painful?"

"Probably because it was as unpleasant for me as the incident that turned you against men was for you."

"I'll drink to that," Andrea declared, swallowing a large gulp of margarita.

"Wanna talk about it, Fletcher?" he prodded.

"Nope, I'm celebrating," she said with a slur in her voice. "I don't want to think about what bastards men can be."

Hal lifted his glass. "To life without women."

"To a world without men," she said, clinking her glass against his.

By the time they finished their meal Andrea's voice

was raspy. She was as nonchalant and uninhibited as Hal had ever seen her. Gone were the tense lines that usually bracketed her mouth. She wore a sleepy smile as she wobbled toward the sink to wash the dishes.

"I'll clean up," Hal volunteered. "Why don't you sit down and take a load off your feet. You're still recuperating from that blow to the head, you know."

"Now who's being a mother hen?" she taunted. "I've got to hand it to you, Griffie, this celebrating bu*sh*iness is beginning to feel pretty darn good."

Hal swallowed a chuckle as Andrea handed him the dish rag. She was beginning to amuse him. Andrea was still her sassy, spirited self, but the defensive mechanisms that kept her distant and remote weren't functioning. She even tossed Hal a reckless grin as she sauntered off with another drink in her hand.

Still chuckling, he glanced down to see himself wrist-deep in dishwater. Good gawd, if Nash could see him he would split a gut laughing at his domesticated younger brother. Damned good thing this was only temporary employment, Hal decided. Bernie Bryant—chief cook, bottlewasher, and handyman at Chulosa Ranch—would have Hal swapping shifts with him in the kitchen if he ever saw this.

For a man who spent most of his time hanging onto bucking broncs and roping and bulldogging calves, Hal did indeed look out of place. Although Andrea had expected Hal to drive home this evening he was content where he was. He was . . . comfortable, satisfied.

His gaze drifted down the hall to see Andrea sprawled on the living room sofa, sipping her drink. After he loaded the dishwasher, he mixed another blender of margaritas.

Refilling both glasses, he sank down at the far end of the couch, granting Andrea plenty of space.

To his surprise, she pulled the band from her thick mass of auburn hair and shook it loose. The silky tendrils tumbled around her shoulders like a waterfall. Hal groaned inwardly, fighting the urge to comb his fingers through the wavy mass.

Maybe it was a good thing Andrea didn't let her hair down too often, he decided. The sight was too distracting. She looked even more alluring than usual—which was way too much already, though she did little or nothing to call attention to her gender.

"I didn't realize how uptight I was," Andrea confided sluggishly. "I'm beginning to feel like a limp mop."

There was nothing limp about the condition Hal suddenly found himself in! He looked at Andrea and asked himself how he ever thought he could relate to her as the sister he never had. He desired her, even if she was too tipsy to notice.

When Andrea switched the TV channel to watch country and western dancing on the Nashville station, Hal could feel the tempo of Vince Gill's song thrumming though him. "Wanna dance?" he asked abruptly.

When Andrea's head rolled back to stare at him, Hal nearly lost it. The way she was draped across the sofa would have been a blatant invitation—if it had come from another woman. Hal tamped down the throbbing sensations coursing through him and told himself to be satisfied with getting Andrea to unwind.

"I don't know how to two-step," she slurred. "I haven't even been to a dance since the high school prom." A grin tugged at her lush mouth. "Tuff was my escort. The clumsy clod stepped all over my feet—it didn't take long to lose enthusiasm for dancing."

"Is that why you dropped him? Lousy dancer?"

Andrea shook her head, causing her long, silky tresses to shimmer like fire in the lamplight. "No, it was because all he had on his mind was sex. I got tired of dodging his hands. I hope Jason—"

Hal grasped Andrea's hand, hauling her to her feet. "Jason isn't Jack the Ripper, and you're supposed to be enjoying yourself."

Andrea braced her hand on Hal's chest to steady herself. Long, spiked lashes swept up to meet his gaze, and Hal felt his heart pounding against her palm.

Damn, it was difficult to remain casual when he reacted to her slightest touch. He must have been too long between women, Hal decided. Either that or Andrea was as radioactive as he thought she was—and his body was as sensitive as a Geiger counter.

"Okay, Griffie, teach me to dance," Andrea mumbled accommodatingly. "All I ask is that you stay off my feet. I've already been trampled once today."

When George Strait crooned about "The Little Bitty Teeny Weenie Thing They Call the Lovebug," Hal settled his hand on Andrea's waist and placed her arm on his shoulder. When she didn't object, he counted the steps aloud so she could follow the rhythm.

"One . . . two—and . . . Slow . . . quick-quick . . ."

The words reminded him of far more intimate and arousing activities than two-stepping. When Andrea miscounted, their bodies collided and Hal swallowed air. He could feel every luscious curve of her body molded to his, knew the instant Andrea became aware of the rigid bulge beneath the zipper of his jeans.

She tilted her head back, staring at him with an impish grin. "Carrying a concealed weapon, Griffie?"

"A hazard of dancing with a beautiful woman," he told her frankly. "But that's not your problem, it's mine. You're just learning to dance, and I'm not expecting fringe benefits."

"It doesn't matter," she slurred out, easing away. "I'm no good at either one."

Hal didn't know how to interpret the comment so he simply kept time with the music and concentrated on teaching Andrea to move with the tempo. Things were progressing smoothly until Garth Brooks's voice filled the room. As the country star sang "The Dance," an unexpected stillness overcame Andrea. She melted against Hal, her head resting against his shoulder. Without thinking, he cuddled her closer, wrapping her so tightly in his arms that he could feel her breathing, feel her body gliding in perfect rhythm with his.

Hal swallowed uncomfortably when Andrea's thigh brushed against his throbbing manhood. "Fletcher?"

"Hummm?" she murmured against the front of his shirt.

"Are we dancing too close for comfort?"

"Not anymore," she said on a sigh. "You feel so good that I don't want to let go."

That careless admission had Hal groaning low in his throat. It wouldn't take much to make him forget he was dealing with a woman who'd had one too many margaritas—at his instigation.

When Andrea looked up at him with that dazzling smile Hal knew he should have been content to leave her sprawled on the sofa. The sultry scent of her was like an aphrodisiac. She was entirely too close, too vulnerable, too attractive.

Damn it, Hal wanted to kiss her senseless, to touch her familiarly, to lose himself in the taste and feel of her. If he did he would be taking unfair advantage, confirming Andrea's beliefs about men.

When her lips parted on a contented sigh, Hal forgot everything except the elemental need pulsating through him. He'd had just enough to drink to take the edge off his conscience—and Andrea had had more than enough.

"Happy birthday, baby . . ."

His dark head descended ever so slowly. He savored the margarita-laced kiss and her uninhibited response. His hands splayed across her hips, pressing her into the cradle of his thighs, imagining what it would be like to feel nothing but her soft flesh surrounding him.

The image was too poignant, too vivid. Hal had to force himself to break their kiss, to retract his wandering hands.

To his disbelief Andrea frowned in disappointment as she wobbled over to collapse on the couch. "Sorry, I forgot I'm just the time you're killing between rodeos. And anyway, you're way out of my league."

Hal towered over her as she lounged temptingly on the sofa. "I told you I make it a practice not to get emotionally involved," he reminded her gruffly. "As for killing time—"

Andrea waved him off with a limp flick of her wrist. "Spare me. I may be a little tipsy, but I'm not entirely stupid. I know you're feeling sorry for me. That's what all this loosening up with margaritas is all about. I'm supposed to be grateful that a hot-shot celebrity is spending his Saturday night with a plain female like me."

Plain? Hal bit back a crack of laughter. Andrea Fletcher

wasn't plain. It was true that she didn't call attention to herself, but she didn't have to. She was naturally alluring and sexy. Even in a gunny sack, nothing could disguise her beauty.

"I'm sure you expected me to treasure that birthday kiss forever and ever." Andrea grinned up at him, and Hal wondered how many of him she was seeing. "Truth is, I'll probably remember it for a long time to come. You kiss as well as you ride, cowboy. I've never had better, but then, I'm sure a worldly man like you has already figured that out."

"Andrea—"

"It's okay," she interrupted as she squirmed into a more comfortable position. "Tonight I don't mind your pity quite so much. Must be the drinks . . . Is it hot in here?"

When she rolled up her sleeves and unbuttoned her flannel shirt, Hal swore under his breath. As usual, she was wearing an unflattering sports bra rather than the sexy little scraps of lace other women used to seduce men.

The fact that Andrea was dismissing him had Hal wondering whether he was pleased or annoyed. At any rate, watching Andrea make herself more comfortable made him decidedly uncomfortable—anatomically speaking. When she peeled away clothing so she could cool down, he went hot all over.

"You can find someone to satisfy you at Slim Chance Saloon. That's Hochukbi's hot night spot," Andrea informed him.

Hal scowled at her. "I'm not interested in a quick lay."

Andrea peered owlishly at him. "You're not? I thought you said you only needed women for—"

"Will you forget what the hell I said," he muttered irritably. "We're celebrating your birthday!"

"You don't have to yell, Griffie," she said with a playful grin. "I may be drunk but I'm not deaf."

"I am not yelling!"

"What'd ya call it then?"

"I'm trying to get your attention, damn it!" he boomed.

Andrea nodded sagely. "I know this benefit birthday bash isn't your idea of a grand time. You're here because you feel sorry for me."

"Damn it, woman—"

"Please fix me another drink," Andrea slurred, grabbing her empty glass.

Hal glared at the glass and then at her. "You've had your limit."

"Never mind, Griffie, I'll get it myself." Andrea pushed herself upright, staggered, and then realigned herself. "Whew, this room is really spinning, isn't it?"

Hal sighed in exasperation when she weaved toward the kitchen, using the wall for support.

"You better take it easy with those margaritas," he warned as he followed in her wake. Andrea showed her defiance by filling her glass to the brim and then taking several gulps.

"Wanna teach me to play poker?" she asked. "I feel lucky tonight."

"You feel *drunk*," Hal corrected as she retraced her wobbly path to the living room. "You're going to hate yourself in the morning."

"I may as well feel a year older tomorrow," she chortled. "After all, I will be."

When Andrea started to snicker, Hal grinned reluctantly. If the boss lady was determined to acquaint herself with a hangover, more power to her. She couldn't say he hadn't cautioned her. But she was strong-willed and determined to do everything her own way, even if it meant making a fool of herself.

For the next hour Hal sat on the floor, teaching Andrea to play poker. When she was dealt a winning hand her face always brightened. Hal usually folded, watching her rake the poker chips into a pile near where she lay sprawled on the carpet.

"I've got a confe*th*ion to make," Andrea slurred out. "I've been cheating you."

"Do tell . . ."

A sharp clap of thunder rocked the house. When rain began to pour down in torrents, Andrea's devil-may-care smile became a worried frown. She clambered to her knees and then to her feet. Staggering noticeably, she approached the window.

"The roads will be slick and dangerous," she mused aloud. "Just like the night Mom died."

Hal strode up behind her, listening to the clatter of huge drops glancing off the window. The hurricane that had wreaked havoc on the Gulf coast had rolled northwest, drenching the wooded hills of Kanima County. Hal found himself wondering where Jason was, hoping the kid wasn't so busy fantasizing about the girl of his dreams that he wasn't paying attention to road conditions.

Odd, Hal had never worried about his own family the way he stewed about Andrea and Jason. Of course, Hal's uncle and brother were experienced and competent. That wasn't true of the Fletchers, even though Andrea proudly maintained that she could take care of herself.

Hell, just look at her. The little lady was drunk. She couldn't even stand up without swaying. And Jason didn't have nearly as many miles under his belt as Hal had. The Fletchers needed someone to watch over them. Too bad

Robert Fletcher had taken the easy way out. What kind of man would let his family down like that?

"Dad must have suffered nine kinds of hell every time it rained," Andrea mused, staring into the darkness. "It must have reminded him of Mom . . ."

When Andrea's breath caught in her throat, Hal wrapped a comforting arm around her. She didn't shy away from him as usual. Instead, she leaned back against him, feeling his compassion.

"Hal?"

"Yeah?"

"Will you hold me . . . ?"

The words no sooner tumbled from her lips than Andrea spun in his arms and cuddled against him. The chunk of rock Hal called his heart turned soft as a marshmallow. He propped his chin on the top of Andrea's head and listened to her breathe and struggle to control her emotions.

"Some birthday celebration this is," she mumbled. "First I get soused and then I blubber all over you. No wonder you feel sorry for me. I'm pathetic."

Hal had heard enough about this pity he supposedly felt. True, he did sympathize with her, but the desire sizzling through him had nothing to do with pity. If she would have let him, he would have sent her troubles up in flames for the night—because he wanted her like hell burning. But, Hal reminded himself, tonight wasn't about what he wanted, it was about what Andrea needed.

Gently, he reached beneath her chin, lifting her face to his. Tears glistened like diamonds in her eyes. Mercy kissing? Hal didn't think so. Holding Andrea felt as right as easing down into the chute and settling onto a saddle cinched to a wild bronc. A cowboy instinctively knew when he had a good fit and was about to make a good ride. Hal knew he would be well satisfied if he could share what Andrea wasn't prepared to give . . .

When she took the unprecedented initiative and rose on tiptoe to kiss him, Hal swore the lightning flashing outside the window had stabbed into him. Andrea kissed him without reserve, as if she were starving for the taste of him.

Hal decided, there and then, that dissolving Andrea's inhibitions in margaritas wasn't one of his brighter ideas. Inexperienced though she seemed to be, she was like a lighted fuse and he was sheer dynamite. Sparks crackled through his bloodstream when she leaned into him, her lush body molding itself to his.

His hands suddenly acquired a will of their own, sweeping across the flare of her hips, skimming beneath her gaping shirt. When his thumbs brushed the tips of her breasts, Andrea moaned softly and strained closer.

"God, I didn't know . . ." she mumbled against his lips.

Hal couldn't resist. His unruly body was running two gears ahead of his brain. His lips abandoned hers to trace the column of her throat. When he lightly tugged at her bra to unveil her breasts, Andrea trembled in his arms. When his tongue flicked at her nipples she groaned aloud. Mindlessly, he suckled her, his hands gently kneading the sweet flesh that filled his hands.

Hal wondered if she knew what she was allowing him to do, if she was long past caring. He was taking advantage, and he should've known better, but the taste of her skin, her wild responses triggered something hot and reckless inside him. He spread moist kisses over her breasts and, meeting no resistance, his hands swept to her abdomen, tracing the band of her jeans. He felt Andrea shiver against him, heard another ragged moan mingle with the sound of thunder and driving rain.

The storm brewing inside the house rivaled the swirling winds outside. Hal's hand dipped inside Andrea's jeans to trace the elastic band at the top of her panties. His fingertips glided lower, feeling the wet heat of her desire. Hot chills skittered down his spine, and his body clenched with need.

When she cried out at the initial touch of his fingertip against her secret flesh, Hal's lips came down hard on hers. His tongue invaded her mouth at the exact moment his fingertip slid into the hot, slick channel between her legs. He groaned aloud when he felt her body shudder around his finger, felt the warm rain of her desire bathing his hand.

He wondered how long it had been since Andrea had let a man touch her intimately. If her response was anything to go by, it had been a good long while. Knowing her feelings toward men, her heated reaction truly surprised him. Whatever secrets Andrea concealed about her past, there was no question that she was still a deeply passionate woman.

"Oh, God . . ." Andrea gasped against his mouth. "Oh, God, what's—?"

Hal felt the wild spasms reclaim her as he stroked her intimately. She cried out when the contractions spread through every part of her being, leaving her shaking in his arms.

Jaw clenched, eyes squeezed shut, Hal reminded himself that he had broken every term of their agreement. Strictly business? No hanky-panky? *Famous last words, Griffin,* he thought as he yielded to the need to tease another shimmering response from her.

He and Andrea were explosive together—she was gasping in ragged spurts that bordered on hyperventilation, calling his name in a disbelieving whisper . . .

And then she passed out!

Hal clamped his arm around her before she crumpled to the floor. Hot and bothered though he was, an amused chuckle rumbled in his chest. Now here was a first, he thought, scooping Andrea up and heading for the stairs. He'd never had a woman black out on him before, even in the wildest throes of passion. He and Andrea hadn't even gotten to the best part, and she was down for the count. He supposed the margaritas, and the blow to her head, were responsible.

Hal probably should have been grateful. There was no telling what might have happened if Andrea hadn't lost consciousness. The last thing he needed was to have Jason walk in on them. Hal had lectured Jason about being respectful to women. Wasn't he a fine one to talk!

Grimacing at the strain on his sore ribs, Hal veered toward Andrea's room. After he put her to bed he stood there for a moment, studying her intently, watching the flashes of lightning illuminate her features.

Okay, so what he was thinking was outrageous, but it would make an important point after Andrea got over being embarrassed and had time to analyze the incident.

With no help whatsoever from Andrea, Hal propped her up against his shoulder to remove her gaping shirt. The ace of hearts tumbled from her shirtsleeve. Hal smiled to himself.

After he tossed the garment over the chair he tugged at Andrea's jeans. Hal devoured her shapely contours for several minutes before he pulled up the sheet and tucked her in bed. She had been lucky tonight, he mused. Things had gone too far—and might have gone even farther if she hadn't passed out!

Bracing his hands on either side of her shoulders, he planted a kiss on her unresponsive lips. "Happy birthday, honey," he whispered.

The flash of headlights and the roar of an engine indicated Jason had returned. Hal scrambled down the steps to destroy the evidence of too many margaritas. No need to arouse Jason's protective instincts, he decided.

With undue haste, Hal spiffed up the kitchen and managed to greet Jason with a nonchalant smile that disguised the unappeased hunger still growling through him.

Seven

Jason Fletcher came through the kitchen door, dripping wet, wearing a smile as wide as a football field. Hal, who had just stashed the booze and blender out of sight, propped himself casually against the wall and sipped a glass of water.

"Man, it's a real toad strangler out there," Jason declared.

"According to the weather reports, we can expect a few days of heavy downpours until the hurricane rains itself out."

Jason glanced curiously toward the living room. "Isn't Andi waiting up for me? She usually does. I expected her to be full of questions."

"Your sister went to bed." *And not under her own power,* Hal didn't bother to add.

"After she suffered that blow, do you think she'll have a headache?" Jason questioned.

"I can almost guarantee it." Hal swallowed his grin with a gulp of ice water. Prolonged visits to Margaritaville made for miserable hangovers—as Andrea would soon find out. "Did you enjoy the company and the movie?"

Jason nodded his damp head vigorously. "The evening was great, except that Tony showed up at Hard Times Cafe. Luckily, the place was jam-packed with adults so he couldn't start any trouble. Brenda and I drove around town to lose him before we headed to Keota Flats."

Jason strode through the kitchen, pausing directly beside Hal. "I heard the latest gossip being whispered in the cafe booth behind me. I thought you might want to know Tony Braden was saying that you and my sister were . . . um . . ." He looked down at his soggy boots. "The word is that the two of you—"

"I get the picture, kid," Hal interrupted. "I wouldn't put much stock in gossip. People think and say what they please. If nothing else, the rumor will keep men like Tuff Seever from coming around to pester your sister. That should be a relief to her, even if the reason leaves a lot to be desired."

"Still, I don't like hearing Andi is an easy lay," Jason muttered. "While you're here, I doubt guys will bother her, but when you leave, some of them might try to see how far they can get."

Hal winced inwardly. He hadn't considered that possibility. He had never gotten involved enough to care about the women who came and went in his life. Obviously, Andrea's protective brother had considered future possibilities.

Whether Andrea approved or not, Hal might find it necessary to make it known around this small town that Andrea was his personal property. He could almost hear her objections. Well, hell, Hal mused, it would be for her own protection.

"Are you going to church with us tomorrow?" Jason questioned.

Hal hadn't been inside a church in twelve years, not since he'd lost faith in just about everything. Besides, he usually spent his Sundays at some far-flung rodeo arena, grooming and exercising the horses and mentally preparing himself for the afternoon finals.

"Wouldn't miss it, kid."

When Jason ambled toward his room, Hal made a beeline for the telephone. After calling information, he dialed Crista Delaney's number. Three rings later, she answered.

"It's nearly midnight," she mumbled.

"I can tell time, thanks," Hal smirked. "I figured my brother would be there. Did I figure right?"

Hal smiled to himself when he heard muted whispers and the rustle of the receiver being fumbled from one set of hands to another.

"Don't you have anything better to do than badger me?" Nash muttered in place of a greeting.

"Why should I let you enjoy what I'm doing without?" Hal fired back. It frustrated him that he'd turned out to be a damned gentleman—of all things!—where Andrea was concerned. He could have taken her and she wouldn't have offered any resistance. So why hadn't he?

"Does this prank call have a purpose?" Nash wanted to know.

"Yes, as a matter of fact. I didn't want to bother Choctaw Jim at this late hour—"

"—But I'm fair game."

"Right," Hal confirmed, undaunted. "Just because you're practicing being married doesn't mean I won't call when I feel like it."

"Get to the point before I expire from old age," Nash growled impatiently.

"I want you to tell Uncle Jim to enter me in bull riding, and every extra event he can schedule, when he sends in my entry fees for the rodeo at Mesquite."

"What the hell for?" Nash hooted. "You're not in topnotch condition yet. If you break a few bones in extra events you could spoil your ranking in your key events and ruin your standings for all-around cowboy of the year."

"I've ridden hurt plenty of times. So have you," Hal parried.

There was a noticeable pause. "What's going on, Hal?"

Hal glanced toward the staircase to ensure his privacy. "I'm going to loan Andrea Fletcher the prize money I make at upcoming rodeos. The extra thousand or fifteen hundred dollars I can make if I win—or place—in extra events could come in handy."

"What!"

Hal jerked the phone away from his ear before Nash blasted his eardrum. "From what I've been able to read between the lines, the Fletchers are close to bankruptcy because of funeral expenses and outstanding loans. If Andrea has to sell the calves—*and* the cows—to pay the debts, she won't be able to produce a livestock crop next year, much less pay property taxes in December. She already sold her own pickup and has been driving her father's old clunker. I suspect she and Jason are living on the money she made from selling her vehicle—and little else."

"And the banker probably isn't eager to renew a loan to a young woman and her kid brother," Nash speculated.

"Probably not, but she's determined to hold onto this ranch, come hell, high water, or both," Hal reported.

"If Andrea objected to me hauling her cattle to the stockyards without pay, how do you think you're going to convince her to accept your charity?"

Good question, thought Hal. "If I'm standing between

her and the wolves beating down the door, she may over-look her stubborn female pride."

"I think it's a mistake to overload yourself with extra rodeo entries. Crista had to wrap up your ribs and dope you with painkillers once already. Those tender tendons and ligaments can't take much abuse on the backs of rank bulls, especially not when you've worn-and-torn them chasing down Fletcher cattle in your spare time."

"You've been around Crista too long," Hal grumbled. "You're starting to sound like a doctor. We both grew up tough, avoiding hospitals whenever possible. I'm not plan-ning to change my habits anytime soon."

"No? Sounds like you're breaking a few of your own rules now," Nash pointed out. "You're making all these arrangements to save your *boss lady*. So what's Andrea Fletcher to you?"

"None of your damned business," Hal snapped irrita-bly. "Just see that I get entered in the extra events.

"And bring me a couple of horses in the morning," Hal added. "If this rain sets in, I don't want to risk having Popeye and Bowlegs take a fall."

"Why not? You don't seem too concerned about your own safety," Nash cracked. "And why the hell can't you come swap out the horses yourself in the morning?"

"Because I'm going to be where everybody's supposed to be on Sunday morning. At church, damn it! Any more stupid questions?"

"You?" Nash chirped. "Since when did you start be-lieving in anything except the evils of women? And one more thing, you better clean up your language between now and tomorrow morning—"

The line went dead. Nash stared at the phone.

"Did he hang up on you again?" Crista questioned as she cuddled close to Nash.

"That's the second time in one day." Chuckling, Nash replaced the receiver. "My brother has become damned touchy all of a sudden."

"Must be the company he's keeping," Crista said wryly. "After the misery Hal caused me, I'm enjoying this."

Nash grinned scampishly as he drew Crista down on top of him. "I'm enjoying *this* even more . . ."

"Is Hal coming home tomorrow?" Crista murmured, distracted.

"Hal who?" Nash's lips settled on Crista's lush mouth, and he forgot everything—and everyone—he ever knew.

Andrea awoke to the amplified sound of rain pounding inside her sensitive head. When she tried to roll over, her stomach pitched like a barrel of acid. Groaning, she slithered toward the edge of her bed, discovering that every bone and muscle that had been trampled the previous day was screaming in objection. But breakfast had to be prepared before attending church . . .

The smell of food drifted up the staircase. Andrea struggled to gain her feet, despite her dizziness. Lord, she thought, she'd have to be dead a week before she felt better. Miserably, she glanced around for her clothes.

Befuddled, Andrea staggered out of bed to confront her reflection in the full-length mirror hanging beside the door. There seemed to be a gap in her memory. She remembered the giddy feelings brought on by the margaritas, the poker game in which she'd cheated outrageously, the approaching storm, the erotic feel of Hal's hands and lips flushing her body with wild, ineffable heat . . .

Andrea swallowed the unpleasant taste in her mouth and watched the hot blush spread up her neck to her pallid face.

"Oh, my God, what did I do?" she croaked.

Frantically, she spun around to see her clothes folded over the chair at her desk. Grabbing them up, she thrust one shaky leg and then the other into her faded jeans. She racked her brain, mentally clicking off the previous evening's events in chronological order. Unfortunately, her mind stalled out at the thought of Hal's masterful caresses. Andrea definitely remembered the burning pleasure of his touch. She remembered experiencing white-hot tingling sensations and then poof! The rest of the night was a blank.

Embarrassed by what she was very much afraid had happened, and even more humiliated that she couldn't remember, Andrea wobbled down the hall. She was reluctant to face Hal, certain he knew things about her that she didn't know about herself, afraid she had behaved like the rodeo groupies who trailed after him.

Dear God in heaven! She had probably confirmed Hal's cynical beliefs that women were either after his body, his bank account—or both!

Clinging to the banister for support, Andrea pulled in a steadying breath. After the traumatic ordeal she had endured four years earlier, she couldn't believe she had allowed a man to . . . Her breath caught when a flashback skittered across her mind.

It must have been those damned margaritas, she decided. That was why she remembered feeling a little wild and reckless.

"Fine, Fletcher," she muttered on her way down the stairs. "Now you know why you slipped out of character—and the good sense you were born with. Question is: Did you actually enjoy the intimacy you've avoided all these years?"

Andrea paused in the hallway to watch Hal moving back and forth between the sink and stove. A stack of steaming pancakes sat on the counter, while slices of ham sizzled in the skillet. In amazement, she shook her throbbing head—carefully. Doing domestic chores didn't fit this cowboy's image.

When Hal glanced sideways and smiled, Andrea's face flamed like a blowtorch. If she wasn't mistaken, their relationship had changed drastically last night, and she felt unbelievably self-conscious because of it.

"Happy Birthday," Hal said, wearing a grin Andrea couldn't account for.

"Was it?" she bleated, cursing her liquor-logged vocal cords.

Hal set the pancake turner aside, still smiling wickedly as Andrea approached. "I assume you don't remember much about the celebration."

Andrea dropped bonelessly into the chair and raked the wild tangles of auburn hair from her face. As if by magic, a cup of coffee appeared before her. "Thank you. Is Jason up yet?"

"Haven't seen him. I was just getting ready to call both of you to breakfast."

When Hal pivoted around, Andrea grabbed his arm. He lifted a dark brow as he glanced down at the hand clamped around his elbow. She knew he was making note of the symbolism of her gesture. It was evident in the rugged lines of his face, the lopsided smile playing on his lips. This was the first time Andrea had reached out to touch him, for any reason. She had made physical contact, when words would have served just as well. She had obviously become so familiar with Hal the previous night that touching him this morning was automatic reflex.

Andrea swallowed hard at the thought of what reaching out to touch him implied.

"Can I talk to you for a minute before we call Jason to breakfast?" Andrea requested, withdrawing her hand from his shirtsleeve.

Hal sank down across the table. "Got a problem, Fletcher?"

Andrea clamped both hands around the cup and took a cautious sip. "I don't know. I was hoping you could tell me if I do."

Sparkling obsidian eyes riveted on Andrea, making her squirm awkwardly. "How much do you remember, Birthday Girl?"

"Damn it, don't make this more embarrassing than it already is," she muttered into his devilish grin.

"Do you remember cheating me at poker?"

Andrea nodded slightly. "I had all four aces up my sleeve at one time or another."

"Do you remember worrying about whether Jason would arrive home safely during the storm?"

Andrea nodded again.

"Do you remember asking me to hold you before you kissed the breath out of me?"

Andrea's face turned fruit-punch red and Hal burst into chuckles. "You're enjoying this, aren't you?" she muttered.

"It's not every day that a woman who practically runs through walls to avoid me initiates that kind of kiss."

Andrea's fingers itched to wipe that ornery grin off his face. She decided to stop beating around bushes and blurt out the burning question before Hal thoroughly mortified her. "How far did we go?"

"You don't remember?"

"I wouldn't have to ask if I knew." Her lashes swept up to meet those dark, dancing eyes. Damned cowboy. He intended to drag this out until she had no pride and dignity left. "I can well imagine the kind of women you're accustomed to on the circuit," she said in a rush. "But I don't live in the fast lane—never wanted to. If I overstepped my bounds it was because I'm not used to drinking. The simple fact is that I wasn't myself last night."

"No? Who were you?" he asked in mock innocence.

Andrea glared at him. "I don't have the foggiest notion."

"So you think your Dr. Jekyll-Mr. Hyde tendencies were triggered by margaritas," he teased relentlessly. "Is that why you keep your distance from men? Because you can't keep your hands off them when you finally let loose?"

"No!" Andrea burst out, then flinched when her voice echoed inside her skull. "I usually freeze up around men," she said in a softer voice.

"I think it's time we discussed why that happens," Hal insisted. "I could deal with your mood swings if I understood where you're coming from."

Andrea watched the mischievous twinkle vanish from his eyes. He was asking her to reveal information that was personal and confidential. She didn't want to remember the unpleasant ordeal from her past, but, because of what happened the previous night, Hal needed to know there could be far-reaching consequences.

"I want to know what happened during your first year of college that makes you so leery of men," Hal insisted.

She swallowed nervously and forced herself to proceed. When she glanced discreetly at Hal, he was watching her intently, the look on his face indicating he intended to have an explanation—here and now.

"I was working overtime at the vet clinic on campus. We'd had an emergency case with a foundering, high-dollar mare that kept me out past midnight. I was walking back to the dorm when four boys—"

Andrea took a sip of coffee, unable to meet Hal's penetrating stare. "They were driving down the street I was crossing. Suddenly, a set of headlights were coming at me, blinding me. Before I realized what was happening, two boys leaped from the backseat and dragged me into the car. They ripped my clothes and . . ." Andrea put a stranglehold on her coffee cup—and her composure.

Hal rose from his chair to remove the ham from the skillet, graciously turning his back while she got herself under control. For that, Andrea could have hugged the stuffing out of him. Though he had teased her unmercifully earlier, he was aware of her distress in rehashing the incident.

"They had been drinking heavily—like Tony Braden and his thugs," Andrea said, her voice barely more than a whisper. "There were beer cans everywhere. While they held me down, they poured beer on me and then licked it off—"

Andrea's voice cracked and tears spilled down her cheeks. Hal sank down in his chair, reaching across the table to clasp her shaking hands in his.

"Go on, honey," he encouraged softly. "Let it all out. It's been a long time coming.

The compassionate timbre of his voice was like a soothing balm that encouraged her to speak the unspeakable that had been buried deep inside her. "One of the boys insisted on taking his turn first, while the others pinned me down and kept watch. He was poised and ready to do his worst, when the driver spotted the campus security police car.

"I was screaming my head off, biting every finger within reach. And then suddenly I was tossed out the door to the pavement. The boys drove off before the security policeman could get a description of the car or the license plate number.

"I was still crying and struggling to fasten my clothes when the officer stopped to help me. Like too many humiliated women, I didn't want to go through the ordeal of pressing charges and facing counter-accusations that suggested I had *invited* near-rape. I was merely thankful the patrolman arrived when he did."

Andrea muffled a sniff and clung to the callused strength of his hands. "I stopped dating, stopped dressing in any manner that called too much attention. I spent my weekends babysitting the policeman's young son and daughter. Dan Rogers had been my salvation, and I wanted to express my gratitude. He and his wife are the only ones who know about my terrifying ordeal.

"I never saw the boys again. I always wondered if they had come to attend the college basketball game and then hightailed it out of town."

"You were very lucky," Hal murmured.

"It didn't seem like it at the time." Andrea forced a feeble smile. "The emotional scars turned out to be every bit as painful as the physical bruises. But last night, after too many margaritas, I let myself forget everything—the past, my parents, the financial burden."

Andrea raised her tousled auburn head, staring at Hal

through a mist of tears. "If I threw myself at you, I didn't mean to. If I went to bed with you then you were the first, and there's a chance I could have gotten pregnant, because I don't—didn't—have any protection."

He stared at her as if she were a strange and curious creature from another planet.

"What happened was my own fault," Andrea hurried on. "I want you to know I don't hold you responsible and I won't—"

"Andrea," Hal cut in quickly.

"Let me finish—"

"We didn't go to bed together," he interrupted.

"We didn't?" Owlishly, she stared at the unexplainable scowl that claimed his bronzed features. "Why not? Close as I can recall, I wasn't protesting, because you made me feel things I've never—"

"Enough," Hal growled abruptly. "Things went a little too far in the living room and you passed out."

"Good grief," Andrea groaned, mortified.

"I carried you to bed, pulled off your outer clothing, and left you to sleep off the margaritas," Hal said.

When Andrea simply stared at him, trying to comprehend why this self-professed philanderer hadn't taken advantage when she had been so susceptible, Hal scowled again. She could only assume that she had made an utter fool of herself. She had undoubtedly repulsed him with her naive kisses. Why else would Hal Griffin turn and walk away from a blatant invitation? Hadn't he made it clear that he limited himself to superficial relationships with women?

"I'm sorry for making you uncomfortable and unloading my hangups on you," Andrea said miserably. "Last night will be my first and last encounter with margaritas."

Before Hal could comment, Jason bounded down the stairs. "I smell food—I'm starved!"

Andrea watched Hal withdraw and felt the full measure of her humiliation. Though he hadn't said a word, she knew she had ruined what might have been a new beginning for her. Cautious though she had been, she was drawn to Hal, intrigued by him. Too bad the feelings weren't mutual.

It was just as well that he would be gone soon, she told herself sensibly. She could wear her heart out on a man like him. If she began to care too much, it would only make him uncomfortable. He didn't want or need restrictions or commitments.

At least one good thing had come of her association with Hal, Andrea reminded herself. She had climbed one significant hurdle this morning. She had discussed the tormenting incident from her past. She had even reached out to a man, even invited his touch the previous night. She was making headway. There was that, she thought as she sipped her coffee and accepted Jason's wishes for a happy twenty-fifth birthday.

While Hal lay in bed, Andrea's words rang through his mind. *If I went to bed with you then you were the first . . .*

His attempt to prove to Andrea that some men could be trusted seemed a dim shadow compared to the light of revelation that had shone on him at the breakfast table. He had presumed Andrea had some experience, though not much. But a virgin? Good Lord!

Hal turned over on the king-size bed and stared at the west wall, wishing sleep would come. With Jason underfoot throughout the day and rain pouring down in torrents,

Hal had no opportunity to spend a moment alone with
Andrea. After the church services, he had taken the
Fletchers to lunch at Hard Times Cafe. That afternoon,
Andrea had fallen asleep on the sofa while Hal and Jason
watched the San Francisco Forty-Niners clash with the
Dallas Cowboys. Andrea had awakened in time to eat a
sandwich for supper and then trudged off to bed.

In Hal's opinion, her birthday had been uneventful. He
had wanted to do something special, but inclement
weather, and her bout with margaritas, had permitted little
besides church and a lunch that Andrea had tried to pay
for herself.

Rolling sideways, Hal stared at the east wall. *He would
have been the first.* The thought kept eating away at him
like battery acid. Good gawd, Andrea Fletcher was virtually
untouched, untried, inexperienced . . . Damn it, why
couldn't she have been like his usual women? It would have
simplified matters. Hal found himself questioning his own
perspectives, revisiting unpleasant memories of a wedding
engagement gone sour. He, who hadn't trusted a woman
in years, wanted to be trusted. He, who made it a practice
never to get involved, found himself involved up to his
eyebrows in a situation revolving around a struggling family that needed help.

Andrea Fletcher needed someone. What she had was a
man who could do little more than slap a Band-Aid on
her financial problems before he drove off to keep his
own commitments. In order to assist Andrea financially—
and he could hear her loudly protesting that!—Hal had to
remain on the grueling rodeo circuit. If he didn't, he might
lose his standings in the race for a berth at National Finals,
and he would be unable to give Andrea the money he won.

Hal propped himself up on his pillows and glared at

the north wall. How and when had he gotten in so deep? A week ago he was perfectly satisfied to wallow in his cynicism, to remain emotionally detached, to live his life on the road. Now here he was, acting like the Fletchers' guardian angel. Well, not exactly an angel, he amended. An angel wasn't supposed to lust after an independent, headstrong virgin who believed she was repulsive because she'd gotten a little tipsy and passed out.

"Well, shit." Hal pummeled his pillow and then stared at the ceiling for awhile.

His frustrated gaze drifted toward the bedroom door. How could he reassure Andrea that he hadn't lost respect for her? Damnation, how could she ever think he had? *He* was the one who practically shoved the drink in her hands to get her to relax. If not for him, she would have been sober as a judge last night.

But they had gotten up close and very personal, and Hal had felt the fire raging inside him, tormented by the knowledge that the pleasure Andrea could provide had to remain beyond his reach.

And why was it that—of all the women he *could* have— he found himself wanting one who didn't indulge in meaningless, one-night flings? This must be one of the tortures designed for the damned, he decided.

Hal flung his bare legs over the side of the bed and grabbed his jeans. Okay, so maybe he was turning out to be a gentleman with a conscience, and all that crap. But crazy as it was, he wanted to be with Andrea now—this very minute. He didn't care to analyze the specifics of that need, he just wanted to be with her. Being cooped up because of incessant rain was making him restless. He needed her, even if he knew he couldn't have all the intimate pleasures he craved.

Quietly, Hal twisted the doorknob to let himself into Andrea's bedroom. The moment he stared down at her shadowed form in bed, an odd sense of peace stole through him. He didn't try to define the reason for the sensation, didn't care to. He simply accepted its existence, accepted his need to be with Andrea in a way he had never allowed himself to be with another woman.

Hal eased onto the edge of the bed to gently rouse Andrea from sleep. She automatically shrank away, until the sound of her name on his lips dissolved her instinctive fear.

"Is something wrong?" she whispered.

"I can't sleep."

"Margaritas make great sedatives."

Hal cupped her chin in his hand, his thumb brushing lightly over her petal-soft lips. "I'd rather have you than Margarita."

She chuckled at his pun. "Yeah, right, Griffin."

"I mean it," he told her honestly.

Luminous orchid eyes peered up at him. "Why?"

She always asked why, Hal realized. He didn't know why. He just wanted to cradle her in his arms, to feel her settling familiarly against him. Sure, he would have preferred more, but Andrea wasn't ready to thoroughly explore the intimacy she had discovered last night.

Although Hal refused to answer, Andrea scooted sideways, making room for him in her double bed. That trusting gesture would have brought him to his knees, had he been standing. He and Andrea had passed another milestone, and he felt oddly humbled by her simple act of faith.

"Hold me," Hal whispered as he stretched out beside

her, returning the words that had touched him so deeply the night before.

"That's all I know how to do." Andrea, wearing her long T-shirt and cotton panties, wrapped her arms around his waist and burrowed her head against his bare shoulder. "But don't hold on too tight, or for very long, okay?"

After hours of flopping like a landed fish, Hal felt himself relax. He smiled, thinking he felt as contented as Goldilocks, having found a bed that wasn't too hard or too soft, but just right.

As many places as Hal had laid his head, his own bed at Chulosa Ranch didn't feel as welcoming as Andrea's. As he drifted off to sleep, he kept hearing her quiet words of acceptance. She would hold him, not too tightly, for a short space in time, until he was ready to leave. She didn't ask for much, didn't expect much. Hal should have felt relieved.

So why the hell didn't he?

On the heels of that question came the words of advice he had offered his own brother—not that Nash had paid a damn bit of attention before he handed his heart and soul over to Crista Delaney. Hal had insisted that if a man wasn't in it for the sex, then he should forget it. Ironic words coming from someone who found himself sleeping in the arms of a woman who knew absolutely nothing about the intimate techniques of passion.

Go figure, Hal thought before he let forbidden fantasy take him where reality could not.

Eight

Andrea opened her eyes and found herself sleeping single in her double bed. Sometime during the night Hal had returned to his room, eliminating the risk of an embarrassing encounter with Jason. Andrea glanced from the raindrops on the windowpane to the digital clock. She had just enough time to prepare Jason's breakfast before he drove off to school.

Anticipation thrummed through her as she donned a pair of faded jeans and a flannel shirt. Today she was going to deliver the partial loan installment to the bank and request an extension so she could keep the family ranch. The incessant rains had spoiled any chance of rounding up cattle in the north pastures and transporting them to town. But surely Tom Gilmore would take the bad weather into account.

Yet, the longer it rained the less chance Hal would have of completing the job, Andrea reminded herself. Hal had rodeos to attend. She would have to handle the remaining round-ups by herself.

On her way out the door, Andrea paused to stare back at the bed. Warm tingles skittered down her spine as she remembered the feel of Hal's powerful body stretched out beside hers. He had restored her belief in men. For years she had blamed the entire male population for the cruel and insulting behavior of four drunken college boys. If Andrea had learned nothing else the past few days, it was that all men weren't ruthless and abusive. She had nothing to fear from Hal Griffin. She felt she could trust any man who put a woman to bed with no more than a pat on the head, and then lay down to sleep beside her without asking for more.

Of course, Hal was operating on pity, Andrea reminded herself on the way to the kitchen. Who would have thought that beneath that hard shell was a tender, generous heart?

Truth be told, Andrea felt oddly disappointed that Hal had made no attempt to touch her the previous night. She had found herself wanting to explore the sizzling sensations he had aroused in her. She ached to discover passion with only one man, the very same one who religiously avoided commitments and complications.

"Forget it, Fletcher," Andrea lectured herself. Hal had managed to heal a few of her emotional wounds. She should be grateful for that. She didn't have time for involvement, either. She had a ranch to salvage, and she was still miles from accomplishing her goals.

Andrea jerked herself to attention when the kitchen door swung open to reveal Hal's bulky frame wrapped in a yellow rain slicker. The mere sight of him incited warm, fuzzy feelings. She was getting too attached, she realized, too comfortable in his presence.

"Morning," Hal murmured as he peeled off the coat. "The horses have been fed. It's still raining."

Andrea grabbed the skillet and set it on the stove. "You may as well go home. This weather isn't supposed to let up for two days. I'm sure you've got better things to do."

"I'm staying," Hal announced as he poured himself a

cup of the coffee he'd made before venturing outside. "I intend to hear what your banker has to say about the delay."

"It's not your problem," she reminded him.

Hal slammed his hand down on the Formica counter and glared at her. "Damn it, Fletcher, what's it going to take to get you to accept help when it's offered?"

Andrea's brows knitted at the sharp tone of his voice. If she didn't know better, she would swear Hal was mad at her. What had she said or done to provoke him?

"I'm letting you go," she declared, a proud tilt to her chin. "When I cash the cattle check, you'll be paid for your services, plus an extra bonus for wasting your valuable time the past two days—" Her voice dried up when he loomed over her like a granite mountain.

"Hear me and hear me well," Hal growled, teeth bared. "I'm sticking around until I do the job I'm being paid to do."

Andrea met his glittering, black-eyed gaze with forthright honesty. "The longer you stay, the harder it will be for me to watch you walk away. Don't you understand, you thick-headed cowboy? I'm afraid I'm on the verge of falling in love with you . . ." Andrea snapped her mouth shut so fast she nearly clipped off her tongue. That was the very last thing she intended to tell him—the very last thing she knew he wanted to hear.

Hal recoiled, clearly stunned. "In three days? This ain't no fairy tale, Cinderella, and I ain't nobody's Prince Charming," he muttered. "You aren't falling in love with me. Lust, maybe, but love? No way."

Andrea bristled immediately. "Don't tell me it can't happen in a matter of days, because it most certainly can. I didn't want it to happen any more than you did. I've got enough problems already. I don't need to love you, especially when you don't want somebody like me complicating your life."

"Call it what it really is, Fletcher," Hal demanded. "You got a little taste of sex and you've mistaken it for something else. My being here night and day, without posing a threat, has made you realize that what happened four years ago doesn't have to spoil the rest of your life. Just because I helped you over the hump, don't start confusing gratitude with love."

"So you think this has been like a therapy session, is that it?" she paraphrased.

"Yes," he said frankly.

"And I'm just too young and inexperienced to know it. Right?"

"Yes," he said with great certainty.

Andrea found herself amused by his surly disposition and clipped replies. She grinned at him. "Can't handle it, huh?"

He towered over her while she scrambled a half-dozen eggs. "Can't handle what? I managed to sleep beside you last night without touching you. You think that was easy?"

Andrea dumped eggs in the skillet and then pivoted to face his dark scowl. "Is that what's ruining your disposition this morning?"

"Geezus!" Hal exploded irascibly. "We have the damnedest conversations before breakfast."

"Well? Is that your problem or isn't it?"

"No!" he bit off.

Smiling at the inconsistency of the male psyche, Andrea let out her customary whistle to summon Jason to the table. It was amusing to watch a man flounder when he encountered the prospect of being loved by a woman he didn't love in return.

Nonetheless, Andrea experienced a strange kind of comfort in knowing she actually could fall in love, without fearing disastrous consequences—if that made the slightest sense. Oddly enough, it made perfect sense to her. Because she honestly did care about Hal, she didn't want to be a burden to him. She didn't want to become a responsibility that he had accepted because she was down on her luck. Her affection stemmed from an admiration for the competent, dynamic man he was. She respected him because he treated her like an individual, not an object. She trusted him because he had earned her trust on several occasions. Hal Griffin was more man than she had ever known.

"This discussion isn't over," he murmured when he heard Jason trotting downstairs. "It's only being postponed."

"You should be accustomed to being adored by female admirers," Andrea remarked. "I'm sure there's a passel of them."

"Don't start speculating on how many women I've had," he growled at her. "I hate it when women do that."

"Why?"

"Don't you know any other words besides *why,* Fletcher?"

She ignored the question and grinned impishly. It had been years since she had felt safe enough in a man's presence to tease so playfully. It felt good.

"All I got to do was share a bed with a famous, hot-shot rodeo star. I'll always wonder what I missed."

"Is that a fact?" Hal snorted sarcastically.

"Fact," she confirmed while stirring the eggs.

Hal grabbed her wrist, demanding her full attention. The pressure of his steely fingers forced her to drop the wooden spoon. He spun her around to thrust his scowling face into hers. "You wanna know something, Fletcher? I think I liked you better when you were avoiding me. Where I come from, women like you are a nickel a dozen. And you're right. I can snap my fingers and get a quick lay after every go-round at any rodeo, if I'm so inclined. The difference is that you don't know the first thing about pleasing a man, and I like it hot, hard, and fast—with somebody who knows the score."

His fingers dug a little deeper into her flesh. He leaned closer, his furious face a mere inches from hers. "What you *missed* was pure and simple sex, not lovemaking. That's all I want or need. You got that, Fletcher? Don't make something out of this physical need that isn't there."

Andrea massaged her wrist when he finally let go. His harsh rejection hurt. She didn't know what to make of him. When she avoided him he was gentle and considerate. When she was open, honest, and playful he turned cold and abrupt.

Andrea reclaimed the spoon and turned back to the stove, unsure how to behave around this lumbering grizzly bear who had stalked in from the rain. She would ignore him and see how that worked, she decided. For sure, she wasn't going to use the teasing, playful approach again. It set him off like a case of explosives.

Pretending Hal Griffin wasn't sitting across the table, Andrea ate her breakfast and visited with her brother. Hal seemed to appreciate eating in silence, so she left him to his brooding. The four years she had spent avoiding men had obviously impaired her ability to relate to them, she reasoned. Hal's about-face attitude made her wonder why she had bothered to poke her head from her self-imposed shell. All he had done was bite it off!

* * *

Andrea dashed through the downpour, refusing to wait for Hal to open the passenger door of his pickup for her. There was so much silence in the cab of the truck during the drive to town that the windshield wipers sounded like percussion instruments. With the cattle paycheck in her purse, she strode into the bank, opening yet another door for herself. If the door slammed shut in Hal's face, all the better.

"Hal Griffin?"

Andrea glanced sideways to see a willowy blonde staring owl-eyed at Hal. Although Andrea didn't know her by name, she had seen the bank employee at the teller's desk when she had come to speak to Tom Gilmore a few weeks earlier. Leaving Hal to renew old acquaintances, Andrea propelled herself toward Gilmore's office. To her surprise, Hal didn't tarry long. He was two steps behind her.

When Tom glanced inquiringly at her, Andrea made a quick introduction. "Tom, this is Hal Griffin. He rounded up the stray cattle so I could make the installment on the loan."

Tom gestured for Hal and Andrea to take a seat. She studied the banker as he levered into his padded leather chair. There was an air of superiority about Gilmore that instinctively annoyed her, Andrea decided.

The banker, who dressed impeccably, distanced himself from his customers. At age forty-five, Gilmore appeared to be keeping himself physically fit. His intense green eyes shifted from Hal to Andrea as he steepled his fingers and flashed the expensive rings that encircled both pinkies.

"I see no sense in misleading you, Andrea," Tom said point-blank. "Even if you have managed to make a partial payment on your father's loans, you must realize that we consider you a risky investment."

Andrea's fists clenched around the arms of her chair, bracing herself for the discouraging news she hadn't wanted to hear.

"Quite honestly, you would do yourself a favor if you simply accepted foreclosure and cut your losses. Managing a ranch is difficult these days, what with the market price on grain and livestock scraping bottom. Without experience, you face more than the usual problems. If we sell your ranch to the highest bidder, you and Jason will have enough money to make a down payment on a home."

Everything in Andrea rebelled against the cool dismissal of what she had struggled so valiantly to save. "This first cattle check should assure you that I intend to make future payments," she said, with as much politeness as she could muster. "I would have had another check in your hands tomorrow, if not for this monsoon season. As soon as weather permits—"

Gilmore flung up a bejeweled hand to forestall her. "Andrea, I admire your spirit, just as I admired your mother's while she was working for us. But Maggie could see the handwriting on the wall. Fletcher Ranch has been in debt for several years, and the situation has become progressively worse."

That was because of Andrea's astronomical tuition and college fees, which Robert insisted on paying, Andrea thought miserably. That, added to final expenses for both parents, had crippled the ranch. And let's not forget that Gilmore and her father had it out, right here in this office, Andrea mused. Gilmore had no intention of cutting her any slack.

"I intend to sell every calf on our property," Andrea declared. "Every cow if need be."

"And how do you plan to provide an income without cows to produce more calves?" he quizzed her.

"I'll take an outside job."

"And attempt to borrow money to restock your pastures?" Gilmore shook his head. "It's a vicious cycle, Andrea. I don't want to see you repeat the mistakes your father made. He obviously saw the hopelessness of his situation and chose to escape the embarrassment of foreclosure."

Andrea felt her temper straining at the bit. Gilmore's reference to her father's suicide hit every sensitive nerve. "Perhaps my father's sense of despair was triggered by his fiery confrontation with you," she gritted between clamped teeth. "Is that the reason you won't give me the chance to prove myself? Because my father lost his temper with you?

"The ranch means everything to me. Maybe you can't understand that—"

"Or perhaps I do," Gilmore cut in, "You feel obligated to continue with tradition, because you think it's your duty. I can understand that, but you aren't being realistic."

"If Andrea can pay off the delinquent interest and part of the principal by the end of this week, will you give her one month to raise the rest of the money?" Hal questioned.

Gilmore shifted in his chair. "I don't see what difference a month is going to make. She'll have to sell the cows—that herd is her only prospect. No other bank is going to lend Andrea money if she doesn't have cattle for collateral. The land can't become collateral, because it's already mortgaged to us."

Hal stared directly at Gilmore. "You're avoiding my question."

"What interest do you have in this?" Gilmore asked, looking down his patrician nose.

"I'm her genie, straight from Aladdin's lamp, and I'm here to grant her wish," Hal said flippantly. "Answer the question. Either you're going to give Andrea a month's grace period after she lost both parents in less than four months, or I'll be thinking you have some particular interest in selling her ranch."

Gilmore scoffed at the insinuation. "Why would I want that ranch? It can't pay for itself without a hefty cattle herd."

"Then I should think you would want to give Andrea the chance to sell her calves, keep the cows, and find outside employment."

"And if she doesn't come up with the money she owes by the end of the month, will you be here to question my ethics again?" Gilmore smirked.

"No, I'll be here to pay what she owes so you'll back off and give her the chance she deserves after what she's been through—without much consideration and understanding from you," he added candidly.

Andrea gaped at Hal as if he had three heads. "You can't—"

Demanding silence, Hal's hand clamped over her fist, which was still gripping the arm of her chair. "Yes or no, Gilmore. Simple questions deserve simple answers."

The banker's chest heaved beneath his expensive three-piece suit. Attempting to stare Hal down, Gilmore drummed blunt-tipped fingers on his desk. "All right, yes," he said finally. "One month. If nothing else, it will prove that I'm willing to make allowances for Andrea's difficulties. But if the money is so much as one day overdue there will be no more excuses. I do not expect to be taken apart at the seams again as I was when I told Robert I couldn't carry him and his loans indefinitely."

Hal arched a dubious brow. "For *that,* he lit into you?"

"He became unstable and irrational after Maggie died," Gilmore explained. "Ask anyone in the bank if Robert didn't lose his cool when I told him I had to foreclose if he didn't pay up."

Andrea bit her tongue as the urge to rush to her father's defense overwhelmed her. She endorsed the check and then handed it to Gilmore. "You'll have your money on time, even if I have to work double days at minimum wage to compensate for the difference between the payment due and my future cattle sales," she assured him crisply.

Head held high, Andrea marched through the office door. Raindrops splattered on her flushed cheeks as she headed for Hal's pickup. Once inside, she stared squarely at Hal. "I don't believe in being dishonest," she rapped out. "You had no right to lead Gilmore to believe you're going to pay my loan."

Hal cranked the engine and then veered toward Hard Times Cafe. "I plan to do just that."

Andrea's jaw dropped open. "Why?"

"Why not?"

"You don't even like me all that much. You made that clear before breakfast."

"You need help, Fletcher, and I'm in a financial position to give it."

Andrea crossed her arms over her chest and sat there like a cigar-store Indian. "I won't allow it . . . Why are we stopping here?"

Hal directed her attention to his wristwatch. "It's eleven-thirty. I'm hungry."

Andrea's gaze followed Hal as he slid off the seat and

shut the door. The man was such an enigma. In the past few days he had changed moods so often that she couldn't keep up with him.

Andrea quit trying to figure Hal out and dashed through another downpour to reach the cafe. The instant she plopped onto the red vinyl seat in the corner booth her mother's oldest, dearest friend hurried over to give her a sympathetic hug.

Laverne Gable clutched Andrea close. "I'm so sorry, sugar. You've had a rough go of it, haven't you?"

Her slim figure encased in traditional waitress-white, Laverne scuttled over to pour two glasses of water. Andrea glanced at the menu she had placed in front of her.

"I've been meaning to stop by to see you after I finish my shift," Laverne said. "But it's been so busy around here that I'm dead on my feet by quitting time." Her fake-lashed gaze settled on Hal, indicating that she was waiting for an introduction.

"Hal Griffin," Andrea complied, "this is Laverne Gable. She and Mom went to high school together."

"Had our first babies together, too," Laverne added, giving Hal a thorough once-over. "My son had the worst crush on Andi in junior high, but then, what boy didn't? Prom queen, homecoming queen, you name it and she *was* it. Of course, a man would have to be blind in both eyes not to figure out why boys stumbled over themselves to get Andi's attention." She winked conspiratorially at Hal. "I heard you and Andi are an item. Tuff Seever was in here this morning, grumbling about you beating his time."

Andrea hurried to set the record straight. "Actually, we're—"

"Getting along splendidly," Hal interrupted, flashing Laverne a knock-'em-dead grin.

Andrea glared at him, exasperated. The man was purposely nurturing the fruit on the proverbial grapevine. One of Laverne's greatest talents was spreading information around the small community. As good-hearted as she was, she had the fastest jaw west of Fire River.

When Tuff Seever lumbered into the restaurant, chewing on his unlit cigar, Andrea groaned silently. Coming here wasn't a good idea. Sure as the world, she would be labeled as Griffin's latest fling—between rodeos. And she wasn't even getting to enjoy the benefits!

"I'll have coffee and chicken fried steak," Hal requested.

"That was Robert's favorite," Laverne recalled, smiling remorsefully. "He ordered the same entree every Friday when he met Maggie for lunch. Hamburger and fries on Monday, hot beef sandwich on Wednesday, chicken fried steak on Friday, just like clockwork." She frowned pensively. "Except for the Friday that he—"

She glanced sympathetically at Andrea. "Sorry, sugar, but I never have figured out why Rob ordered a grilled cheese sandwich that particular Friday. Chicken fry was his favorite. You wouldn't think a man who was about to do what he did would order the cheapest item for his last meal—"

"I'll have fried chicken strips," Andrea interrupted hurriedly.

"There I go again," Laverne muttered, scribbling the order on her notepad. "I never know when to shut up. My ex-husband certainly told me that often enough. 'Course, he just sat there in front of the TV and belched his beer. Couldn't hold down a job to save his lazy soul. Best move

I ever made was kicking him out and raising my son without that freeloader's bad influence."

When Laverne wheeled around and whizzed off to take Tuff's order, Hal smiled dryly. "I admire anyone who can pour out her life story in the time it takes to place an order."

"Laverne's life is an open book—always has been."

Andrea glanced sideways when a broad figure of a man halted beside the booth. Amos Harden glanced down at her, his pudgy hand coming to rest on her shoulder. "Confound weather is playin' hell with your round-up," he mumbled. "Did you manage to get Gilmore off your back until the storm blows over?"

"He reluctantly agreed to an extension," Andrea confided to her nearest neighbor.

Amos nodded his bald head in silent greeting to Hal. "With this cowboy on your side, you'll meet your deadline," he assured her. "How ya doin' on the circuit, boy?"

"Can't complain," Hal replied with a lackadaisical shrug.

"Where's the next rodeo?"

"Mesquite, Texas."

Amos hiked his sagging overalls over his pot belly. "Well, good luck to ya. I'll be in my easy chair, rootin' for ya while you're jarrin' your teeth on those wild broncs."

"I appreciate all the moral support I can get, Amos."

His hazel eyes twinkled as he glanced momentarily at Andrea, then back to Hal. "I knew you were the man to solve Andrea's problems. Not every job provides such pretty scenery, does it?" he added with a wink.

Hal peered at Andrea so longingly that she nearly burst out laughing. Why Hal wanted to convince everyone in Hochukbi that they were a genuine item she could not imagine. Probably some spiteful prank to amuse himself. With Hal, nobody really knew what he was thinking.

At least Andrea didn't have a clue. He hadn't behaved like an infatuated boyfriend this morning, that was for sure. He'd been downright blunt. So what was this walking contradiction up to now?

"If there's anything I can do to help out, hon, just give me a holler. Your dad and I struggled, side by side, for years. Helped each other out by borrowing farming equipment when we got in a bind." Amos leaned down, quietly adding, "We even got drunk together a couple of times and cussed the bank for those high interest farm loans. Your dad had his—"

"What are you doing over here, pestering these lovebirds," Laverne clucked at Amos. "Can't you tell when young folks want to be alone? Get back to your own booth, you old goat."

Andrea grinned when Laverne shooed Amos on his way. She had missed this small town atmosphere while she was at college. At least here, people cared enough to be interested in their neighbors.

The thought made Andrea even more determined to hold onto her heritage, to remain a part of this community. Now, if only the leak in the sky would stop dripping so she could gather another trailer-load of calves and transport them to the stockyards!

Laverne set two cups of coffee on the table. "Lunch will be out shortly. Better eat up before you float away. Jess Burton was in here an hour ago, telling everybody to keep an eye on the river. The water has been rising so fast that some of the folks down in Tin Can Alley are heading for higher ground. Flood plains are the worst place in the world for trailer parks. But you know Tuff—

he'd sell his own mama to make a few bucks. How that man has managed to make a living selling real estate and insurance I'll never know. Guess it proves there's a sucker born every day."

When Laverne scuttled off, Hal eased back in his seat. His gaze settled on Tuff, who had wedged his rotund body into a booth on the opposite side of the cafe. From the look of things, Tuff was passing along information—probably about Hal and Andrea.

Andrea shook her head at Tuff's high-school mentality. She doubted the man would ever grow up. Jason Fletcher was already more emotionally mature than Tuff ever thought about being.

After a hastily eaten meal, Andrea led the way outside. "I need to stop for some groceries before we head home."

When she reached for the door handle, Amos poked his bald head outside the cafe to flag her down. "Better check those cattle down by the river" he advised. "We've had enough rain to sink Noah's Ark. You could lose several head when the river hits flood stage."

Andrea flounced onto the seat, feeling Hal's probing gaze. "Go ahead and say you told me so," she grumbled begrudgingly.

"Told you so, Fletcher. The Wild Bunch will be hell to drive into the pens. We should have rounded them up with the rest of the herd."

With a sense of urgency, Andrea squirmed in the pickup, watching rain saturate the countryside. Ponds were forming where grass once stood. She needed to get those cattle to higher ground—fast.

So much had happened the past few days that she had forgotten about those contrary Brahmas. She would like to sell the whole lot of troublesome misfits—if they didn't drown themselves first.

"I'm going to the river when we get home," Andrea announced as Hal negotiated another winding curve. "I may not be able to get to the strays at all if I wait until the rain lets up."

"You *may* need an ark, *Noah,*" Hal smirked.

"Maybe, but I can't afford to lose a single cow or calf. Gilmore is waiting for any excuse to foreclose."

"He seems *too* anxious to me."

"My dad didn't endear himself to the man," Andrea commented. "Amos confirmed that. Dad obviously resented the fact that Gilmore was holding the ax. On top of everything else that Dad had been through, the possibility of losing the ranch was obviously too much . . . Be careful on this winding curve," she added hastily. "You can lose control in the blink of an eye."

Andrea hated this stretch of road. It was a constant reminder of how quickly a life could be snatched away, of how much heartache those left behind had to endure.

"Do you know the woman working at the teller's desk?" Andrea questioned, anxious to change the subject.

"Yeah, I know her," Hal said flatly.

"Old girlfriend?"

"No, old fiancée."

Andrea clamped her mouth shut and stared at the huge raindrops that splattered against the windshield. The woman, who looked to be somewhere around Hal's age, was definitely attractive—stunning, in fact, Andrea could understand why he had fallen so hard. What Andrea didn't know was what had broken the engagement and left Hal so cynical. It must have been something drastic, she speculated.

"Aren't you going to ask why the plans fell through?" Hal muttered.

Andrea stared at his rigid profile. "I don't have to—it's not any of my business. But I think she was nine kinds of fool for betraying your trust."

"How do you know I wasn't the one who betrayed?"

"Because I know you better than you think," she said with an air of certainty.

"You don't know me at all, Fletcher. You only want to believe you do."

Andrea stared straight ahead, listening to the wipers slap against the windshield. There it was again, that abrupt, dismissive tone of voice that warned her to back off. There were times—like now—when Andrea wondered why she had fancied herself in love with this man. Maybe it was just an illusion, an attempt to reach out and care about someone, hoping to compensate for the emptiness in her life.

"You're right," Andrea murmured belatedly. "I don't know what makes me think I know you at all . . ."

Nine

Hal was as cross and cranky as a junkyard dog and had been for more hours than he cared to count. The reason? He was forcing himself to do without something his brother was enjoying—in limitless supply. Sex. Really good sex.

How was a man supposed to function normally when he was in a permanent state of arousal? Hal asked himself as he stalked into the barn. Riding wasn't going to be easy. The last thing he wanted to do right now was straddle a damned horse.

So much for a man getting what he wanted.

Grimly, he slid the saddle in place. The gelding called Bandit shifted sideways when Hal fastened the cinch. The mare, Sweet Pea, had the same reaction when Hal abruptly tossed the second saddle blanket into place.

The two sure-footed horses Nash had exchanged for the highly prized rodeo mounts were rolling their bits, staring through the barn at the pouring rain. Hal shared their lack of enthusiasm. He would have preferred to cozy up in the house instead of tramping through waterlogged pastures to round up those cantankerous Brahma cattle.

Hal grumbled to himself when Andrea appeared on the elevated deck outside the kitchen. "Face it, Griffin, the woman is driving you nuts."

Hal had hoped the night he had spent cuddling Andrea would appease the gnawing ache. No such luck. Sleeping beside her only made the hungry need more pronounced.

A man could only be so noble and restrained before he blew a fuse. Hal was lusting after an inexperienced virgin who had been out of circulation for four years. If and when Andrea decided to test the waters of passion, she was going to need a man with inexhaustible patience and a tender touch.

That man was not Hal Griffin.

He had made that crystal clear this morning when Andrea tried her hand at playful teasing. It had been like nudging a rattlesnake with a blade of grass.

Hal had awakened so hard and hungry he could barely tolerate the discomfort. Everything Andrea said and did thereafter had rubbed him the wrong way. He practically bit her head off with very little provocation. And when she declared she thought she was falling in love with him he wanted to shake her.

Andrea's emotions were in such a befuddled tangle that she couldn't distinguish between gratitude, loneliness, and desperation. So what did she do? She called it love.

As if Hal wasn't having enough trouble dealing with his frustration and Andrea's ridiculous conclusions about love, he had run smack-dab into Jenna Randall—or whatever her last name might be by now. Of all the rotten luck!

Seeing Jenna had unearthed another heap of feelings and frustrations that Hal was in no mood to deal with. The woman from his past, and the woman in his present, were causing him entirely too much grief. Thoughts and memories were churning inside him like updrafts in thunderstorms. Clearly, the best course of action was to complete this job at Fletcher Ranch and get the hell out of town—pronto.

Andrea walked into the barn, her beguiling orchid eyes riveted on him. Hal noted the uncertainty in her expression—uncertainty that his bad-tempered comments had put there. He was tormented by conflicting urges: to kiss her breathless and simultaneously curse her for being so damned inaccessible. These riotous feelings were spoiling his disposition, coloring every thought and tainting every conversation.

"Shit," Hal muttered, turning his back on Andrea. He hoped the steady rain would cool him off. The cold shower he had taken this morning—when wanting her had him aching so bad he had to get up and leave—hadn't worked worth a damn. Neither had a long walk in the pouring rain.

"Hal?"

"What?" he snapped crankily.

"There was a call for you on the answering machine."

"From my brother? What did he want?"

"No, from a woman named Jenna," Andrea informed him. "She asked you to call her back when you had the chance. Is that your—?"

Hal wheeled to slap Sweet Pea's reins in Andrea's hand, his abruptness startling her into silence. "You delivered the message—now let's get on with this, shall we?"

Andrea ducked her head and nodded. Hal silently cursed himself for making her life more difficult than it was. But damn it, knowing what he now knew about her past and her lack of sexual experience, he had to protect her—from himself.

Gawd, the irony was killing him. The older brother routine had turned out to be a flop. His body hadn't cooper-ated with that scenario. Then he had tried to think of himself as Andrea's mentor . . . but he ached to be her lover—and knew he shouldn't, couldn't. Hal didn't consider himself the gentle, patient, compassionate type of man. Detached, emotionally uninvolved, and blunt to a fault better described him . . .

A forbidden memory slipped past Hal's defenses as he stared down at Andrea. All too well, he remembered the night his intimate fondling had left her shimmering like warm honey on his fingertips. He had aroused her until she literally passed out . . .

His body clenched. Irritating, untimely sensations rushed through him, exasperating him to extremes. Caged rage, Hal thought as he swung onto Bandit's back. He could identify with rodeo bulls confined to metal chutes while uncomfortable flank straps were wrapped around them. The instinct to snort, buck, and kick loose was overwhelming. That was exactly how Hal felt—restrained by his own conscience, tormented by primitive male instinct.

And Andrea thought *she* was a basket case? Ha! She didn't know the half of it!

Ignoring Andrea, who rode at his side, Hal trotted through the swampy pasture. She had the good sense to keep her mouth shut. For that, Hal was thankful.

Just get this job done and go back to the life you know, Hal kept repeating to himself.

"Oh damn," Andrea groaned, gesturing west. "I should have checked on those Brahmas this morning."

When she gouged her boot heels into Sweet Pea's ribs and galloped off, Hal muttered several coarse expletives. Putting his mount into a canter, he headed toward the underbrush that stood in rushing water. The cattle—having the collective IQ of a tree stump—were stranded on a sandy knoll surrounded by frothy water. They were huddled like a wolf pack, milling in a circle.

Hal swore under his breath when Andrea charged her mount into the swift current, determined to rescue the bawling calf that had been knocked into the river by the panicky herd.

Hal scowled, kicking Bandit into his swiftest gait. That idiotic woman would lay her life on the line to save that calf, to save this ranch and all the sentimental ties she had to it.

Above the roar of water spilling from its banks, Hal heard Andrea curse the horse as it balked at the overpowering current. Sweet Pea flung her head in objection, but Andrea was relentless. She forced the horse toward the tiny isle in midstream.

"Damn it, woman!" Hal roared. "You'll do your little brother a lot of good when you drown! Let me handle this."

"No!"

There it was again—that uncompromising syllable that Hal was beginning to detest. He ground his teeth and cursed Andrea's daredevil nature. That female was as daring as he was. Worse, Hal amended. His daring was tempered with experience and common sense. Hers was sheer stupidity!

If Andrea didn't swallow a river of water during this shenanigan, Hal swore he'd hold her head under until she was so waterlogged she would have to take orders from him.

With the coiled rope in one hand and the loop in the other, Hal sent Bandit into the boiling current. While Andrea's mount floundered to gain footing on the island, Hal swung his lariat. The loop settled over the wild-eyed calf's head. Urging Bandit to reverse direction, Hal dragged the calf toward safety.

The mother cow, hearing the calf's distress call, plunged into the water. The jittery herd, anxious yet apprehensive about following the cow's lead, bolted one direction and then the other, searching for the safest route.

Hal tugged the soggy calf ashore, but he kept his gaze glued to Andrea. He couldn't shake the uneasy feeling that calamity was riding this bubbling current. All it would take to get Andrea into serious trouble was one sideswipe from a terrified cow. If Sweet Pea went down in the river, Andrea would have trouble jerking her foot from the stirrup and swimming free. Bearing that in mind, Hal's gaze leaped back and forth from Andrea to the calf that struggled to gain its footing.

With experienced ease, Bandit slopped to higher ground. Hal had taken his eyes off Andrea for only a moment while he unloosed his lariat. It was a moment too long. Her yelp of alarm bolted through him and froze his very soul. He glanced across the river to see Sweet Pea scrambling in shifting sand. Milling cattle collided with the floundering horse.

When Sweet Pea bucked and then kicked out at the cow crowding her space, Andrea went flying. Clawing air, she latched onto the first stable object within reach—a Brahma cow. Eleven hundred pounds of startled bovine came unhinged when a body sprawled on its back. The cow dipped her head and flung out both hind hooves in an act of enraged defiance.

Despite oncoming disaster, Andrea accomplished her original purpose. The cattle herd was forced to clear a path for the outraged cow. The braver members of the herd splashed into the water, summoned by the bawling calf and cow that had separated from the others. Tentatively, the cattle fell into a line to battle the current.

Hal grimaced when Andrea lost her grasp on the cow's rain-slickened hide. With a twisting lurch and plunging dive that would have done a rodeo bull proud, the cow ejected its hapless rider. Andrea did a belly buster in midstream, directly in the path of the swimming herd.

"Hal!" Her terrified screech hung in the humid air. Hal coiled his rope and urged Bandit knee-deep into the current. Before he could toss his loop, one of the cows swam directly over the top of Andrea. The instant her wet head popped to the surface, Hal flung the loop.

At no time in his life had he prayed so hard. He discovered Andrea was correct on one count. Rodeo—rough and rugged though it was—was entertainment compared to the situation they were in. He wasn't merely out to claim prize money for turfing a steer—he was trying to save a life that had somehow become entirely too precious to him.

Hal sighed in relief when the lasso dropped over Andrea's extended arm. Dallying the rope to the saddlehorn, he signaled for Bandit to back up. For several minutes Hal played cat and mouse with the rope, pulling Andrea sideways in the powerful current, hoping to avoid flailing hooves. He barely had time to scoop her onto his lap and rein Bandit out of the way before the herd lunged toward higher ground.

While anxious cows bawled to summon their missing calves, Hal swatted Andrea's soggy butt for scaring several good years off his life. With an abrupt jerk, he shifted her around until she was straddling his thighs on horseback, facing his thunderous scowl.

Hal glared into the peaked face surrounded by a mop

of wet hair. "Damn it to hell, woman!" he bellowed. "Don't you ever listen? That's the second stupid stunt you've pulled in less than a freaking week! You wanna kill yourself? Do it on your own goddam time. Hear me!"

Andrea pulled in a ragged breath and then had the audacity to smile at him.

Smiled, damn it!

"I retract what I said about rodeo being entertainment. Anybody who can stay on the back of a bucking bull—or cow—for eight seconds has my respect. And, by the way, you really are something else with a rope in your hand, Griffin."

When Andrea impulsively flung her arms around his neck and hugged him, Hal crushed her against him. Like a damned fool he buried his head against the side of her neck, his lips brushing the rapid pulse beat in her throat. She lifted her head and peered at him with those glorious orchid-colored eyes and her arms slid around his neck, her fingers spearing into his wet black hair. For the life of him, Hal couldn't find the will to reject her when she pressed her soft lips to his. Despite what she had endured at the hands of drunken college boys she was offering herself to him—he could sense it. Gone was her mistrust, her apprehension. Right or wrong, she was his for the taking.

Hal closed his eyes and drank the sweet nectar of her kiss. Her honest, hungry response sent his mind reeling. Instinctively, he wrapped her legs around his hips, cursing the barrier of wet fabric between his throbbing manhood and her tender flesh. He felt Andrea shiver as he pressed her against him—and held her there as his tongue plunged into her mouth.

Hal groaned aloud when Andrea shifted closer, her hips

gliding provocatively against him. Hands shaking, he caressed the wet flannel that covered her breasts. But it wasn't enough. He wanted to feel her flesh beneath his hands, to warm her cold skin and feel the fire of passion sizzling through her—and into him.

At first touch, Andrea quivered against his hand, arching into his caress. Hal was oblivious to the rain, the rushing waters fifteen feet away, the milling cattle around him. He was so attuned to Andrea's responses that nothing else registered. When he thrust against her, she spread her legs farther apart, until his aching flesh was separated from hers only by that cursed denim.

It was almost more than he could bear—being so close and yet so intolerably far away.

Heaven and hell at once . . .

The splattering sound of Sweet Pea floundering ashore to nudge Hal's leg brought him back to his surroundings. Sweet Pea shook off the water and tossed her head. Reluctantly, Hal reached out to grab the mare's trailing reins.

"We better move this herd to the barn while they're still in a submissive mood," he rasped.

When Andrea didn't immediately slide onto her horse, Hal glanced down at her. Slowly, but without her customary hesitation, she uplifted her hand to limn the curve of his lips with her forefinger. Her gaze held him captive, an unspoken invitation in those spell-binding depths.

"Fletcher," he said, summoning the remains of his self-control, "you're playing with fire. Unless you want to find yourself flat on your back with all your idealistic illusions shattered, I suggest you haul your fanny onto your horse and steer clear of my lap."

"Why do you do that?" she questioned, searching his scowling face.

"Why do I do what?"

"Try to frighten me away now that I've come to trust you?"

Because wanting you this badly scares the living hell out of me, Hal replied silently.

He was trying to do the honorable thing here. Why couldn't she figure that out?

Hal struggled to breathe normally. These close encounters were wearing his disposition onion-skin thin. He kept lashing out at Andrea because lashing out at himself no longer helped. She was damned hard on his willpower, not to mention what she was doing to the most sensitive part of his anatomy. The sooner he gathered the rest of her cattle and left this ranch the better off they would both be.

Hal was going to put in a call to Nash and Uncle Jim—PDQ. By tomorrow night, Andrea's cattle would be waiting transport to the stockyards. Hal was spending only one more night at her place.

Now that Andrea's responses were becoming more inviting, Hal was suffering every kind of hell. He couldn't have sex with a damned virgin. It would demand more than he was capable of giving, so that was that. He didn't know how much longer he could trust himself with her. Running like hell was his only option.

With grim resolve, he deposited Andrea on her mount, then reined Bandit toward the herd. The swim through fierce currents had taken the starch out of the contrary Brahmas—thank God. The herd moseyed toward the corral beside the barn without causing Hal any more trouble.

He never once glanced at Andrea while she rode on the far side of the herd. He didn't want to see the hurt and rejection he knew he'd caused. All he could offer her was his cash winnings—she was welcome to his money. That he could give without his conscience nagging him to death.

Andrea was too damned good for the likes of him. He had become a hell-raising rounder, a card-carrying womanizer the past decade. She deserved better—a helluva lot better. Someday the right kind of man would come along. Hal had done what he could to help her overcome her irrational fear of men, but he couldn't cross that dangerous line that loomed in front of him.

Now that Andrea had learned to reach out to *him,* she could reach out to another man—a better man, not some rough-edged, hard-ass cowboy who understood bulls and broncs better than he would ever understand women. Hal would do the charitable thing by giving Andrea financial footing. Once the herd had been converted to cash she could put her life back together and make a fresh start—and he would be history.

Besides, he was feeling restless again. It was time to hit the road. There was another long stretch of highway awaiting him, another luck of the draw at the arena, another willing female who agreed to play by Hal's rules for the night.

Andrea stood beneath the warm, pulsating mist of the shower. Her thoughts weren't centered on the ordeal at the roiling river. She was lost to another vivid memory, full of sensations that wouldn't go away. Inexperienced though she was, she had felt Hal's desire for her while they were straddling his horse. She had heard his rumbling groan when she instinctively sidled closer, savoring the close contact, the pure pleasure that he aroused in her.

Andrea hadn't taken a risk with a man in four years, because fear wouldn't permit her to trust a man's intentions. The fact that Hal had backed away from their intimate encounter indicated that he was an honorable man. Other men might have taken advantage, but not Hal. She loved him all the more for that. In his own way he was trying to protect her, just as he had done twice before when she faced impending danger.

Andrea had discovered how lonely she had become inside her shell. She longed to explore the tantalizing sensations that Hal excited. She didn't need complications in her life, but her awakened womanhood had taken on a life of its own.

Though Hal hadn't said so, Andrea sensed he was anxious to finish the job and move on. She detected it in the way he had gone about cutting out the calves to a separate pen for loading and transport. She had also overheard bits and pieces of his phone conversation with his uncle.

The thought of Hal walking out of her life without sharing the intimacy she had begun to crave was unthinkable. A quiet inner voice urged her to seize the moment before it was lost forever.

Andrea switched off the shower and grabbed a towel. She was ready to discover exactly what she had been missing. This was not an impulsive surrender, it was a conscious acceptance of a need that had remained dormant for years. One special man had come along, and she couldn't deny wanting him. Time was running out. It was now or never.

No strings, no promises, only the pleasures of the moment, Andrea reminded herself. She knew better than to expect commitment from Hal. She would play by the rules he demanded from the women who came and went in his life. She just wanted to fill her aching loneliness.

Her hands shook as she hurriedly dried her hair. What if she didn't possess the skill to satisfy an experienced man like Hal? How would she react if he used that gruff voice he relied on when he tried to keep her at arm's length? How could she make him understand that she didn't want his protection or his money, but rather the freedom to give of herself—for once—to one special man?

Andrea set the blow dryer aside and stared at her reflection in the mirror. She had only one answer to the many questions plaguing her. Honesty, she decided, was the only sensible policy. No games, no pretense. It was a part of what she was, what she had been brought up to be. Hal Griffin could make all the harsh remarks he wanted, but he couldn't argue with the truth of her feelings for him or the desire she knew he felt for her.

With that reassuring thought, Andrea wrapped the over-size towel around her and padded down the hall to Hal's room.

One more day, Hal mused as he dried off from his quick shower. He had cut the weaning calves from the herd with fiendish haste, and then put in a call to his uncle. Reinforcements would arrive in the morning to haul off the load and gather up the remaining herds. His family would be underfoot, making it impossible for him to get close enough to Andrea to torture himself again.

Soon he'd be gone and he wouldn't be fighting this never-ending battle against his worst enemy—himself.

His basic instincts had become so ungovernable that Hal felt as if he was walking on live coals.

A grim smile played about his lips as he tied the towel around his waist. Andrea Fletcher had found her place to fall apart when her emotions finally erupted. He, on the other hand, needed to find a place to cool off.

One more day and he could do exactly that . . .

Hal halted outside his private bathroom when he heard the creak of his bedroom door. The sight of Andrea in her towel—and nothing else—hit him like a Mack truck. "Aw, damn," he muttered.

He had hoped his ominous scowl would send her into retreat, but he should have known better. Despite her hang-ups, Andrea was a daring and courageous woman. This afternoon's events lent testimony to that.

Hal valiantly tried again to discourage Andrea from making a crucial mistake with the likes of him. "What the hell are you doing in here?" he snapped.

To her credit, she met his glare without blinking, without flinching. "I want you to teach me what it's like to make love—"

"Sex," he corrected abruptly. "Don't go getting idealistic on me, honey. And don't feed me, or yourself, that crap about thinking you've fallen in love. The simple fact is that we experimented a little, over a round of margaritas. Now you're curious."

Hal scoffed as sarcastically as he knew how. "You think a quick hop in the sack is going to cure you, after what happened to you in college? Well, experiment with someone who'll be around next week or next month. I'm a fly-by-night rodeo ride at best. I doubt you'll like the kind of sex I'm used to."

Despite his discouraging comments, Andrea took a bold

step forward. "I'm not asking for preferential treatment, so you can drop your negative sales pitch. I want very much to be with you . . . I need to be with you."

A towel, Hal was damned sorry to say, didn't do much in the way of concealing a man's response to an alluring woman. He had tried to come off as hard and cynical to deter Andrea, but *hard* was all he had managed. She knew it, too. He saw her gaze dip below his waist, and he cursed the lack of cooperation he was getting from his body.

"Little innocents who play with fire always get burned. Go away, Fletcher."

Muttering, Hal presented his back to her. Bad idea, he realized, exasperated. He had given her the chance to approach without seeing his expression, even though his erection stood in blatant contradiction to his rejection.

Hal winced when gentle fingertips skimmed his flesh, measuring the wide expanse of his shoulders. He could feel the track of fire sizzling along every nerve ending. He dragged in a breath to steady his wavering resolve—and inhaled the clean, alluring scent of the forbidden . . .

Damnation, how much was a man expected to tolerate? Why did he have to suffer the tortures of the damned to spare the loss of her innocence? *He* seemed more interested in protecting her purity than *she* did!

The light whisper of her lips across his shoulder blades was pleasurable—and tormenting. The touch of her hands gliding down the muscled contours of his back was divine torture. His entire body went rigid in response to the tingling sensations that zigzagged through him like an electrical current.

"Don't touch me," he growled, not daring to glance at her.

"Please don't ask me not to do the very thing I want

to do more than I want to breathe," Andrea whispered against his skin. "I know I'm not experienced, but I can truthfully say you are the only man I have ever wanted the way I want you. I'm only asking for what most women my age already have."

He couldn't endure her gentle caresses another instant. It was doing impossible things to his body. He had to scare her away *now*—a second later would be too late. Scowling—at himself, at her—he wheeled around.

"Fine, honey, you want what I'm used to giving? Well, don't say I didn't warn you. You haven't been around enough to know you would have been better off wondering what you've missed instead of messing with a man like me."

His arm snaked around her waist, purposely jerking her flush against him, pressing the bold evidence of his desire against her thigh. His mouth came down in a ravenous, bruising kiss meant to jolt her to her senses, to reestablish a few of those reflexive mechanisms she had always used to keep her distance. Hal groaned inwardly when Andrea melted trustingly against him, accepting his plundering mouth. He cursed himself down one side and up the other for resorting to scare tactics that, as of yet, weren't working worth a damn.

Scarred and cynical though his heart was, he couldn't bring himself to hurt this woman who had been pawed and mauled during the impressionable years of her life. She felt too good in his arms, tasted too innocent and sweet to be forced to bear more pain or rejection.

Yet, that was what this situation demanded, he reminded himself. Fright was a strong motivater. It was also the only available ploy he knew how to use.

Hal clamped his fist in her towel and gave it an abrupt

yank. Andrea gasped beneath his rough kiss, her body tensing in response to haunting memories of another time and place. Hal made the mistake of staring into those wide eyes that swept open to focus on him. He saw the flicker of fear—a fear that quickly transformed to a glow of trust he didn't deserve, didn't want.

"It's all right," she assured him quietly. "You told me how you liked it."

That soft acceptance did Hal in. Andrea was prepared to accept him on his own terms—hot, hard, and fast. He'd all but told her he only chose to have sex with his body, giving nothing of himself in return. It had always been so uncomplicated before. Nothing seemed simple now.

"Damn you," Hal groaned in hopeless defeat. "Damn you, woman . . ."

Ten

His lips settled over hers as his arms relaxed around her bare hips. His hands glided over her silky flesh as gently as if he were unwrapping a delicate package. It was impossible to miss the bruises left by flailing hooves—souvenirs of Andrea's daring escapade. Hal couldn't bear the thought of leaving another mark on her, couldn't exert the force needed to frighten her away.

For the first time in forever he felt inadequate—he wasn't sure he possessed the kind of gentleness Andrea deserved. The rough and tumble rodeo life hadn't prepared him for this moment. The harrowing ordeals he'd undergone during military service certainly hadn't taught him to be tender. So how did a man display gentleness when it was foreign to him?

Hurriedly, Hal thumbed through the chronicles of his wayward life, searching for the sources of the quiet pleasures he remembered encountering along the way. The warm breath of a summer's breeze against his cheek, the stillness of sunrise, the beauty of a crimson moon. All that was pure and sweet and untouched by human hands. That inexplicable feeling that burgeoned in a man's soul when he found the essence of inner peace for a few brief moments.

Hal became all things gentle and pure—those things a

woman like Andrea deserved—as he lifted her in his arms and carried her to the bed. He solemnly vowed to soothe away each mark of her pain. He promised to teach her what she wanted to know about passion—and intimacy. And that, Hal discovered, was a lesson he was learning right along with Andrea. With each tender kiss and caress, he found his own pleasure and satisfaction expanding, intensifying. Arousing her by gentle increments was an in-depth study of erotic sensation.

Each time she trembled beneath his hands and lips he felt his body calling out to hers. Pleasing her excited him, mesmerized him. Each moan that escaped her lips was like a heady sip of whiskey. Feeling her uninhibited response echoing into him became an instant addiction. The more Andrea surrendered to his intimate caresses, the more he wanted to explore the dimensions of this thing called desire.

When his fingertips glided over the bud of her breast he smiled at her breathless response. When he took her nipple into his mouth, flicking his tongue against the rigid peak, her breath flooded out in rasping sighs. With the tenderest of care, he splayed his hand down her belly to trace the soft flesh of her inner thigh. Hal groaned inwardly when he felt her feminine heat so close to his exploring fingertips. All too well he remembered how Andrea had shimmered around him the first time he had dared to touch her so familiarly.

Memories of her explosive responses brought another smile to his lips. Although he suspected too many margaritas were responsible, having a woman pass out did crazy things to the male ego. Hal found himself wanting to take Andrea back in time—to that wild, breathless instant—to offer her that same intense pleasure before he buried himself inside her and gave himself up to the wonders of this new brand of passion.

With the gentle nudge of his elbow he opened her legs to his light caresses. He studied her shapely body like the work of art it was. Perfection, he found himself thinking. Pure, natural perfection. And for one brief, ecstatic moment she was his, and he would be hers.

When he cupped her in his hand, tracing the dewy petals of her womanly secrets, he felt the honeyed fire summoning him. When he slipped his finger inside her, Andrea cried out his name. He stroked her, aroused her, until her labored breathing became a whisper.

"Hal, please," she moaned as she all but melted beneath his caress. "Come here . . . now . . ."

He grinned rakishly when he felt the shivering spasm consume her, felt her nails clench on his forearm to anchor herself against the swirling sensations.

This odd sense of power was heady stuff.

"Demanding little thing, aren't you?" he teased.

Her sooty lashes swept up to meet his grin, and then her passion-drugged gaze settled on his hand as he stroked her once again. Hot pink blotches stained her cheeks as she watched him ignite the white-hot blaze that left her burning around him.

"You've never been as cruel as you are now," Andrea gasped as another wild convulsion engulfed her. "Damn me?" She sighed in a shuddering breath as her body arched helplessly toward him. "Damn you . . ."

He chuckled devilishly at her curse. "You aren't ready to accept me yet," he told her.

"Wanna bet——?"

Her voice fractured when he inserted two fingers, spreading her, filling her. He watched her eyes widen, felt her stiffen and then relax as he caressed her until she was bathing his hand with the liquid heat of her desire.

"Oh, my . . ."

Hal saw shock register on her lovely features, felt her all-consuming surrender echo through her, spill into him. Her breath came in such ragged, gasping spurts that Hal wanted to laugh aloud in triumphant satisfaction.

Sweet mercy, he had never known a woman could become so overwhelmed by passion that she could lose consciousness. Maybe it hadn't entirely been the liquor that sent her over the edge that first night, he thought as Andrea suddenly grabbed at him. She was so out of breath that her chest heaved and her face paled.

"Please!" she choked out. "Hal?"

He made a hasty grab for his wallet on the night stand to retrieve the foil packet. Andrea must have assumed he was about to abandon her, for she cursed him between panting breaths.

"I'm not going anywhere, sweetheart," he said with a grin. "Have a little patience."

"I don't have any left and you damn well know it!"

The look of longing on her face was an aphrodisiac to Hal. Desire burgeoned anew as she reached for him. Hal came to her, his body trembling with eagerness. But even as he drew up her knees to position himself above her, he was vividly aware of that age-old adage about the first time not necessarily being a woman's best time.

Yet, that was what Hal wanted, knowing the *first* time with Andrea would also be his *only* time. He would be gone in twenty-four hours. He couldn't solve her financial problems if he didn't return to the circuit.

Hal tried to hold himself in check when Andrea instinctively arched up to welcome him. He had been doing a damned fine job of restraining himself . . . until primal instinct sank in its sharp claws. His body surged toward hers, aching to become a part of her softest flesh. He heard Andrea's gasp, felt her flinch reflexively as he thrust into her.

"I warned you," he murmured, withdrawing helplessly, only to plunge again, too deep, too fast.

"It doesn't matter because I love you . . ." Andrea whispered as she gave herself up to him.

Be gentle, Hal chanted to himself. But his hungry body was paying no attention to the order from his brain.

He cursed the instinctive rodeo skills that taught him never to let go, to glide with rhythmic grace while he matched the movements of a wild bronc . . .

Helluva time to be thinking about that! Hal thought as unspeakable pleasure streamed through him. He didn't want to consider Andrea just another go-round at some nameless rodeo, especially considering the glorious ride she was taking him on.

"Good . . . gawd," Hal wheezed when the most astonishing rush of sensual pleasure tumbled over him. Ecstasy drenched him as he thrust mindlessly against Andrea's yielding flesh. The silky arms that had wound around his shoulders suddenly fell away. Hal felt the soft whisper of her sigh against his chest at the same instant that he shuddered above her.

For several seconds—or several centuries, he couldn't tell which—the world spun around him in a fuzzy blur. And then ineffable sensations exploded, pouring forth in such a wild rush that he felt himself collapsing upon her.

Hal struggled to draw breath, levering onto his forearms to keep from crushing Andrea beneath his weight. To his amazement, he saw her outflung arms lying limp on the

sheet, her long lashes against her cheeks like folded butterfly wings.

Damned if she hadn't done it again, he thought, grinning suddenly.

Hal dropped a kiss to her lips. "Hey, sleeping beauty,
are you still with me?"

After a moment, Andrea blinked. When she realized
what had happened, her face blossomed with profuse
color. "I ruined everything, didn't I?" she said, humiliated.
"I'm s—"

He pressed his index finger to her lips. Hal couldn't
begin to explain the satisfaction he derived from something that thoroughly embarrassed Andrea. "The two
things ruined here were my good intentions and your
virg—"

Hal shut his mouth—fast. Swell, he thought. Fine time
for his guilty conscience to start nagging him again.
Where had the voice of reason been when he needed it?
Belated badgering wasn't going to help now, was it?

Andrea reached up to smooth away his frown. "I'm not
sorry about *that,*" she told him sincerely. "I'd do it all over
again, but only with you."

"You know the rules," Hal reminded her, feeling uncomfortable with the honesty in her gaze. He eased away,
all too aware that the residual evidence of her lost virginity
clung to him.

"Yes, I know the rules," she affirmed as Hal turned his
back and sat up on the edge of the bed.

"Not everything you expected?" he asked, knowing he
must have unintentionally hurt her when he lost himself
in the throes of passion. At that crucial moment, Hal had
forgotten his vow to be gentle. Male instinct had taken a
fierce and mighty hold on him.

"Even better than I imagined," she said truthfully. When he tried to reach for the towel he had hastily discarded, Andrea clutched his elbow to detain him. "I never knew there was such a thing as more pleasure than I could bear. What hurts most is knowing I lost touch. That wasn't fair to you."

What it was, was a relief to know Andrea was unaware of the frenzied impact of pleasure that had engulfed him. She had taken him so far over the edge that *he* had nearly blacked out! Now, wouldn't that have been a fine how-do-ya-do!

It was damned scary to be so totally obliviously lost in passion. *Shared* passion, Hal thought shakily. In her unselfish giving, Andrea had taken more from him than she could possibly imagine.

Good thing she'd passed out before she discovered the truth. Hal never wanted her to know the extent of her effect on him—not in bed or out. He'd learned long ago that letting a woman know she wielded power over a man was dangerous business. He absolutely refused to let himself become a gold-plated fool again.

Hal wrapped a towel around his hips and then tossed Andrea her own towel. He had preached the evils of women and the disasters of emotional involvement for years. Yet, here he was, breaking his own commandments. He'd let his uncontrollable lust run the show.

The loss of Andrea's virtue tormented him. He had never been anybody's first before. And how had he handled it? Sure as hell *not* with the finesse the situation deserved. He couldn't even force himself to glance at her now. Guilt hounded his every step.

Maybe Andrea had been right all along, he thought. Maybe he *was* a male chauvinist coward. He could take every spinning, lurching, bone-jarring buck on a bronc, but he couldn't take the innocence this woman offered him without beating himself black and blue.

"Hal?"

He halted, staring at the bathroom door as he was about to enter. "What?" He didn't look back, especially not when he heard the bed creak as she came to her feet. He didn't need to. Her image was—and would forever be—engraved in memory.

"Let me return the good piece of advice you gave me a few days ago."

He glanced over his shoulder to see her ambling toward him, the towel wrapped around her. As if he couldn't see through the terry cloth barrier, couldn't remember the sight of her lush body, the silky feel of her skin beneath his hands and lips. "What piece of advice is that?"

"Lighten up, Griff. I'm not going to beg you to stay when it's time for you to go. No ties, no promises. You have no reason to feel guilty. If I can live with being another notch on your belt, surely you can, too."

Hal laughed as she closed the door behind her. The thing he hated most about Andrea—and paradoxically admired, in an exasperated kind of way—was her spirited sass. He stepped into the shower to wash away his guilt and the evidence of Andrea's lost innocence. *Because I love you . . .* When the words whispered through his mind Hal squeezed his eyes shut. The little lady was very much mistaken about her feelings for him. She would come to her senses when he walked out of her life.

He had helped her pick up the pieces and get back on track. And he had helped her overcome old fears. When she had the time to think it through she would know—as he did—that he was just the same passing fancy he became for every other woman who fantasized about bedding some dusty, beat-up rodeo cowboy who was something of a celebrity.

The hard, cold fact was that Hal had nothing to give, was too set in his ways. He didn't believe in love, even if his starry-eyed brother had become a recent convert. Nothing in Hal's experience confirmed the existence of lasting emotion. Passion was a bodily reaction he could understand. But love? It was a fool's invention, an excuse to glorify the simple act of sex.

As for Andrea, she was looking for something to believe in, something to restore her faith and revive her spirit. Hal had been her crutch when the going got tough. If he and Andrea were lucky, they could come away as friends.

Hal had never had a female friend before. He had come closer to that experience with Andrea . . . until he had stepped over the line.

It wasn't going to happen again.

After his much-needed reality check, Hal donned his clothes and then went downstairs. He was hell-bent on pretending nothing earth-shattering had happened.

He did exactly that when he met Jason at the kitchen door, after his day of school and football practice. Hal also avoided Andrea that evening, still baffled that she had accepted what had happened better than he did. *She* had lightened up, Jason had pointed out. Hal wished the hell *he* could. But suddenly, he was the one who was taking life too seriously.

Andrea smothered a smile, paradoxically feeling flattered by Hal's lack of attention. He had made a grand spectacle of spending all his time with Jason. Both of them had spent the evening munching on popcorn and watching a game. She could have been a stick of furniture, but she didn't mind. She knew Hal was having trouble coping with what had happened between them.

That gruff, grizzly bear of a man had tried to discourage her even though his body had been responding strongly to her. And for all his barking and snarling and preference for impersonal sex, Hal Griffin had been incredibly gentle and caring.

Andrea felt a flush of heat spiraling through her body as she automatically went through the steps of preparing Jason's breakfast. After years of being petrified of a man's touch—and his brutal intentions—she had welcomed every stroke of Hal's hands, the warm whisper of his lips. Ineffable sensations had suffused her. Even the initial stab of pain had seemed a small price to pay for all the wondrous feelings.

Her deepest regret came in knowing she would have no opportunity to return the immense pleasure Hal had bestowed on her. She wanted to learn to arouse him to the point of oblivion—only then could he understand how much she treasured those wild, sweet moments in his arms.

Of course, there would be no more stolen moments, because Hal was careful not to find himself alone with her. Andrea suspected he had delayed coming down to breakfast in hopes of avoiding her. Early riser that he was, he was probably pacing around upstairs, punishing himself for accepting her invitation and stealing her virginity. But before he left, Andrea intended to speak privately with him. She wished Hal would stop dillydallying around upstairs and get down here before Jason barreled down the steps.

Muted sounds from the hall caught Andrea's attention. She glanced up as she turned the ham and cheese omelets in the skillet. Hal strode in and halted beside the coffeemaker.

"Good, you finally showed up. I wondered how long you planned to avoid me."

"Good morning, Fletch," he muttered, without a glance in her direction.

Andrea quickly cut to the heart of the matter. "I want to discuss this business about you backing my loan."

"Forget it, we aren't arguing the point," he said in no uncertain terms. It was a waste of breath.

Andrea spun around, brandishing the pancake turner in his face. "If you try to cover my debts I'll feel as if I'm being paid for what happened yesterday—something that *you* can't seem to cope with as well as I can. *You* wish it didn't happen. It *did* happen. *I* liked it, but I don't expect financial compensation because of it."

Hal set his coffee cup aside and then turned back around, looming over her. "The financial compensation I'm offering is all you're getting from me," he told her bluntly. "I won't be back. Yesterday wasn't the beginning of anything."

"I realize that," she assured him.

"But do you believe it?" he growled, midnight-black eyes glittering down on her.

"Yes," she affirmed.

"No, I don't think you do. Since I got here I've been the shoulder you leaned on. At first you were too proud, too afraid, because you didn't trust men in general. I helped you through difficult times and you were grateful—so grateful that you offered me something you could give only once."

"That's not true—"

"Bullshit," he scowled, overriding her protest. "Let me analyze the situation for you before you get the facts distorted again. I *did* feel sorry for you. I looked at you as a charity case, my good deed for the year. I gave you a mercy kissing one night in the kitchen and a mercy screwing in the bedroom. That's all it was."

Andrea blanched at the cruel, insulting comment. She wanted to deny his ruthless, vulgar declaration, but he looked so angry that it was hard to find the nerve to argue.

"Sure, I wanted you, even when I didn't want to want you. And sure," he went on gruffly, "I went easier on you than I have on other women, because it was your first time. I may be a heartless bastard, but I tried to give you what you wanted without hurting you any more than I had to.

"I'm a hell-raiser with a checkered past. I've gone through more women than I can count, just for the sport of it. I'm no damned good for you. You don't want to believe it, because you idiotically assured yourself that you were falling in love with me in less than a week."

"I—"

"Shut up and listen," Hal demanded sharply. "We've been living in each other's pockets, and we let things go too far while we were conveniently sharing the same space. But what happened was lust, pure and simple. You've been battling tough times and I became your temporary escape. Accept it for what it is, Fletch. And accept the money I plan to mail to you. Thank your lucky stars that I'm leaving, because I've got nothing you really need."

Andrea opened her mouth, but Hal's stony expression warned her not to interrupt again.

"Have I made myself clear or do I need to be more blunt than I've already been?"

"If you send me so much as one penny I'll mail it back," she gritted out, fighting tears.

"You'll take it and be glad you've got it," he snapped brusquely. "Hear me well, Fletch. When I pack up and leave I don't like to have any unfinished business. I don't want to be paid for rounding up and transporting your cattle. I just want a clean break, along with your admission that you made a mistake with me that can't—and won't—be repeated."

Andrea found it impossible to keep her mouth shut. "I didn't make—"

Hal grabbed her arm, forcing her to meet his relentless gaze. *"Say* it," he hissed at her. *"Believe* it."

Andrea winced at the biting pressure on her wrist. He looked so cold and hard that she wondered if she had ever really known him at all. Her silly romantic notions were shattering to bits.

The hero worship she unwillingly felt, the inexpressible gratitude, the respect was still there, but she was beginning to realize that love was just what he claimed it was—a fanciful illusion. She had let herself see what she wanted to see in this hard-as-nails cowboy. She had needed someone to help her recover. He had been her crutch, she regretfully admitted.

He wanted realism, did he? Fine, he'd get it, right down to the last desolate drop. "I made a mistake," she muttered at him, misty eyes flashing. "I'll be glad as hell when you're gone so I can get on with my life."

He let her go then, reaching behind her to pull the skillet

off the stove before the omelets burned. Without another word or glance, he turned around and walked out the kitchen door.

Andrea muffled a sob and then inhaled very deeply, battling for control. Damn that bastard. Whatever made her think Hal Griffin was everything she had ever hoped for—or desired—in a man? He was welcome to the rodeo circuit that took him miles away—and kept him there. She hoped one of his wild, high-flying rides took him to the edge of the planet—and bucked him off!

Hal said his last good-bye to Jason before stalking into the barn. His stomach churned as his emotions boiled. He barely noticed the low-hanging clouds had parted to reveal the first spears of sunshine that had graced the sky in several days. His own brutal words stabbed him like a spike. He could well imagine the impact they had on Andrea.

He had forced himself to come down hard on her, trying to dispel the mistaken affection she thought she felt for him. But saying those hateful, belittling words tore him up inside. For damned sure and certain, cruelty—even when it had a purpose—was mighty hard on the perpetrator.

He had needed to make a clean break, leaving Andrea with no illusions. He couldn't focus on the long string of upcoming rodeos if he felt he had left unfinished business behind.

When Hal heard the roar of a pickup engine and clatter of the stock trailer, his rigid shoulders sagged. Reinforcements had arrived. Hurriedly, he saddled Bandit and Sweet Pea, then he strode outside to greet his brother.

Nash sat behind the steering wheel of his flashy red

extended cab pickup. Choctaw Jim and Bernie Bryant were wedged shoulder to shoulder with Nash—like the Three Musketeers coming to the rescue. Leon, the best cowdog in Kanima County, sat on Bernie's lap, his nose stuck out the window, sniffing the air, the customary red bandanna tied around his neck.

When Nash stepped down Hal didn't waste time with trivialities. He wanted to get underway. Cattle were scattered over three thousand acres of waterlogged pastures.

Bernie Bryant unfolded his bulky frame and stretched his creaking bones. "Well, this is a mighty fine-looking place," he observed. "Almost as scenic as Chulosa."

"Did you come to work or sightsee?" Hal popped off.

"My, aren't you in a joyous mood, little brother," Nash smirked.

"You know how cranky I get when I'm stuck in the same place too long," Hal muttered. "Bridle the horses so we can get rolling. Who knows when the sky might spring another leak."

Nash glanced quizzically at Choctaw Jim, who usually had all the answers. Jim stared pensively toward the kitchen door and then shrugged. After a moment he smiled that mysterious smile that oftentimes drove the Griffin brothers crazy.

Nash was reminded of those weeks when his frustrated feelings of divided loyalty between his closest friend and Crista Delaney had driven him up the wall. Jim had merely smiled the same way he was smiling now.

Nash met his uncle's enigmatic expression and grinned. Same song, different verse, he speculated.

"What the hell are you two supposed to be? A matched set of grinning idiots?" Hal asked grouchily.

"Was I this bad?" Nash asked his uncle.

"Too close to call," Jim replied before he ambled over to unlatch the trailer gate.

Two saddled horses clambered to the ground. Impatiently, Hal watched Jim and Nash slip the bridles into place. In less than two minutes all four men were mounted and ready to ride. Leon was sniffing the air, anxious to perform his duties.

"We aren't calling it a day until every cow and calf has been gathered up and separated for transport," Hal growled, leading the way through the pasture.

Bernie glanced curiously at Choctaw Jim. "Some mood Hal's in. He looks like he'd like to kill somebody."

Jim chuckled as he swung onto his horse. "May the Great Spirit help anyone who gives him an excuse."

Nash hurried to catch up with Hal, who set a swift pace. "Is the banker still breathing down Andrea's neck?"

"Yes. After the rest of these calves are sold, the Fletchers can still call this house their home—for a month," Hal explained. "If they can't meet the overdue payments, the bank will foreclose."

"Tough month," Nash murmured.

"No shit."

"For the Fletchers, too," Nash said wryly.

Hal jerked up his head, glaring thunderclouds at his brother's sunny smile.

"Being a guardian angel must be difficult work," Nash went on, undaunted. "In order to finance the Fletchers you'll have to bust your butt in every rodeo time will permit. If you push too hard for extra prize money you might get reckless. An injury could cut you out of the standings for National Finals. If you ride too carefully you may make a poor showing with the judges. That puts you between the devil and the deep."

"I've already considered all the possibilities, but thanks for the wrap-up," Hal said sarcastically. "By the way, you look half-dressed without Crista draped over one shoulder. Where's the love goddess?"

"She's working at the hospital," Nash said, ignoring Hal's snide tone. "She, of course, sends her regards to you—and her utmost sympathy."

Hal snapped his head up and scowled at his brother's ornery grin. "I hardly need that curly-headed therapist's sympathy. I'm feeling no pain."

Nash stared pointedly at the house in the distance. "No? Then what do you call that thorn in your paw? You seem pretty damn irritable to me. I may have been out of circulation for the last five years—"

"Exactly right, and you ain't the only one around here who thinks he knows everything—and doesn't know shit from shinola," Hal cut in cattily.

Nash frowned. "Meaning?"

"Meaning: Don't offer advice on topics you know nothing about."

When Hal gouged his spurs into Bandit's hide, the gelding shot off. Nash twisted around to grin at Choctaw Jim. "You've spent the past few years as Hal's traveling companion. Does he seem extra touchy to you?"

Dark eyes gleaming, Jim's features crinkled in a smile. "Worst mood I've ever seen him in."

"Even worse than when Jenna Randall cut him to bits?" Bernie questioned interestedly.

Nodding, Jim settled himself more comfortably in the saddle. "Traveling the circuit with Hal isn't going to be pleasant. It's hard for a man to ride bulls and broncs with a chip on his shoulder. I wonder if he's figured out what put it there."

"When he takes off my head for asking a simple question he's definitely got something bothering him," Nash remarked.

"Or *someone* bothering him," Choctaw Jim corrected quietly.

Nash urged his mount toward the herd grazing in the distance. Hal was circling and doubling back to put the livestock in motion. A quiet command from Nash sent Leon racing off to keep renegades from breaking rank.

After watching Hal work with hurried impatience, Nash smiled to himself. Now why would a man who had no use for women—who never let any female since Jenna get under his skin—be in such a flaming rush to complete this assignment and leave town? Hal had learned to handle every make and model of female that came his way. So why was he practically running from a woman, especially after he'd offered her financial backing?

There was only one reason Nash could think of.

He chuckled in amusement. It appeared that Andrea Fletcher knew Hal better than his own family did. That rough-edged, hard-living cowboy was turning out to be a real coward. He couldn't run fast enough to escape the mysterious hold his boss lady had on him.

Eleven

Hal had left Fletcher Ranch in a foul mood. Two weeks later his disposition hadn't improved. He still felt like a wild bronc chafing at a flank strap. Only it wasn't physical restraint that made Hal edgy. It was those damned invisible chains, the miserable memory of what he had been forced to say in order to jolt Andrea to her senses.

During every event at the Mesquite Rodeo, Hal had forced himself to rout Andrea from his mind and concentrate on the challenge at hand.

Somehow, despite his frustrating distraction, he did manage to win his go-rounds in bareback, saddle bronc riding, and timed events. He had scorched the steer roping competition by turfing a calf with an 8.7-second run, collecting a hefty prize purse for his top scores.

It was his rusty bull-riding techniques that had given him problems. Hal had scratched on the first go-round at Mesquite, and then listened to Choctaw Jim's repeated lectures on the idiocy of jeopardizing his rankings by riding bulls.

Ever since Hal had landed hard on the rodeo turf, his ribs had throbbed like aching teeth. Muttering at his stubbornness, Choctaw Jim had bound him up with so much adhesive tape and padding that he looked like a mummy. But Hal's determination had paid off. He had finished fourth in bull-riding bonanza and collected an extra eight hundred dollars from the pay window.

At Phoenix, Hal found himself pitted against the cream of bull-riding connoisseurs and mounted on brutal rough stock. The techniques of remaining on a bull had begun to come back to him and his scores improved. Not only had he won first in his usual events, but he had a good chance of winning the bull-riding competition with scores in the eighties.

Riding high, Hal had been tempted to call Andrea just to see how she was managing. He suppressed the urge in the nick of time. He hadn't talked to her in sixteen days.

He was determined to make it seventeen.

Hal wanted to give Andrea time to realize how wrong for her he was. His harsh rejection would cure her eventually. Too bad his conscience was riding him so hard, even when he knew he had done the right thing. He didn't believe in those three little words any more than he believed in Santa Claus.

Hal had lain awake at too many cheap motels, remembering what he had vowed to forget the instant he drove away from Andrea. But the feel of her silky body joined intimately with his had burned like brands on his flesh—and his mind. There had been nights when he couldn't even breathe without wanting her, without remembering the hot tidal waves of pleasure that rolled over him when he was buried so deep inside her that he had become a living, breathing part of her very essence.

Yet, he was realistic enough to know the love she claimed to feel was only an outpouring of the emotion caused by her desperate situation. Though Andrea refused to admit it, she had needed compassion. She had been searching for someone to care about, hoping somehow to compensate for losing her parents.

Passion had become her crutch, that was all. Hal had driven home that point before he left. He had also offered himself up as the object for Andrea's anger, another kind of outlet for her bottled emotions. In so doing, Hal was left to bear the guilt of his own words, remembering the hurt he had seen in those orchid eyes . . .

"Pay attention," Choctaw Jim muttered as he and Hal strode toward the rodeo chutes. "If you're hellbent on bull-riding to make extra money, then you better keep your mind on your business."

"Yes, ma'am," Hal smirked at his uncle, who had been treating him like a rebellious child.

Choctaw Jim's obsidian gaze pinned Hal like a butterfly in an insect collection. "If you aren't smart enough to admit to me—and yourself—that you've been dangerously distracted the past two weeks, then at least listen to the word that's going around about the bull you've drawn for the final go-round."

Hal sighed impatiently as he reached for the coiled rope. He checked the rigging and handhold carefully before he powdered the gear with resin. "Okay, Mama, what's the good word on Crocodile?"

Choctaw Jim stared grimly at Hal. "Croc will eat you alive if you aren't totally focused on him. Since nobody else has managed to keep a seat on this twelve-hundred-pound package of fury, you have a chance to collect the prize money you're after—or to punish yourself for something you're keeping private," he added with a pointed glance. "But no matter what, it's going to be eight seconds of living hell between the first leap from the chute and the buzzer."

Jim gestured toward Hal's shirt—more specifically at the layers of adhesive bandages beneath it. "You can expect to strain every sore muscle you're favoring. Croc is the worst spinner on the circuit. This Brahma-Hereford cross is a powerful mass of violent kicks and twists."

Hal listened as he recoiled the bull rope and then slid the leather glove onto his riding hand. He knew by his uncle's tone of voice that this veteran cowboy was concerned about the upcoming ride.

Maybe he was privately punishing himself. *Maybe? Be honest, Griffin,* he thought to himself. He had taken a pure and innocent woman and spurned her for claiming she cared for him. All the jolting, bone-jarring bucks on the back of a bull couldn't make him forget that.

"Watch out for Croc's cropped horns," Choctaw Jim cautioned. "That sorry bastard would just as soon hook you as look at you. When you finish your ride, get out of his way—fast—no matter how much you're hurting. He's notorious for coming after cowboys. He already landed that rookie from Montana in the hospital. Justin Simms has a twisted knee and a bruise the size of his home state on his hip."

Hal nodded somberly as he climbed the chute railing. He focused single-mindedly on the task ahead of him. Crocodile's reputation—and the fifty points awarded for a bull's performance—was worth good money. According to Jim, Croc was more than willing to do his part. All Hal had to do was hang on and look good doing it.

Jim's lean fingers clamped on Hal's arm before he could swing a leg over the top rail. "You don't have to do this," he murmured. "You've racked up plenty of points in the all-around standings at Mesquite, and here at Phoenix.

You can walk away from this devil. You better be damned certain you believe in what you're doing—and why."

Hal met those dark eyes so like his own, surveying the wrinkles and creases that hard living had placed on his uncle's bronzed face. "I'm very sure this is what I want and need to do."

Jim studied him for a long moment. "She means that much to you?"

Hal quickly looked the other way. He hated it when his uncle's questions sounded like statements of fact. This wise old buzzard was too damned perceptive.

"You don't understand the situation," Hal muttered.

"If you're bound and determined to do this *for* her, *because* of her," Jim said all too astutely, "then it better be her face you see when Croc sends you spinning. You could find yourself launched all the way across the arena."

Hal focused all thought on the bull that slammed restlessly against the chute beneath him. With the help of Choctaw Jim and the wrangler working the chute gate, Hal pulled his bull rope around the massive animal. Positioning himself above Croc, he slid his gloved riding hand through the handhold. He laid the loose end of the rope across his upturned palm, wrapped it securely around the back of his hand, and then cinched it between his ring finger and pinkie.

The rope—with its brass bell dangling beneath the bull's belly—was all that held Hal in place. Helluva time to consider that, he thought. As a precautionary measure, he took up the slack in the rope until it all but cut into his gloved hand.

"Not so tight," Jim advised. "You've got to be able to free your hand and bail out if the need arises. With your strained ribs, you don't need to get hung up in the rope and tossed around like a rag doll on the side of this devil bull."

"There are two topnotch rodeo clowns waiting to pull me loose if I get tangled," Hal reminded his uncle.

"Well, don't make their jobs more difficult than they already are," Jim grumbled. "Bullheaded cowboys and half-crazed bulls can scare the britches off clowns."

Grabbing the top rail with his free hand, Hal eased down on Crocodile. It was like straddling a granite mountain. The bull's loose hide twitched beneath Hal's denim-clad hips. Internal rumbles indicated Croc intended to erupt like a volcano the instant the chute gate opened. The drooling bull snorted impatiently, kicking at the metal cage, more than ready to eject Hal from his precarious perch.

Hal drew in enough air to inflate his chest like a balloon, then nodded to the gatekeeper. When Choctaw Jim yanked the flank strap tightly against Croc's belly, the bull slammed against the chute, attempting to take off Hal's left leg before they bolted into the lighted arena.

"Mean son of a bitch, aren't you?" Hal growled at the ton of rigid muscle beneath him.

"They don't come much meaner than Croc," the gatekeeper informed him. "There's no sweet spot on this bull. Croc comes out with two whiplashing jumps and then takes a hard right. He'll try to leave you in the corner, so you'll have to jockey to find the center of his back. After that, Croc begins his wild spins. He has no defined pattern. He'll play you, and your reactions, by ear.

"When you unload, run like hell. Croc will be on your heels. You turn your back on him and he'll mow you down. The Montana Kid may be the new rookie sensation, but he learned his lesson the hard way with Croc."

"Thanks for cheering me up," Hal smirked.

"Just trying to keep you alive, Griff," the gatekeeper replied, grinning. "I plan on seeing you in Glitter Gulch in December. Any cowboy who rides bulls when he doesn't have to do it to keep his standing for all-around champ has my vote . . . You ready to let him rip?"

When the gate banged open, Hal settled on the center of Croc's humped back, hoping to avoid as much of the twisting and kicking as possible. Croc's eyes rolled back and his mouth frothed as he blew himself high in the air and then circled back hard to the right, trying to slide his rider to the outside.

Hal gritted his teeth and squeezed the handhold in a death grip. He tried to synchronize his movements with the winding jumps by thrusting out his spurs to grab hold of Croc's loose hide. It was like spurring concrete. Croc had no *sweet* spot or *soft* spot.

When the bull wheeled left, Hal scrambled to keep his weight above the handhold. The bellowing bull came down on all four hooves with such a jarring thud that Hal's bones rattled and his teeth ground against each other.

Damned good thing he had brushed up on his skills at Mesquite, he thought fleetingly. The rough stock in Texas had prepared him for the demon monster he had drawn in Arizona.

"Six seconds!" the announcer informed the audience jam-packed into the grandstands.

And then Crocodile wound himself up in preparation for his famous disorienting spins. With a drooling snort, he leaped up and threw himself sideways in one whirring motion. Hal's world became a jarred blur. He straightened to prevent being sucked into the vortex of the tornadic spin the bull created.

He would never get his hand loose, Hal thought frantically. The feeling in it was no more than a numb ache. The vertebrae in his spine were being fused with each fierce landing—and then ripped apart with every whirling lunge.

Hal felt himself getting dizzier by the millisecond. Croc was twirling like a washing machine. When the enraged bull tried to turn himself inside out with plunging leaps and high-flying kicks, Hal recalled his uncle's words. *Focus. Find that one image that keeps your world right side up while the bum is trying to turn you upside down and fling your sorry ass in the dirt.*

Hal willed himself to concentrate on the one thing he had spent sixteen days—and nights—trying to ignore. In a world where pain and violence threatened to destroy his resolve, he focused on a cloud of silky auburn hair and hypnotic orchid eyes. Though his body was one excruciating ache, he detached himself from it all. He concentrated on a forbidden memory, that one moment of glorious pleasure.

"Three seconds, ladies and gents!" the announcer said excitedly. "No wrangler has stayed on Croc this long in Phoenix. Let's let Hal Griffin know we're rooting for him!"

Hal didn't hear the enthusiastic cheers. There was nothing but the pounding thumps and snorts echoing just beyond the perimeter of his focus.

For her, because of what I did to her, he whispered. *Hang on, Griff you miserable bastard . . .*

The tearing sensation that sliced through Hal's arm threatened to distract him. Croc had broken himself in little pieces beneath Hal, trying to fling him head-over-heels. Hal reached deep inside himself, demanding everything he had to give.

"One second!" the announcer shouted.

The buzzer sounded and Hal automatically jerked on his numb arm, trying to free himself from the ropes bound around his wrist.

"He's done it, ladies and gents!"

At a moment when Hal would normally feel nothing but relief, he was frantically trying to loosen his riding hand, which was knotted in rope and anchored to the handhold. He hadn't intended to ride this power-packed mass of outrage for more than the necessary eight seconds, but he wasn't about to dismount without taking his right arm with him!

A collective gasp brought the crowd to their feet. Croc wheeled in another dizzying circle that left Hal sprawled on the bull's hump. Centrifugal force threatened to send him cartwheeling out of control.

"Shit," he muttered, wrestling with his tangled hand.

When the clowns rushed forward to distract the snorting bull, Hal worked his fingers feverishly. It was now or never, he told himself. He couldn't take another spin cycle on this crazed beast. He had lost his balance point as well as his focus.

Teeth gritted, Hal jerked his hand sideways, feeling the sharp pain spearing from shoulder to wrist. Croc took another unhinged leap in the air and Hal went airborne. He saw the colorful clowns' costumes rushing toward him—and past him—to divert Croc's attention. Hal's breath came out in a whoosh when he made his crash landing on the turf, every bone and muscle quivering like a tuning fork.

Get on your feet, Hal silently demanded of himself. *Get the hell out of that maniac's way!*

Another collective gasp from the crowed indicated

trouble loomed behind him. Hal twisted around on the ground to see those devilish black eyes and frothing mouth at close range. Preservation instincts burst to life as the monster bull charged at him.

"Watch it, Griff!" one of the clowns yelled as he tried to deter the bull by whacking it on the shoulder.

Hal wondered if Satan himself could loom more menacingly than Croc. Hal's scent was thick in the animal's flared nostrils. Croc was out for blood—Hal's.

When the bull lowered his horned head, Hal reflexively flung up his left arm to protect his vital organs. Pain crashed through his forearm as he scrambled to his feet amid the frightened shrieks from the grandstands.

When he stumbled on unsteady legs, the clowns swarmed to his rescue. Hal was shoved toward the fence, his breathing labored, his body throbbing with aches he couldn't pinpoint. He wasn't sure which part of his body hurt worse, but his left arm seemed to be demanding considerable attention. Dully, he stared down at the bloodstains on his forearm.

"Helluva way to make a living," the rookie news reporter said as he swaggered up beside Hal.

That flippant tone, compounded by the way the cocky kid was looking down his freckled nose, brought out the worst in Hal. "I'd ride Croc again before I'd switch places with you," he snorted. Though his arm was beginning to hurt like a sonuvabitch, he'd be damned if he let this snotnosed reporter know it.

The reporter was brushed aside by a crowd of cowboys who had come to check Hal's condition and congratulate him.

Rooster Anderson, the bulldogger from South Dakota,

was the first to arrive on the scene. "Dandy ride," he said. "Now let's see that arm."

Hal carefully unbuttoned his cuff and rolled up his sleeve.

"Christ!" Rooster crowed. "You broke the damned thing."

Hal stared at the broken flesh and protruding splinter of bone. It wasn't the first time he had suffered breaks, but obviously it was the first time the rookie reporter had seen one firsthand. The kid's face turned Clorox-white.

"A souvenir," Hal told the kid with a smirk. "Nice of Croc to leave me with something to remember him by."

The reporter swallowed visibly and then wobbled away.

When Hal saw Choctaw Jim cutting through the crowd, he hurriedly smoothed his sleeve over his forearm, but not quickly enough. Jim stared at the injured arm and then glowered at Hal.

"Satisfied?" he scowled as he herded Hal toward the locker room to retrieve his gear. "You may have picked up a sizable purse for that ride, but you just earned yourself a box seat at the nearest hospital."

"No hospitals," Hal growled defiantly. "I don't like those medical types hovering around me, telling me what I can and can't do, when I can or can't do it."

Choctaw Jim stopped short. "You want to end up with a deformed arm like Bernie Bryant?"

"No." Hal was all too familiar with the unnatural bend in Bernie's arm.

"Then don't argue with me," Jim insisted, hustling Hal up the ramp toward the pickup. "That arm needs immediate attention."

Hal allowed himself to be whisked away and driven to one of his least favorite places. Much as he hated to admit it, his arm was killing him. He knew he wouldn't be able to compete at the next rodeo. He would have to skip Billings, Montana, and let the horses earn as much mount money as possible.

Broken arm or no, he would sit out the rodeo in Billings, and then climb back aboard in Bismarck, Hal promised himself. It would give him two weeks to grow accustomed to working around the cast that would inevitably be plastered on his left arm.

As soon as Hal picked up his cash winnings from Phoenix he would mail them off to Andrea—same as he had done after the rodeo in Mesquite, Texas. By the end of this month, Tom Gilmore would have to agree to give Andrea an extension on the mortgaged property.

"Hal?" Choctaw Jim said as he slid beneath the steering wheel.

"This isn't going to turn into another one of your long-winded lectures, is it?" Hal asked tiredly.

"Nope," Jim replied as he drove to the hospital.

"More of your philosophy then?"

"Yep. Remember what a devil of a time you had getting loose from the bull rope you anchored too tightly around your hand tonight?"

"Yeah," Hal murmured, cradling his throbbing arm against his aching ribs.

"It's going to be the same way as long as you're trying to get loose from that pretty little cowgirl back in Oklahoma. You wrapped yourself too tight *then,* just as *now."*

"You know the code I live by," Hal said and scowled at his uncle.

"Sometimes rules get broken, just like arms." Jim countered, smiling that infuriating wry smile. "A smart man could save himself considerable trouble—"

"You don't understand, so don't butt in," Hal grumbled, staring at the street lights as they whizzed past the pickup.

Jim glanced sideways at his billy goat of a nephew. One of two, as it turned out. "It's you who doesn't want to understand that there are some forms of power in this world that a man can't fight. But you'll understand one day," he predicted.

"Damn, I think I'd rather visit the hospital than sit through your malarkey."

"Whatever makes you happy," Jim accommodated, still grinning. "I look forward to the day when it dawns on you what *will* make you happy."

Hal clamped his mouth shut. It was useless to fence with Choctaw Jim. Hal always lost. The wise old owl had an answer for everything. In fact, Jim was the only man on the planet Hal had ever allowed to have the last word. Sure 'nuff, Jim had gotten it again.

Andrea plopped down on the sofa and then propped up her aching legs. It had been another long, exhausting week. She had run herself ragged, looking for a job to pay off her debts. There wasn't much to be had near Hochukbi. The vet clinic was already staffed to capacity.

Andrea had found herself over-educated for the jobs available. Bad as she hated to do it, she had taken a job as secretary at Tuff Seever's real estate and insurance agency—a small, two-room office on Main Street. It was temporary and would only last as long as his permanent secretary was on maternity leave. Liz Thurman, a friend from high school days, was the proud mother of a bouncing baby girl, and Andrea was holding down the fort until Liz returned.

Despite Andrea's distaste for the kind of jobs she had avoided for years, she had been moonlighting as a waitress at Slim Chance Saloon. She had Hal Griffin to thank for making it possible for her to mill around the rowdy male patrons without recoiling.

She owed Hal that much, she thought as she sipped her soda. Although he had hurt her deeply, she wasn't as leery of men as she had once been. She simply ignored the wolfish whistles and seductive growls that followed her from one table to another. Andrea had learned to survive. She had also learned that love could be reduced to a sexual equation by a man who had exited her life without a word—only a personal check . . .

Andrea well remembered the day she had opened the envelope from Hal. Despite her objection, he had sent her partial payment on the loan. He had obviously finished high in the standings at Mesquite—hence the hefty check.

Proud and defiant, Andrea had mailed the check back to Chulosa Ranch, in care of Nash Griffin. She had followed the same procedure when she received the envelope postmarked from Arizona.

Under no circumstances was Andrea going to accept money from that damned cowboy. If he refused to accept her affection—no strings attached—then she didn't want his money. Or him. Hal had offered cash because he considered her some kind of charitable obligation, not because he honestly cared about her. He sympathized with her situation, and he had allowed himself to become more involved than he originally intended—that was all.

"Confounded cowboy," Andrea muttered to the empty room. She glanced at her watch, wishing she had time between shifts to stop by the football stadium in Hochukbi. Jason's team was playing their biggest rivals in the district play-offs. While Jason was hurling passes she would be dodging a few of her own.

Tiredly, Andrea got to her feet. The phone rang before she could climb the stairs to change clothes.

"Andrea?" It was the same sexy voice Andrea had heard a few weeks earlier on the answering machine. "This is Jenna Randall. Hal never got back in touch with me. Is he still around?"

Andrea silently cursed Hal. "No, he's back on the rodeo circuit."

"When do you expect him to return?"

The question indicated that Jenna had heard the gossip about Andrea being Hal's latest romantic interest. Boy, was that a laugh. Andrea was Hal's latest rejection.

Why did Jenna want to track Hal down? Andrea wondered curiously. Was she trying to rekindle an old flame despite local gossip that linked Hal and Andrea together?

"I can't say exactly when he'll be back," Andrea hedged. "Would you like me to give him a message?"

Which would be *never.*

There was a slight hesitation. "Uh . . . no. Just tell him I called."

Andrea hung up the phone, cursing the willowy blonde. Ten to one, that femme fatale wanted to torment Hal for old time's sake. Maybe Jenna planned to bolster her own confidence by breaking up what she presumed to be a budding romance between Hal and Andrea. Wouldn't Jenna be surprised to learn that Hal wanted nothing to do with Andrea!

Andrea hurriedly changed into jeans and a baggy blouse. She wasn't anxious to report for work at the bar. She constantly had to listen to the local yokels attempt to boost their egos by trying to beat Hal's time.

Hal's attempt to keep other men at bay had worked in reverse. She had become a challenge to the Neanderthal-mentality males who hung out at Slim Chance—which ironically was more chance than they would ever have with her.

No chance at all, Andrea reminded herself. She had fallen in love with that brawny cowboy, and he had trampled on her heart. She wasn't about to stick her neck out again, not for anybody.

Despite the hassle, Andrea was making good tips at the bar. She could tolerate the men because she desperately needed the money.

A quick glance at her reflection had Andrea raking her fingers through her hair and reaching for an elastic band to confine her unruly tresses to a pony tail. Hurriedly, she bounded down the steps. She would plaster on an artificial smile and drive off to do her job for the next four hours. And be able to pay off the second loan at the end of the month.

In two or three months, she might be able to breathe easier. Until then, she was a secretary and a waitress who scrambled around to keep up with the farm chores in what little spare time she had left. At least she didn't have time to pine for that blasted cowboy.

For that, Andrea was grateful.

Hal paced in his room at Ho-Hum Motel in Billings, Montana. He felt like a caged tiger. Hanging around the rodeo arena was wearing on his disposition. What was left of it, that is. The cast on his left arm didn't do much to brighten his moods, either. He wasn't accustomed to being on the fringe of rodeo activity, the way his uncle did. He was used to being in the thick of things, testing his skills, trying to shave a few more seconds off the steer roping events.

Loitering around beer stands and remaining behind the scenes at the chutes made Hal so restless he could barely sit still. The highlight of his week was giving the rookie cowboy from Montana a ride home after the Arizona rodeo. With Justin Simms in the truck, Choctaw Jim couldn't spout as much philosophical mumbo-jumbo.

Justin had been dismissed from the hospital the night Hal was admitted. When Justin asked to hitch a ride north, Hal had readily agreed.

Too bad Justin had wandered off to enjoy the rodeo night life this evening, before his father picked him up the following morning. Hal could have used the kid's boisterous company. It beat the hell out of having Choctaw Jim sprawl on the bed and smile that stupid damned smile.

"Restless?" Jim questioned.

Hal scowled as he dropped into the chair beside the scarred table.

"You could call her, you know, just to see how she's managing and to find out if she received the checks."

"I have complete faith in the postal system," Hal snapped.

"You may be the only one I know who does," Jim said, his aggravating smile still intact.

"Wonder how the Hochukbi football team is doing against Kanima Springs," Jim said five minutes later. "Didn't you say the Fletcher boy was the quarterback?"

"Yes," Hal answered shortly.

"I wonder what Nash and Crista are doing tonight?"

"Probably giving each other physicals," Hal said sarcastically. "No sense interrupting them—"

The rap at the door came as welcome relief. Hal bolted up to find Justin bookended by two well-endowed females with varying shades of platinum hair. The skimpy halter tops called attention to their generous cleavage, while the painted-on jeans emphasized the flare of their hips. Their heavy makeup gave Hal the impression that both women were wearing masks. Typical groupies, he decided, with "willing and eager" plastered all over them.

"We're on our way to the Silver Stallion Saloon to wet our whistles," Justin drawled. "Thought you might like to come along."

Hal glanced over his shoulder, noting his uncle had raised his brows and was grinning smugly. The old goat thought Hal was too stuck on Andrea Fletcher to carouse the way he used to, did he? Well, Jim could damned well think again. Although neither bottle blonde was Hal's type, either one would do. A third-rate romance was just what he needed.

"Sure, why not?" Hal said carelessly.

When Hal pivoted to scoop up his hat, Jim was staring speculatively at him. "It won't help," he murmured confidentially.

Defiantly, Hal set his Stetson at a jaunty angle. "Wanna bet on it?"

Choctaw Jim nodded. "If I'm wrong, I'll match whatever you win in the competition in Bismarck."

"Good—you can practice writing your signature on your check while I'm gone." Hal wheeled away, sliding his good arm around the woman delegated as his date for the evening.

"Don't look back, Hal," Choctaw Jim called out.

Hal stared out the open doorway. "Why not?"

Jim's quiet laughter floated across the room. "Because

the bridge you're trying to burn is still on fire, and all the beer between here and Oklahoma won't put it out."

Hal gritted his teeth and surged off. When the champagne blonde's full breasts rubbed provocatively against his arm, he felt an odd sensation of betrayal. There was no reason for it, he assured himself as they drove to the bar. He was footloose and fancy free. No ties to bind, no commitments, no emotional attachments. He could do as he damn well pleased, as many times as he pleased, with whomever he pleased. It made no difference that the eyes peering up at him were brown rather than orchid. He didn't care that the woman's hair was brittle blond instead of wavy auburn.

This was Hal's way of life—an uncluttered existence. He liked to travel light, with no unnecessary emotional baggage. Tomorrow he would be on his way to Bismarck, and the busty blonde would be a vague memory. There would be another female on the horizon, another sunrise shimmering on another part of the country.

Tonight, he was bound and determined to get Andrea off his mind and out of his system—once and for all. He'd purge himself in the fires of impersonal passion, Hal told himself as the accommodating blonde sidled closer.

He poured himself another drink from the pitcher in the middle of the table, letting the brew quench his thirst. Plenty of booze and a willing woman would cure him.

With that optimistic thought, Hal took another drink.

Twelve

Smiling in satisfaction, Jason Fletcher propped himself against the outer wall of the locker rooms. He had played his heart out for four grueling quarters. For three of them, Hochukbi and Kanima Springs had been deadlocked— equally matched, no score on the scoreboard. And then Jason and his wide receiver had connected on a long pass and the short sprint into the end zone. Suddenly, it was as if the home team could do no wrong. Jason threw two more touchdown passes in the fourth quarter, outdistancing their rivals by twenty-one points.

Checking his watch, Jason glanced around the abandoned area. Brenda had promised to meet him after she drove home to change out of her cheerleading uniform. He started toward his truck, wondering if her parents had refused to let her leave. Maybe he'd just stop by to say hello before driving to the ranch.

Before Jason could reach his truck, a dark figure leaped from the shadows beside the building. As Jason wheeled around, a musty canvas tarp floated over his head. He struck out to defend himself when he heard the scrambling of more footsteps.

Unseen fists pelted his head, his ribs. When he doubled over, he was kicked forward, stumbling on the trailing ends of the tarp, sprawling on the pavement. Blow after punishing blow rained down on him. Jason struggled to remain conscious, cursing the unseen faces of his attackers . . . until the world turned a fuzzy shade of black . . .

Andrea climbed into the old-model truck that had once belonged to her father. As had become her habit before leaving the bar's parking lot, she counted her tips. Not bad, even if she'd had to avoid more moves than an open field runner.

News of Hochukbi's resounding victory had reached the bar. Andrea had asked to leave work a half-hour early so she could celebrate with her brother. She expected Jason would be out on the town with Brenda, but Andrea wanted to touch base with him.

She glanced down the street, watching the floodlights at the stadium evaporate into the shadows. Hurriedly she drove to the far side of town, hoping to catch Jason before he left on his date.

A sense of uneasiness settled into Andrea's bones as she veered into the parking lot. Her brother's truck sat alone in the deserted area. Had Jason driven off with Brenda, planning to swing by and pick up his vehicle later . . . ?

Andrea's breath stuck in her throat when she saw the crumpled form lying beside the sidewalk. "No!" she shrieked, mashing her foot on the accelerator. Frantic, she stopped the truck beside the fallen body and leaped out. Jason didn't move a muscle when she shouted his name. Angry outrage consumed her as she squatted down beside her brother.

"Jase?" Hands shaking, Andrea eased him onto his

side. His mouth was swollen and his left eye was puffy. "Jase!" she wailed, trying to jostle him to consciousness.

Tears spilled down her cheeks as she clutched him to her. Jason was all she had left. *Please God, don't take him, too!* she pleaded between sobs.

A groan tumbled from Jason's lips. "Andi . . ." Tentatively, he licked his swollen lips, then tried to lever onto an elbow. The movement demanded more strength than he could muster. His body involuntarily collapsed on the pavement. "God, I hurt all over."

"Who did this to you? Tony and his thugs?"

"Don't know," he rasped as Andrea hooked her elbows beneath his arms to prop him up. "Couldn't see who. They tossed a tarp over me."

Swearing under her breath, Andrea braced her legs to hoist Jason to his feet. He staggered dizzily, bracing an arm against the side of the idling truck. When his knees folded up like a card table, Andrea tried to provide support.

Once she managed to get him into the truck, she shoved the gearshift into drive and rammed her foot to the floorboard. She laid rubber on the asphalt in her haste to get Jason to Kanima County Hospital. He had been beaten to a pulp after a physically grueling game. Jason needed medical attention—immediately.

Andrea didn't even consider the extra costs she would have to pay in deductibles before the insurance kicked in. She would work three jobs, if she had to. No matter what, Jason would receive the best care.

Although she exceeded the speed limit in her haste to reach the hospital, Andrea was cautious as they reached the treacherous curve that had killed their mother.

"Sis," Jason gasped. "I think I'm going to be sick."

"Be sick out the window," she told him, her gaze glued to the curve. "I'm not taking time to stop, much less slow down more than I have to. Just hang on, Jase. We'll be there in a few more minutes."

Nash Griffin picked up the phone in Crista's office at the hospital to place his late-night call. At Andrea's request, he and Crista had arrived there while Jason was being examined.

Although Hal had insisted he would have no further contact with the Fletchers, Nash felt compelled to tell him about the beating. Glancing at the number of the Ho-Hum Motel in Billings, Nash dialed the phone. After two rings, Jim's drowsy voice came over the line.

"How's it going in Billings?" Nash questioned.

"Except for your brother going stir-crazy with his broken arm, you mean?" Jim said. "Not bad. Popeye, Blue Duck, and Bowlegs have been bringing in good mount money. How are things going at home?"

"Things at Chulosa are fine," Nash said hurriedly, "but things at Fletcher Ranch are not. A bunch of hoodlums attacked Jason after the football game. They left him unconscious in the parking lot. Andrea found him and brought him to the hospital. Helluva way to celebrate winning the district play-offs."

"Damn," Jim muttered. "Is the boy going to be okay?"

"It's too soon to tell. He's being kept for observation tonight. They'll run tests in the morning," Nash reported. "Jason has one grand-prize shiner and a few stitches on his lower lip. I won't know much else until tomorrow."

"How's Andrea taking it?"

Nash recalled the haunted look in Andrea's eyes, the

pinched expression on her pallid face as she wore a path in the waiting room. The little lady was a walking knot of tension, and it worried the hell out of Nash.

Nash and Crista had offered plenty of compassion and support, but Nash suspected Andrea needed something more—from another source. Whether Hal was inclined to give Andrea what she desperately needed, Nash couldn't say. He could only convey the news and hope his pig-headed brother made the right decision.

"Nash? Is Andrea all right?" Choctaw Jim prodded.

"I think she could use more than casual acquaintances right about now." Nash replied. "She hasn't mentioned Hal, but I thought he should know what's going on, even if he doesn't think he cares."

"I'll pass along the news and call you back while we're on the road to Bismarck."

Nash replaced the receiver and then ambled down the hall. When he returned to the waiting room, Andrea was still wearing ruts in the floor and wringing her hands. Nash could see why Hal had gotten attached to Andrea and Jason. His protective instincts were kindled at the sight of her stricken face.

As for Jason, Nash cringed, thinking how the teenager's handsome features had been swollen and distorted. Jason's passing arm didn't look to be in good condition, either.

Strong-willed and determined though Andrea repeatedly tried to be, she needed a shoulder to lean on, someone who would be there for her, someone to take command.

As competent and skilled as Crista Delaney was in this kind of situation, her comforting smiles and appropriate words were useless. Andrea refused to sit down and relax. She was operating on frayed nerves and adrenaline, worrying herself sick about her brother—the only family she had left in this world.

It was going to be a long night, Nash predicted as he propped himself against the nearest wall.

Hal turned onto his back and stared at the ceiling, try-ing—as usual—to remember where he was. Another mo-tel room in another rodeo town, he finally recalled. Ho-Hum Motel. Good a place as any, he assured himself. He had slept like the dead, compliments of too much beer. His head felt like a melon. Any abrupt sound was sure to split his rind.

Dully, Hal propped himself up on his good arm and tried to focus his eyes. He and the buxom blonde had closed down the bar sometime after midnight. Hal had had every intention of doing his manly duty when she led him to her apartment, but he had come down with the worst case of cold feet ever recorded in the annals of rodeo-night-life history. What the empty-headed blonde had to offer Hal hadn't wanted.

Since when had he gotten so damned particular?

When Hal levered upright, his stomach pitched and rolled. He needed a shower and several doses of caf-feine—straight into the vein—to get him jump-started. Bleary-eyed, he glanced toward his uncle's bed. There was a note on the pillow that indicated Jim had gone to the arena to load up the horses and fuel the truck.

Thank God, Hal thought as he weaved toward the bath-room. He needed as many minutes of reprieve as he could get.

Hal groaned in relief as the soothing water rained down on him. Although he was forced to bathe with his left arm stuck outside the shower curtain, the rest of his body appreciated the curative effects. Five minutes later, reasonably sure he would survive, he grabbed a towel. He heard the motel door click shut, heard the rattle of paper sacks. Jim had returned with breakfast-to-go.

Hal wrestled his way into clean briefs and blue jeans. Without bothering to shave, he emerged from the bathroom, anxious to get his hands on food and coffee.

"Sausage and egg biscuits," Jim announced, tossing one of the sacks on Hal's unmade bed. "How was your big night on the town?"

"Never better," Hal said hoarsely, reaching for the biscuits. "Coffee?"

"On the dresser," Jim replied. "Everything is ready to go."

Hal munched on his breakfast, hoping to settle his queasy stomach.

"Nash called last night."

Hal continued to eat in silence.

Astute eyes zeroed in on Hal, waiting to gauge his reaction. "Some hoodlums roughed Jason Fletcher up last night after the game with Kanima Springs. Andrea found him in the deserted parking lot and rushed him to the hospital. Crista and Nash spent the evening there."

Hal's dark head jerked up, his bloodshot gaze fixed on his uncle.

"I guess Andrea needed someone to be with her while she waited for the doctor's diagnosis."

"How is the kid?" Hal demanded impatiently.

Jim shrugged noncommittally. "Won't know for sure how serious his condition is until they run tests. Laid the poor kid out pretty good, though, from what Nash said.

Good thing Crista will be around to console Andrea. Nice to know somebody cares enough to be there for her."

Hal was on his feet in the blink of a bloodshot eye, tossing clothes into the suitcase with record speed.

"Relax, boy," Jim said, smiling slyly. "You have time to eat before we shove off to Dakota. After the night you had on the town—"

"Damn it, Choctaw, why the hell didn't you tell me all this last night?" Hal growled disdainfully.

"I debated about even bothering to tell you this morning. If memory serves, you didn't want to think about—or see—Andrea Fletcher for the next hundred years."

Hal halted in the act of tossing his extra pair of boots in the suitcase. "Not going to tell me?" he croaked.

"Why should I? You went out last night to get cured—or something—with that cosmetic creation in skin-tight clothes. Besides, you have already gone above and beyond the call of duty with the Fletchers—or so you said. You gathered their cattle and sent them your winnings.

"The money replaces your presence in their lives, right?" Jim asked. "Besides, nobody showed up to console you when you busted your arm . . . So, do you want me to take the first shift while you catch a catnap?"

"No, I want you to take me to the airport so I can catch a flight to Oklahoma City," Hal muttered, slamming his suitcase shut.

"What about your return debut in Dakota?"

"Screw the rodeo," Hal snapped, jerking up his suitcase. "Can you handle the horses at the rodeo and drive home by yourself?"

"No problem," Jim said with a wry smile.

Hal was out the door, making a beeline for the pickup. Grinning, Choctaw Jim scanned the room for personal items that might have been overlooked. That was a customary ritual for those who lived out of a suitcase and followed road maps to earn a living.

Despite Hal's mutters and growls, Jim took his own sweet time piling into the truck. After all, he knew exactly what time the plane departed for Denver and Oklahoma City. Hal would reach the airport in time—no sweat.

It would be a pleasant drive to Dakota, Jim assured himself. Hal wouldn't be there, squirming in his skin, grumbling and scowling. A little peace and quiet for a change, Jim thought, grinning. Thus far, this road trip hadn't been a damned bit of fun, not with a grizzly bear of a nephew as his sidekick.

Hal grimaced and then swiftly schooled his expression as he walked into Jason's hospital room. The teenager's handsome features were bruised and swollen. According to Nash, who had picked Hal up at the airport, it had been touch and go during the night.

Jason's bruised kidney had temporarily shut down, leaving the medical staff to speculate on whether the injured organ would ever function properly. As for Jason's passing arm, it was a mass of black and purple bruises.

Strained ligaments, according to the latest report. It was improbable that Hochukbi's star quarterback would be allowed to suit up for the state playoffs in two weeks. At present, the staff wasn't optimistic.

Poor kid, Hal mused as Jason stirred in his sleep. The teenager had fallen for the prettiest girl in high school, and the rutting stags couldn't tolerate his fame and good fortune. Although Jason couldn't identity his assailants, Hal had a pretty good idea who was responsible.

That pimply-faced little bastard was going to pay for this, Hal vowed fiercely.

"Jason is a nice kid, isn't he?" Crista Delaney murmured as she entered the room. "Tough as a boot, too. He told me he intends to gut it out, just like you do." She stared directly at the cast on Hal's arm. "Does anything ever stop you in your tracks, Hal?"

Hal appraised the shapely, curly-headed therapist who had stolen his older brother's heart. There was a time not too long ago when Hal hadn't trusted Crista or her motives. He wasn't too keen on the wedding scheduled the week before the rodeo clinic at Chulosa Ranch. But he had to admit his brother seemed happier, more himself, than he had in years.

Crista met his eagle-eyed gaze as it swept over her. "What is it going to take to convince you that I love your brother dearly? You're as skeptical about me as ever."

"Fifty years of wedded bliss should do it," Hal replied. "Can you guarantee that, Curly?"

"As a matter of fact, I can. I'm not as pessimistic as you are. And by the way, there's someone around here who has suddenly become as cynical as you, if that's possible. Andrea doesn't believe in much of anything anymore." Crista smiled ruefully. "Except, of course, that her family is under some kind of curse."

"Where is she?"

"She's been at the hospital every minute she has between her jobs," she informed him. "Did Nash tell you she's working as a temporary secretary at a real estate and insurance agency in Hochukbi and moonlighting as a waitress at Slim Chance Saloon?"

"No." Hal continued to stare at the sedated teenager.

"All Nash said was that the checks I wrote to Andrea were returned—torn to pieces."

"She's quite a woman," Crista murmured as she checked Jason's charts. "I like her a lot. She's spunky, gutsy, and proud."

"She's a lot like you," Hal replied. "But—"

His voice trailed off when Jason's heavily-lidded eyes fluttered open. At least one of them did. The other was swollen shut.

"Hal?" Jason rasped groggily. His gaze drifted to the plaster cast that had been signed by every cowboy who competed in Phoenix and Billings. "What happened to you?"

"Looks like we both had a tough go-round." Hal eased his hip onto the side of the bed. "How are you feeling, kid?"

"Like I'm in a holding pattern over an airport," Jason mumbled out one side of his mouth. "The pain's gone, though."

The pain, Hal presumed, lay just beneath the strong medication that left Jason floating around the room.

"So's mine," Hal said with a dry smile. "It only hurts when I breathe."

Jason tried to grin, but the stitches in his lip wouldn't stretch that far. "Has Andi been here yet? I didn't sleep through her visit, did I?"

"No," Crista said, approaching the bed. "I told her not to come back tonight because I was going to see that you slept soundly after we took your vital signs. The truth is your sister didn't go to bed at all last night. She was here until noon. I thought she needed some rest after her twelve-hour workdays."

Jason nodded slightly, and then tried to shift into a more

comfortable position—without tangling his I.V. "That's good. Andi has been meeting herself coming and going for two weeks. And now this."

When Jason yawned, wincing at the pain in his lip, Hal smiled compassionately. "Better save your strength and get some rest, kid. I'll come by to see you tomorrow."

"What about the rodeo circuit?"

Hal shrugged. "There's always a rodeo next week and the week after. I'll catch up when the time is right."

"Thanks for coming, Hal," Jason murmured gratefully. "I've . . . missed . . . you . . ."

"Bad case of hero worship," Crista remarked as Jason dozed off. "I've had to listen to him sing your praises for a full day."

"Me, too," Nash added as his powerful frame filled the doorway. "You've really done a number on this kid. I lived with you my whole life and I never did think you were all that special."

"You're just jealous," Hal flung back playfully.

"Like hell," Nash chuckled as he automatically curled his arm around Crista's waist. He dropped a greeting kiss to her lips. "Hi, honey."

"Jeezus, the two of you are pathetic," Hal snorted as he headed for the door. "Those sappy smiles and slobbery kisses are making me sick."

"Going home?" Nash inquired.

"Why do you need to know? Is this your day to keep tabs on me?"

"Just brotherly concern," he said, grinning wryly.

Hal scoffed on his way out the door. "Don't worry, big brother, I'll try not to interrupt you and my sister-in-law-to-be—wherever I am."

"Thanks, we would appreciate that," Crista and Nash chorused.

Hal paused in the hall to heave a weary sigh. He'd started the day with a hellish hangover, hopped one plane and then another, skipped two meals, and hurried to the hospital. Tired and hungry though he was, he felt compelled to find Andrea, to know how she was holding up. She was probably hiding out in the tack room in the barn, crying. Hal wondered how she was going to react to seeing him after he had left on such a cruel, insulting note.

There was only one way to find out. Hal borrowed Nash's truck and drove south.

Andrea slid onto the seat of her truck, then draped herself over the steering wheel. She was unbelievably tired. Worrying about Jason and staying up all night was hell on someone holding down two jobs and doctoring sick cattle.

The deadly bacteria, left over from the days when buffalo herds grazed and bedded down on the prairie, was more prevalent during rainy seasons. Andrea had found two collapsed calves beside the fence row, and had given them the injection for Black Leg.

The disease, known to spread to epidemic proportions, forced Andrea to inoculate all the yearlings. That was another expense she couldn't afford but had to meet if she wanted to keep her livestock healthy enough to sell.

Fate had a nasty way of tossing one stumbling block after another in her path, making it difficult to keep her spirits up.

She had pulled herself up by her bootstraps so often the past few months that she had begun to ask herself why she bothered. Maybe it would be easier to admit defeat, sell the ranch, and move away. She and Jason could make a new start somewhere else. Considering all the trouble he was having, it might be better if he completed his senior year elsewhere.

Life would be simpler for her, too. She could hold down one job instead of two. There would be no more ranch chores, no sick livestock. It was the easy way out . . .

The thought reminded Andrea of her father.

Hurriedly, she switched on the ignition and drove away from Slim Chance Saloon. She had doubled her tips this evening—sympathy seemed to be worth a considerable sum, Andrea decided. Word of Jason's assault had spread through town. Men who usually flashed her come-hither grins had become courteous and generous.

Must be a quirky male characteristic. Hal was a prime example of pity resulting in monetary compensation—just like the patrons at Slim Chance.

Andrea drove home, her high-beams flashing against the metal guard rails that lined the hilly curves. In the distance she could see a thin swirl of smoke curling into the cloudless night sky. The closer she came to the arched gateway of the ranch, the more anxious she became. My God, in her haste to eat and change clothes—in between dashing from the hospital to work—had she neglected to turn off the stove?

Wild with desperation, Andrea veered off the highway. The truck fishtailed in the gravel as she stamped on the accelerator. She topped the hill at sixty miles an hour, cursing like a trooper. Flames leaped from the wooden barn that her great-grandfather had built at the turn of the century. He had erected that building with his own hands, using lumber from the trees growing on the ranch.

The horses! Andrea's heartbeat tripled as she zoomed toward the barn. Not only were the sick calves and horses penned in the stalls, but more than four hundred square hay bales—her whole supply of winter forage—were stacked in the loft. And the tack room, Andrea thought frantically. Replacing the vet medicine, supplies, and saddles would cost another fortune!

Andrea slammed on the brakes with both feet. In a flash, she bounded from the truck and dashed madly toward the barn to salvage what she could.

It would serve no purpose to call the volunteer fire department in Hochukbi, she realized. By the time the firefighters assembled and drove from town, there would be nothing left but the stone foundation.

Tearing off her blouse, Andrea covered her face and forged inside, compelled by the terrified screams of the horses and bawling calves penned in the burning inferno.

Hal saw the same curl of smoke that had sent Andrea racing against time. Swearing colorfully, he floorboarded his brother's truck and skidded through the arched gateway. Gravel flew like bullets as he sped down the half-mile driveway. With reckless haste, Hal ground to a stop, and then launched himself from the truck.

"Fletcher!"

No answer, only the hiss and crackle of flames that crawled toward the north peak of the barn. Desperately, Hal glanced toward the house, wondering if Andrea was inside, calling for help.

When he heard the thunder of hooves, he wheeled toward the barn. "Crazy woman," he muttered.

He didn't need X-ray vision to know Andrea was responsible for sending the string of horses and wobbly calves through the smoke and flames. He saw her trim silhouette staggering toward fresh air—with her blouse over her head. There was nothing to protect her upper torso from the intense heat except one of those damned sports bras she insisted on wearing.

As Andrea pushed away from the wall of the barn, sputtering and wheezing, Hal stalked toward her. "What the hell are you doing? Trying to kill yourself again?"

Andrea gasped for breath and ignored him. She stumbled toward the door of the tack room to retrieve the saddles.

"Damn it, Fletcher, just let it go!" Hal bellowed.

"No!" Andrea choked out. "The fire hasn't reached the tack room yet. There's still a chance!"

Hal took off at a dead run, intercepting Andrea before she plowed into the rolling smoke. "There are pesticides and fertilizer in there. I saw them myself. They could blow sky high."

When Andrea tried to twist loose from his grasp, Hal towed her backward.

"Let me go!" she railed at him.

"No way," Hal snapped. "If you get yourself killed, what the hell is your brother supposed to do? He's stuck in the hospital, in case you've forgotten. If you don't give a damn about yourself, at least think about what losing you would do to him."

When Hal's words penetrated her frantic desperation, all the fight went out of Andrea. She slumped against him in utter defeat.

"Why did they have to destroy our property?" she cried in frustration. "Wasn't it enough that they knocked the window from Jason's truck, slit the tires, and scattered our cattle to kingdom come? Did they have to beat Jase down in order to build themselves up? And this—" She gestured helplessly toward the smoldering barn.

Tears streamed down Andrea's sooty cheeks as she stared helplessly at the fountain of orange flames that spurted through the roof. "What did we do that was so horrible that we deserve this?"

Hal didn't have any answers. All he could do was hold Andrea close while she watched the smoke and flames belch from the old barn.

"Did you call the fire department?" he questioned.

"Call them what? *Too late?* " she muttered sarcastically. "They couldn't have helped." She stared at the barn with fatalistic resignation. "I barely had time to get the livestock out."

Reluctant though Andrea was to leave the scene, Hal shepherded her toward the wooden deck. She seemed compelled to watch, even if there was nothing she could do to stop it.

Once inside, Hal pulled out the nearest chair. "Sit," he ordered sternly.

Disheartened, Andrea slumped into the seat, staring at the far wall of the kitchen, saying nothing. Hal dialed the emergency number and gave directions. When he turned around, those beautiful orchid eyes that had haunted his nights and tormented his days were brimming with tears.

"The hay is gone, too," she said on a muffled sniff. "It'll smolder among the debris for days—"

An explosion shook the windowpanes, testifying to the existence of pesticides and fertilizer in the tack room. The sound was the final straw for Andrea. She buried her face in her hands and finally succumbed to her tears.

"I d-don't want to s-stay here anymore," she wailed

through her sobs. "No m-matter what I do it's n-never enough. Why fight it?"

Hal dropped down on one knee in front of her chair. Gently, he reached out to pry her hands away from her flushed face. "I'll take you away from here—right now, this very minute—if that's what you want. But make damned sure it isn't just the anger and frustration talking."

"Why shouldn't I walk away?" she asked in a tortured voice. "It's only a damned house, a lousy piece of land. Why should I care? My own father didn't stick around to try to save it. Why should I?"

When her shoulders shook and tears spilled in torrents, Hal suffered right along with her. He didn't know what to say, didn't know what was best for her.

Too bad Choctaw Jim wasn't here. The man always had good advice and a few proverbs to dole out in any situation. All Hal knew was that his heart was twisting in his chest. Andrea never seemed to be able to recover from one staggering blow before she was pelted with another. How much was she supposed to take?

And damn your soul for making her battles more difficult, Hal cursed himself.

"Your arm is broken," Andrea burst out suddenly. "What happened?"

"I had a little trouble with a bull called Croc," Hal said blandly.

"You haven't shaved lately, either," she noted, rerouting the salty streams that dribbled down her cheeks.

"I was in a hurry to see Jason."

"I'm sure he appreciated that. He thinks you hung the moon," Andrea mumbled. "I guess your ex-fiancée thinks so, too. She called a couple of days ago." She glared accusingly at Hal. "Just because I have become *Tuff's* fill-in secretary doesn't mean I intend to convey messages between you and your old flame, too . . ."

Andrea glanced away, staring through the window, watching the firelight glow in the darkness. "I don't suppose I'll have any more luck seeing that Tony and his hoods are punished for starting this fire than I'll have connecting them to Jason's assault," she mused aloud. "Those creeps must have known I would be at work tonight. They sneaked out here when I wasn't around."

The screaming siren heralded the firemen's arrival. Although Hal tried to discourage Andrea from venturing outside, she bounded from her chair and hurried toward the door. As so often happened in rural areas, the raging fire could only be prevented from spreading to the other outbuildings. The barn was so consumed with flames that there was nothing left by the time their streams of water sizzled on the charred rafters.

Completely defeated, Andrea turned back to the house. Hal watched her go, feeling her frustration as if it were his own. He recalled his uncle's haunting words the night Hal had broken his arm.

Remember what a devil of a time you had getting loose from the bull rope? It's going to be the same with that pretty little cowgirl back in Oklahoma. You wrapped yourself up too tight—then as now.

How and when, Hal wondered as he ambled over to speak to the fire marshal, had Choctaw Jim gotten so damned smart?

Thirteen

Andrea tossed her smoky clothes aside and stepped into the shower. She didn't know how long she stood there, didn't really care. Nothing seemed to matter anymore. The harder she fought, the more trouble she encountered. At the moment, she would give all her tips and wages from both jobs for one—make that *five*—of Hal's margaritas. Although she had never believed that the best way of dealing with trouble was to drown it in liquor, Andrea would welcome the numbing sensations she had experienced a few weeks earlier.

Temporary relief at best, Andrea thought realistically. But then, temporary was better than nothing.

That's it, Fletch, wallow in self-pity. You deserve to. Just throw up your hands and walk away. Leave it all behind.

Even as the defeatist thoughts echoed through her mind, Andrea knew she couldn't turn her back on her heritage. She hadn't thrown in the towel when male vet students razzed her about finding another career that better suited her shapely body and good looks. She hadn't allowed herself to sacrifice the ranch when she lost her parents. She would hang on, because the ranch was all she and Jason had left—a tradition, a way of life, family pride.

She wasn't going to call it quits because the damned barn burned down. She wasn't about to let those four cocky little bastards ruin her brother's senior year or drive her from her home.

Andrea stood up a little straighter and marshaled her resolve. She would thumb her nose at those creeps—and Tom Gilmore, too, while she was at it! She would take the insurance compensation for the barn and pay off another chunk of the loan. She would find someone to sell her enough hay to get the cattle herd through the winter. But *nobody* was going to drive her off this land. She was from pioneer stock, and Fletchers were made of sturdy stuff—most of them, anyway.

Her determination rejuvenated, Andrea shut off the shower. Beginning tomorrow, she was going to . . .

Andrea scrambled to grab a towel when a shadow loomed by the door. When Hal appeared, she covered herself as best she could. Damn, she thought in her shock and desperation, she had forgotten that she never intended to speak to Hal Griffin again.

Too late for that, she reminded herself. She had even gone so far as to cry on his shoulder while her barn burned. But now that she had her head on straight she would treat him with the careless indifference he expected.

"I'm staying the night, Fletch," Hal announced in a business-like tone. "If you still want to leave in the morning—"

"I've decided to stay," she cut in, her chin tilted to a defiant angle. "I'm not calling it quits, even if those thugs send the whole damned place up in flames."

Hal smiled faintly, his gaze never dropping below her neck. "I figured you would say that after you calmed down."

When Hal spun away, Andrea swallowed a portion of

her injured pride and said quietly, "Thank you for helping me."

He turned his head a fraction, the five o'clock shadow making him look like a renegade from the Old West. Andrea felt an unwanted rush of affection pouring through her—affection Hal didn't want or need. He had told her—and quite explicitly—that he regarded her as his charity case. The Fletchers were his good deed for the year, nothing more.

"I would appreciate it if you would call Jenna while you're here," she insisted. "I think she's determined to break up this affair you and I *aren't* having. I would also appreciate it if you would ask her not to call here anymore. I'm too busy to run your phone service."

"Fletch—"

"I'm dead tired," Andrea declared, shooing him out of the way. "Let's save this conversation for next week. Next year would be even better. Don't expect breakfast in the morning. I have to see Jase before I go to work."

"Will you shut up—for once?" Hal said and scowled at her.

"Will you go away—for*ever?*"

Intense black eyes riveted on her, burning wherever they touched. "Is that what you really want? I remember a time not so long ago when you came to my room, dressed exactly as you are now. You were in no hurry for me to leave *then.*"

With spiteful defiance, she tossed back the words he had hurled at her when he left. "Well, I made a mistake, didn't I? And you were a man of all kinds of *mercy* back then, weren't you?"

Hal had the decency to wince at the reminder. Wonders

never ceased, Andrea thought. The man did have a conscience, after all.

"But don't you fret now, sugar," she drawled sarcastically—she had learned the technique from the master. "I I find myself in need of another mercy—"

Hal's good hand shot out, giving her a hard, quick shake. "Don't say it."

"Why not?" she flung back. "Too crude for your delicate senses, cowboy? I thought harsh words were part of your everyday vocabulary."

His arm snaked around her waist, plastering her against him. Andrea felt the tremors of desire and struggled to ignore them. It was pay-back time. She was going to treat him the same way he'd treated her. It was petty and spiteful, but it was also damned gratifying.

"Or maybe *you're* the one in need of mercy now," she smarted off, forcing herself to remain rigid and unfeeling in his one-armed embrace. "What's it been? A couple of days since you got laid?"

"Stop it," Hal growled.

"Stop it?" Andrea parroted. She was just getting warmed up. It felt good to blow off a little steam. "I rather like this don't-give-a-damn-what-I-say-or-do attitude I've learned from you. I kinda like behaving like a bitch, too. It's ever so much easier when you're dealing with a real bastard."

"Damn it, woman," he muttered down at her.

The personification of cool indifference, Andrea twisted from his grasp. "Aw, come on, Griffie. Don't turn into a stuffed shirt. Not you, not the hard-ass cowboy I've come to know. You're the one who taught me. Don't you enjoy looking at me and seeing your own reflection?"

"You're really starting to piss me off," Hal snarled, eyes glittering.

Now that was the best news Andrea had heard in months. "Am I? Well, hot damn!"

And then Hal did her the discourtesy of grinning, thereby spoiling all her spiteful pleasure. "Is this something new—shooting off your mouth and talking dirty?"

Andrea veered around him and sauntered into the hall. "Nope," she said breezily. "This is my way of letting you know that I'm not the same naive woman you left behind a few weeks ago. I got over my infatuation and all that hero-worship nonsense. It wasn't first love—just a simple case of first lust. Soon as I find somebody else who catches my eye, I'll be in it just for the sex—like you."

On the wings of that brash remark, Andrea sailed into her bedroom and slammed the door.

Swearing under his breath, Hal stood in the hall. He had the feeling his cynical attitudes really were contagious—and he didn't like what he saw.

God, had he really done a number on her? Little Miss Sass and Spirit was out to show the world that nothing could touch her, nothing could hurt her, nothing could affect her. She reminded Hal of somebody he knew all too well. She was right. It *was* like staring at his own reflection.

Scowling, he went to look up Jenna's phone number. He was in the perfect frame of mind to deal with his devious ex-fiancée.

Jenna answered on the third ring. When her soft, seductive voice came over the line, Hal recalled the time in his life when he had been blinded by a pretty face, taken in by flattery, and then used to hook a bigger fish. The experience had taught him that the rules of civilized society didn't apply in love or war.

The experience had been a rude awakening, the worst of all possible humiliations. Hal had taken his pent-up frustration out on women, and the world. Now Andrea was trying to do the same thing . . .

The thought made him wince.

"Hello?" Jenna said a second time.

Hal jerked himself back to the present. "This is Hal Griffin. You have something to say to me?"

"Can you come over tonight?" Jenna murmured provocatively.

Hal's gaze drifted down the hall to Andrea's closed door. He wasn't leaving her alone. Didn't want to leave her alone, even if she would have preferred that. He had traveled hundreds of miles to be here, and here he was going to stay. Jenna lost the right to his loyalty and consideration twelve years ago.

"Sorry, Jen, I've got better things to do and somebody I prefer to do them with," he told her frankly.

"Hal, I need your help."

There was a strained undertone in her voice. Hal suspected it was deliberate. The woman should have been an actress. "Really? I thought women were supposed to turn to the men they married when they needed help."

"I never married," she informed him. "I know you have every right to hate me, but this really is important. When you walked into the bank a few weeks ago I thought there was a chance for me to get out of this mess I'm in."

Hal gnashed his teeth. Why, he wondered, did the woman always perceive him as part of her grand schemes to better herself? He had played the sucker for her once before. Never again.

"Not interested," Hal told her point-blank.

There was a noticeable pause before Jenna sighed into the phone. "If you care anything about Andrea Fletcher, you'll be here."

That got Hal's attention. He didn't like the sound of it, even if it was just a lure.

"Not tonight," Hal muttered.

"Tomorrow then? It has to be soon."

Hal muttered to himself. "Okay, tomorrow night. Seven-thirty. Give me directions to your place."

Once Jenna had told him where to find her, Hal replaced the receiver without so much as good-bye. He didn't trust her any farther than he could spit. She was the reason he mistrusted women, after all. Chances were Jenna hadn't changed all that much in the past decade. If anything, she had probably become more deceitful.

Hal pulled off his shirt on his way to shower and shave. There was only one woman he felt he could trust. She was lying in bed, waiting for the last corner of her world to cave in on her. She needed and deserved help. Jenna didn't.

Hurriedly, Hal scrubbed himself squeaky clean and scraped off his five o'clock shadow. For fifteen minutes, he paced his room, telling himself he should crawl into bed—and stay there. Problem was, he didn't want to sleep alone. He wanted what he had spent weeks assuring himself was over and done.

The truth was, he hadn't been able to forget Andrea, no matter how hard he tried—and he'd tried pretty damned hard. Still, she was the ache that wouldn't go away, the memory that haunted him.

Wearing nothing but a clean pair of jeans, Hal padded barefoot down the hall. When he opened Andrea's door, she bolted straight up in bed.

"Now what? Is the house on fire, too?"

Hal felt a smile working its way across his lips. "No, I'm the only one on fire around here. Now that you've decided you're in it for the sex, too, I thought we may as well—"

"You really are an ass," Andrea hissed.

"Perfect match for a sassy little bitch like you," he flung back.

"Is this how all your one-nighters play out, Griff?" she smirked.

"No," he said honestly. "I'm usually fawned over and praised for my skills—in the arena, that is."

"Forgive me if I don't fawn. Somebody shattered all my idealism when he walked out the last time he was here."

"Yeah, somebody did," Hal agreed. "He was a genuine bastard."

"You certainly got that right."

"Since when did you start agreeing with everything I said?" he asked, chuckling.

"Since I decided to be like you."

Hal ambled over and sank down on the edge of the bed. Although Andrea recoiled when he reached for her, he was tender but persistent. With delicate care, he traced her high cheekbones, the lush curve of her lips with his forefinger. "Emulating me would be a gigantic mistake," he murmured.

"I seem to be making mistakes on a regular basis these days," she tossed back, her voice wavering beneath the onslaught of his light caresses.

Hal bent his damp raven head and realized—right there and then—that he had been starving for the sweet taste of her for weeks on end. The battles he had fought with himself in hopes of remaining emotionally detached had been a waste of time and effort. All the burning hunger, the deep desire, came crashing down like a rock slide.

The woman had gotten to him, even though he knew she had only reached out to him when trouble threatened to swamp her. He had led her to believe she had been just a convenient outlet for his physical needs, but it was the other way around. Andrea just refused to believe it—until Hal had forced her to accept the fact that circumstances were responsible for her distorted feelings.

Of course, Andrea hadn't intentionally tried to deceive him, not the way Jenna had. Andrea had needed to be held, needed something to hold on to. Hal couldn't fault her for that, because she'd had such a rough go of it.

"No more words about love," Andrea promised as his lips skimmed her throat. "Just uncomplicated sex."

"Uh-huh." Hal wasn't paying enough attention for her words to register. He was too lost in her fresh, clean scent, the silky texture of her skin.

"Teach me another lesson," she requested, her voice dropping to a velvety pitch.

His hand glided beneath the hem of her oversize T-shirt, making him want to hurl it out the second story window. He wanted to feel her supple body pressed to his—with nothing in between.

"What lesson is that?" he asked, hopelessly distracted.

"Teach me to please a man."

Hal blinked, suddenly aware that he hadn't kept up with her train of thought. "Why?"

Andrea laughed softly as she reached up to explore the

muscled terrain of his chest. "I thought that was supposed to be *my* question."

"A little of you must have rubbed off on me," he murmured, nipping at the sensitive point beneath her ear.

Despite the tingling pleasure he had felt shivering across her skin, Andrea withdrew. She stared up at him with those impossibly beautiful eyes.

"You really want to know why?"

He nodded. "Why?"

"So I can show you how good *you* make *me* feel when you touch me."

Hal had always appreciated her honesty. He just wasn't sure she needed to discover what kind of power a woman could have over a man. Andrea aroused him without even trying.

"Hal?" Andrea prompted, her fingertips gliding through the hair on his chest.

"I'm thinking it over." His voice dropped to a husky pitch when his body quivered beneath her curious explorations.

"I'd appreciate a snap decision here," she teased playfully. "I've got my heart set on fooling around tonight. It's a little late to dash off to find another guinea pig to accommodate me."

"Can't have you running around in your nightshirt," Hal agreed, smiling scampishly. "Oh, what the hell. Since you're all-fired determined to experiment with somebody's body, may as well be mine. Just go easy on the broken arm."

When he stretched out on the bed, Andrea propped up beside him. "Now then, Love Doctor, how does a woman go about turning a man on?"

Laughter rumbled in his chest. Never once in thirty-two

years had he found himself in any encounter that remotely compared to this. She was making sex altogether new and intriguing.

"I've never been a clinical study before," he confided.

"Good," she said, her forefinger tracing figure eights around his nipples. "I like being your *first* at something."

Hal threw her a wary glance "You aren't thinking of writing a sex manual, are you?"

"Sure, why not? How-to books have been selling like hotcakes for years. How do you think I managed to tackle the plumbing leak under the sink?"

"You put the pipe collar on upside down," he didn't hesitate to remind her.

"I'd have gotten it right eventually," she assured him as her hand trailed down the firm muscles of his belly, making his breath quicken. "Either that or I would have completely flooded the kitchen floor . . . so . . . Griff, how do I excite a man?"

"You're doing a damned good job already. Just remember the steps you followed with your plumbing."

Andrea burst out laughing. "Good sex is like good plumbing? Next I suppose you're going to tell me that my hand is a pipe wrench."

"Could be," he said, quickly losing interest in playful banter.

Hal found himself wanting something from Andrea that he had never permitted with other women, because he usually preferred to remain in control of his sexual liaisons. He wanted her to take the initiative, to touch him, explore him . . .

He forgot to breathe when Andrea's thick, wavy hair cascaded over his chest and her lips skimmed his ribs. He could feel the tips of her breasts teasing his skin. Impulsively, he reached out to return the pleasure of her touch.

"I can't concentrate when you do that," Andrea murmured. "I'm the one who needs to practice. How am I doing so far?"

"Mmm . . ." Hal moaned as her teasing hand followed the wedge of hair that dipped into the waistband of his jeans. The fact that she came just shy of touching him where he was most a man was pure and simple torment.

"Could you define *mmm . . .*" she requested.

Andrea was clearly enjoying herself. So was Hal, in a frustrated sort of way.

"Good," he translated. "That feels good."

"What does it take to make you feel *great?*"

"Andrea, this is—"

"You aren't being very cooperative," she admonished.

"Lower . . ." he rasped and then flinched when her first experimental touch sent scalding chills over his flesh.

Hal felt the trail of fire blaze through every muscle and nerve ending. Intense need burgeoned with each sweep of her fingertips. She stroked him, traced him . . . until he was arching helplessly toward her, craving more.

"Sweet Jesus," Hal groaned as the pad of her thumb brushed the blunt tip of his sex. "Show a little mercy!"

He heard as much as felt her reply as her lips skimmed the aching length of him. "Never for mercy, Hal," she quietly assured him, reminding him of his cruel words when he rejected the affection she had once offered. "If I'm killing you with pleasure then you're beginning to understand what you do to me. But there's a distinct difference. I have no mercy, only the need to return the exquisite pleasure you gave me . . ."

Hal would have said something in reply—he wasn't

sure what. But then, she took him into her mouth, her tongue gliding over him, sending him cartwheeling toward the edge of restraint.

"God!" he gasped on what little breath he had left.

She was making a feast of him, tasting, touching, exciting him wildly. Hands like velvet drifted from chest to thighs. Lips like moist silk measured the hard length of his manhood, pausing at irregular intervals to nip and tease almost beyond bearing. Hal battled for self-control, but a silvery drop of need betrayed him.

And when she sipped the taste of his passion he groaned aloud. When she shifted to touch her lips to his, sharing the taste of his desire, Hal felt himself swirling toward the vortex of a whirlwind stronger than anything he'd experienced in a rodeo arena. Though practice had taught Hal to hold on despite pain for that eight seconds of eternity, he found himself falling helter-skelter through time and space. He wanted, needed Andrea—now. One more moment and it would be too late.

"Lord, woman," Hal hissed through clenched teeth as his good arm curled around her, lifting her above him so she could straddle his hips. He cursed the need that refused him time to arouse her. He was taking without giving. With Andrea, that seemed vital and necessary.

Fierce and uncontrollable need bombarded Hal as Andrea reached between them, caressing him, encouraging him to take what his body demanded.

Hal gritted his teeth and battled primal instinct. "No, not like this," he gasped.

Andrea guided him to her as she bent over him. Her lush mouth sought his, just as she sought the hard length of him to fill her, complete her.

"Exactly like this," she insisted, her orchid eyes glowing with passion. "I want you out of control, as I was . . ."

When he felt her softest flesh shimmering around him Hal gave himself up to mindless ecstasy.

Paradise, he caught himself thinking. He had come home, after years of aimless wandering. Paradise was having Andrea in his arms, feeling her eager body welcome him. She was what had been missing, the need that even his fast-paced, challenging lifestyle couldn't satisfy. Home, coming home . . .

Hal's thoughts spiraled like the cloud of smoke that still hovered over the smoldering barn. The immense pleasure that consumed him demanded all his strength and energy. He thrust against Andrea in wild desperation, aching to bury himself so deep that he couldn't tell where his passion began and hers ended.

Hot, pulsating need drove him, destroying every ounce of control. Hal shuddered against her, spilling himself into her like a raging river. For what seemed like forever, he clutched Andrea to his heart, yielding to the brain-scrambling aftermath of a desire that created its own terms of existence.

A while later Andrea stirred above him, her lips feathering across his eyelids and then his mouth. "Mmm . . ."

"Define *mmm,*" he murmured, grinning in contentment.

"It translates differently from male to female," she said, playful amusement rippling in her voice.

"What's the feminine translation?"

"Better than lemon chiffon pie," Andrea declared, raising her head from his shoulder to grin impishly at him.

"Where's lemon pie on the scale from one to ten?"

"Do you always rate sex after one-nighters? Is that another of Griffin's Commandments? What did the last fling

ate? I don't want to risk blowing any holes in your ego."
he smiled mischievously. "I thought you said you hated
when women wanted to compare—"

His index finger brushed her lips to silence her. Hal
ooked through the shifting shadows to stare her squarely
n the eye. "There hasn't been anybody since you," he
dmitted.

Andrea blinked, stunned. "There hasn't?"

"Nope."

"Why?"

Hal raised his left arm, directing her attention to the
cast. He watched her face fall in disappointment. Once
before, he had tried to discard the affection she claimed
she felt for him and he had hurt her badly. He had also
discovered just how much it tormented him to be deliberately cruel to her. Though he still knew it was best that
she accept sex for what it was, he couldn't mislead her.

"Actually," he confessed, "having a cast to cramp my
style isn't the reason."

"It's not? Then why?"

Hal smiled wryly. "Gimme a break, Fletcher."

"You've already had one." She gestured toward his arm.
"Why?"

Hal eased onto his side, taking Andrea down beside
him. Forehead to forehead, breast to chest and hip to hip,
he pressed a lingering kiss to her responsive lips. "Figure
it out for yourself, boss lady," he challenged her.

"You're beginning to like me a little?" she ventured,
eyes twinkling.

"Yeah, I'm beginning to like you."

"Griff?"

"Hum?"

"I like you, too," she whispered before she cuddled up

next to his heart and gave way to the exhaustion that ha
become her very existence.

Hal lay awake, listening to Andrea's methodical breath
ing, his good arm wrapped possessively around her. H
wondered if he was experiencing the same sensations tha
had become his brother's downfall. He also wondered i
the overpowering force Choctaw Jim had mentioned wa
trying to grab hold of him. Hal had the uneasy feeling
that the force *was* with him—or at least close enough t
devour him if he let it.

Andrea awoke, feeling as if she had a new lease on life
She and Hal had passed a new milestone. Although she
hadn't mentioned the L-word that made him go ballistic
last time he was here, Andrea was assured of her feelings
for that brawny cowboy. She had expressed her affection
with each bold touch, marveling at the pleasure she received from learning to arouse him, from making him
want her until he was shaking with need.

When she had awakened with a smile, Hal had returned
it. Then he had made love to her with the same playful
enjoyment they had shared the previous night. For the first
time, and despite the obstacles she still faced, Andrea felt
at peace with herself. Hal had brought joy back into her
life, put a smile on her lips. She would always love him
for that. It was going to kill her when he packed up and
went down the road to another rodeo—and the temptations
of women eager to please him.

Maybe she had read too much into Hal's admission that
there had been no one else since the first time they had
made love. And maybe his injured arm and bruised ribs

ad required recuperation, without the strain of bedroom
ymnastics.

"And maybe you're getting carried away with wishful
hinking," Andrea criticized herself.

"Wishful thinking?" came the deep, resonant voice be-
ind her.

Andrea wheeled away from the smoldering remains of
he barn that she had been staring at the past few minutes.
Her gaze swept down Hal's powerfully-built physique with
possessive intimacy. She knew this man better than she
knew herself. He had become a living, breathing part of
her, and she had touched him in all the familiar ways
overs shared . . .

When the thought put a blush on her cheeks, Hal's left
eyebrow elevated and his sensuous lips quirked. "Just
what *were* you thinking?" he quizzed her.

Despite her embarrassment, Andrea answered him honestly. "I was thinking how much I like touching you."

"Good gawd, woman," Hal groaned, impulsively reaching out to tug her into his arms. "You really don't believe
in any kind of mercy at all, do you?"

"I thought we covered that topic last night," she tossed
at him "Never for mercy only for—" Andrea stopped
short, determined to maintain a light, carefree tone that
wouldn't leave Hal feeling hemmed in. "For experimental
purposes," she finished belatedly.

Hal peered at her for a long, pensive moment. Then he
kissed her hard and fast before he stepped back into his
own space. "Let's go see Jason."

Andrea nodded agreeably. "Soon as I call Tuff about
filing an insurance claim for the barn, I'll be ready. I'd
like to have the adjuster appraise the damage as quickly
as possible."

When Andrea strode toward the deck, she sensed Hal
eagle-eyed gaze following her. She wondered what he wa
thinking, wondered if he was already feeling restless an
anxious to move on. Did he have the slightest idea hov
badly she wanted him to stay?

Ah well, she thought as she punched in Tuff's hom
phone number. Maybe she and Hal could have one da
together. She longed to spend her one and only day of
with him, to simply be herself and enjoy being with him

She would have that much, Andrea promised herself
She would have one day to remember always.

Was that asking too much?

Fourteen

Hal visited with Jason for an hour before he left brother and sister together in the hospital room. He was greatly relieved to hear that Jason's kidney was now working properly.

Although the boy had been sedated to ease his pain and ensure plenty of rest, he would be released the following morning. However, Jason's throwing arm required Crista Delaney's expertise. She had promised to stop by Fletcher Ranch each night after work to give hot and cold pack treatments, massages, and strengthening exercises.

Hal had noted the strained lines on Andrea's face when she informed her brother of the burned barn. The woman had been under tremendous stress lately. She definitely needed a diversion, Hal decided.

Striding down the hall to use the phone, Hal placed a call to Bernie Bryant—the ex-rodeo-cowboy-turned-cook at Chulosa Ranch.

"Bern, I'd like to ask a favor," Hal said when Bernie answered.

"What's up, Hal?"

"What's up is that Fletcher's barn was purposely burned down," Hal reported.

"Well, damn, those poor kids are having the worst string of bad luck I ever saw."

"I wondered if you could fix a picnic lunch for th afternoon. I'd like to take Andrea down to our fishing hol on the river. She needs to get away for a few hours. Mayb you and Nash would like to come along."

"Nash won't be around for lunch. He and Crista ar driving up to the City to shop for wedding bands"

Hal smirked at the news. "I figured Curly would insi: on Nash having a ring through his nose so she could lea him on a leash."

Bernie snickered at that. "I don't think she needs a rin and leash. Your big brother looks to be trained to hee already."

No kidding, thought Hal. Nash melted like a snow ban in July whenever Crista winked those cedar-green eyes o hers and flashed him a smile. These days, the man was hopeless cause. The fire-breathing wolf-dragon of Kanim Springs had become domesticated.

"What time do you want your picnic basket, rods an reels, and bait ready?" Bernie questioned.

"Around noon. The nurse came in to give Jason anothe sedative. He'll be out like a light pretty quick, I suspec We'll be at the house in an hour. Are you coming alon; with us?"

"I appreciate the invitation, but I . . . um . . . was goin to drive over to Keota Flats to pick up supplies. See yo later."

Hal hung up the phone, reasonably certain Bernie's trip was a spur-of-the-moment inspiration to ensure Hal and Andrea's privacy. Although Hal could have used a chape rone to make sure he kept his hands to himself, he had t admit he was anticipating this little excursion to his child hood haunt, and Andrea desperately needed to forget he troubles for a few hours.

Forty-five minutes later, when Jason's droopy eyes slammed shut, Hal ushered Andrea from the hospital.

"Where are we going?" she asked as Hal put her in the truck.

"Fishing."

"I haven't been fishing since I was a kid."

"Me, either. We'll make a contest of it."

Andrea raised a curious brow. "What grand prize does the winner receive?"

"Bragging rights," Hal announced as he drove off.

"Thanks."

Hal took his eyes off the road long enough to cast her a quick glance. "What for?"

"For knowing what I need," she murmured.

Hal refocused on the road and drove toward home. It was becoming increasingly apparent that somewhere along the way he had become attuned to Andrea's needs. That wasn't surprising, of course. He had spent more time with her than any woman alive.

All part of being charitable, Hal quickly assured himself. After all, this was his good deed for the year.

Andrea pulled up short when the thick clump of trees lining the river opened to a peaceful cove, complete with a delta of sand at the river's bend. "It's beautiful," she breathed in awe. "Just like the rest of your ranch."

Hal set the picnic basket aside, and then shook out the quilt. "Nash and I used to come here on days when our mother was confined to bed with migraines."

"Did your dad come along with you?"

Hal laughed humorlessly. "Dear old daddy had better things to do, and other women to do them with. He ran

off with one of his lady friends when Nash and I were i
grade school. Haven't seen or heard from him since, nc
even when Mother died."

"I'm sorry," Andrea murmured sympathetically.

"Don't be." Hal handed her a fishing pole. "Choctav
Jim quit the rodeo circuit, took over raising us, and helpe
Mom as long as she was alive. Jim was the best thing tha
ever happened to Nash and me."

Andrea reached into the tin can to dig out a worm fo
her hook. "My parents always went fishing with Jaso
and me. We did things as a family for as long as I ca
remember. Whether it was working cattle, attendin;
church, or going to Jason's ballgames, we did it together."

When Andrea hurled her line into mid-channel witl
skillful ease, Hal raised a dark brow. "I may have spoke
too quickly when I challenged you. You look as if yo
know what you're doing."

Andrea grinned impishly as she tightened the line. "
can catch 'em, clean 'em and cook 'em. When I reel i
the biggest fish, you better believe I'll brag about out
fishing the hot-shot rodeo celebrity."

"All this and modesty, too," Hal chuckled, casting hi
line. "I—"

Hal shut his mouth in a hurry when Andrea's line wen
taut. He watched her battle the channel cat that had mad(
its quick strike. When she had hauled the fish ashore, Ha
appraised the two-pounder she held up in playful triumph
"Damn, lady, you don't mess around, do you?"

"Nope, we Fletchers take our fishing quite seriously,"
Andrea replied as she placed her catch on the stringer.

When Hal's line shot sideways, he reeled in his fish
Andrea burst out laughing when he hoisted a scrawny
perch from the water.

"Robbing cradles, Griffin?" she teased unmercifully.

Grumbling, Hal tossed the little beggar back in the river, and then aimed himself toward the picnic basket. Andrea's stomach growled the instant the aroma of fried chicken and baked beans filled the afternoon air. She braced her pole beside Hal's, then sat down cross-legged on the quilt.

After the meal she stretched out on the quilt to soak up the sunshine and savor the peaceful pleasures of the afternoon. The tension melted away and Andrea fell asleep, content where she was.

While she dozed contentedly beside him, Hal stared up at the cloudless sky. Something had been niggling him since the previous night when he topped the rise of the driveway to see the barn in flames. The conversation he'd had with Jenna had aroused a few more questions, for which he had no answers. He had the unshakable feeling that the difficulties that constantly cropped up in Andrea's life were too well timed.

If you care anything about Andrea Fletcher, you'll be here.

Jenna's words played over and over in Hal's mind. What was that conniving female up to? Hal sure as hell intended to find out. He also intended to look Tony Braden—and Company—up. What had been jealous rivalry between teenagers had suddenly become brutally destructive.

Hal was the first to admit that bad luck struck occasionally, and was known to descend in sets of three. He had his arm in a cast to prove that bad luck did occur, but the Fletchers seemed plagued with one disaster after another. It disturbed Hal that the barn had been set afire while Jason was hospitalized and Andrea was busy running between jobs—and the hospital, to visit her brother. Tony Braden hadn't tried to conceal the fact that he was harassing Jason. And then, it was as if the rules had suddenly changed. Jason had been covered with a tarp so he couldn't identify his assailants. The barn was targeted while the ranch was untended.

Was it because the criminal acts were punishable?

A premonition of danger rippled through Hal. Something was simmering beneath the surface of the Fletchers' *supposed* bad luck. Hal couldn't shake the feeling that things weren't exactly as they seemed.

Andrea, he realized, had been too busy and upset by her daily battles to analyze the procession of events. She was simply struggling to survive.

When Hal stumbled over that thought, a pensive frown plowed his brow. Tony's spiteful tire slashing and his attempt to scatter the cattle could've made it impossible for Andrea to sell her livestock and pay the overdue interest on her father's loans. If Hal hadn't put in a call to his brother to transport the cattle to the stockyards, the payment wouldn't have been on time.

Hal scowled to himself as he reflexively cuddled Andrea against him. If he followed that path of logic, then why burn the barn? Andrea could expect swift compensation for her loss—which could be paid toward the outstanding loans. That fact shot his theory of premeditated sabotage all to hell.

Glancing at his watch, Hal nudged Andrea awake. Contented though he had been, a restless, edgy feeling prompted him to get up and get moving. He wanted to rehash the Fletchers' problems and try to make sense of them.

"Let's stop by to see your brother," Hal suggested as he gathered their gear.

"Is something wrong?" Andrea questioned perceptively.

"No," Hal hedged. "I just thought Jason would appreciate a short visit before the nurse dopes him up for another good night's sleep."

Later, when Hal dropped Andrea off at her ranch, she glanced quizzically at him. "Aren't you coming in?"

"There's some unfinished business I need to take care of."

Hal watched Andrea's shoulders slump in disappointment, but then she forced a smile. She was still hoping for things he wasn't accustomed to giving, but he had given her more than she knew. This afternoon's excursion was one of a kind. He had never taken anyone to his private haunt by the river. It was his *querencia*—his safe haven, a monument to the innocence of his youth.

Hal refused to delve into the significance of taking Andrea to his favorite fishing hole, for fear of what he might discover. He had already unintentionally allowed a bond to develop between the two of them. It held him as securely as the handhold and rope held him while he straddled rodeo bulls. Hal couldn't get loose, at least not when Andrea needed him. Not until she realized *why* she let herself get a little too attached to him, *why* she had allowed herself to become intimate with him.

Despite what Andrea said, Hal knew she was still stuck on that idea of a knight in shining armor—or rather, shining *spurs*. Undying gratitude colored her thinking. Until she realized passion came and went, taking short-term commitment with it, Hal would simply enjoy the pleasure she gave him, the satisfaction he derived from helping this strong-willed woman hang on to what was rightfully hers.

"Before you returned to the circuit I had hoped we could—" Andrea began hesitantly.

"Don't go getting all sentimental on me, Fletcher. I'm not leaving yet. I just have something I need to do."

"I wanted to be with you every spare moment," she whispered.

It was all Hal could do not to reach across the seat of the truck and kiss the breath out of her.

"I'll be back tonight," he said, staring through the windshield. "But it will be late."

Andrea nodded pensively. "I'm expecting too much again, aren't I?" Again, she smiled for his benefit. "Sorry, Griff. I keep forgetting the rules."

"Yes, you do," he affirmed before he put the truck in reverse.

Hal drove away, aware that he was having one helluva time remembering the rules himself. Andrea had him— and his previous philosophies—tangled in knots.

He stopped breathing when a sudden thought hit him right between the eyes. Last night, when he had granted Andrea free license to experiment with him, he had been too oblivious to anything but his own need to remember to use protection. He had been desperate for her. He had wanted nothing between his aching flesh and her soft, responsive body. And this morning he had . . . done it again, damn it!

A frustrated groan tumbled from his lips as he drove toward Hochukbi. Hell's freakin' bells! If he got in any deeper, he'd be up to his eyebrows! Sweet mercy, he had never been so reckless and irresponsible in all his born days.

The image of orchid eyes staring up at him from a tiny face rattled Hal momentarily. A child, his child, one he could spoil rotten and love the way his father had never loved him and Nash. A sweet little girl with her mother's determined spirit and striking beauty to . . .

Holy shit! Where had that thought come from?

Hal shook himself from his trance, determinedly focusing on his upcoming encounter with the Queen Bitch from his past. First things first, he told himself as he took the dangerous curves that rimmed the wooded hills of Kanima County. He was going to find out what Jenna meant by the comment she murmured over the phone.

Andrea dropped down in the kitchen chair, listening to the carefully worded explanation from the insurance spokesman who had called. Disbelief registered on her face while Evan Hudson elaborated on his company's position in reference to her claim.

"After we received a tip that insurance fraud might be involved, we have decided to investigate. No compensation will be made until we have all the facts," Evan reported.

"Are you suggesting that I deliberately burned down my own barn?" Andrea choked out.

"The fire marshal reported that arson was involved," Evan said dispassionately. "I've been on the phone this afternoon, gathering facts."

"And what has your fact-finding mission turned up?" Andrea demanded in outrage.

"The first thing I learned was that you've been unable to meet past-due payments on your bank loans," Evan said matter-of-factly. "Our anonymous caller also advised us to make note that you have recently taken temporary employment with our agent in Hochukbi."

"What has that got to do with anything?" Andrea muttered.

Evan cleared his throat. "You have a history of association with Tuff Seever that dates back to junior high and high school. It is possible that you have used your influence with him, hoping to send the paperwork through his office without the usual questions being asked about claims of this nature."

Andrea couldn't believe what she was hearing! She was supposedly buttering Tuff up so he would approve payment for damages?

"I suggest you seek legal advice, Miss Fletcher. Considering the time of night you finished your shift at the local bar, you had ample opportunity to set the fire and make sure it was raging *before* you called the fire department," he emphasized heavily. "Without your injured brother at home to verify the time of your arrival, certain questions arise. I do not need to mention that the medical expenses, combined with defunct loan payments, provide ample motive for insurance fraud."

Andrea's fist clenched around the receiver. Never in her life had her integrity been suspect. Suddenly, everything she had done to save her ranch was being questioned. She wanted to scream to high heaven.

When Hudson hung up, Andrea swallowed anxiously. Her stomach twisted in nervous knots. When news of an investigation spread through town Jason would catch the brunt of it at school, and Andrea would be labeled as an arsonist!

Lord, how could so many good intentions go so wrong? She hadn't taken time to call the fire department because she had livestock to rescue. How could anyone misconstrue that as an attempt to give the barn ample time to catch fire *before* Hal arrived to put in the call for assistance?

Dazed and miserable, Andrea strode onto the deck to revive herself with a breath of evening air. She clutched her jacket tightly around her to ward off the soul-deep chill. She couldn't afford legal representation in a court case. If she withdrew the insurance claim she would all but verify her guilt, and she would have no cash to replace the hay that had been destroyed by the fire.

Taking the case to trial would not only be expensive but time consuming. How could she keep both jobs and still make court appearances?

Frustration ate at Andrea. She didn't know which way to turn, what to do next. If Hal had been here, she would have run straight into his arms. He was the only stable force in this careening world of hers.

Damn it, all she was trying to do was save her home and provide a stable environment for her brother. What was the crime in that?

The jingling phone caused Andrea to freeze. She wasn't sure she could endure another helping of bad news tonight. Reluctantly, she re-entered the house to discover what else could go wrong in her life.

"Andrea? This is Jenna Randall. Is Hal there? I'd like him to come by my place a little later than we originally planned this evening."

Andrea steeled herself against the feelings of betrayal that thrummed through her. Hal had obviously called to schedule a tryst with Jenna last night—before he came to her room. How could he have done that?

Because she had all but challenged him with her reckless attitude, Andrea realized.

And men like Hal Griffin thrived on challenge.

"Hal has already left," Andrea managed to say without her voice cracking.

"Well, I guess I'll just have to work around it."

You do that, Andrea raged silently.

Hands shaking, she replaced the receiver. Wasn't it enough that she was being accused of insurance fraud and was about to lose everything she held dear? Did she have to find herself playing second fiddle to the only woman Hal Griffin had ever asked to be his wife, too? God, how many kinds of fool was she, anyway?

Every kind, obviously.

Andrea wheeled around and dashed outside. It felt as if the world was closing in around her again. Chasing the wind on the back of a horse seemed vital and necessary. Riding would scatter the thoughts from her cluttered mind and give her the chance to decide what she was going to do with the rest of her life.

Whatever she decided to do, she thought bleakly, she couldn't do it here. The cards were stacked against her. She was going to lose the ranch . . . and the one man she could have loved with all her heart and soul.

Damn him, she was—and always would be—just killing time for Hal. How could she convince herself otherwise when Jenna was waiting for him?

Fifteen

Hal glanced at the directions he'd jotted down. He was curious about this mysterious appointment with Jenna. In truth, he wouldn't be the least bit surprised to learn that she was in the middle of some clandestine plot to drive Andrea off her property.

But why were the Fletchers being targeted? Who wanted to see the bank foreclose on their ranch? If Hal knew the answers to those questions he'd be one happy man. It was difficult to request an investigation based on instinct and suspicion. But at the moment, Jenna was heading his list of those who could provide some answers.

Hal stared down the darkened street leading to Jenna's apartment. He instantly recalled what happened to Jason while hanging around deserted locker rooms. Damn, Hal should have brought Nash along. A man with a broken arm and bruised ribs could become easy prey.

Hal killed the engine, then glanced cautiously around him. In a town the size of Hochukbi, the twelve double-stacked apartments that opened into a central courtyard were considered a high-rise. He would have expected grander accommodations for a high-roller like Jenna. Knowing she was out here in the boondocks was certainly cause for suspicion.

To be on the safe side, Hal grabbed the hammer from

the leather tool pouch that Nash kept behind the pickup seat. With the tool tucked inside his jacket, he ambled along the shadowed sidewalk. If somebody jumped him, he intended to hammer a few heads on his way down.

Warily, Hal stared at the darkened apartment where Jenna lived. This was a far cry from the ritzy condo she had in Oklahoma City when he first met her. He had been so crazy about that blond bombshell that he hadn't known ass-end from head-up. But he had found out soon enough.

Shoving his bitter thoughts aside, Hal rapped on the door, ever mindful of his shadowy surroundings. The door whined open.

When no one appeared in the darkened doorway, Hal waited, his trusty hammer wedged against his tender ribs.

"Come in, Hal."

All five senses went on alert as he stepped inside. When the door swung shut, Hal's gaze narrowed on a well-filled, silky white negligee. God, he would have given his first place winnings to see Andrea decked out in a little number like this!

When Jenna stepped close, gliding her hands up his chest to toy with his hair, Hal stood immobilized. Full lips, coated with passion-red lipstick, whispered over his.

"It's been a long time," Jenna murmured, brushing her breasts provocatively against his chest.

"Yeah, well, time passes," Hal said flippantly.

He remembered the old days when Jenna's spell had blinded him. He had fallen hard. It had taken him a few months to realize that her sensuality was carefully rehearsed.

When he finally discovered the truth he could have strangled the bitch. He had learned not to trust her *then,* and he damned sure didn't trust her *now*. Hell, the woman probably lied in her sleep.

Jenna pouted prettily in response to his snide remark. "Surely you aren't still angry at me over something that happened almost twelve years ago," she whispered.

Hal made a neutral sound as he set her hands away from him. "I was led to believe that my coming here had something to do with Andrea's situation."

Jenna shrugged a partially bare shoulder. Her striking gray eyes twinkled up at him. "It got you here, didn't it?"

Hal gnashed his teeth. Same old games. Same old Jenna. Here was the original Bitch Goddess, he thought to himself. All sultry, deceptive beauty—with claws attached. The fancy clothes didn't disguise the tramp she was.

Hal had played Jenna's games already—and lost. He wasn't about to be a fool twice. Besides that, his patience was short. He could have been enjoying the company of an honest, sincere woman right now, not playing mind games with this lovely but devious tramp.

When Jenna curled her hand into the band of his jeans, Hal grabbed her wrist, bending her hand backward until she shrieked in pain. "You had your chance a long time ago, but you traded me for a sugar daddy," he snarled.

"You're hurting me," Jenna whimpered.

"I came here to find out what you know about the incidents plaguing Fletcher Ranch. And don't fool yourself into thinking it was for any other reason."

"I don't know what you're talking about," Jenna hissed, her face puckering beneath the carefully applied coat of makeup.

"Wrong answer, honey. Try the truth for a change," Hal sneered, tempted to apply more pressure to the slender hand tipped with dragon-claw nails. "What are you doing in this podunk town?"

"Making a living the best way I can," she insisted.

"Horseshit," he scoffed sarcastically.

"I don't have the faintest idea what you're trying to get me to say. I was looking for a new job and a position opened here, so I took it. All I know from gossip around the bank is that Fletcher Ranch will soon be up for sale because Andrea can't meet the payments."

Hal's eagle-eyed gaze drilled into the shadows surrounding him. He noticed the way Jenna's eyes darted sideways as she scrambled to answer his questions. Someone was probably in the bedroom, eavesdropping on this conversation. Jenna couldn't admit the truth, even if she wanted to, without jeopardizing her own safety.

What was going on here? Hal wondered. And why was Jenna trying to seduce him? If she had gotten him into the bedroom, what trap was waiting to close around him?

Scowling, Hal flung Jenna's hand away. Touching her was repulsive. This scheming bitch was trying to use him for one reason or another. Hal didn't doubt that for a minute, and he wasn't hanging around for another second.

"You have it all wrong, Hal," Jenna called after him. "I only wanted what we never had in the past. I thought maybe I could do something right for once. Losing you was the biggest mistake I ever made, my deepest regret. I was young and foolish."

The snide remark on the tip of Hal's tongue went unspoken. He closed the door behind him, and then positioned himself beside the window. He waited a full minute, plastered against the brick wall.

When he heard the muffled male voice inside the apartment he knew for sure that Jenna hadn't been alone.

Who was with her? Hal didn't have a clue, but he wasn't sure that barging back inside was the wisest thing to do. And worse, he couldn't positively swear whether Jenna had *wanted* him to see her glance toward the darkened hall, or if she was trying to be discreet. Was she trying to warn him? Or had she simply given her devious game away?

Quietly, Hal inched away from the window to return to his pickup. Glancing into the rearview mirror, he swiped at the lipstick on his mouth, though he couldn't do much about the flowery scent that clung to his flannel shirt and denim jacket.

Driving away, Hal asked himself what other complications were waiting for Andrea Fletcher—and for him. He had nearly stumbled into a well-laid snare tonight. He wasn't going to do it again.

If nothing else, the encounter with Jenna left him thanking the Lord for unanswered prayers. There had been a time when he thought Jenna was a man's every dream come true. Nowadays, he wouldn't trade Andrea's oversize nightshirts, sports bras, and forthright honesty for one tumble in the sack with that scheming siren-of-a-blonde. Having Jenna drape herself all over him left Hal feeling contaminated—as if he had just wallowed with a lowlife slut.

And speaking of lowlife, a visit with Tony Braden seemed appropriate. Hal veered into the nearest service station to call his brother. There were times when older brothers were nice to have around, especially brawny brutes like Nash. They had survived a number of barroom brawls together in their glory days on the circuit.

"Hello?"

"Nash? This is Hal," he said hurriedly. "Did you and

my sister-in-law-to-be find the correct size ring to hook through your nose this afternoon?"

Nash chuckled at his brother's customary cynicism toward the institution of matrimony. "Actually, we bought matching bands . . . for our fingers. What are you up to?"

"I was wondering if you might be in the mood to flex a little muscle."

"Sounds interesting."

"Leave Curly at home," Hal insisted.

"I plan to. I take great care of what's mine."

Hal found himself sharing a similar sentiment. There was no question that Andrea was his—and his alone. In this day and age, who would have thought a beat-up, jaded cowboy would be so damned old-fashioned?

"Hold on a minute while I look up Tony Braden's address," Hal requested as he thumbed through the phone book. "I want you to help me get to the bottom of these incidents with the bad boys of Hochukbi. I suppose Bernie told you about the Fletcher barn burning down last night."

"Yes, I was sorry to hear that. You think this Braden brat had something to do with it?"

"That's what you and I are going to find out."

"Give me forty-five minutes.

"I'll give you fifty," Hal allowed generously. "Watch those winding roads between here and Chulosa."

"Your concern is real touching," Nash drawled.

Hal hung up the phone, deciding to swing back by Jenna's apartment building in case the mystery man was still wandering around.

To Hal's surprise, he saw the carload of hoodlums cruising through the apartment parking lot. The pudgy blond kid that Hal had pulled from the back seat a few weeks earlier climbed out. Bobby Leonard glanced cautiously in every direction, then scuttled toward Jenna's door.

Hal couldn't see who answered the knock. The door opened, just as it had when Hal arrived. Bobby Leonard stepped inside momentarily, then reappeared. After the teenager climbed back in the waiting car, Tony drove away.

Maintaining a discreet distance from the car, Hal followed the teenagers for thirty minutes. One by one, Tony dropped his scuzzy friends off at the run-down dumps they referred to as home. Tony cruised through town, turned off into the classy residential district, then stopped in front of a well-manicured brick home.

When Hal passed the house a few minutes later a grim smile pursed his lips. According to the name on the mailbox, this was where Brenda Warner lived. The kid from the wrong side of town was still mooning over Jason's high school sweetheart.

Tony might be doing his mooning in a detention center very soon, Hal predicted.

After following Tony back to the dilapidated shack on the outskirts of town, Hal waited for Nash to show up. As it turned out, Hal wouldn't have had to call on his brother. Even a one-armed, busted-up cowboy could handle one punk. Yet, Hal wanted to go for effect. Scaring the living daylights out of Tony was essential.

Fifteen minutes later, Hal was glad he had called his brother. He saw the other three hoodlums slinking down the dark street, scampering from one tree to another to avoid being noticed. They converged on Tony's house and disappeared inside.

Nice to have all his ducks in the same pond, Hal decided as he watched his brother pull up behind him in the rattletrap truck, its hay spear protruding from its bed.

Hal grinned as he watched Nash step down. Wearing leather glows, chaps and spurs, Nash Griffin cut the same striking swath he had during his rodeo heydays.

"I brought along your gear," Nash said as he halted beside Hal. "I thought it might be effective to get these punks' attention."

Hal fastened himself into his rawhide chaps, cursing the plaster cast that impaired what was usually a fluid and practiced procedure. Donning the spurs, Hal led the way toward Tony's house.

As luck would have it, the fearless foursome were on their way out when Hal and Nash strode to the door. Four pairs of eyes registered shock when the Griffin brothers plowed through the front door. When Tony grabbed the nearest object, Hal flung up his left arm. The flying textbook lanced off his cast and fell open on the floor.

"Get outta here, you motherfuckers, or I'm calling the cops," Tony sneered.

"Good idea," Hal sneered right back at him. "Then you can tell Sheriff Featherstone all about how you broke windows, slashed trailer tires, spooked the cattle, and assaulted a fellow student after the football game. Then we'll discuss that little campfire you started at Fletcher Ranch."

"Where's your mother?" Nash questioned in a cold, gruff voice, his tawny eyes glittering with menace.

"Out screwing whoever will have her," Tony spat bitterly.

"Did the rest of you boys sneak away from your homes after curfew?" Hal demanded in the same ominous tone.

Three scruffy heads nodded in defiance.

"Good." Hal chuckled devilishly, making a spectacular

production of pulling his leather gloves into place around each fist. *"You* aren't out after curfew and *we* aren't here. That makes things easier."

Nash swallowed a grin as he watched four teenage Adam's apples bob apprehensively. "I usually pick on somebody my own size, but it's going to be pure pleasure to beat these scumbags to a pulp. What do you think, little brother?"

The boys' gazes leaped back and forth between the muscular hulks that blocked their escape route. Evidently the punks had a hard time imagining Hal as anyone's *little* brother.

"What were you doing at Jenna Randall's apartment tonight?" Hal demanded, looming a step closer.

"Nothing," Bobby Leonard jeered, and then squealed when Hal's hand shot out, jerking him up by the ribbing on his T-shirt, twisting the fabric around his neck like a noose.

When Tony tried to break and run, Nash pounced. Dragging Tony backward by the hair, Nash's arm twisted in a vise-like grip that had the teenager yelping in pain. "You better start answering my little brother's questions" Nash snarled down Tony's neck. "It took a twelve-hundred-pound rodeo bull to break Hal's arm, but it won't take much to splinter you in two or three places."

When Bobby Leonard opened his smart mouth to spit an expletive, Hal lifted his knee, catching the slow learner in the crotch. Bobby sucked air in huge gulps.

"Is the lady paying you to harass the Fletchers?" Hal growled. When Bobby refused to reply, Hal kneed the punk once again. "Answer me, asshole, or you'll be singing soprano in the church choir."

"Yes," Bobby bleated, his face the color of paste.

"For how long?" Hal demanded to know.

When Bobby opened his mouth to sing like a canary, Tony hissed at him. "Shut up, Bobby—"

Tony's terse command became a pained wail when Nash hooked a powerful arm around his neck and tilted his greasy head to an agonizing angle.

"Then suppose *you* tell us, sleazebag," Nash sneered, applying persuasive pressure.

"Let go!" Tony squawked like a plucked chicken.

"Dream on, dickhead," Nash scoffed, squeezing Tony's neck in the crook of his elbow.

"We were only trying to get even with Jason at first," the red-headed kid in the corner burst out. "Jason stole Tony's girl."

"Seems to me that Tony tried to come on a little too strong to interest any girl, especially one like Brenda," Hal muttered, glaring at the helpless teenager caught in Nash's grasp. "You're going to have to learn a little consideration and respect before you ever hope to get a date, pal. Cleaning up your bad-ass act wouldn't hurt, either."

"Go on, kid," Nash ordered the redhead. "What happened after you started badgering Jason?"

"Then we decided to get back at Hal for interfering," Brad Latham reported. "I don't know how that lady from the bank found out about us scattering the cattle during round-up, but we didn't slash anybody's tires. The lady came by Tony's house one night after school and said she'd pay us to harass Jason."

"How much?" Hal muttered, his ebony eyes glittering.

"A hundred dollars," Bobby squeaked.

"What did she pay you for when you went by her apartment tonight?"

"We're supposed to drive out to the ranch to break a

few windows," Sammy Pikeston, the freckle-faced kid, replied.

"How much did it cost Jenna to get you to pulverize Jason and set fire to the barn?" Hal wanted to know.

"We didn't do that," Sammy insisted. "We were paid to scare Brenda off that night so she couldn't meet Jason after the game."

"What did you do to that girl?" Nash growled, tipping Tony backward until his spine crackled like popping knuckles.

"We just scared her back home," Tony gasped. "That's all, I swear to God!"

"You better be swearing to my big brother," Hal snorted sarcastically. "He's the one who'll break that stupid neck of yours if we find out you're lying."

"We didn't lay a hand on Brenda," Tony panted, his eyes squeezed shut against agonizing pain.

"What about burning the barn?" Hal questioned.

"We didn't have anything to do with it," Brad Latham insisted. When Hal pinned him with an icy-black stare, Brad hastily added, "It's the truth."

Hal glanced quickly at his brother. "You know something, Nash? I was just thinking about adding four more names to the list for next month's rodeo camp."

"To do what?" Nash smirked, still keeping Tony in a painful backbend. "Scooping shit from the arena or learning to ride and rope?"

"Maybe a little of both," Hal said thoughtfully. "Maybe these clowns could earn respectable wages by caring for the livestock while learning to be as tough as they seem to think they are."

"Why would we want to mess with a bunch of smelly

livestock?" Bobby scoffed, though not as defiantly as usual.

Hal grinned wickedly. "Because agreeing to come to rodeo camp might be the only way to make sure the four of you walk out of this house in one piece. Since I don't have much faith in the juvenile court system I plan to exact my own punishment for breaking windows and damaging horse trailers. And in case you naive little pricks haven't figured it out yet, you've been set up to take the rap for assault, battery, and arson."

That got the boys' attention—in a hurry.

"Because you let yourselves be taken in for cash, you've become prime suspects for more serious offenses against the Fletchers. With your history and reputations, nobody will believe you weren't responsible."

Four young faces paled noticeably.

"I'm beginning to think Jenna Randall has some seedy connections," Hal said pensively. "If you're smart you'll lie low until we find out who's behind this."

"You've gotten yourselves in one helluva fix," Nash added gravely. "Unless you change your ways—and fast—you'll do time in a detention center with some dyed-in-the-wool hardasses who'll have you wishing you'd listened to good advice when you had the chance."

The boys glanced at each other for a long moment.

"Well?" Hal prompted. "What's it going to be? Are you going to tell Sheriff Featherstone what you know, lie low for a few days, and then show up at our rodeo camp? Or do you prefer to be sent off to a place where the hard-core creeps of this world like to initiate new arrivals with perverted sexual tortures too hideous and disgusting to describe?"

Four faces grimaced at the thought.

"Where do we sign up for rodeo camp?" Tony mumbled.

A slow smile replaced Nash's ominous glare. "You just did, kid."

Subdued and convinced, the boys awaited instructions. When Hal had laid down the rules, he strode off to call Andrea.

Nash smiled wryly. "Checking in?" be teased.

Hal's gloved hand hung in midair. He glanced over his shoulder to see his brother grinning in amusement. Yes, Hal guessed he was checking in. He had told Andrea he would be back by this time. Funny, Hal had never felt the need to check in with anybody else before.

Hal didn't take time to analyze the gesture—he simply placed the call. Frustrated, he waited as the phone rang six times before the answering machine clicked on. He supposed Andrea had driven to the hospital to visit Jason.

At least Hal hoped that's where she was.

"Fletch? It's Hal," he spoke to the machine. "I'm going to be detained longer than anticipated. We'll talk when I get back."

Hal hung up, turned, then scowled at Nash's twinkling, amber-eyed gaze. "I've always appreciated a man who knows when to keep his mouth shut," Hal said to Nash on his way out the front door.

Nash's broad shoulders shook in amusement as he brought up the rear as they headed for Sheriff Featherstone's home.

Sheriff Featherstone blinked owlishly when he found the Griffin brothers and four scruffy teenagers on his doorstep. "I'm beginning to wonder if there's such a thing as 'off duty' in the Kanima County department," he grumbled.

Without wasting time, Hal explained the gist of the situation and prompted Tony—and Friends—to give their statements to the sheriff. Featherstone's bushy gray brows furrowed and then rose like exclamation points as he listened to the teenagers tell about their feud with Jason Fletcher and the payments they'd received.

"You boys had better keep your noses clean from here on out. And you better make yourselves scarce the next few days, unless *I*'m the one who needs to contact you," Featherstone said sternly. "You let a feud over a girl get you wound up with some pretty sorry individuals. From now on, don't answer the door without checking to see who's on the other side. Don't use the phone without using signals to each other. You got that?"

The boys nodded bleakly.

"I'm telling you flat-out—you've gotten your butts in a sling on this one," Featherstone continued solemnly. "This case is a top priority, but it's still going to take time to track down whoever is behind this scheme. Until I do, stay clear of Jenna Randall and watch your backs."

He glanced meaningfully at Hal and Nash. "That goes for you, too. Fletcher Ranch is most likely being cased. Otherwise, this female contact wouldn't have known who to pay. She's used these boys as a smokescreen to hide more serious crimes."

After Featherstone shooed the boys on their way and ordered them to drive Tony's clunker at a reasonable speed, the sheriff focused grimly on the Griffins. "I would like to set up a stakeout at Fletcher Ranch, but any suspicious traffic at this stage of the game will be monitored. All the precautions I can take aren't enough. The Fletchers need protection. I don't know how I can—"

"I'll keep an eye on the Fletchers," Hal volunteered.

Featherstone raised a thick brow. "With a broken arm?"

"This cast makes a helluva weapon," Hal assured him.

"And I'll be around to back Hal up," Nash insisted. "I've been at the ranch enough lately not to draw suspicion."

Featherstone nodded agreeably. "That's good. New faces make perps nervous."

With the promise that Featherstone would check Jenna's ties first thing in the morning, Hal and Nash strode toward their trucks.

"I'll take the rattletrap so you can have your new truck back," Hal offered.

Nash nodded as he veered toward the fire-engine-red extended cab pickup. Halting, Nash glanced at his brother. "Do you think the banker might be involved?"

"It's possible. There appears to be several ties to the bank. Andrea's mother worked there before her accident. Robert Fletcher was reported to have roughed up the loan officer. And then there's dear, sweet Jenna."

Nash shook his head. "I always thought she was bad news, though you refused to believe it twelve years ago."

"Don't remind me," Hal scowled. "Believe me, I've thought about it often enough. If Jenna is somehow involved, then there has to be big money at stake. She doesn't operate for peanuts."

Nash was silent for a moment, then he smiled dryly. "Kinda makes a man appreciate what he *could have* if he wasn't such a bean-brained billygoat, doesn't it?"

Hal glared at his brother. "I love you too, butthead."

Chuckling, Nash opened the pickup door. "I don't have time to exchange insults—got to check in with Curly. I've discovered how nice it is to be wanted, needed, and loved for all the right reasons. Try it sometime, little brother. You might be surprised."

Hal watched Nash drive off, thoroughly dismayed by the drastic change that had overcome the wolf-dragon of Chulosa Ranch. Crista Delaney really had sunk her claws into Nash's tough hide—and made him like it!

Hal wondered what it would be like . . . He immediately squelched the thought. *Forget it, Griff,* he told himself as he drove away. Despite his involvement with Andrea, it was only temporary. Hal had been too cynical for too long. He knew no other way. And besides, Andrea was too good for the likes of him. He could never be anything but a strong shoulder to lean on through the worst months of her life.

Sixteen

Andrea brought the laboring mare to a walk and reined along the ridge overlooking Fire River. Riding at breakneck speed in the darkness had been a daredevil stunt, but the fast-paced romp had scattered her troubled thoughts and rejuvenated her spirits. She was still mad enough at Hal Griffin to spit rusty nails. Although she couldn't blame him for rekindling an old flame that hadn't burned itself out, it still hurt—badly.

Damn it, why couldn't Hal have sneaked around with Jenna Randall *before* Andrea found herself so emotionally attached to him? Why did he have to wait until she cared so much?

As for her conflict with the insurance company, Andrea was still simmering. The call from Evan Hudson had put her in turmoil. No matter what she decided to do, it would cost her more than she could afford . . . .

Andrea frowned when a set of headlights flashed across the pasture. The blinding light zeroed in on her, making the mare prance nervously. To her disbelief, the car veered around the deep ravine left by recent rains and sped directly toward her.

Driven by panic, Andrea gouged her mount and thundered toward the house. The roar of the car's engine growled like a snarling monster in pursuit. When Andrea tried to veer east, the car bounced across the pasture, cutting off her escape.

The blaring of the horn startled the mare. Andrea clamped herself to the rearing horse and hurriedly switched directions to avoid the blinding lights. Her arms encircling the frightened animal's neck, Andrea held on for dear life. She was sure she was about to be thrown from the horse's back and run over by the speeding car.

Damn Tony and his mean-spirited friends! she thought bitterly. Hadn't those punks tormented her and Jason enough . . . ?

When the roar of bad mufflers and another set of headlights appeared on the rise, Andrea breathed a sigh of relief. The car that had been chasing her across the pasture backed up and sped off in the opposite direction. She supposed Tony and Company were trying to be sure that she didn't identify the car, but Andrea was pretty sure who had been harassing her, even if the blinding headlights prevented her from making a positive ID.

The mare halted to catch its breath, staring uneasily at one set of headlights and then the other, uncertain which direction to take. When Hal's brawny silhouette appeared in front of the lights in the driveway, Andrea muttered to herself.

Did it have to be Hal who arrived to scare off her assailants? After he had gone running to Jenna, Andrea hated to have to thank him for saving her.

"What the devil is going on out there?" Hal demanded as he strode back to the truck to switch off the lights.

Andrea trotted to the corral to pen up the horse. When she turned around, Hal was blocking her path.

"What happened?" he demanded impatiently.

"Somebody tried to run me down."

"Why were you riding at this time of the night?"

"I needed fresh air." She veered around him toward the wooden deck.

"Damn it, woman—"

Andrea rounded on Hal the instant he followed her into the kitchen. "Damn, *you*," she spluttered.

"Me? What the hell did I do?"

Outraged by his mock-innocent expression, Andrea grabbed the closest object. She didn't bother to break off one banana, she hurled the whole bunch at Hal's broad chest. A two-liter Coke bottle found its way into her hand and she heaved that, too.

To her bitter disappointment, he glided away with practiced ease, catching the Coke bottle before it hit the door. Damn him.

"Get out!" Andrea screeched, reaching for the roll of paper towels.

Hal caught the roll and set it on the counter beside the Coke. His lips twitched as he surveyed Andrea's flushed face. When he had the audacity to smile, Andrea itched to slap the grin off his face.

"How could you?" she railed at him. "You know how I—" Andrea bit down on her words and looked away.

"I know how you *what?*" Hal wanted to know, still grinning at her.

"Just leave me alone! I'm furious because I let myself trust you, depend on you. I—" Andrea's mouth slammed shut. Hal lifted a dark brow and grinned at her. "Oh, shut up!" she sputtered.

"Did I say anything?"

Andrea didn't reply. She glared at him, kicked off her boots, and shucked her jacket. "Kindly leave," she demanded. "I'd like to get undressed and go to bed. I have to be at work at eight in the morning."

"If you're going to undress, I'd rather stay," he said waggling his eyebrows at her.

"Why? So you can compare notes?" she tossed casually. When he simply stood there holding up the doorjamb, Andrea glowered. "Now what are you doing?"

"Thinking."

"Don't overload your circuits, Griff."

"Aren't you going to ask me what I'm thinking about?"

"I'd have to care to ask," she sniped.

"If you don't care, then what was that little tantrum with the fatal bananas, Coke bottle, and paper towels all about? Lucky for me you didn't have a loaded gun lying around."

"I was simply letting off steam after a miserable evening and a frightening chase. It had nothing to do with you and Jenna," Andrea assured him.

After a long moment of silence, Hal held up the door and Andrea stared at the air over his head.

"I didn't touch Jenna," he told her finally. "I stopped caring about her years ago."

"Yeah, right," Andrea scoffed. "Next I suppose you're going to sell me some oceanfront property in Oklahoma."

Andrea refused to remain in the same room with this smiling rascal. Whirling around, she stalked through the hall, intent on reaching her room and locking her door. She heard Hal muttering, but she didn't look back. She stamped up the stairs, cursing him with every step.

"I hope you realize you're acting like an idiot," he called up to her.

"I obviously *am* one," Andrea flung back.

When she heard Hal leaping up the staircase, Andrea

plunged forward. She was determined to slam her door
on that snake—who couldn't keep his hands off the lost
love in his life.

Hal didn't need her. He'd *had* Jenna tonight. Andrea
would be damned if she was going to sit still and listen
to him explain that he and his ex-fiancée had decided to
give their relationship a second chance.

Andrea thought she was home safe—until Hal blocked
the doorway with a sinewy arm. Curse him, he had spoiled
her chance of slamming the door in his face.

"Don't throw anything else, wildcat," Hal ordered.
"I've already got a broken arm."

"I'd like to break the rest of you into little pieces,"
Andrea hurled snidely. Her arm shot toward the door, as
if he was too stupid to know where it was. "Get out and
don't come back. Jenna called to make sure you would
be keeping your rendezvous, so you don't need to break
anything to me gently. I already know you and Jenna are
seeing each other again."

Hal propped himself against the doorjamb, smiling.
"You're in a huff because you think I slept with Jenna?"

Pushing away from the doorjamb, Hal ambled over to
retrieve the jacket Andrea had thrown on the floor. Folding
the garment, he laid it over the back of the chair. "I have
no interest in Jenna," Hal said matter-of-factly.

Andrea didn't call him a liar but her skeptical look said
as much.

Hal casually straddled the chair—backward. "Although
we usually have these discussions before breakfast, I think
we'd better clear the air here and now."

Andrea waited anxiously, certain she was about to hear
the details of Hal's involvement with Jenna—something
he'd been hesitant to discuss. It was gratifying to know

he intended to open up to her, that he trusted her enough to divulge an unpleasant part of his past.

"I first met Jenna at a collegiate rodeo in Oklahoma City. I was a senior with a top ranking and I had received a lot of publicity. Sort of the man of the hour," Hal explained with a self-deprecating smirk. "My brother had graduated and was touring the pro circuit with Choctaw Jim. I was on my own for the first time."

Andrea sank down on the bed to listen.

"I was riding high after winning two events and placing second in two others. Then, out of nowhere, the most attractive female I'd ever laid eyes on came sashaying toward me—all smiles and charm."

Andrea winced. It hurt to hear that Hal considered Jenna a veritable goddess.

"She was the kind of girl who could have had any man she wanted, and I fell in over my head. We wound up at her ritzy apartment in the city and—"

When Hal looked away, Andrea swallowed over the lump in her throat. She was pretty certain where the twosome had ended up, and what they had done when they got there. Andrea tried to remind herself that the incident had taken place more than a decade earlier, but her feelings for Hal made her possessive. She didn't want to deal with the fact that there had been another woman in his life who had meant more to him than she ever would. It was silly and idealistic, but she couldn't help what she felt.

"After that night, I spent my spare time driving from the college campus in Weatherford to Oklahoma City to see Jenna. A few times she asked me to drop packages off at a friend's house while I was on my way back to school. She said it had something to do with her job with cosmetic wholesalers and distributors."

Hal shook his head and scoffed at his own naiveté. "It never occurred to me that I was the mule who was delivering dope to her sugar daddy dealer, or that Jenna used me to make him jealous. I thought I was in love and I was too blind and stubborn to realize I was being manipulated."

Andrea's heart went out to Hal. She could imagine what the affair had done to his pride and self-esteem.

"I called Jenna twice a week while we were away at rodeos, drove the eighty miles from campus to see her, and nearly ruined my grade point average because of her. I was ready to marry her. The night we returned home from college rodeo finals I was sporting two championship titles and an engagement ring. I was all set to surprise Jenna at two o'clock in the morning."

Andrea tensed. She could guess who had received the surprise of a lifetime.

Hal's face contorted with self-disgust. "I sneaked into the bedroom with the ring in my hand and found her in the sack with the man who was paying the rent on her apartment. He wasted no time in informing me that he was reclaiming his property and leaving his wife for Jenna. She had effectively managed to make the bastard jealous, even if he was almost old enough to be her father."

"I'm sorry," Andrea murmured sympathetically.

"Yeah, so the hell was I," Hal snorted disdainfully. "That's when I discovered love was a distortion of the mind, an illusion. I had been fed a pack of lies—I was so young, idealistic, and gullible. I had an expensive ring to remind me what a fool I had made of myself. I couldn't face my brother and uncle, who had repeatedly told me Jenna was bad news, just like I've told you I'm no good for you. You didn't listen any better than I did."

Andrea averted her gaze when Hal's dark, probing eyes focused on her. Despite what he kept telling her, she refused to believe he was bad news. She had more faith in him than he did.

"I was too humiliated to join the pro circuit and take the ridicule," Hal continued. "I wanted to get as far away as I possibly could. I needed to find an outlet for my frustrations, so I joined the army and requested overseas duty—ASAP."

"That's where you learned to handle a helicopter," Andrea presumed. "Amos Harden told me about last year's 'copter round-up. He said that was the most amazing piece of flying he had ever seen—scared the pants off him a time or two."

Hal shrugged off the compliment and continued. "Because I had to block out the bad memories, I was daring enough to gain my superior officer's notice. I ended up flying into places and situations that I would just as soon forget, doing things on hush-hush missions that were never recorded. The only kind of citations and medals awarded in those armpits of the world were pats on the back and a quiet thank you."

Hal paused, as if to close the door on the torment of the past. "When all the memories made it impossible to sleep, I returned to the States to join Nash and Uncle Jim on the rodeo circuit."

He stared at Andrea for a long moment. "The hell I survived was like being purged by fire. I had learned to exist, to take whatever life offered without any illusions. I became a self-indulgent hellion, caring only about myself.

"When Levi Cooper was injured and paralyzed at National Finals, I readily turned my winnings over to pay for his rehabilitation. The money meant little to me. Only family and good friends mattered. As for women, I never lost my heart to the string of glossy rodeo groupies. I've lived hard and fast, doing things that would embarrass and offend a good and decent woman like you. The fact is I don't have much heart left, and I have vowed to take what life can offer—without looking back, without regret."

"But you have just enough heart left to take on an occasional charity case," Andrea whispered, eyes downcast. "I guess I didn't realize how fortunate I was to have your assistance when you have so little regard or respect for my gender."

"There was a difference between you and the other women," Hal did admit, managing a semblance of a smile. "From the onset, you made certain I knew that all you wanted from me was my professional expertise. That was a unique experience for a man who usually has women flocking around him because he's something of a novelty, a celebrity."

His expression sobered. "And then along came the very same woman whom I could have cheerfully choked more than a decade ago. I should have realized Jenna was mixed up in some kind of underhanded scam the first time I saw her in the bank. But I was too distracted by the problems you and your brother were facing to make the connection. I simply preferred to forget I ever knew that devious vamp."

Andrea frowned, puzzled.

"The only reason," he said emphatically, "that I went to see Jenna tonight was because your string of bad luck no longer seems coincidental. The timing has been all too perfect. When I talked to Jenna on the phone last night, she insisted I come to her apartment—if I cared what happened to you."

Andrea went very still, her wide eyes transfixed on Hal's craggy features.

"Jenna was all decked out in one of those provocative little garments that are meant to tantalize and entice. She tried to feed me all that crap about making mistakes in the past and starting over again. I didn't buy any of it. I simply demanded to know what she knew about your problems with the bank. She denied knowing anything, insisting she had only made the comment to get me to come by her apartment."

Andrea stared at Hal in astonishment. "That's so devious!"

"That's the way Jenna operates," Hal replied. "After I left her apartment I decided to look up Tony and his thugs. I even called my brother to help me make a strong impression on those hoodlums. It turns out that Jenna has been paying them to harass you and your brother."

Andrea half-collapsed against the headboard. "Paid?" she parroted in disbelief. "But why would Jenna do that? I barely even know her."

Hal reached out to sketch Andrea's astonished expression with his forefinger. "I'm not sure yet, but I would bet my chances at National Finals that it has something to do with the value of this property. Whoever is behind this scheme wants you to think Jason's rivals are responsible for your woes. Despite what you think, Tony and his friends weren't chasing you around the pasture tonight. Nash and I escorted them to the sheriff's house for a private conference. Those punks have been set up to take the heat. Someone around here doesn't want you to keep this ranch, and Jenna has been paying those kids to cause you misery every time you turn around to divert attention from whatever scam she's part of."

"They've been exceptionally good at it," Andrea grumbled. "They even placed an anonymous phone call to my insurance company and insisted that I purposely set fire to the barn so I could collect money."

Hal did a double take. "How do you know that?"

"Because a spokesman from the insurance company called earlier this evening to inform me that a question of fraud has been raised. I can expect to have my day in court—if I request any compensation for the loss of the barn."

Hal muttered under his breath. "You better check with Tuff to see if this so-called spokesman is legitimate. This may be just another tactic to prevent you from making your payments. Everything indicates that someone is anxious for the foreclosure and sale of this property."

"For what possible reason?"

"It could be speculation on oil and gas wells in the area," Hal said pensively. "It could be a number of things that are being kept quiet so the property can be acquired at rock-bottom prices. But whatever is going down, the county sheriff has been alerted and has promised to check it out."

He smiled encouragingly at Andrea. "I've been delegated as your bodyguard, so I'd appreciate it if you wouldn't slam doors in my face or hurl objects at me. We're supposed to be on the same side, and I'm not going anywhere until this matter is resolved."

"I can't afford a bodyguard," Andrea insisted.

"You can afford me. I work cheap."

Andrea appraised his wry grin. "You'll have to charge a guardian angel's going rate if I'm to afford your services.

All that's standing between me and bankruptcy are the tips I get from Slim Chance Saloon."

"I want you to quit that job," Hal demanded. "I don't like the idea of barroom patrons undressing you with their eyes and groping when you walk by—especially not with that sexy walk of yours."

Andrea blinked. "I don't walk—"

"You're right," he cut in, grinning rakishly. "You don't walk, you *move . . .*"

"I do not!" Andrea objected loudly.

"Not intentionally," he clarified, "but the results are the same. You can't help being attractive. That's just the way it is."

A compliment from a man like Hal was inordinately flattering. Andrea blushed. "Well, I'll have to learn to swagger like a cowboy and dress down more than I already do, but I can't quit my job. I need the money."

"I told you I was going to pay the loan at the end of the month," Hal reminded her. "I do not appreciate having my personal checks sent back in shreds. Don't do that again."

"Don't ask me to accept your money," she countered, tilting her chin to a stubborn angle. "You may have saved my life a couple of times, but that doesn't give you the right to control it, or to pay me off because I wanted you to—"

Hal put a finger under her proud chin, forcing her to meet his intense gaze. "Retract your claws, wildcat," he murmured. "I intend to have my way in this matter, even if I have to hand the check over to Gilmore myself. I'm going to pay your debt and you're going to swallow that damnable pride of yours and thank me kindly."

"No."

There was that uncompromising word again.

"I am not your problem—and I am certainly not one of your expenses," Andrea said stiffly.

Hal came off the chair to draw her to her feet. His hand glided down her back to settle familiarly on her hip, pressing her against him. "You are definitely a problem," he murmured, letting her feel the evidence of the problem *he* had when her body was meshed to his. "There is also the matter of a few unfinished chapters in your how-to sex manual."

"Have I left out a few things?" she asked, her breath wobbling in response to his nearness.

"Uh-huh." Hal reached between them with his injured arm, his fingertips moving clumsily over the buttons of her flannel shirt. "Damned nuisance of a cast. Really cramps my style."

Heat sizzled through Andrea's body as his hand nestled familiarly between her breasts. She studied his handsome face while he fumbled with the buttons of her shirt.

Dear Lord, how had she come to care so deeply for this man? Did he realize she would give him all within her power to give, just for the asking? Ah, if only she could convince him that love did indeed exist and that it was simmering inside her, leaving her aching to share it with him, to reassure him that she was nothing like Jenna Randall.

What, Andrea wondered as her shirt fell by the wayside, would it take to earn the love of a man like Hal Griffin? How could she teach him to trust in her, to believe that she would never intentionally hurt or betray him? If nothing else, she wanted Hal to return to the rodeo circuit, assured that someone cared deeply for him, cared uncon-

ditionally. She wanted him to know there was a place he
could come when the world crowded in on him.

"Just once," Hal murmured, tugging at her elastic
sports bra. "I would like to see you in one of those lacy
scraps of lingerie that would do you justice. You're far too
lovely to conceal your beauty from appreciative eyes."

Andrea grinned impishly as she helped him doff the
clinging bra. "You want me to take a job as a stripper to
flaunt my figure?"

Hal scowled at the very idea. "Hell no, you are for my
eyes only, honey. I'd just like to see you in an eye-catching
outfit like the one Crista wore to bewitch my brother—the
one I accidentally got a glimpse of last month." His dark
eyes gleamed in sensual anticipation. "Peeling you down
to your silky skin is another of my erotic fantasies . . ."

Whatever sassy retort Andrea intended to voice was
lost forever when Hal's warm mouth skimmed her shoulder and then drifted over the rigid peaks of her breasts.
The world threatened to slide out from under her as he
took one aching bud between his thumb and index finger,
plucking, teasing, tormenting her with pleasure.

Helpless to restrain her uninhibited responses, Andrea
leaned into him, her body silently begging for more.

"You like?" he whispered, smiling against her quivering
skin.

"Mmm . . ." Andrea moaned.

"We're back to that again, are we?" Hal chuckled softly
as he cupped one breast and lowered his dark head to feast
on her nipple.

Andrea's quick gasp and reflexive shiver prompted another husky laugh. "I've always been curious to know if
a wildcat can purr as well as she hisses and pounces. Shall
we find out?"

As his hands and lips flowed over her skin, Andrea felt scalding chills consuming her.

"Hal?" She barely got out his name before another raspy moan tumbled from her lips.

"Too much?" he questioned. "Not enough?" He flicked his tongue over the proud peaks while his hand scaled the zipper of her jeans and glided languidly over her inner thighs.

"Too much," Andrea managed huskily.

"Are you paying close attention so you can write this down for your soon-to-be bestseller?" he teased devilishly.

"I need directions to locate the mind you've caused me to lose—" Her words became a groan when his hot mouth devoured her sensitive nipple. "Dear God, Hal . . ."

"Just pretend this gorgeous body of yours is an open book," Hal playfully suggested as his head moved to the other rosy peak and his fingertips worked the snap and zipper of her jeans. "I'll spell out the techniques . . . Every last one of them . . . All in the name of education, of course . . ."

Andrea's pulse pounded like hailstones when his hands scaled her ribs and then swirled over her abdomen, pushing fabric out of his way to make contact with ultrasensitive skin. Each place he touched sizzled and burned. When he crouched in front of her and his hands and lips moved down her body slowly, deliberately, Andrea was sure her knees were going to fold up like a tent. Heat pooled in the very core of her being when he ran his thumb along the elastic leg of her panties. When his thumb glided beneath the sheer fabric to brush the delta of feminine curls, Andrea tried desperately to draw breath. Air filled her chest like thick fog. The instant he traced her softest flesh, Andrea clamped her hands on his broad shoulders

for support. The world was spinning out of control, threat
ening to take her with it.

Andrea swayed as indescribable sensations burs
through her like fireworks. She felt his deep laughter vi
brating against her skin, his warm breath, the fluid motio
of his hands and lips.

"Hal . . ."

"I'm glad you still remember my name," he raspec
against her scented flesh.

His name was all she *could* remember as his kisses
coasted from thigh to ankle. His hands and lips savorec
every inch of her with such tender caresses that Andrea
had to dig her nails into his shoulders to maintain her
balance. The pleasure consuming her was enough to stagger mind and body.

"What are you doing?" she whispered in broker
breaths.

He didn't reply as his thumb traced the heated petals
of her femininity. His seeking lips followed, driving her
mad with pleasure. "If you make me pass out again, I'm
never going to forgive you."

Andrea swore this seductive devil intended to do jus
that. His cheek brushed against her abdomen, his breath
hovered over her with murmurs of shocking, titillating
promises. She felt herself losing touch with reality, orbit-
ing a universe of incomprehensible sensations that converged into burning pinpoints of sensual heat . . .

Hal smiled when Andrea's nails scored his shoulders
She was so unbelievably responsive to his touch that he
wanted to share the kind of secret intimacies with her tha
he had never shared with anyone else. He wanted to teach
Andrea things about herself that she didn't know.

Mesmerized by the pleasure he received from loving

her so thoroughly, Hal traced the muscles of her calves, her thighs. When he nudged her legs farther apart she obeyed his silent command. His wandering hand drifted over the delta of curls once again. She shivered, her breath riding on a ragged sigh. When he replaced his hand with his lips he heard Andrea's muffled cry.

"Don't. I—"

"I want to touch you," Hal murmured as his fingertips glided up to test the dewy heat of her response.

"You already are."

"Not enough to satisfy me," he insisted. "I want all of you, to taste you, to experience you every way imaginable."

When his fingertips feathered over the sensitive nub of passion Andrea all but came apart—from the inside out. When his tongue moved over her silken flesh she choked for breath.

He tasted her desire for him, felt his own body answering the secret shivers coursing through her. His intimate kiss, the thrust of his tongue, triggered ecstatic convulsions that left her shaking. Her response echoed through him with such intensity that he was thankful he was already on his knees. If he hadn't been, the pleasure he was experiencing would have driven him there.

She didn't realize how it delighted him to arouse the profound sensations undulating through her. He had never experienced the heady satisfaction of leaving a woman to burn alive—for him, because of him.

Discovering the extent of the power he held over Andrea brought him incredible pleasure, made him crave more. He derived unbelievable enjoyment from watching her divine torment. He controlled her reactions, filled her with rapture. He had acquired the skills to make this one exceptional woman respond to his touch in the most intimate and erotic ways imaginable.

As he stroked her he could feel her body coil around him like liquid fire. Hal withdrew his fingertips to trace the scented heat of her desire across her belly, to the tips of her breasts. Then his hand brushed her lips, moist with her desire for him.

His name tumbled from her tongue, over and over, as he caressed her, tasted her, sensitized her. And when she begged him to end the sweet torment Hal couldn't trust his legs to support him. When one more wave of rapture drenched her body, Hal guided Andrea to the carpeted floor. She was grasping at his clothes, so impatient to take him into her and hold him that Hal couldn't hide his smile of triumph.

"You devil," Andrea rasped, tugging at the band of his jeans. "Do something—quick!"

Hal wrestled out of his jeans—with Andrea's eager assistance. He reached for the foil packet in his wallet with shaking hands. As he knelt between her bent legs, Andrea took the packet and then covered him with the kind of artful and inventive techniques that had Hal gasping for air.

The feel of her hands on his hard flesh had him trembling. When she drew him to her, Hal braced himself on his good arm, cursing the inhibiting cast even as he buried himself within her.

Andrea arched up to him with a wild cry, her body gyrating beneath his in an ancient, instinctive rhythm. He plunged within her silky depths and rode out the storm of passion that raged inside him.

Wild desire, vivid and intense, shattered all rational thought. Pleasure stole through Hal like a wildfire in the

ind. He clutched her to him as need consumed him, mak-
g no attempt at restraint. He simply reveled in each and
very mind-boggling sensation that making love to Andrea
oused in him, savored their joining, and held on as if
e never meant to let go.

When the last fiery surge took him over the edge into
finity, Hal heard Andrea's soft words, accompanied by
is own rapid heartbeat. "I . . . love . . . you, love . . .
ou . . ."

When Andrea collapsed beneath him, Hal chuckled to
imself. Damn if she hadn't done it—again! He waited a
w seconds for her to come to, for those luminous orchid
yes to focus on his still-smiling face.

"Well, for Pete's sake," Andrea muttered, humiliated.

"Pete who?" he couldn't resist asking.

Andrea whacked him on the shoulder. "You're enjoying
is, aren't you?"

"Immensely," he said unrepentantly.

"Think you're some sort of super stud, don't ya, cow-
oy?"

"Whatever you say, ma am," he said in his best drawl.
I never argue with a woman who's got my—"

"Don't say it," she warned, frowning in mock disap-
roval.

"Utmost respect," he finished. "My, what a dirty mind
ou have, Little Red Riding Hood."

Andrea met his ornery grin. "My, what a big—"

Hal howled with laughter, realizing that it was the first
ime in his life that he'd had great sex and laughed at the
ame time. He hadn't thought it possible to enjoy a woman
his much.

"My, what a big *ego* you have, you big bad wolf," An-
rea said, smiling impishly.

Hal's head moved toward hers, his lips skimming he petal-soft mouth. His expression grew serious. "Promis me you won't take any more unnecessary risks aroun here until we find out who's behind all this. I don't wa to lose what I have with you—I don't want to lose *you* . .

"Why not?" Andrea asked, searching his shadowe face.

"Because you're not only too good for the likes of m but you're amazingly good for me," he murmured.

Andrea shook her head, sending a splash of aubur waves across the carpet. "That's where you're wrong, she contradicted. "I'm the kind of trouble you don't nee You have a chance at world championship titles in La Vegas. You need to be with your family right now, prac ticing. You also have expenses that—"

"Are you back to harping about me lending you mone again?" he interrupted.

"How can I make you understand that it's importan for me to handle this situation by myself instead of leanin on you? You won't always be here, Hal. You've said s yourself. I have to cope with this alone, just as I will whe you're gone."

"Then sell me part interest in your ranch," Hal sug gested. "I'll pay your loan and you can include my nam on the deed."

"And risk having the mysterious third party use thei scare tactics on you? No way," Andrea said adamantly "If I get roughed up, I won't have to climb on the bac of a bull, but *you* will. And don't tell me you don't wan those national titles. You've hung tough on the circuit a year. I couldn't bear knowing your chances were jeopard ized because of this charity case."

Hal had learned that arguing with Andrea was like rid

ng into a brick wall. He would simply have to do what
vas best—and let her throw a conniption later. For now,
ae wanted to make his way from the floor to the bed. That
vas something he hadn't been able to manage during the
hroes of passion.

When Andrea snuggled up beside him, her cheek rest-
ng on his shoulder, Hal felt himself sinking into the mat-
ress as if it were a fluffy white cloud. Knowing she cared
about him, even when she shouldn't, knowing she would
risk losing her ranch to protect him was humbling and
reassuring. No matter where or how far he roamed, there
was one place where he would be welcomed and accepted
for what he was.

Watching Andrea being chased across the pasture ear-
ier tonight, seeing her driven too close to the ridge where
her father had leaped to his death, had shaken Hal pro-
foundly. Every protective instinct had burst to life.

He couldn't bear to see her hurt. She had been hurt
more than enough already. Hal had made his own contri-
butions to that—in spite of his good intentions. But Andrea had come to matter to him and he was compelled to
help her any way he could.

Without conscious thought, Hal dropped a kiss to her
forehead and pulled her close. He fell asleep on a wild,
sweet memory that led him into dreams of each sizzling
sensation they had shared—for however long this would
last . . .

Seventeen

The jingling phone roused Hal from peaceful slumber. He reached toward the nightstand, aware—for the first time in years—of where he was. The satiny, womanly warmth beside him was satisfying, reassuring.

"Hello?" Hal said drowsily.

"Morning, sunshine."

Hal lifted an eyebrow at his brother's cheery tone. He glanced at Andrea's alarm clock and saw that it was set to go off in fifteen minutes. Andrea stirred, too tired to be fully awake. Hal stroked her bare shoulder and spoke softly to Nash, giving her a few more minutes of needed rest.

"What's up, Nash?"

"I had to drop Crista off at the hospital early since her car is in the shop," Nash explained. "I decided to swing by Featherstone's office."

Hal tensed when Andrea's wayward hand glided down his torso. It was difficult to concentrate when she caressed him.

"And?" Hal managed in a level voice—somewhat level, at least.

"Featherstone put some of his technical experts on the computer."

Hal muffled a moan when Andrea's warm lips skimmed

ver his belly, her tongue circling his navel. When her
dventurous hand moved lower to explore the muscular
extures of his thighs, Hal's breath hitched.

"You okay, Hal?" Nash inquired. "You sound like
ou're in pain."

"Sort of," Hal croaked.

"Ribs still aching? Arm itching under your cast?"

"Mmm . . ." Hal scrambled to retrieve the remains of
is self-control when Andrea's hand enfolded his hard-
ned flesh, measuring him with curious fingertips.

"Do you want me to have Crista prescribe some pain
ills?" Nash questioned in concern.

"I've got more medication than I need already—" Hal's
oice fractured when Andrea's lips feathered over his
lesh, causing the kind of throbbing intensity that bordered
n torment.

He wondered if Andrea knew she was driving him
razy. Probably. The little imp had to be aware of the dev-
.stating effect she was having on him. How could she
ot?

Hal expected he was getting exactly what he deserved
or interrupting Nash and Crista—on purpose—and heck-
ing Nash about it. But the sweet torment of Andrea's
ouch left him aching for more, not less, of her tender
:aresses. Had this not been an important call, Hal would
ave told Nash to take a flying leap and then would have
lad Andrea on her back in the time it took to blink.

Nash's quiet chuckle came down the line when Hal
;roaned again. "I wouldn't happen to be interrupting you
or a change, would I, little brother? How convenient that
oor Jason is cooped up in the hospital and you volun-
eered to be the bodyguard for that knockout little cowgirl.

Maybe you aren't that eager to hear what I have to sa
right now."

"You started, now finish it."

"Well, according to—"

"Not you!" Hal moaned aloud when Andrea assume
he was eager for more of her sensual explorations. Whe
she took him into her mouth, caressing him with the flic
of her tongue and playfully nipping teeth, Hal squeeze
his eyes shut and battled like hell for control. His han
glided under the sheet to stroke her nipples—he wante
to arouse her as thoroughly as she was arousing him.

"I'm getting confused here," Nash snickered.

"Imagine how I feel," Hal said between clenched teeth

"Hot and bothered, from the sound of things," Nash
teased unmercifully. "When you got mixed up with An
drea I think you bit off more than even you could chew
Mr. Hot-Shot Rodeo Champ."

"Nash . . ." Hal growled warningly.

"Okay, okay. I've had my fun—not that you aren't hav
ing yours," he couldn't help but add wickedly. "Feather
stone had one of his deputies check out Jenna's license
tag number last night. They ran the ID through the com
puter.

"Sure enough, Jenna still has a permanent address in
the City, but not the one where she lived when you firs
met her. She has an expensive condo on the north side o
town. Featherstone called in a favor to OKCPD and ha
a cruiser swing by the condo. There was a flashy Mercede
parked in Jenna's spot. The department is checking ou
the car to see who might be associated with her."

Hal stilled Andrea's roaming hands and forced himsel
to concentrate on what his brother was saying. "Go on.

Andrea escaped his restraint to torture him with ye

another dose of erotic pleasure. That, Hal decided, was definitely *not* going into her how-to manual. There were some secret techniques lovers had to discover—and experience—for themselves. Andrea's tactics would have sizzled the pages off a book.

"Featherstone requested information about Jenna's bank accounts and credit card services. He's trying to make a connection that involves transfers of large amounts of cash in case someone intends to purchase Fletcher Ranch—if and when it faces foreclosure. At the moment that's all the sheriff has, but I expect we'll find Jenna working with another wheeler-dealer like the one you stumbled onto years back."

"Tell Featherstone to keep digging, as fast as he can," Hal urged in an unsteady voice.

"I'm going to hang around the office to see what else he turns up." Nash paused to snicker. "I'll try to call you back when you aren't so preoccupied."

Hal hung up the phone and focused his attention on the woman who had turned him every which way but loose.

"You're going to pay dearly for this prank," Hal promised, reaching down to draw Andrea up beside him.

Her heavily-lidded orchid eyes fluttered up. She smiled at Hal with the kind of sensual honesty that slammed into his solar plexus like a doubled fist.

"I had every intention of finishing what I started," she assured him. "You aren't just an experiment. Never were. Never will be. I love touching you—"

The alarm clock blared and Hal cursed colorfully.

Andrea was jolted from her dreamy trance. She stared at the clock, then at Hal. "I'm sorry, I didn't realize it was so late. I didn't mean to—"

"—Tease me until I all but came unraveled in your hands?" Hal finished for her. "I'll bet you didn't."

Andrea blushed. "I'll admit I like knowing I can arouse you, but—"

"That's the understatement of a lifetime," Hal interrupted.

When Andrea touched him he went hot all over. When she bathed him with those soft lips his body burst into flame. This saucy little wildcat had his number, all right. He had watched the transformation from cautious and hesitant female to skillful seductress. Hell, he was partially responsible. He had become her mentor, her instructor—and *she* had taught him things *he* had never even dreamed of.

Her generous sensuality was a rare gift—one he had never received, had never wanted to return, until Andrea came along. Her love was his for the taking—if only he could overcome his long-harbored cynicism and mistrust. She claimed to love him now, but what about next month when he was a thousand miles away? What about ten years from now when the newness of passion had worn off? Would he be man enough to intrigue her, excite her, please her then?

When Andrea leaned across his chest to silence the alarm Hal groaned at the feel of her breasts brushing his hair-roughened skin. "You owe me—big time—boss lady," he insisted.

"Deal," Andrea agreed without the slightest hesitation.

When she rolled from bed to make a fast dash to the shower, Hal's hawkish gaze devoured every well-contoured inch of her body. "Deal. Any time, any place I say."

Andrea glanced back at him as she breezed through the door. "You certainly drive a hard bargain, don't you?"

"You're the one who left me that way," Hal reminded her, smiling scampishly. "And next time *you* answer a telephone call, you better pray like hell that we aren't alone. We'll see how well you can concentrate when I'm doing the kind of things to you that you were doing to me a few minutes ago."

"You'd stoop to such a vengeful prank?" Andrea quizzed, smiling at him with such happiness and laughter in her eyes that it took his breath away.

"In a New York minute, sweetheart," he confirmed, wearing an idiot's smile—and not caring that he was.

"No matter who's calling?"

"Anybody, any time," Hal insisted.

"It will be interesting to see which one of us can carry on the most intelligent conversation under those circumstances," she tossed back at him. "I didn't think you were doing such a hot job of it earlier. Your voice was wobbling noticeably."

Hal snatched up a pillow and hurled it at her. The missile thumped against the doorjamb where she had been standing the split-second before. The sweet refrain of Andrea's laughter flowed into the room, settling over Hal. She was deliriously happy, he realized. After years of isolating herself from men, he had managed to make her smile again.

The thought triggered an enormous sense of accomplishment. It was more than the triumph he experienced after riding a bronc to the buzzer. It was more than hearing a crowd's enthusiastic applause for a good performance.

Hal shook himself from his daze, then crawled from bed. Something very peculiar had happened to him in the past month. He had undergone a decisive change, an attitude adjustment. Considering his lightning-quick reaction to Andrea he had to wonder if he was revisiting puberty. Yet, it was more than a physical response to this unique woman. The attraction had taken a mystical hold on him.

Dressing on his way to the door, Hal hurried downstairs to fix Andrea breakfast before she left for work. A few minutes later, Hal found himself hovering over the stove like Aunt Jemima. Suddenly he was as much at home in Andrea's house as he was in his own, fussing over a meal to make sure Andrea had enough nourishment to get through her double days.

Blankly, Hal stared at the ham and egg sandwich cooking in the skillet. After years of going on the road, meeting the challenges of rodeo, *and* enjoying the wild night life Hal was turning into a regular homebody.

When Andrea bounded down the steps in her rush to leave for work, Hal called her attention to the breakfast sandwich and glass of orange juice. She skidded to a halt, staring at the food and then at him. Then she flung her arms around his neck and kissed him full on the mouth.

"I—" she said and stopped abruptly, peered up at him, and plowed on in a rush. "I love you, Hal Griffin. You may not like the idea. You might not want to hear it. You may not choose to believe it, but you might as well get used to it. I can't help the way I feel."

Before Hal could voice a reply Andrea scooped up her breakfast and scurried out the door. For a long moment Hal stood there, listening to the rumbling motor of the farm truck as it sped down the driveway.

A month ago he had dragged Andrea over blazing coals when she confessed she loved him. A month ago, he had written off her misguided feelings as gratitude, as a physical release for all the emotional upheaval in her life. And now, after he had let her become so much a part of his life, he couldn't imagine what it would be like not to see her smiling up at him, whispering those three little words.

Hal grabbed the skillet and immersed it in dishwater. Damn, he *was* turning into one of those sensitive, cooperative, ultramodern males. Next thing he knew he'd be sewing lace on the hem of his blue jeans and tying ribbons on his chaps. That would draw howls of laughter from the rowdy rodeo crowd.

Let 'em laugh, Hal thought as he plunged his callused hands into the dishwater. One of Andrea's lighthearted smiles meant more than a high-scoring rodeo ride. Being the reason for her bright, ringing laughter was fast becoming Hal's most treasured experience. He never dreamed such things could make him happy.

Go figure . . .

Hal veered into Jason's hospital room to see the bruised teenager dressed and sitting on the edge of his bed. A stunningly attractive young woman with long, blond hair and vivid blue eyes was seated in the chair beside the window.

"Hi, Hal." Jason gestured toward his companion. "This is Brenda Warner."

Hal appraised the situation in one glance and then smiled wryly. "Did somebody call off school?" he quizzed the fetching blonde.

Brenda grinned guiltily, causing becoming dimples to crease her cheeks. "I called in sick today."

Hal's dark-eyed gaze shifted momentarily to Jason before settling on Brenda. "Sympathy pains?"

She nodded. "I thought I'd keep Jason company. That is, if you don't mind."

"I'd appreciate the help," Hal replied as he grabbed Jason's suitcase. "I have some errands to run, but I had planned to postpone them because I didn't want to leave him alone on his first day home." He leaned close to Jason to add confidentially. "But no fooling around while I'm not there to chaperone, kid. Your sister would have my butt."

Jason blushed beneath his bruises.

"I'll follow you to the ranch," Brenda said, rising from her chair.

"Good idea," Hal replied. "Considering all the accidents that keep occurring around the place, I wouldn't want to take any chances. We're better off if we travel in groups."

"I'll tell the nurse that Jason is ready to leave," Brenda volunteered.

Jason smiled dreamily when Brenda disappeared into the hall. "Isn't she the prettiest thing you ever laid eyes on?"

Almost, Hal thought. These days his tastes ran toward curvaceous, auburn-haired females who didn't flaunt their stuff.

After the nurse wheeled Jason out the door, Hal assisted his patient into the old farm truck. With Brenda trailing behind them in her compact car, Hal headed to Fletcher Ranch.

"How is the passing arm feeling?" Hal questioned his distracted companion.

"Sore as all get-out. The doctor said it was questionable

whether I could start in state playoff game," Jason mumbled. "But Crista Delaney promised to stop by after work to try some physical therapy. She knows I don't want to miss the last game of my high school football career. College scouts will be there . . . Damn those thugs!" he burst out bitterly.

Hal studied Jason's puckered expression. "The fact is, Tony and Company weren't responsible for your injuries or the burned barn," Hal told him.

"Yeah, right," Jason snorted skeptically.

"The situation isn't what it seems, kid. There is another party involved, someone anxious to see that you and your sister lose the ranch. At least that's my theory. Nash and I cornered Tony and his friends last night and we came up with some interesting facts."

Wide-eyed, Jason stared at Hal's rugged profile. "But why would somebody do that?"

"That's what I'm trying to find out. Those high school hoodlums were paid to harass you. They didn't realize they were being framed. I don't expect any more trouble from them."

"Probably not, since you know where Tony lives," Jason mused aloud. "I would've liked to have been on hand when you and Nash cut those creeps down to size."

"Tony is so damned envious of you it's pathetic."

Jason blinked, bemused. "Envious of *me?*"

Hal nodded. "I followed Tony after he dropped his friends off last night. He drove by Brenda's house and sat there staring into the distance for several minutes. Although Tony's background doesn't give him much of a chance with a girl like Brenda, it doesn't keep him from wanting and wishing." Hal glanced pointedly at Jason. "I think you might be able to identify with that, after you waited several months to work up the nerve to ask her out."

"So what am I supposed to do? Feel sorry for the jerk who has been making my life miserable?"

"Would that be too much to ask? Put yourself in Tony's place, kid. He doesn't have much going for him—a father in prison, his mother a drunken prostitute. He has no guidance to speak of, no one who cares, no claim to fame. He acts tough because he's overcompensating for feelings of inferiority. And worse, the girl of his dreams seems to be pretty damned interested in the hot-shot, high school star quarterback."

Jason frowned thoughtfully as he mulled over Hal's words.

"How frustrated do you think *you* would be if some good-looking, studious, and athletic senior classman was *your* competition for the girl of your dreams?"

Jason heaved a sigh and slumped against the seat. "So what am I supposed to do, Hal?"

"Bury the hatchet somewhere besides Tony's back," he advised. "It's in your own best interest, especially in light of the problems you and Andrea have. If whoever's behind this scheme tries to make contact with Tony again, he might be persuaded to give us the information. We can use all the help we can get. I, for one, would like to know who is responsible for all this—and why."

Jason nodded agreeably. "Okay, I'll try to let bygones be bygones, but don't expect me to sing Tony's praises to Brenda. I'm not feeling *that* charitable."

Hal chuckled in amusement. "You do have it bad, don't you, kid?"

Jason half-twisted to stare at the driver of the car behind

im. "Do you think I'm too young to know what love really is, Hal?"

Hal squirmed in his skin. Since Jason had looked up to him like an older brother or father figure, Hal had found himself in the middle of some pretty awkward conversations. He should be getting used to it by now.

He wasn't.

"You may not be too young to know how you feel," Hal said and purposely avoided using the word *love*. It wasn't a concept he was all that comfortable with yet, though Andrea insisted he accept her feelings for him rather than deny them the way he usually did . . .

Hal gave himself a mental slap for derailing his original train of thought. "Don't rush headlong into a relationship," he advised. "That's one thing you *are* too young for, even if premarital sex among high school students is on the rise."

Jason grinned outrageously. "Darn. I was all set to practice safe sex this afternoon—"

Hal rounded on Jason so fast that the truck swerved toward the ditch. "You will practice *no* sex or I'll break your sprained passing arm into two equal pieces!"

Jason chuckled at Hal's outburst. "Is that what happened to *your* arm?"

Hal reluctantly smiled, realizing—too late—that Jason was teasing. "Yeah, kid, that's the way it happened. It just sounded more impressive to let everybody think a ton of bull ran over me."

Jason was silent for a moment. "Mind if I ask you something, Hal? Man to man?"

Hal's fingers clenched around the steering wheel. He didn't like the sound of that. "You're full of questions, aren't you?"

"Is there something going on between you and my sister? Lately I've noticed the way Andrea looks at you when you aren't watching. The way you look at her. I mean you're still here when you don't have to be."

Yes, he was still here, Hal thought. He didn't have to be. He *wanted* to be, *needed* to be.

"Well?" Jason prompted when Hal didn't respond immediately. "Is there something going on that I don't know about?"

"Ah, here we are," Hal said with more enthusiasm than necessary. "Home sweet home."

"You're avoiding my question," Jason noted.

"Yeah," Hal admitted honestly. "There is something going on between Andrea and me. We sort of have a thing for each other—temporarily. You aren't going to get all bent out of shape about it and try to beat the shit out of me, are you?"

Lips twitching, Jason glanced down at his bandaged arm, and then stared at Hal's cast. "I may not be too bright, but I don't think either of us is in any condition for an all-out fight." His eyes twinkled as he stared directly at Hal. "Besides, I've decided I would rather be a lover than a fighter."

Hal met Jason's stare, feeling the impact of respect and acceptance that was being directed toward him. "Me, too, kid. It saves wear and tear on the body." He hitched his thumb toward the compact car that had pulled in behind them. "And if you're smart, you'll soak up all this sympathy and concern. You can rest assured that poor ole Tony Braden is literally eating his heart out, wishing he could exchange places with you, despite the sorry shape you're in."

"I guess a guy should appreciate how good he's got it," Jason said as he eased gingerly from the truck. "Not that you need it, Hal, but you have my permission to date Andi. She seems happier than she's been in years." He paused to stare directly at Hal. "Just don't hurt her. I might decide to take you on, battered body and all."

Hal sat there like a slug while Brenda hurried to assist Jason up the wooden deck. A date? he thought to himself. He and Andrea hadn't even been out on a date. The improvised picnic and fishing trip didn't count. That had been his way of distracting Andrea from all the turmoil.

A date. What a novel idea, Hal mused. Maybe when he got to the bottom of this ugly business he could ask Andrea out. *She* hadn't dated in four years. *He* hadn't dated in twelve years; he'd been screwing around for the hell of it when the mood suited him. Gawd, when he recalled the kind of life he had been leading, it reminded him—all over again—that he didn't deserve a woman like Andrea.

He didn't want to remember that right now. He was satisfied in this place out of time, away from the demands of the rodeo circuit and the raucous night life that accompanied it.

Speaking of novel ideas, Hal wondered if Andrea had ever allowed herself to be picked up. He was curious to know how she would react to his outrageous flirting. Maybe he'd show up at Slim Chance during her shift. It was the perfect excuse to see for himself if Andrea was being harassed by the bar patrons.

In the meantime Hal intended to do a little pushing and shoving—to see what turned up, without alerting Andrea. He wanted to keep her in the dark and out of harm's way until the smoke cleared. With any luck he could expose the culprits and force them into the open.

And if Jenna was as involved as Hal suspected she was, he was going to hang that devious tramp out to dry!

Eighteen

Andrea stared in disbelief at the crowd of men and women hovering around the corner booth of Hard Times Cafe at high noon. She had hurried over from the real estate and insurance office to grab a sandwich, and there Hal sat, holding court and signing autographs. When he saw her, he excused himself and ambled toward her.

Her heart slammed against her ribs—and stuck there.

As he approached, every pair of feminine eyes monitored his graceful movements. And *he* said *she* had an attention-catching walk? Well, look who was talking!

Andrea couldn't stifle the smile that blossomed on her lips when Hal gave her the once-over, despite the modest dress she was wearing. Her body instantly responded to the devilish sparkle in those coal-black eyes. An odd sense of pleasure unfurled inside her, and she wondered if this was how her mother had felt when Robert joined her for lunch three days a week.

Andrea lifted her gaze when Hal halted directly in front of her. She was tempted to reach out to trace that seductive smile on his lips. Instead she asked, "What are you doing here?"

"Waiting for you, wildcat," he murmured as he guided her toward the corner booth. "Sure hope your boss doesn't try to get in touch with you. The patrons might get an interesting lesson straight from your bestselling how-to."

Andrea felt the blush working its way up from her neck to splotch her cheeks. Hal's wicked laughter erupted behind her. "Behave yourself," she muttered aside.

"You're the one who put the thought in my head," he countered as he sank down on the padded vinyl seat across from her. "And anyway, I'm not supposed to behave. You know cowboys have cantankerous dispositions. It goes with the territory."

Andrea frowned when an unnerving thought struck her. "I thought you were going to stay with Jason today. Is there a problem? Didn't the doctor release him? His injured kidney didn't shut down again, did it?"

"Jason hasn't suffered any complications. He's doing fine. Better than fine, actually," he amended as he settled himself on the seat. "His girlfriend played hooky so she could fuss over him."

Andrea blinked. "You left the two of them alone at the house? *Unchaperoned?*"

"Don't get your feathers ruffled, mother hen," Hal taunted. "I gave Jason my best lecture, complete with all the bells and whistles. He's not in any condition for sexual gymnastics, but I reminded him to keep his hands to himself. But I expect a few steamy kisses would help cure him."

"Hal," Andrea admonished.

When Laverne Gable scampered over to take the order, Andrea had to field her rapid-fire questions about Jason's condition and listen to commiserations about the burned barn.

"Those sorry little hoodlums should be locked up," Laverne grumbled. "The whole town wants their heads

n a silver platter. The football team needs their star quar-
erback for the state playoffs."

When Andrea opened her mouth to set the record
traight, Hal reached across the table to clasp her hand in
is, giving it a silencing squeeze. He obviously didn't want
he latest information sent down the grapevine yet.

"You can bet Jason will be suited up and anxious to
lay," Hal inserted. "If the doctor gives the okay, Jason
von't let a bruised arm keep him sidelined."

"Well, that's a relief," Laverne said with a gusty sigh.
The town is planning on chartering a bus and driving up
o Oklahoma City to watch the game. We want to see
ason and his teammates in action."

When Laverne swept off, Hal stared curiously at Andrea. "Did you check on the insurance spokesman who
alled you?"

"I had Tuff call the main office," Andrea reported. "No
ne by the name of Evan Hudson works for the company.
Tuff filed my claim for the damages and requested that
he appraiser come by the ranch this week."

"Good," Hal murmured. "Hopefully, you'll be able to
ollect on the hay, ranch supplies, and the building lost
n the fire."

"Tuff said he would make sure there were no delays. I
an use the money to pay off the interest and principal on
he outstanding loans."

She waited to see if Hal was going to offer to make the
ayment for her. She was primed and ready to object if
he did. Thankfully, he kept his mouth shut. Andrea hoped
she had made it crystal clear that she wasn't going to
accept another nickel of Hal's charity. He'd worked too
hard—risking injuries like the one that hampered him
now—on that grueling circuit. Andrea couldn't live with

herself if she accepted his money to save her home. It sounded like something Jenna might do, and Andrea never wanted to be lumped in with that deceitful mercenary.

When Laverne returned with burgers and fries—and the latest gossip—Andrea caught up on local news. Laverne was an absolute marvel. How she could file, store, and process all that information in her brain, Andrea could not imagine. Laverne made computers look outdated!

When Laverne whizzed off again, Hal chuckled and shook his head in amazement. "You should be grateful that you don't live in town, under the watchful eyes of that well-meaning busybody. Does anything go down in this one-horse town that Laverne doesn't get wind of it."

"Very little," Andrea replied, munching on her French fries. "Laverne considers her friends and neighbors part of her extended family. To hear her talk, she knows everybody personally, even if she only takes their orders at the cafe."

Andrea glanced at her watch, then picked up her hamburger and ate hurriedly. "Thanks, Hal," she said between bites.

"For what?"

"For joining me for lunch. It was a welcome surprise. I'm enjoying the company."

He smiled at her. "Don't start reading all sorts of hidden meaning into it. I told you, three would have been a crowd at your ranch today."

Andrea lifted an eyebrow. "What's the matter? Afraid I might think you actually cared enough to join me for lunch?"

Hal reached across the table to wipe away the drop of catsup that pooled at the corner of her mouth. His tender touch sent frissons of heat rippling through her bloodstream. When her face flushed, Hal grinned at her helpless response.

"I can think of other things I'd rather have for lunch besides this burger . . . and it isn't served on a bun." His eyes twinkled. "On second thought, it could be . . ."

Andrea swallowed, blushed profusely, and snatched up a French fry. The provocative comment had her steaming like a clam. Hal's gaze smoldered, promising intimacies that she was eager to see fulfilled. Andrea knew she had placed herself in the most vulnerable of all positions when she admitted how much she cared for Hal.

Not that he couldn't have figured out by the way she reacted to him, she reminded herself. She had always been open and honest. But even now, she sensed that what she called love, he regarded as passion.

Stubborn man. He refused to believe that he was exactly what she wanted and needed. He was still too cynical to admit there was such a thing as tender feeling—straight from the heart. Somehow, someday, he would realize that what she felt for him ran soul-deep. Too bad this once-burned, twice-cynical cowboy was afraid to return her affection. It would probably choke Hal Griffin to voice those three words.

"A dime for your thoughts," Hal probed, studying her intently.

Andrea flashed him an impish smile. "I thought a penny was the going rate, big spender."

He ignored that. "I can't decipher your expression. What are you thinking?"

Andrea dug into her purse to retrieve her billfold. "I don't think you really want to know. It always makes you nervous. Dinner is on me," she announced abruptly.

Hal smiled rakishly. "If dinner had been *on* you, I

would have enjoyed it far more than I did. I'll have to remember to garnish you with mustard and ketchup the first chance I get."

Andrea flushed at the erotic picture he painted.

"Now *that* I can read loud and clear," Hal chuckled, tossing a tip on the table.

"You're outrageous," Andrea muttered.

"Is that a complaint?" he murmured as he assisted her to her feet.

His close physical contact affected her the same way heat affected a stick of butter. Andrea stepped away before she blushed all over. There were too many curious eyes on the celebrity cowboy whose presence had graced the small town of Hochukbi. She wondered if everyone in the cafe knew she had fallen head over boot heels for this roguish rascal who could turn on the charm when he felt like it.

When they stepped outside the door, Hal's lips grazed her forehead. "I trust Tuff has accepted the fact that we're an item and he isn't chasing you around the office. Do I need to sit your old boyfriend down and tell him what's what?"

"He's behaving like a gentleman," Andrea reported. "Of course, I laid down the law the first day on the job."

"I hope you used my name as a threat."

"Didn't have to," Andrea told him saucily. "I can take care of myself. I plan to continue taking care of myself after you ride off into the sunset. Thanks for meeting me for lunch," she added as she strode across the street.

Hal watched the hypnotic sway of Andrea's hips as she strolled toward the office. Every time she walked away he kept feeling that strange tug of possessiveness, that need to protect and defend. Gawd, that woman had the damnedest effect on him. Even though she was the most independent woman he had ever known, Hal found himself constantly rushing to her aid. He couldn't remember the last time he had been so aware of a woman, so attentive to her needs.

Turning away, Hal headed toward the clunker truck. While Andrea was filing and typing up insurance claims at her office, Hal was going to go behind her back and take the pressure off her.

She would throw a tantrum when she found out, but time was running short. Hal couldn't dillydally around Hochukbi indefinitely. He had a must-ride rodeo to attend the following weekend, and he couldn't concentrate if he was worried about Andrea. He had to find out who was behind this scheme.

With grim resolve, Hal switched on the blinker and veered into the bank parking lot. He expected that what he was about to do was going to shake things up. Good. He wanted quick results.

Hal had to give Jenna credit when he walked through the door. She flashed him a two-hundred-watt smile, even after he had pretty much told her off the previous night. She was still trying to project that air of false innocence that had lured him so successfully a decade ago.

If there was one thing Jenna was exceptionally good at, it was performing. Unfortunately for her, Hal was wise to her.

With little more than a nod of greeting Hal propelled himself toward Tom Gilmore's office, ready to drop a grenade in the loan officer's lap and see how he reacted.

"Got a minute, Gilmore?" Hal said without preamble. "I've got some business with you."

Hal noticed that Gilmore cast a quick glance toward the teller's deck, behind which the attentive Jenna stood. Hal couldn't help but wonder if Gilmore might have been the man lurking in the shadows of Jenna's apartment last night. That scenario seemed to fit. Gilmore was in a position to turn a profit if he foreclosed and then bought Fletcher Ranch. And where there was money to be made, Jenna wouldn't be far away.

"What can I do for you?" Gilmore questioned as he leaned back in his leather chair and steepled his fingers.

Hal reached into his back pocket for his checkbook and took great satisfaction announcing, "I'm paying off the interest on Andrea's loan. I am also giving notice that I intend to pay the balance on the property Robert Fletcher mortgaged to keep his ranch in operation while sending his daughter through vet school."

To Hal's surprise, beads of sweat immediately popped out on Gilmore's forehead. A strained expression pinched his features. It was the damnedest thing Hal ever saw.

"You can't do that," Gilmore choked out. "The loan was in Robert's name and the responsibility falls to his children."

"Horseshit," Hal snorted. "It doesn't matter who pays the loan. If you're going to quibble over technicalities I'll write Andrea a check and then have her give it to you. But either way, the interest payment will be paid in full—today."

"Why are you doing this?" Gilmore muttered. "This is none of your concern."

"Haven't you heard?" Hal asked flippantly. "The little lady is my girlfriend."

"That's hardly the point."

Hal wrote out the check and signed his name. When he thrust it at Gilmore, the man stared at the check as if it were a coiled rattlesnake.

"Take it," Hal demanded. "If you don't, I'm going to assume you're responsible for the all-too-convenient catastrophes plaguing the Fletchers. And don't make the foolish mistake of thinking I'm not suspicious about why you're anxious to foreclose on a family that has been a respectable part of this community for generations." Hal looked Gilmore squarely in the eye. "Are you planning to buy this property?"

"Of course not," Gilmore adamantly denied, still sweating like a marathon runner on the Fourth of July. "I'm only doing the job I'm paid to do."

Hal scoffed sarcastically. "Do I look like I was born yesterday? I know damned well there's something going on between you and Jenna. That woman can smell money before a man opens his wallet."

Gilmore swallowed so hard that Hal was sure the man was going to choke on his own spit. "You don't know what kind of trouble you'll get yourself into if you force me to accept this check," he wheezed.

When Gilmore's gaze darted toward the open door, Hal sank back in his chair to appraise the situation. Gilmore was so fidgety he couldn't sit still. The man was definitely involved, but to what extent, Hal couldn't say. Gilmore had *scared* written all over him. Scared of what? Meeting with an untimely accident because he hadn't carried out his part in whatever shady dealings he had gotten himself into?

The thought sent a stab of uneasiness through Hal's gut. *Untimely accidents.* Hal decided to shoot from the hip.

"Maggie Fletcher knew too much, didn't she? How convenient that your former employee took a wrong turn through the guard rail."

Bull's eye!

Gilmore's face turned white as yogurt.

So there was a connection, Hal speculated. Andrea's problems *were* connected to the death of her mother, and maybe even her father. Hal predicted the whole thing had to do with money. After all, that was Jenna Randall's middle name.

Given Gilmore's reaction, Hal decided to press harder, especially after he remembered something Laverne Gable had said the first time he and Andrea had eaten lunch at the cafe.

"I wonder what would happen to you if I spread the word that Robert Fletcher's suicide might have been a cleverly devised murder. Just like his wife's supposed traffic *accident,* maybe?"

"That's preposterous," Gilmore muttered, his hands knotted into white-knuckled fists. "There's nothing to substantiate such conclusions."

"There isn't?" Hal smiled goadingly. "Then tell me why a man who established a pattern of eating his favorite meal at the cafe every Friday—just like clockwork—chose to settle for a grilled cheese on the very day he planned to throw himself off a cliff—and miss his son's ball game for the first time in his life.

"I don't know about you, Gilmore, but if I had decided I would be eating my last meal, I would have ordered my favorite food. And furthermore, I would have watched my son's game and done the cowardly deed *afterward.*"

Hal leaned forward, pinning the blatantly nervous Gilmore with an eagle-eyed stare. "Whoever killed Robert

Fletcher knew he would be alone at his ranch after his son had driven off to the game."

"You can't prove any of that," Gilmore hissed, still sweating profusely. "It's all speculation, wishful thinking to explain a suicide, to save face. The fact is that Robert couldn't handle the loss of his wife. Everybody knew he was crazy about Maggie. When she was gone, nothing was as important, not his loans, not football games, not a daughter in vet school—nothing. Robert had lost his reason for living. Ask anybody in town."

Hal braced his elbows on the desk, staring unblinkingly at the banker. "I'm asking *you*, Gilmore. Did Robert suspect that his wife may have been murdered because of something she knew? Is that what the fracas between the two of you was really about?"

When Gilmore opened his mouth to voice what Hal expected to be a denial, he quickly cut the banker off. "And before you try to feed me a crock of lies, let me assure you I haven't kept my suspicions to myself. If I meet with an untimely accident there will be others showing up here to ask questions, others who will follow up on my suspicions, others who are aware that I paid off Andrea's loan—just in case my check is *misplaced* or *accidentally shredded*."

"Don't do it," Gilmore whispered urgently, his apprehensive gaze leaping toward the door where Jenna stood watching.

Hal studied Gilmore's face, picking apart his facial expression like a specimen under a microscope. "I think you and I need to have a private conversation. If you don't agree, I'm calling Sheriff Featherstone right now so he can ask you a few questions—on the record. I've already contacted him, by the way."

Hal got the results he wanted.

Gilmore nodded bleakly. "All right, we'll talk."

"Tonight," Hal insisted. "Late, very late."

Gilmore's head bobbed in agreement. "I'll meet you on the dead end road by the river. By Fletcher's holding pens."

Hal remembered what Jason had said about seeing several vehicles using that remote path lately. Obviously, Gilmore had been there himself.

"Three o'clock in the morning," Gilmore murmured.

Hal studied the man astutely. "A dead end road sounds like a good place for a man to get his business in bad shape. I'll be watching to make sure you come alone." Hal slid the check across the desk, leaving it under Gilmore's nose.

"You're asking for more trouble than you can possibly imagine," Gilmore whispered.

"Then I'll be in familiar territory. Write me a receipt." When Gilmore hesitated and glanced at the door, Hal snarled, "Do it. I'm not leaving without one."

Reluctantly, Gilmore signed, dated, and filled out the receipt.

"A pleasure doing business with you," Hal announced, tucking the receipt in his shirt pocket. "Have a nice day."

When Hal strode through the door, Jenna was studying him curiously. He expected she was champing at the bit, eager to discover what this transaction was all about. Hal also suspected that he couldn't have jeopardized himself more if he had pinned a target on his chest.

Whoever wanted the Fletcher property—for whatever reason—had gone to some pretty deadly extremes. Although Gilmore had said nothing to incriminate himself, his apprehension was a dead giveaway. Hal's stab in the dark had connected. Maggie and Robert Fletcher were expendable; the clever mastermind had found ways to dispose of all his obstacles without arousing suspicion.

Hal wasn't about to take Andrea into his confidence. Knowing what a daredevil she could be, she was liable to go off half-cocked. He had offered himself as bait, and he wasn't going to let Andrea know until the worst was over.

Paying off the interest on the loan would sure bring this situation to a head in a hurry. All Hal had to do was stand back and wait. Until then, he would make damned certain Andrea suspected nothing. He would have to keep her occupied.

Hal smiled wryly as he piled into his old truck. A perfect solution was forming in his mind. It was going to be a pleasure keeping that little wildcat occupied.

Jenna ambled into Gilmore's office under the pretense of getting his signature on a paper. Her intense gray eyes zeroed in on his pinched expression. "Do we have a problem?"

Gilmore raked a shaky hand through his salt-and-pepper hair and then exhaled deeply. "Afraid so. Hal Griffin just paid off the back interest and a portion of the principal on the Fletcher loan."

Jenna swallowed an oath. "You should have foreclosed weeks ago. The longer you drag this out, the riskier it is. I hope you realize that."

Gilmore was fully aware of what happened to anyone who got in the way of this land deal. Now he was caught in a trap with no way out. That thought had him swearing again.

"You look a little shaken," Jenna observed with a smirk. "You have every reason to be, of course. Since you're the one who botched up this transaction, making something difficult when it should have been simple, you're going to have to *remove* the problems yourself. You do understand me, don't you?"

Gilmore's throat constricted when his gaze met her cold granite eyes. He wondered if he would live long enough to regret letting himself be taken in by this alluring but treacherous black widow.

"You do understand, don't you?" Jenna repeated, staring him down.

Gilmore nodded grimly. "I'll take care of the complications."

Jenna braced her hands on the desk and smiled icily. "That's good. I would hate to see something happen to you or your family. It would crush your wife if word got around that you haven't exactly been a model husband and father. News of our affair could be disastrous to you personally and professionally."

Gilmore grimaced as Jenna pushed herself upright and then plucked up the paper she had brought to the office. She retreated—one hip at a time—reminding him of intimacies that never should have happened. Gilmore cursed himself for falling into this hopeless snare. He was frantic to escape, hated what he was forced to do. He had been in a living hell for months.

Hands trembling, Gilmore stuffed Hal's check in the pocket of his slacks. He wondered how he would be able to live with himself after tonight, wondered how he would be able to *live* at all!

* * *

Jason Fletcher swore he'd died and gone straight to heaven. He would remember this afternoon as long as he lived. Brenda had been with him, serving him sandwiches for lunch, keeping the glasses of ice water and Cokes filled to the brim, cuddling up beside him to watch movies on TV. For the past several hours his aches and pains hadn't bothered him at all.

He had stolen a few kisses here and there. Well, not actually stolen them, he amended. Brenda had been a willing participant. She had also been careful not to aggravate his injuries when she looped her arms around his neck and nestled against him—face-to-face—as they stretched out together on the living room sofa.

"Brenda," Jason murmured before he dropped another kiss on her inviting lips. "There's something I've been wanting the two of us to do."

"What's that, Jason?" she questioned warily.

Jason inhaled a deep breath, feeling the strain across his bruised rib cage. "You probably think it's too soon, but—"

Brenda withdrew, her pretty face a mask of disappointment. "What is it with you guys?" she muttered resentfully. "That's the last thing I would have expected from you. I thought you were different."

Seeing the look of angry disappointment on Brenda's face damned near broke Jason's heart. How could heaven turn to hell so quickly?

"Wait!" he called as Brenda bounded to her feet, flashing him a glare.

"No, *you* wait," she snapped. "I've been waiting six months for you to ask me out. When you finally did, I thought I had found a guy who liked me, not because I

happen to be head cheerleader, not because I'm moderately attractive—"

"Moderately?" Jason laughed aloud and then groaned
at the unintentional pain he had inflicted on himself.
"You're the prettiest girl in school, in the county, probably
in the whole darned state."

"And the latest conquest, right?" Brenda asked bitterly.
"And you think just because I like you, and because I feel
absolutely terrible about what happened to you, that I'll
sleep with you so you can brag to your friends. Well, it's
about time you found out what every other guy I've dated
knows—I don't put out. And if you believed the cruel lies
that I do, then you're going to be disappointed!"

"Brenda, hold on a minute!" Jason called as she
snatched up her purse and stalked toward the kitchen.

"I'm not *holding on* for another second and you can
wait on yourself, Jason Fletcher!"

Jason struggled to sit upright and then staggered to his
feet. Problem was, he tried to rise too fast. Dizziness
swirled around him like a whirlpool.

"Well, damn . . ."

His legs collided with the coffee table, knocking him
off balance. With a hiss and a groan, he collapsed on the
couch. To his surprise, Brenda was beside him in a flash,
her lovely features etched with concern.

"Are you okay?" she demanded to know.

"No," Jason grumbled.

"Should I call the doctor?"

Jason didn't waste a second. He had to correct Brenda's
misconception—now. He slid his high school ring off his
finger and presented it to her, with a smile that boasted
blue-tinged lips. "I only wanted to know if you would go
with me, nobody but me," he rasped, cursing his light-

headedness. "I wasn't going to ask anything besides that. Swear to God, Brenda."

Brenda stared at the ring resting in the palm of her hand, then peered into Jason's pallid face. She opened her mouth, but no words came out. She simply stared at him.

"Truth is, I disputed every guy who claimed you were an easy mark. I knew it was male ego talking, because you're not like that," Jason hurried on. "You're like my sister when she was in high school. There was a lot of wishful thinking going on before Andi graduated, too. She got so fed up with it that she swore off men for years."

"You understand?" Brenda questioned, tears shining in her lake-blue eyes.

"I think I do," Jason murmured. "Hal says girls like to be treated with courtesy and respect, to be appreciated for what they are. That's how I feel about you—because you're the way you are. I just want to be with you. I want to let those clowns know we're going together and that they'll answer to me if they bother you."

Tears dribbled down Brenda's flushed cheeks. "Oh, Jason, I'm sorry I went ballistic. I thought you were taking advantage—"

"I don't blame you," he interrupted, grinning. "I was stumbling around, trying to work up the nerve to ask you to wear my ring."

Despite the tears, Brenda smiled back. "I'd like that—a lot."

Jason propped up on an elbow and leaned toward her. His lips brushed hers in a feathery kiss. "So would I," he whispered genuinely, sincerely. "I've never given anybody my ring before, never wanted to—"

A sudden movement by the door caught Jason's attention. He jerked back so quickly that he winced. A mortified groan tumbled from his lips when he saw his sister staring at him with a disparaging frown.

Brenda turned all the colors of the rainbow.

"Jason Wayne Fletcher, what is going on here?" Andrea demanded. "I hope you're treating this young lady with the respect and consideration she deserves."

Jason grinned at Brenda. "See what I mean?"

Brenda nodded her blond head.

"Actually," Jason said as he levered into a sitting position, "I just asked Brenda to go with me."

"Go where?" Andrea smirked. "You're too banged up to go out."

"You know what I mean," Jason grumbled at his dense sister.

"The ring thing, you mean?" Andrea inquired.

Brenda's head bobbed, her face still pink with embarrassment.

Andrea pushed away from the wall and then strode into the room, eyeing the blushing blonde crouched in front of Jason like a servant before her king. "Don't get accustomed to sitting at my brother's feet," she advised, her eyes dancing with amusement. "All of a sudden men star getting the idea you'll heel and fetch."

When Jason peered up at his sister, silently requesting that she cut him some slack, Andrea broke into a grin "Shall we celebrate over supper? It has to be fast, because I have to leave for my second job in an hour."

"I'll help," Brenda volunteered eagerly, clutching the ring in her fist.

"Thanks." Andrea gestured to Brenda to follow her into the kitchen "We've got to keep up Jase's strength. It's n fun having a steady boyfriend if you can't go out with him."

"Nope," Brenda agreed, tossing Jason a saucy grin. "Couch potatoes are a dime a dozen."

Andrea chuckled when Brenda joined in to tease Jason. "Mind if I use the phone to call my folks?"

"Go ahead, Brenda. Phone's on the kitchen counter."

When Brenda and Andrea disappeared around the corner, Jason slumped onto the sofa. He was back in heaven again. The girl of his dreams had accepted his ring and his sister had lightened up enough to tease him the way she used to in the old days.

Life could be difficult, Jason decided, but it did have its bright moments.

Nineteen

Andrea grinned at the petite blonde who had slippe
the oversize ring on her thumb before preparing the dinne
salad. If Andrea wasn't mistaken, Brenda was as infatu
ated as Jason was. It was gratifying to see two peopl
equally enamored with one another. Andrea wished sh
found herself in the same kind of relationship. Unfortu
nately, it was a one-sided love affair with the restless cow
boy who had taken her on as a charity case.

"Jason says you and I are a lot alike," Brenda said a
she sliced up the tomatoes. "But I guess you decided me
weren't so bad when Hal Griffin showed up. He's reall
something, isn't he?"

Brenda's attempt at conversation amused Andrea. Sh
was curious to know why Jason had linked her with th
young blonde as kindred spirits. And what was it abou
Hal, Andrea wondered, that made women of all ages sit u
and take notice? Did he have the same effect on femal
from eight to eighty? Probably. There was something abou
a rugged cowboy that seemed to attract feminine interes

"High school boys can be a real pain," Andrea repli
belatedly, turning the fried chicken in the skillet. "They'
always trying to keep score, to outdo each other. Kin
makes you want to give up on the entire gender until th

mature mentally and emotionally. For some of them, that never comes."

"I was ready to give up on boys before Jason came along," Brenda confided, tossing cucumber slices in the bowl. "But he's different, special."

"I can't argue with that," Andrea said, grinning. "He's my brother. I think he's terrific—"

The roar of a faulty muffler heralded Hal's arrival, followed by footsteps clattering across the deck. To Andrea's surprise, Hal barged through the door as if he owned the place. She wondered at what point in time he had begun to consider Fletcher Ranch his territory, and if there was any hidden significance in that.

Andrea's welcoming smile changed to disbelief when Hal whipped his good arm around from behind him to display a dozen red roses. "They're beautiful," she exclaimed. "I'm sure Jason will be touched."

"Hi, Brenda," Hal said, casting the blonde a quick glance before he refocused on Andrea. "The flowers aren't for Jason. I don't give flowers to other men. It goes against my code. These are for you."

Andrea's mouth dropped open. "Why?"

"You're welcome," he prompted with a lopsided smile.

"Thank you," Andrea murmured. "But why?"

Hal glanced wryly at Brenda, avoiding Andrea's persistent question. "Nice ring. Looks a little too big for you, though."

Brenda blushed beneath Hal's teasing grin. "It's Jason's."

"No kidding," Hal chuckled, his obsidian eyes dancing with mischief.

Andrea's knees wobbled as she watched Hal turn on his charismatic charm. Cynical though Hal Griffin could be, he had a natural way with women. Even Brenda wasn't immune to him.

"Jason and I are going together," Brenda announced, returning Hal's contagious smile.

"How much did the kid have to pay you to get you to agree to that? Must've cost him a bundle."

Brenda's face flushed at the rodeo superstar's playful razzing.

"I'll help Fletcher with supper," Hal volunteered. "Why don't you keep Jason company."

Brenda glanced back and forth between Andrea and Hal, and then broke into the kind of dimpled smile that had melted Jason's heart months ago. "Is that a hint for me to get lost?"

"Smart little lady," Hal said with a wink. "No wonder Jason is crazy about you."

When Brenda strode off to rejoin Jason, Hal rummaged through the cabinets looking for a vase. Andrea watched him covetously, wishing she could be alone with him instead of skedaddling to work at the local bar. She knew their hours together were numbered. Hal would be gone soon. Only a fool would expect him to return, but that didn't stop Andrea from wanting to be the place he came between rodeos, even if she knew she was inviting heartbreak.

"What's with the flowers?" she questioned as she removed the chicken from the skillet to make cream gravy

Hal shrugged his shoulders. "Impulse. Just like this . . .'

When he hooked his arm around Andrea and bent her over backward, she giggled at his playful mood. "Are you feeling all right?"

"Why don't you feel me and find out for yourself," he growled devilishly.

"Hal!" Andrea sputtered. "For heaven's sake—" Andrea swallowed her tongue when Brenda appeared in the doorway, carrying Jason's empty glass.

Brenda's brows arched in amusement as she appraised the situation. "Oops."

Reluctantly, Hal tilted Andrea upright, then flashed Brenda a mock scowl. "Can't even enjoy a simple kiss without all these kids underfoot."

"Jason is thirsty," Brenda explained, refilling the glass. "Sorry to interrupt."

"Don't let it happen again," Hal said in mock seriousness.

When she scurried off, Hal monitored her departure. "Your brother has excellent taste. He's also right about Brenda having the kind of walk you're famous for. Drives guys nuts."

"You, of course, are a connoisseur of seductive walks, I suppose."

"Yes," he said. "In my book you still have Brenda beat by a mile. Nobody else I know fills out a pair of jeans and looks as good walking away as you do."

"Thank you, I think," Andrea murmured as she sprinkled flour in the skillet.

"You're welcome." Hal stepped close, nuzzling the side of her neck. "Are you going to quit your night job?"

Andrea shivered beneath his seductive assault and tried to concentrate on the gravy. "You know I can't quit. My day job is only temporary."

"You know I don't like having you flitting around bars late at night. Some pickup artist might make a play for you."

"Right, like that's going to happen," Andrea scoffed.

"You never know." She could feel his lips curving into

a smile against her neck, and she wondered what he found so amusing.

"I thought you were here to help me fix supper," Andrea prompted, worming out of his grasp. "Make yourself useful by setting the table."

"I'd rather make love to you on the table," Hal confided devilishly.

Andrea rolled her eyes and shook her head at Hal's outrageous mood. But truth be told, she delighted in his playfulness. His surprising arrival at the cafe and giving her flowers this evening had added spark and pleasure to her long days. Andrea wondered how she would endure life when Hal left. Wondered if she would have a home to come back to in the weeks that followed . . .

That thought threatened to dampen Andrea's spirits, but she resolved to live for the moment, to be thankful for Hal while he was with her. There would be plenty of loneliness in the months ahead.

Andrea cast aside her concerns. She had discovered what love was—for the first time in her life. And she still had her brother, bruised and battered though he was. She should appreciate life's blessings instead of fretting about the moment when the things she held dear would be stripped away from her.

Andrea called the troops to dinner with a loud whistle, taking quiet enjoyment in watching Jason and Brenda looking shyly at each other. Her brother was deliriously happy, and Andrea took comfort in knowing Brenda shared the same magical feelings that Jason was experiencing for the first time in his life.

Young love, Andrea mused over fried chicken, mashed potatoes, and gravy. She was glad her brother was enjoying what she had missed out on. She hoped that wherev er four assailants were, they had matured and regretted their actions. They had deprived Andrea of so much. It had taken a man like Hal Griffin to put her back in touch with herself and teach her to trust again.

Too bad Hal didn't trust *her* enough to believe in love.

While Andrea was moonlighting at Slim Chance Saloon, Hal entertained the teenagers with anecdotes about rodeo life. Being in mixed company, Hal stuck to incidents that happened in the arena, not after hours. When he heard a knock at the kitchen door, he answered it armed with Andrea's pipe wrench—just in case. Hal remembered, all too well, the desperation and anxiety in Tom Gilmore's voice, the quiet warning he murmured before Hal left the bank that afternoon.

To Hal's relief, he found Nash and Crista. Nash arched a thick brow as he stared pointedly at the wrench.

"Having plumbing problems, Mr. Fix-It?"

"Nope." Hal set the tool aside. "Just being cautious."

Crista strode inside and draped her jacket over a kitchen chair. "How is our patient doing?"

Hal noted the way Nash's golden gaze wandered over Crista's T-shirt and trim-fitting jeans. That hungry, possessive look was hard to miss. There had been a time when Hal scoffed at his brother's mindless obsession, but these days he was beginning to understand it all too well.

"Cat got your tongue?" Crista teased Hal.

He shook himself from his thoughts. "Jason and Brenda are in the living room. The kid seems to be doing fine, except for floating around on cloud nine."

Crista frowned bemusedly. "Did his doctor prescribe strong painkillers?"

"The girlfriend," Hal explained wryly. "Those two love-birds are staring at each other the way you and Nash do. I've been on a steady diet of Pepto Bismol. First you two and now them."

Crista stared at the long-stemmed roses on the table. "Who brought those?"

Hal shifted awkwardly from one foot to the other. "I did," he mumbled.

"For Jason?" Nash inquired, grinning devilishly.

Hal shifted again, uncomfortable with his brother's piercing scrutiny. "No."

Crista beamed in impish delight. "Well, what do ya know, Mr. Tough-as-Leather has a sentimental streak. Who would have thought it?"

Hal glowered at the pert blonde. "I thought you came by to check on Jason, not badger me."

"Curly is multi-talented," Nash put in. "She can do both at the same time."

Hal hitched his thumb toward the living room. "Get to work, miracle worker," he demanded grimly "The kid has a state playoff game in two weeks. The whole town is praying for his speedy recovery."

When Crista ambled off to examine her patient, Hal grabbed Nash's arm. "Have you heard anything from Featherstone?"

Nash nodded his dark head. "He's been checking Jenna's description. Turns out the lady has been spotted in various parts of the country the past few years, and not with the most respectable of citizens."

"Does Featherstone have specifics?" Hal questioned intently.

"Not yet. He's waiting for a call from a sheriff in Colorado. It seems that a swank resort was built on a secluded piece of property purchased after a foreclosure. The family involved with the sale had a string of bad luck."

"How convenient," Hal muttered. "I don't suppose Jenna was working at the nearby bank at the time."

Nash nodded gravely. "Featherstone thinks there may be a connection. Except the ravishing beauty at the bank in Colorado was a redhead."

"Amazing what a bottle of dye can do," Hal muttered.

"A real con artist, isn't she? I'm not surprised to learn that she's up to her old tricks. She learned them at an early age."

"The original bitch goddess," Hal continued. "Gorgeous but deadly. I think she has the loan officer at Hochukbi bank by both balls. The man's scared shitless."

"Did you wring any information out of him?"

"He nearly came apart when I wrote a check for the interest on Andrea's loan."

Nash's tawny eyes widened. "Damn, little brother, you do love to live dangerously, don't you? If Featherstone's suspicions are correct, these land scams have underworld ties. You could have a price on your head for interfering."

"Better than making Andrea the prime target."

"What did she say when you paid off the interest?"

Hal avoided his brother's direct stare by studying the vase of roses. "I didn't tell her."

"Afraid Little Miss Independent will blow her stack?" Nash snickered.

"Or something." Hal peered somberly at Nash. "I'd just as soon keep her and Jason out of this until we know exactly what's going on around here. They've suffered enough already."

"I can't argue with that. So what's the plan?"

"I told Gilmore I intended to pay off the mortgage with

my winnings from National Finals. If that plan falls through, I'm going to mortgage my portion of Chulosa Ranch to clear Fletcher land."

Nash muttered several oaths. "Way to go, Hal. Now those bastards will really be coming after you with a vengeance."

"At least then we'll know who the bastards are," Hal insisted.

"Why are you doing this?" Nash demanded quietly. "For the first time in five years we're free and clear. Your chances of winning championship titles in Vegas are the best they've ever been. You're all but inviting a bunch of thugs to break you in pieces so you can't perform. You've taken this charity case too damned far . . ."

Nash's voice trailed off as he scrutinized his younger brother's expression. "Only it isn't charity anymore, is it, Hal? It's gone way past that, hasn't it?"

Hal turned his back on his brother. "I was always a sucker for strays and underdogs," he answered. "The Fletchers need help."

Nash barked a laugh. "Well, I'll be damned. You are well and truly hooked on that violet-eyed bundle of sass, aren't you? Why don't you just admit it?"

"Why don't you stop heckling me and offer to help out?" Hal snapped. "I have a late-night appointment with Gilmore on a dead end road. If you can stand to miss a little sleep, I could use a backup in case he's desperate enough to show up with a gun."

Nash's bronzed face paled noticeably. "Damned daredevil," he scowled. "I want you to be around to serve as my best man."

"Then be back here at two-thirty in the morning and bring a couple of saddles. Andrea's were destroyed in the fire. You and I are going to take an evening ride and wait for Gilmore."

"Great," Nash grumbled. "I get to be the bodyguard's bodyguard."

Hal smiled recklessly. "That's what brothers are for."

"I would have preferred better odds. We may have more guests than we can handle tonight."

"We always found ourselves up against the odds. Nothing has changed."

"Yes, *they* have," Nash contradicted. "We used to battle drunks in barroom brawls, not thugs with ties to organized crime."

"Times change," Hal said with a shrug.

Nash stared at him solemnly. "Let's just hope you live long enough to change with the times. If this appointment turns sour I hope to hell you have the courage to admit why you're sticking your neck out so far for Andrea Fletcher."

When Nash ambled off to join Crista, Hal stared pensively at the roses. Blood red roses, he thought with a grimace. Not the best choice of colors, considering the circumstances. Next time he would buy orchids—the same color as Andrea's luminous eyes . . .

If there was *a next time . . .*

Hal quickly discarded the thought, but it circled back like a boomerang. No matter what happened during his rendezvous with Gilmore, Hal promised himself to enjoy the time between now and then fully.

Smiling, he rehashed his conversation with Andrea, recalling the way her body had reacted when his lips skimmed the sensitive point beneath her ear. Ah yes, he was going to make damned sure he went to the rendezvous with the ultimate fantasy sustaining him.

The tantalizing thoughts put a wide grin on his lips as

Hal strode off to watch Curly work her magic on Jason. The kid didn't know what a massage was until she set to work with those gentle hands. Hal had enjoyed her talent once or twice himself. As for brother Nash, he was getting more than a bride in his bargain, Hal mused. Nash was getting one helluva masseuse—in boots!

Hal had been tucked in the corner of the bar for almost thirty minutes, watching Andrea wait tables on the opposite side of the smoke-filled room. She had been at the counter filling orders—her back to the door—when he strode inside, his black Stetson pulled low on his forehead to avoid recognition. His busty, red-haired waitress had cast him several interested glances when she sauntered past, to see if he wanted more than one longneck.

What Hal really wanted was to bust some chops. Four citified dudes had been causing Andrea grief the entire time he'd had been sitting in his corner. He had heard "Hey, sweet baby, swing that curvy ass over here and fill the pitcher" too many times already. The fact that Andrea hadn't dumped the pitcher of beer on those knotheads had Hal simmering. She was tolerating sexual harassment in order to keep this lousy job.

Hal nearly squeezed the bottle neck in two when one of the pseudo-cowboys reached out to pat Andrea on the fanny. What irritated Hal was that he had used the same disgusting tactics a few times in nameless towns on the circuit. It made him ashamed to call himself a man. Of course, he reminded himself, most of the waitresses he patted on the butt had already rubbed their breasts against his shoulder under the pretense of filling his mug. They had offered invitations and Hal had accepted.

Andrea, however, was simply doing the job she was paid to do.

Although Hal's initial reason for being there was to spend extra time with Andrea, he felt a compulsive urge to stake his claim for the rest of these half-drunken clowns to see—and remember. Since Andrea had insisted that she'd never let a man pick her up—ever—Hal had the ridiculous desire to be the first. And the *only*.

It looked as though he would have to bang a few heads together in the process. Those four assholes, gussied up in flashy western shirts, bandanna scarves, and straw hats, were really starting to piss him off.

"Hey, babe, what time do you get off?" one of them asked as Andrea walked past.

When she ignored the question, the drunk grabbed hold of her shirt, causing the beer mugs to slide across the tray she was carrying. If not for her graceful agility, the patrons at the adjacent table would have been showered with beer.

"Let go," Andrea demanded.

"Not until you tell me what time you get off."

"Eleven-thirty," she hissed through gritted teeth.

"I'll be waiting," he purred at her.

"You'll die waiting," Andrea assured him loftily.

Despite Andrea's attempt to elude the brazen man, he towed her backward, forcing her into his lap. Hal was out of his chair in the blink of an eyelash. If he had been Andrea, he would have dumped the mug over Bozo Number One's head. Unfortunately, she didn't want to risk losing this crummy job.

"Damn, honey," the man growled as he pressed himself against the back of her thighs. "I'm not sure I can wait until closing time. I'd like to get in your pants—"

Hal took great satisfaction in forcing his way into the

conversation and watching the man's bloodshot eyes widen in surprise. Hal didn't miss Andrea's shocked gasp when she recognized him.

"If you make one more wisecrack about my girlfriend," Hal snarled menacingly, "or if you paw at her one more time, I'll break both of your arms. Got it, dickhead?"

"Get lost," Bozo Number Two sneered.

"You heard him," Bozo Number Three chimed in. "Get—"

Hal's flying left elbow caught Number Three in the mouth, grinding the plaster cast against bared teeth. Hal never took his eyes off the creep holding Andrea in the chair. "I said let her go. She's already spoken for."

Red-rimmed eyes darted sideways to see blood dripping from the broad nose Hal had smashed with one powerful blow of his arm. Reluctantly, the goon released Andrea.

Hal rose to full stature, his dark eyes riveted on his quarry. "If I get wind of you badgering this little lady again, you'll answer to me."

Bozo Number One glared right back. When he started to rise from his chair, Bozo Number Two grabbed his arm. "Back off. We don't need trouble," he cautioned.

Begrudgingly the urban cowboy plunked back into his chair and fastened his attention on the half-empty mug in front of him.

"What are you doing here?" Andrea muttered as Hal strode along beside her.

"Protecting my interest," Hal replied.

"I can take care of myself."

Hal veered toward his table to sit down. His eyes turned as black as chunks of coal as he stared up at the independent expression on Andrea's face. "If I hear that comment one more time, I'm going to strangle you. You don't have to take that kind of crap from those creeps."

"Did you ever behave like that in a bar?" she questioned.

Hal refused to answer.

"Well, did you?"

"If I did, I deserved a beating for it," he scowled.

"You're supposed to be watching my brother," Andrea chastised him.

"Crista gave Jason therapy and I put him to bed. He's doing fine."

"He's injured," she contradicted huffily. "Now what are you doing here?"

Hal conjured up his most engaging smile, for all the good it did him. "You claimed you had never been picked up before."

Andrea gaped at him, then broke down and grinned. "So you think you can get places with me that these other clowns can't, do you, cowboy? What makes you think I'll fall for your line?"

Hal tipped his hat and sprawled in his chair. "Am I being too egotistical? Too chauvinistic?"

Andrea nodded her auburn head. "I absolutely hate that in a man."

"What do you like in a man?"

"Margaritas and roses."

"Yeah?" he said and sat up a little straighter, thoroughly enjoying this lighthearted banter. "What else, doll face?"

Andrea flashed him a sultry smile, then leaned over to retrieve his empty bottle, purposely brushing her breasts against his shoulder. "Stick around till closing time, Love Doctor, and you might be the first to find out what I like— and how I like it . . ."

Hal groaned aloud when Andrea sashayed away, her hips moving in hypnotic rhythm. Damn, that woman could be dangerous. Good thing she didn't know how lethal she was, Hal thought.

Thirty minutes later, Hal followed Andrea to her truck in the abandoned parking lot. She halted, staring at him curiously. "Where's your pickup?"

"I had Brenda drop me off on her way home."

Grinning slyly, Andrea piled into her old truck.

Hal noted her elfish grin and arched a brow. "Got a problem, Fletch?"

"No, you do," she said, as she revved the engine.

"I do?"

"Sure do," she confirmed driving away. "You didn't pick me up after all. I'm the one with the truck. My record is still clean. I've never been picked up."

"Mere technicality," Hal chuckled, giving his hand a dismissive flick.

Andrea veered down the side street, parked the truck, and flung herself into his arms. Hal burst out laughing as she wrested the buttons of his shirt open and slid her hands against his chest.

"Damn, lady, you do get all over a man, don't you?"

Her fingertip skimmed his nipples and then detoured toward the muscles of his belly. "Complaining, hot-shot cowboy?"

"Ordinarily, yes. Tonight, no," he murmured as he wrapped her in his arms.

Andrea tipped back her head, her eyes sparkling. "I've never made out in a parked truck before," she confided. "You?"

Hal kissed the tip of her nose, her cheek. "Well . . ."

Muttering, Andrea scooted beneath the steering wheel,

switched gears, and cruised off. "I've got one request of you, Griffin."

"What's that, Fletch?"

"Before you leave town, I'd like to be your *first* time at something besides hitting you with a clump of bananas."

Although her tone was light and teasing, he sensed she meant what she said. Hal studied her profile in the glow of the dashboard lights. He watched her negotiate the hilly roads that led to Fletcher Ranch, monitored the rise and fall of her breasts beneath her T-shirt.

Hal wasn't sure at what exact moment he realized Andrea Fletcher was the best of every woman he had ever known, but a strange, incomprehensible sensation rippled through him, touching every part of his being.

It must be the mystical pull of the crimson moon burning against the night sky, he told himself. That was why he was feeling so mushy inside, so hungry. He would give the world to see Andrea flash him another smile like the one she had delivered in the bar. It had been playful, yet inviting, impish yet touchingly honest.

Lord, man, get a grip! Hal ordered himself. You know damned well you're not what this little lady needs. Oh sure, you've come to her rescue in one crises after another and you've made her losses easier to bear. But you've become her anchor in a storm-tossed sea. Despite what she *thinks* she feels for you, she's going to recover from her tragedy and then she'll wake up and realize what you've been trying to tell her all along. Gratitude isn't love, passion is new and exciting. People get so caught up in each other erotically that they read more into the encounter than is actually there.

Hal had almost let himself believe Andrea did love him.

But time would test that. Time would also teach her that this was just a phase on her road to recovery. Hal had taught Andrea to want him. She had come to depend on him. Her fierce sense of honesty and loyalty demanded that where there was physical desire, there should also be love. She didn't know better yet.

He did.

"You're awfully quiet," Andrea noted.

"Just thinking," he murmured, staring out the window at the blazing crimson moon.

"I thought we agreed that sort of thing could short-circuit the male brain," she teased.

"Right," Hal chuckled. "Us dumb cowboys only know about broncs, bulls, beer, and broads."

"What's with you tonight?" she persisted. "You seem . . . different. Is something wrong?"

"Horny as hell," he said for shock value.

Andrea shook her head in amusement. "Do you have to be so blunt?"

"You're the one who got me hot and bothered when you sauntered off and left me smoldering in my corner of the bar."

"You mean my attempt at seduction was effective?"

Hal glanced ceilingward. Lord, didn't this woman have the slightest idea how wildly desirable she was, how much power she wielded over a man?

"One hundred percent," Hal murmured, studying her as she navigated the curves.

Quietly, Hal sat on his side of the truck, oddly content to study Andrea. Passion was prowling through his body, linking with his erotic fantasies. He wanted her curled up beside him in that king-size bed—warm and yielding and eager for his touch, his touch alone. He wanted to lose himself in her, to savor a few moments of blissful eternity just in case his conference with Gilmore didn't meet his optimistic expectations.

Hal had offered himself as bait because he wanted to protect Andrea. He was determined to discover who was holding the ax over her head—and why. He owed her that much for the pleasure and contentment he'd found with her.

Somehow or another, Hal vowed to leave Andrea with something she could hold onto in the years to come. Something lasting, enduring—her land, her inheritance. That would be his gift to her, he reminded himself as he surveyed her moon-drenched profile. That, he added silently, and the memories of passion so hot it could burn down both ends of the night.

Twenty

"I love you . . ."

When Andrea eased from bed to pad barefoot down the hall to her own room, Hal lay awake. Her words swirled around him, pleasing him, tormenting him. Her scent clung to him like the memory of the wild tide of passion that had engulfed them. Leaving her was going to be one of the most difficult things Hal had ever done. He hadn't meant to let her get to him, hadn't meant to become so involved in her life. Hadn't meant to care quite so much . . .

Hal forcefully cast aside his thoughts and donned his clothes. He had an appointment with Gilmore—Nash was going along for the ride in case trouble broke out.

With the silence of a shadow Hal descended the stairs. He smiled as he sidestepped the spot where the boards creaked. Funny, this house had become as familiar as his own home. And if he had anything to do with it—and he damn well intended to—this house would remain home to the Fletchers.

Once outside, Hal cut out two horses from the herd in the corral. To Nash's credit, he was a quarter of an hour early in case the rendezvous was also being monitored by that mysterious third party.

In silence, and with practiced ease that bespoke of years of handling livestock, the Griffin brothers saddled and bridled the horses. Nash and Hal had passed through the second pasture gate when headlights beamed in the distance.

"Your late-night appointment," Nash presumed as he watched the driver switch off the headlights and navigate by the light of the moon.

Hal's scalp prickled when he heard the crunch of gravel that indicated a second vehicle had arrived on the scene. The lack of light made it difficult to see the car. "Looks like we've got extra guests," he muttered. "I suggest we take Gilmore for a scenic ride along Fire River to ensure privacy."

Nash reached into the pocket of his jacket to produce the cellular phone. "Shall we call for backup? Choctaw Jim and Bernie said they would be glad to pitch in if we needed reinforcements. They're only a phone call away."

"Helluva world we live in," Hal smirked. "We can make calls on horseback these days."

"Yes or no," Nash demanded impatiently. "It'll take them over thirty minutes to make the drive."

Hal surveyed the dark shadow of the car as it tried to remain undetected by creeping down the road at a snail's pace. "Call in the troops," he decided. "We might as well wrap this up as tightly as possible tonight."

Nash punched in his home phone number and Choctaw Jim answered on the second ring. "We could use you and Bernie to block the driveway at Fletcher Ranch," he requested quietly. "You can use our farm trucks to block off the road. Better call Sheriff Featherstone before you leave home."

Hal focused on the man who skulked from the car parked beside the pasture gate. "Gilmore looks to be alone . . . unless he's got backups crouched on his floorboard. I'll swing by to pick him up while you find a hiding place beside the river.

Nash nodded as he reined away. "Don't get careless You've already got a broken arm."

Keeping the roan gelding at a walk, Hal approached Gilmore and kept his gaze on the banker's hands. If he reached toward his pocket, Hal would assume Gilmore was carrying hardware—in which case Hal would have to do some fancy footwork.

Hal halted his mount beside the banker. "Climb aboard," he ordered.

"I don't ride."

"You will tonight. I have to be sure we're alone."

Hal pulled his foot from the left stirrup to give Gilmore a foothold. Reluctantly, Gilmore swung up behind him.

"I don't think I was followed," Gilmore murmured.

Hal didn't reply. He didn't want Gilmore to know they had spotted the second vehicle. As of yet, Hal wasn't sure he could trust the banker.

With snakelike agility Hal reached behind him, his fist clamping over the pocket of Gilmore's coat.

"What the hell—?"

Hal jabbed the banker in the solar plexus with his elbow. While Gilmore gasped for breath Hal extracted the concealed pistol. "And here I thought we were pals," he scoffed sarcastically.

"I only brought the gun as a precaution," Gilmore insisted as they trotted toward the underbrush.

Hal halted the horse and then motioned for Gilmore to slide to the ground. Without looking for Nash, Hal dismounted. He knew his brother was around somewhere, standing sentinel.

"None of this was my doing," Gilmore burst out suddenly. "I swear it wasn't. I was lured in before I realized what was happening."

Hal appraised the banker's taut features and the dewy beads of sweat that clung to his forehead. He said nothing, letting his silence indicate that he expected elaboration.

"Five months ago, I got a call from a developer in the City," Gilmore rushed on. "The corporation was interested in purchasing a remote section of land to construct a resort that caters to diplomats and businessmen, a place with plenty of game for hunting and fishing. The company requested a list of potential properties. If I could come up with a lot of acreage at a cheap price, I stood to make a fortune."

Hal's dark-eyed gaze riveted on the banker, who wrung his hands nervously. "Fletcher Ranch fit the bill," Hal presumed.

Gilmore nodded. "With all the loan payments falling farther behind, the bank officers were debating about foreclosing unless Robert met his interest payments on time. I made the mistake of pushing for a foreclosure, knowing I could turn a huge profit."

Gilmore shifted, his hands balling into fists at his sides. "The corporation spokesman insisted that one of his employees be sent to monitor the situation."

"Jenna," Hal muttered disdainfully.

Hesitantly, Gilmore confirmed the speculation. "I made my second mistake by being taken in by her."

Hal could predict what was coming next. The seduction, the carefully-arranged snare that trapped the unsuspecting banker. "You're having an affair with her."

"I *was*," Gilmore corrected. "In the beginning I didn't realize she planned to use it against me, forcing me to meet the demands ordered by her employer. But when I tried to back out of the deal, she promised to broadcast the scandal all over town, humiliating my wife and family and jeopardizing my reputation at the bank."

"Got yourself in a helluva mess, didn't you?"

"Helluva mess," Gilmore repeated bitterly. "One afternoon while Jenna was badgering me to announce the foreclosure, Maggie Fletcher overheard part of our conversation. When she tore off to tell her husband, Jenna put in a hasty call of coded messages.

"I didn't know what she was up to, but the next morning I received news that Maggie's car had skidded and plunged down the embankment. I didn't think it was an accident, but I was too terrified to ask questions, too trapped by the threat of blackmail to reveal what I knew."

Hal swore under his breath. An innocent woman had died needlessly to protect this mercenary scheme.

"The corporation assumed everything would fall neatly into place after the supposed accident," Gilmore went on to say. "Robert had to sell off part of his equipment to pay for the funeral arrangements. I tried to buy time for the Fletchers, but I was ordered to call Robert to my office to tell him we were going to foreclose. He blew up, with Jenna watching from a distance. Robert set himself up for the supposed suicide. He couldn't handle losing Maggie, and whoever had been tailing him knew he was a devoted follower of his son's football career."

Hal raged silently. Robert's devotion to Maggie and his predictability had been used against him.

"When Robert turned up dead, I knew I was never going to be free of this nightmare until I delivered the land to the developer. I may never be free of Jenna's threats."

"And so your colleagues decided to discourage Andrea

and Jason from holding onto their property," Hal inserted perceptively.

Gilmore sighed audibly. "The cattle herd was frightened and scattered in an attempt to keep Andrea from making the delinquent payments. But then you showed up to get the job done and the payment arrived on time. Jenna was furious that I gave you a month to come up with the money, but I was afraid people might get suspicious and I would be scorned if I foreclosed when the family was suffering through such difficult times."

The banker peered grimly at Hal. "Now that you've made the payment, you're the one at risk. If I were you, I would check my vehicles and equipment before driving. You might find yourself involved in an accident—even launched from a bronc because of faulty gear. There's no way in hell this corporation is going to let you make that final payment. They have already proved they'll do whatever necessary to acquire the land . . . and I can't help you, because my neck is already in a noose."

Hal muttered several succinct expletives. Gilmore had been done in by greed—and by Jenna's wicked charm. She had the banker by the nuts and she knew it. If he didn't dance like a puppet, his personal and professional reputation would be in shambles.

"I don't know what to do," Gilmore whimpered in frustration. "I already have two deaths, assault, battery, and arson on my conscience."

"I need the phone number of the corporation," Hal requested. "I'd also like the names of the thugs who are providing the muscle."

With shaky hands, Gilmore retrieved his wallet and fished out a business card. "It's an unlisted number. I already checked—a little too late. If I'd known the kind of ethics this corporation practiced I would never have gotten involved. And I don't know who's responsible for the crimes against the Fletchers—that's the God's truth. I don't know where to turn, what to do . . ."

"I suggest you pack up and take an unannounced vacation," Hal advised. "But I wouldn't leave without giving Featherstone a number where you can be reached."

"I can't leave without taking the risk of being followed."

"You were followed tonight," Hal informed him.

Gilmore's face turned incandescent white in the moonlight. "Oh, God! They know!"

"You probably have Jenna to thank for that," Hal scowled. "She would have had to be blind not to notice how upset you were while I was in the bank. She probably put a tail on you."

"I still have your check," Gilmore murmured. "I was afraid to endorse it."

Hal stepped closer, looming like a mountain. "That is the one thing you damned well better do before you hightail it out of town. If I'm going to stick my neck out as bait for these hoodlums I want the Fletcher property back in the right hands. Understood?"

Gilmore nodded.

Hal climbed aboard his horse, scooting forward to give Gilmore room. "One more question," he demanded. "Were you at Jenna's apartment the night she got me over there?"

"No," he said quickly. "This is the first I've heard of it."

"You better not be lying to me, Gilmore," Hal said ominously.

"God's truth." Gilmore anchored himself to the saddle as Hal trotted off. "I was at Jenna's apartment twice too

many, but I haven't been back in three months. Jenna was
the worst mistake I ever made."

Hal smiled grimly. He remembered thinking the same
thing a decade earlier.

Lou Gresham squinted into the darkness, keeping surveillance from the side window by the back seat of the
car. "I think I see something," he murmured.

Lenny Walters leaned toward the dashboard, straining
to make out the two shadows on horseback. "Sonuvabitch.
That pussy banker must've spilled his guts to Griffin."

"That damned cowboy rode down from the house,"
Frankie Simpson scowled from the driver's seat. "I don't
like the looks of this. Call Jenna."

Kent Johns grabbed the car phone and dialed the number.
"We've got trouble," he muttered the instant Jenna answered. "Gilmore drove out to parley with Griffin. Looks
like he's running scared."

When Jenna didn't respond immediately, Kent's bushy
brows flattened. "Well? What do you want us to do?"

"I'm thinking."

"Think faster," Kent demanded. "Gilmore is returning
to his car and the cowboy is on horseback. We can't run
em both down."

"Where's Andrea Fletcher?" Jenna questioned.

"Hell if I know. At the house, I guess."

"One of you better track her down," Jenna suggested.
If things go bad, we'll need bait to make Griffin behave."

"He doesn't scare easily," Kent informed her. "We already found that out once tonight."

"He'll behave if his girlfriend's life hangs in the balance," Jenna predicted. "Go get her."

Kent eased the back door open. "I'm going after the Fletcher woman. Lou, you better come along, just in case I have trouble handling her."

"My pleasure," Lou said, grinning wickedly.

Lou wouldn't mind getting his hands on that gorgeous piece of ass again. Having her in his lap at the bar made his nuts ache. He'd like to have his fun with her a few times before they disposed of her.

Couldn't leave eyewitnesses lying around, Lou reminded himself as he scuttled up the road. This wouldn't be as easy as crying wolf and luring old man Fletcher to the edge of the ridge while Kent leaped out to shove him from behind. But this would be a damned sight more enjoyable, Lou reminded himself. Too bad that cowboy wouldn't know Lou had beat his time—the *final* time.

Following Kent's lead, Lou crouched down to waddle through the weeds in the bar ditch. A sinister smile played on his lips while he envisioned how he was going to make that haughty little waitress beg for mercy a dozen different ways.

Hal waited in the underbrush by the river, watching Gilmore blaze off in a cloud of dust, following the dead end road that became a grassy path that led through Amos Harden's pasture. To Hal's surprise, the second vehicle didn't give chase. It remained in the middle of the road.

"Now what?" Nash muttered as he urged his horse up beside Hal's. "I suppose the strong-arms will be coming after you. They probably think they can guarantee Gilmore's continued silence if you meet with a convenient accident."

Hal didn't doubt it. Gilmore was quaking in his skin

The man knew too much, had too much to lose. The banker may have told all to Hal, but that didn't mean Gilmore would admit to anything in court, especially if Hal wasn't around to make him remember what he was trying so hard to forget.

"Got a plan, little brother?" Nash prodded.

Hal surveyed the car for a moment. "Maybe we should be neighborly and greet our guests."

"Sneak attack?" Nash chuckled. "I wouldn't mind identifying those bastards. I suspect they're the ones who beat Jason black and blue. Maybe we should return the favor."

"Sounds like a hell of an idea to me."

Hal nudged his horse toward the protection of the bushes that lined the river. They could travel part way on horseback before resorting to the kind of field training Hal had perfected during his stint in the army. In fact, Hal would like to field-strip the occupants of the car before he turned the thugs over to Featherstone.

Within a matter of minutes Hal had tethered his horse in the trees. Crouching down, he slithered through the grass. Nash was right behind him, moving with the silence of a prowling wolf.

"Choctaw Jim," Hal whispered when he heard the purr of a distant motor. "Perfect timing."

Nash murmured, "Never have quite figured out how he does it. Sixth sense, I guess."

"According to Uncle Jim, it's part of our Choctaw heritage," Hal replied. "He says we'd have the knack, too, if we worked to perfect it. Something about getting in touch with the inner self."

Hal chuckled as he and his brother belly-crawled through the pasture. His attention was fixed on the nondescript black car. Moonlight glinted off the bent chrome bumper, leaving Hal to wonder if this was the vehicle that nudged Maggie Fletcher's car off the road one dark and rainy night.

Hal was pretty sure it was.

Something cold and uncompromising forced Andrea from the depths of sleep. Before she fully roused, a hand clamped over her mouth, quickly replaced by what she assumed was her pillow case.

Her heart hammered wildly as she opened her eyes to see two bulky shadows looming over her. She instantly recognized the man holding the gun to her head when he shifted sideways, bathing his sharp, angular features in the moonlight that speared through the window. It was the creep from the bar!

"If you keep your mouth shut, we won't work that little brother of yours over again," Lou Gresham hissed. "One peep out of you and he's history."

Andrea nodded.

"Smart lady," Kent murmured as he hoisted her upright.

Andrea found herself bookended by two of the pathetically dressed dudes she'd met in the bar. These men had beaten Jason to a pulp, she realized, and were surely part of the conspiracy responsible for torching the barn.

Although her natural instinct was to pull free and scream bloody murder, she didn't react. No way would she endanger her brother or Hal. Slowly, Andrea complied with the pistol that stabbed into her spine and moved silently down the hall.

* * *

Hal motioned to Nash to stay put. Like a slithering snake, Hal slid under the fence wire, then crawled through the ditch. Circling behind the car, he positioned himself so he could attack the driver while Nash made a grab for the front seat passenger. Even odds, Hal mused as he crouched. That was unusual.

Hal charged toward the car like a blazing bullet. Curses erupted from inside when he jerked open the door and grabbed a fistful of the driver's jacket, dragging him from the car while Nash launched a flank attack. Hal swung his cast in an arc, catching the cursing driver upside the head. His uplifted knee caused the man to bend in the middle and howl like a dying coyote.

On the other side of the car, the cohort howled back. Nash was using similar tactics.

Handicapped though he was, Hal managed to drive the man to his knees. A jab of his boot heel sent the driver sprawling in the gravel. Hurriedly, Hal checked for a weapon, finding a snub-nosed pistol. When he rolled the man onto his back and stuck the pistol under his chin, Hal's brows jackknifed. It was Bozo Number Four from Slim Chance Saloon!

Headlights flared in the darkness, thanks to Choctaw Jim's timing. Hal smiled to himself as the truck approached, halting directly behind the car.

"Everything under control?" Hal called to his brother.

"I'm fine, but I can't say the same for this clown in cowboy clothes."

Choctaw Jim and Bernie Bryant stepped down from their truck to appraise the situation. Bernie smirked at the shiny boots and loud shirts the tenderfeet wore.

"City boys masquerading as cowboys," Bernie smirked. "You can spot 'em a mile off."

"Where are your two buddies?" Hal growled at the swollen-faced driver.

"How should I know? It's not my job to keep up with them."

"Where's Featherstone?" Nash questioned.

"He should be here in five minutes," Choctaw Jim replied as he strode over to survey Hal's handiwork. He stared at the downed driver. "Good thing Hal only had one fist to work with. You wouldn't have any teeth left . . ."

Choctaw Jim's voice trailed off when Nash half-dragged the second man around the car, depositing him in a groaning heap. Jim's astute gaze scanned the interior of the car, noting the cellular phone in the back seat.

"Were you boys making calls while you were waiting?" Jim questioned.

"Yeah," Bozo Number Two smarted off. "I called my mama."

Hal stared at the thugs in disgust, suddenly remembering the four teenagers who had been paid to harass the Fletchers. Those four kids weren't going to turn out like these heartless bastards, he promised himself. Maybe he couldn't save every hard-luck kid from a life of crime, but he could sure as hell do something about Tony Braden and Friends. Hal made a mental note to keep tabs on the boys, just as soon as he dealt with these slimy, full-grown thugs.

A foreboding shiver skittered across Andrea's skin while she was ushered down the darkened stairway. Although her oversize T-shirt did little to ward off the evening chill, the prospect of imminent danger caused gooseflesh to pebble her skin.

Soundlessly, she was escorted through the kitchen. Her mind raced, trying to decide what to do. Now that she was downstairs she might risk making the kind of racket that would alert Hal and Jason.

Hopefully, her loud yelp would provoke her captor to hurry her away. When Hal and Jason heard her and realized something was amiss, they would be too far behind for their lives to be in jeopardy, but they could place a call for help. That was all Andrea wanted.

Andrea mentally prepared herself. The instant she stepped into the kitchen, her hand shot sideways to grab the toaster. With one fierce jerk she yanked the cord from the electric socket. Whirling, she leveled her makeshift weapon against Lou Gresham's head. He let out a roar as he stumbled back against Kent, who was behind him in the doorway.

Though her pulse was pounding like a jackhammer, Andrea aimed the toaster at the pistol, knocking it from Lou's hand. The weapon skidded across the floor as their foul cursing filled the air.

While the men were logjammed in the doorway, Andrea sprinted toward the kitchen door, hoping beyond hope to draw her captors farther away from the men sleeping upstairs. The instant before Andrea threw open the screen door, she screamed Hal's name at the top of her lungs.

"Get her," Kent snarled as he shoved Lou ahead of him. "I'll retrieve the gun."

In lumbering strides, Lou dashed after Andrea. She flew toward her old truck, hoping to lock herself inside. But to her dismay Lou leaped off the deck, slamming her into the side of the truck before her hand fastened around the latch.

"You're gonna pay for all this trouble, bitch," Lou sneered, pinning her with the weight of his bulky body.

Andrea struggled valiantly to free herself, but a painful yank on her unbound hair sent her breath hissing through her clenched teeth. Lou had wrapped the long strands around his fist—twice—holding her head at an uncomfortable angle. His brawny arm clamped around her chest as he dragged her against him, forcing her toward the passenger-side of the truck.

Trapped like a rat, Andrea thought in disgust. So much for her brilliant plan of escape.

Hal came to his feet when he heard another vehicle approaching. Dust rolled as the sheriff's car skidded in the gravel and Featherstone bounded out to survey the situation.

"Looks like I missed all the fireworks," he smirked at the city dudes. "Damn, who dressed you boys?"

Hal quickly conveyed the information he had received from Gilmore. The sheriff read Bozos Number Two and Four their rights, cuffed them, and tossed them in the patrol car.

When the sheriff drove off, Hal breathed a sigh of relief. It was short-lived. When he heard Andrea's scream and the revving engine of her old farm truck, the blood froze in his veins.

"Andrea . . ." Hal knew where the two missing men were. He had the sickening feeling the hired thugs intended to take a hostage.

"Oh, shit," Nash muttered, making a mad dash toward

the truck Jim had been driving. "We've got to block the drive—"

No sooner were the words out of his mouth than Andrea's truck lurched forward, circling the charred remains of the barn. The pickup burst through the pasture like a runaway locomotive, leaving the metal gate dangling on its hinges.

"Son of a bitch," Kent hissed when headlights flicked on in the distance. Huffing and puffing from his wild dash from the house to the truck, he tried to navigate across the rough terrain.

Andrea bucked and kicked, then quieted when Lou rammed the barrel of the pistol against her temple. Having her hair wrapped around his clenched fist kept her chin tilted toward the ceiling. In frustration, she watched Kent drive the truck Lou had quickly hot-wired.

"Damn it, hurry up," Lou muttered, glaring out the back window. "Somebody is coming up behind us. Let's take the same route through this pasture that we used when we torched the barn."

"What about Lenny and Frankie?" Kent questioned as he bounced over the bumps.

"They're on their own," Lou insisted. "Just get us the hell out of here—fast!"

Andrea's hope dimmed as the truck jostled across the pasture. Maybe she wouldn't survive this, but she knew Hal would avenge her death.

Perhaps he hadn't come to love her, but he devoted himself to the underdog. For all his gruff ways, Hal Griffin had a generous heart. He also possessed the kind of tenderness Andrea thanked God she had experienced once

in her life. He had taught her to live again, rather than
exist. He had restored her faith in mankind—some of
them at least. Present company not included. Hal was the
best thing that had ever happened to Andrea. She would
remember him always . . .

Hey, Fletch, don't give up, came that defiant little voice.
*You aren't a goner yet. Don't give up. Never give up. Never
say die!*

As the truck roared across the pasture, Andrea marshaled her resolve. She reminded herself that bouncing
over this rugged terrain could cause the occupants of the
truck to flop around like Mexican jumping beans. That
could work to her advantage. She would bide her time,
waiting for the pistol to slide away from her temple. And
then she would strike like a coiled snake.

Hopefully, the deflected bullet wouldn't have her name
on it . . .

Twenty-one

While Nash braced himself against the handholds on the passenger side of the pickup, Hal drove with an urgency that ate him alive. If Nash was concerned that his spanking new truck was being abused as Hal bounced across the rugged terrain, he never let on. He simply kept those intense golden eyes trained on the dark shadow that lumbered across the pasture, knocking gates out of the way as it went.

Adrenaline pumped through Hal at such a frantic pace that he was panting. He was afraid, he realized with a start. He was experiencing ice cold fear. He had seen it on the faces of rookie cowboys as they eased denim down on the wrinkled hides of raging bulls. He had seen it on the faces of soldiers in combat. He had even seen it on Tom Gilmore's face—twice in one day. Sheer panic threatened to divert him from his main purpose.

Hal had learned to control fear years ago, but fear for his own safety was different from this! This was a living hell. Worrying about Andrea had him paying penance for every sin he had ever committed—or even contemplated. He was contemplating several right now. He wanted to launch those two bastards in that clunker truck so deep into hell that they would never find their way out.

Hal thumbed his nose and hissed a curse. Those dan-

dified cowboys weren't going to make it off Fletcher property, not if he could prevent it. He wasn't letting them out
of sight—ever!

The overwhelming need to reach Andrea, to assure himself that she was alive and well, nearly drove Hal out of
his mind. She was probably suffering those tormenting
flashbacks from college. If one of those thugs put his
filthy paws on her . . .

That terrible thought bounced around Hal's mind as he
plunged into a deep rut, causing his hat to slam against
the top of the cab.

"You okay, Nash?" Hal questioned without taking his
eyes off the pasture.

"I feel like a milk shake," Nash muttered, tightening
his grasp on the handhold above the door. "When we catch
up with those sons-a-bitches don't do anything crazy."

"Right, like you didn't go berserk when Crista's life
was threatened," Hal countered.

Nash shut his mouth, knowing Hal was right. The Griffin brothers tended to go a little crazy when those they
loved were at risk.

Andrea stared at the tall grasses waving in front of her.
Her captors didn't know where they were going, but she
had crossed this section of pasture a hundred times. She
knew exactly where the ditch that led into a deep ravine
during heavy rains was located. She also knew it was going to be her prime avenue of escape.

If she wasn't mistaken, Hal was right behind her, his
headlights flaring inside the cab—constantly reminding
her captors that he was giving chase. Andrea was taking
no chances with Hal's life. She loved him too dearly

have him caught in a crossfire. She had lost practically everyone else and she refused to lose Hal!

Andrea forced herself not to tense up as the truck sped toward yet another pasture gate. She refused to give the slightest indication that she was coiling to pounce. Just a few more seconds and the truck would nose-dive into the unseen trench, bucking like a wild bronc. At that precise moment, she would attempt to escape.

Kent cursed foully when the steering wheel spun out of his hands. Andrea's arm shot upward as the truck went airborne a second time. She heard the pistol clank against the back window as she sprawled across Lou's lap, making a desperate grab for the door latch.

The impact of the truck slamming into the deep ditch caused Lou's head to whiplash into the dashboard. Andrea jerked on the latch and the door creaked open. Bracing her bare feet against Kent's hip, she lunged through her escape hatch, pushing against the weight of the limp body doubled over her.

The truck strained and groaned as its back wheels spun up a shower of mud and grass. Andrea performed a semblance of a somersault in her haste to escape. She was on her feet in a single bound, running as fast as her legs would carry her, ignoring the sharp stabs of the brittle grass beneath her feet.

"Stop her!" Kent snarled. "Damn it, she can identify us!"

Lou didn't reply. His head had smacked against the windshield, knocking him unconscious.

Frantic, Kent ground the engine, only to find the truck sinking deeper into the mud. He grabbed for the door latch, clawing his way out of the immobilized truck. He glanced over his shoulder, seeing the headlights bearing

down on him. Kent leaped into the ditch, knowing th
other pickup couldn't follow without getting stuck. He ra
as if the demons of hell were in hot pursuit, cursing th
fact that his pistol had slipped from his pocket during th
rough ride, or during the crash landing—he didn't know
which.

Hal's heart leaped when he saw Andrea flapping he
arms to gain his attention. He stamped on the brake
thankful she was in one piece, even if she had taken
terrible risk by rolling from the truck. At least now Ha
could breathe normally again . . .

Then he spotted the straw cowboy hat floating abov
the rim of the ditch like a headless specter. A killing fur
thrummed through him as he bounded from the truck. N
way in hell was Hal going to let that bastard escape o
the waterway to Fire River! He was going to pay dearl
for scaring Hal half to death!

"Hal!" Nash muttered an oath when he saw Hal rac
along the rim of the ditch.

Hurriedly, Nash checked on the man still sprawled hal
in, half out of the old farm truck. Blood seeped from th
cuts and gashes on Lou's forehead and cheeks as he la
senseless.

Nash glanced sideways, watching Andrea's breast
heave beneath her long T-shirt. Her gaze was fixed o
Hal, who was skirting the ditch, waiting for the right mo
ment to pounce.

"Confound it, Nash," Andrea sputtered. "Stop that hare
brained brother of yours before he gets himself shot! I wen
to considerable trouble to make sure Hal stayed in on
piece, and now look at him!"

Nash bit back a grin as his gaze settled on Hal's fleeting silhouette. Andrea's comment pretty much summed up her feelings—she had endangered her own life to protect Hal from harm.

Quite a lady, Nash mused. Just exactly what a man like Hal needed—once he had come to his senses and quit being such a coward when it came to love and commitment. Hal had been battling a decade of hard lessons and hangups. Jenna had made an absolute fool of him, slashing his pride to shreds.

But Andrea was nothing like Jenna. How could Hal not trust a woman who had laid her own life on the line to spare him?

"Well, damn it!" Andrea spouted off, glaring at Nash. "Do something!"

Nash did something, all right. He scooped Andrea up in his arms and deposited her on the seat of his pickup. "And stay there," he commanded brusquely. "You've done quite enough for one evening."

"Are you going to help your brother or not?" Andrea muttered as Nash circled the truck. "What kind of brother are you, anyway, to let him tear off with his arm in a cast without offering help!"

Nash halted in his tracks, his gaze locking with hers. "I'm *going*," he assured her.

"Not fast enough to suit me. If you don't hurry up, I'm going to have to do something myself!"

When Andrea hopped down, Nash flung up his hand. "Do you know what *stay put* means?"

"Do you know what *hurry up* means?" she shouted back.

Nash wheeled around to follow in his brother's wake,

grinning past the dressing-down he had received from An
drea. "A real spitfire," he mused aloud.

Andrea's spirit and gumption reminded him of Crista
Two of a kind, Nash mused as he charged off. Actually
he doubted that his brother needed an extra hand. Even
with a broken arm, Hal's bottled-up outrage would sustain
him. Nash predicted he would be nothing more than a
spectator in this foot race. Kent Johns had never seen Ha
Griffin furious. Nash had. The thug was about to receive
the full benefit of Hal's anger—firsthand and first*fist*.

Hal monitored Kent's flight through the ditch tha
plunged into a ten-foot ravine. Before Kent could lose
himself in the spiny fingers of brush-choked waterways
Hal launched himself off the ledge. Kent yelped when he
went down beneath Hal's considerable weight.

Kent tried to scrabble to his feet, but Hal rained blows
against his head, sending his straw hat cartwheeling in the
mud.

Pounding Kent flat was just what Hal needed to release
his pent-up fury. This man was taking the brunt for dis
posing of Maggie and Robert Fletcher in the name o
greed. Kent and his cohorts were nothing more than hired
murderers—no consciences, no respect for human life
other than their own. Kent was responsible for Andrea
and Jason's suffering, and Hal was holding the bastard
accountable. This creep may have his day in court, but he
was getting the hell beat out of him—here and now.

Snarling, Hal kicked Kent to his back and plopped
down on his barrel-shaped belly. One-handed, Hal trans
formed Kent's plain features into a punching bag. When
Kent flung up an arm to deflect the blows, Hal resorted

to the tactic wild broncs were famous for—he bit the bastard good and hard. Hal wasn't beneath dirty tricks, not when he was consumed by rage.

When Kent screeched and drew back his bitten hand, Hal stuffed his fist in the man's open mouth. His knuckle slammed into teeth, causing Kent to splutter in pain. When he reached back to deliver another blow, an unseen hand clamped around his wrist. Swearing, he swiveled his head to see Nash behind him.

"That's enough. If you beat the son of a bitch to death, you'll be stooping to his level."

"Maybe," Hal muttered, barely restrained. "But it will save the state from housing this worthless bastard at taxpayers' expense. I'm for cutting expenses." He tried to shake Nash loose—but to no avail.

Stalemate. Hal and Nash were equally matched in strength—and determination.

"Why don't you go check on Andrea while I haul this slimebag back to the truck. She's worried sick that you're going to hurt yourself worse than you already are. She needs to know you're okay. That courageous little lady risked death to keep us from harm's way while we were trying to save her."

The comment was meant to cool Hal down, but it had the reverse effect. He bolted to his feet, glaring in the direction he had come. "That woman could have gotten herself run over by that truck," he scowled. "She was trying to protect us? Is she nuts?"

Nash swallowed a grin while he watched Hal's chest rise like bread dough. "Crazy as hell," Nash readily confirmed. "Daring as a bullfighter, brave as a bank robber, not to mention defiant as a—"

"Shut up," Hal muttered, stalking away.

Fuming, Hal stamped through the ditch. He climbed the steep incline and nearly stumbled back down when Andrea flew into his arms.

"Are you okay?" she demanded, hugging him hard.

Hal pulled her arms loose and gave her a sound shaking. "No, I'm not okay," he snapped, black eyes glittering with fear and fury. "I told you more than a month ago not to try any more stunts. But did you listen?

"Hell, no," he blared, answering his own question. "First it was the cattle stampede, then the flood, then a dash into a burning barn to rescue the livestock. And now this!"

Hal's voice hit such a loud pitch that the cicadas in the surrounding trees screeched in chorus. Nesting birds abandoned their perches to circle overhead.

Chest heaving, Hal's ruthless gaze bore down on Andrea. "I've busted my ass for weeks, helping you out of the scrapes you get into. I even canceled a rodeo competition and deprived other cowboys of riding my horses just so I could come back here and watch over you and Jason. I alerted the sheriff. I even brought you roses, for God's sake!"

Andrea's brows furrowed, unclear as to what a dozen roses had to do with anything. Hell, Hal didn't know, either. All he knew was that he had to do whatever was necessary to break this daredevil female's habit of scaring the living daylights out of him—time after goddamn time!

Then Hal remembered the pistols he had confiscated from the other bozos in the car. The thought ignited his temper like a NASA rocket. "I don't suppose those bastards held a gun to your head while they were abducting you, did they?"

"Well . . ." Andrea stammered.

"Damn it, Fletcher!" he bellowed.

"Hal, the idea wasn't to take Andrea's head off, but rather to——"

Nash, who had come up behind his brother, wasn't allowed to finish his sentence. Before Nash could dump Kent's limp body beside Lou's, Hal rounded on him.

"*You* take her back to the house," Hal demanded. "I refuse to stand here arguing with an idiot!"

"Why? Afraid I won't be able to tell which is which?" Nash smirked.

Hal snarled something foul, stormed toward the old truck that was stuck in mud, and then climbed inside. Those citified dudes may not have known how to unstick a stuck truck, but Hal had done it a hundred times. He shoved the gear into reverse. Wheels spun. Rubber burned. Then he slammed the gear into drive, rocking back and forth until the tires gained enough traction to propel the truck forward. Wobbling, the truck lurched upward, fishtailing up the embankment to sit idling on level ground.

One-armed, Hal dragged Lou and Kent onto the pickup bed. "I'm going to haul these thugs to Sheriff Featherstone's office and then I intend to track Jenna down before she skips town—if she hasn't already."

Without a second glance, Hal sped off in the old farm truck. Nash shook his dark head in dismay. Surely he hadn't behaved this badly when he found himself deeply involved with Crista.

Although Nash had tried to lay all the problems he and Hal were having with Levi Cooper at Crista's feet, he had finally accepted his feelings. To this day, Nash still cringed at the thought of how unjustly he had hurt the only woman he had ever loved. Nash wondered if Hal realized he was doing the same thing. Probably not. A man in love could be pretty damn dense sometimes.

Hal was striking out at the invisible chains that held him captive. He was taking it out on Andrea—the last person on earth who deserved it.

Nash's thoughts trailed off when he noticed the shiny tears in Andrea's eyes. Her gaze followed Hal's speeding retreat across the pasture and her shoulders sagged noticeably.

"He won't be back," she whispered. "He found an excuse to end it." She sighed deeply and wrapped her arms around herself to ward off the chill settling into her soul. "Tell him I'm grateful for everything he's done." Her gaze swung to Nash, tormented, heartbroken. "Tell him I— Tell him thank you."

Nash swore under his breath as he watched Andrea walk gingerly toward the passenger side of his pickup. Poor kid, he thought. Riding high on fear and adrenaline, Hal had teed off on Andrea. Ten to one, Nash's block-headed brother didn't even know why he was so determined to make a clean break from Fletcher Ranch.

Nash was tempted to interfere, to put in his two cents' worth again. But he knew Hal had to wade through his tangled emotions himself. Nash could only hope Hal would realize what he stood to lose, what that hot flash of temper could cost him. Andrea was the best thing Hal had going, but the idiot refused to acknowledge that.

Nash listened to Andrea come down from her own adrenaline high. The desperation and tension that had sustained her for the past hour crashed like a rock slide. In between gut-wrenching sobs, she apologized for snapping at Nash, for collapsing in tears.

Nash cursed his brother soundly for refusing to stick

around, for leaving him to comfort Andrea. He had made all the right noises about how everything was going to be fine, but she wasn't buying it.

Nash couldn't give Andrea what she needed. His arms were the wrong ones. His voice didn't have the same soothing effect.

Put quite simply, Nash was the wrong Griffin brother.

When Nash stopped at the house, Andrea bolted out. He shook his head in dismay as he put the truck in reverse. Then he saw Jim and Bernie mending the gates that had been broken during the high-speed chase and decided to lend a hand.

At least some of his skills could be put to good use.

Hal jerked his freshly cleaned shirts from the hangers and shoved them into his duffel bag. He had been mad as hell when he left Fletcher Ranch the previous night. He was even madder now. By the time he dumped Kent and Lou off for incarceration and drove back to Hochukbi, Jenna had packed up and hightailed it out of town. He presumed she had been tipped off.

Hal hoped the sheriff's APB turned up that missing bitch—soon. He cursed the thought of Jenna running around scot free, setting up more scams that could tear families apart.

As for the ruthless developer who ramrodded this scheme, Featherstone had finally come up with the name of Jim Carlson and turned all the information over to the FBI. There was a warrant for Carlson's arrest, but the man had become as difficult to find as Jenna.

Justice, Hal thought disparagingly. Justice was an idealistic philosophy that served criminals better than victims . . .

Hal felt a familiar presence at the bedroom door. He jerked up his head to see Nash propped against the wall—a favorite habit of his.

"Are you sure you're ready to get back on the suicide circuit?" Nash inquired. "Casper, Wyoming boasts the best rough stock and competitors. All the big names will be there."

"Sounds like the place to be, doesn't it?" Hal said as he crammed his jeans into the bag.

"Choctaw Jim refuses to go with you," Nash reported. "He says he doesn't want to be there when you crash-land on your broken arm. He says it's too soon to compete."

"Fine." Hal wedged his spurs into the bulging bag and then zipped it shut. "I'll find some company. The hot spots in Casper are filled with friendly faces. So is the arena."

"She said to say thank you," Nash blurted out of the blue.

Hal froze momentarily, then he abruptly slung the bag over his shoulder.

"You came down too hard on Andrea," Nash said firmly.

Black-diamond eyes clashed with glittering amber. "I had to make a lasting impression," Hal retorted in his own defense. "Every damn time I close my eyes I see her lying in the grass, her head blown off, tire tracks across her midsection. I did my best to make my point with that female. Next time she gets into trouble maybe she'll remember our discussion and take the safe way out—for a change!"

As Hal made his way past his brother, Nash smiled dryly. "I hope somewhere between here and Wyoming it dawns on you that it's not so much *her* daring that upset you, but rather the effect it had on *you,* little brother. There's a big difference."

Hal snarled a farewell and stalked off. He was anxious to be going down the road again, eager to cure the overwhelming restlessness that hounded him. He had to get away, had to find some place to vent his frustration. He needed a familiar routine. All his perspectives were bent out of shape. The hustle of rodeo would restore his outlook on life. It always had. He had come to depend on rodeo—especially now.

With undue haste, Hal loaded the horses in the trailer. He threw a few curses at Bowlegs in the process. If that damn horse didn't learn to step into the trailer without making a big production of it, Hal was tempted to use the cattle prod on that contrary animal's butt!

Fifteen minutes later Hal drove away from Chulosa Ranch, pointing the stock rig north. He had endless hours to prepare himself mentally for the upcoming competition. He also had a bag of protective gear to take the pressure off his mending arm and tender ribs.

At least the ribs were healing nicely, Hal thought optimistically. Plenty of wranglers rode with broken arms and strained muscles. No big deal. Injury was part of the game.

Physical challenges, his mind whispered. *Is that all you need from life?* Hal scowled as he set the cruise control. He zoomed up the interstate, staring north toward Kansas. He was through playing Good Samaritan. Andrea Fletcher was on her own from now on. When Hal got edgy for the things a woman could provide, he would find an agreeable, uncomplicated female to take the edge off, just as he had in the past.

Simple as that. As of right now, he'd never have to care

what happened to the women who came and went from his life. He wouldn't have to get involved, wouldn't give so much that he left pieces of himself scattered behind him like an unfinished jigsaw puzzle. No ties, only the challenges of a road leading to the National Finals in Las Vegas.

He wanted to claim his title, to match his brother's feat from five years past. He wanted that satisfaction—and the cash prize that would give Andrea the stability to take full command of her ranch. Then he would be free and clear of her, of those orchid eyes that had mistaken charity for love. He would have paid his dues for taking Andrea's innocence.

One of these days Andrea was going to wake up to what he had been telling her all along. She was grateful for what he'd done to put her life back together. She had offered herself to him, trying to repay him with passion—and called it love. But once Hal was gone, Andrea would make her own way with her usual determination. She would come to understand—at last—that he wasn't what she really wanted, needed, and deserved.

And I don't need or deserve her, either, Hal reminded himself—in Kansas, and then again in Nebraska. *Rodeo takes me where I need to go, feeds the restlessness in my soul. There's another bronc waiting to be ridden to the buzzer, another calf to rope and tie in record time.*

Hal had what mankind coveted since the beginning of time—unlimited freedom. Hal Griffin had everything a man needed . . . and he would be damned if he'd hang around, waiting for Andrea to realize that what she felt for him wasn't everlasting love . . .

That was the gist of the problem, wasn't it? Hal asked himself as he drove into Nebraska. He was . . . *afraid* An drea was going to wake up and realize her knight in shining spurs wasn't her Prince Charming after all.

Hal had learned—the hard way—how it felt to be rejected, to know he didn't have what it took to hold a woman's interest. He was too blunt and straightforward, too set in his ways, too much the product of a hard life.

He was *not,* Hal admitted, one of those thoroughly modern males of the 90's. He was a throwback to the Old West, and maybe even to the Neanderthal days—if anybody wanted to get technical about it.

Andrea was seven years his junior—seven light-years away. She hadn't been around the block. She'd been out of circulation, isolated from men. She had shared passion with only one man—him. Once the impact wore off, Andrea would feel obligated to Hal because he had saved her life, her heritage.

He couldn't tolerate the thought of Andrea remaining by his side because of gratitude, or a kind of hero worship. He didn't want to look into those beautiful eyes after the infatuation died. He couldn't bear the thought. He had been hurt badly a decade ago, but it would be even worse now. He couldn't have a permanent relationship with Andrea . . . because he would give his scarred heart away and eventually lose the one woman he cared deeply about. The thought of loving and losing again made a damned *coward* out of him!

Preservation instinct urged Hal to get the hell out while the getting was good!

Twenty-two

Andrea was fit to be roped, tied, and thrown for the count! She had taken the money she had saved from working two jobs, the compensation for the loss of the barn and its contents, and had driven to the bank. To her outraged disbelief, Tom Gilmore—back from his unplanned vacation—informed her that Hal had paid the balance two weeks earlier—didn't she know?

Damn that pigheaded thundercloud of a man! Andrea fumed as she stamped back to her truck. Hal had turned her into one of the highest paid hookers of the century. How dare he do that to her! How dare he reduce her affection for him to a mathematical equivalent and then leave the state of Oklahoma without so much as a goodbye—or even a good riddance!

Andrea had torn up his first check and mailed it back in pieces. Then Hal had gone behind her back to pay her loan. That miserable sneak. He couldn't return her love so he had paid her off. To accept his charity would be admitting that she was after his money, that she *had* become his temporary prostitute, that he was only killing time with her between rodeos. Well, he wasn't going to destroy her precious memories by putting a price tag on them. She wouldn't stand for it!

Andrea was still smoldering when she returned to the

ranch. To her surprise, the old farm truck from Chulosa Ranch had rolled to a stop in her driveway—a few seconds ahead of her. Choctaw Jim's record for perfect timing was still intact.

A sense of panic streamed through Andrea as she approached the older man. Andrea swallowed hard, noting he was alone. So where was that block-headed cowboy she had fallen in love with? Sprawled in some hospital bed somewhere, recovering from another injury?

"Is he okay?" Andrea blurted out without preamble.

Choctaw Jim smiled his enigmatic smile. "If you're asking if he's still in one piece, the answer is yes."

Andrea's rigid shoulders slumped. "That's a relief."

"No, it's a concern," Jim contradicted, studying Andrea pensively. "He's pushing himself on the suicide circuit, entering events that he doesn't even need to keep his ranking. I was hoping I could impose on you to talk some sense into him."

"It's hard to talk to a stone wall," Andrea muttered. "I told Hal not to pay off my loan and he did it anyway, so you can see how much influence I have over that stiff-necked, rock-brained billygoat."

Choctaw Jim's onyx eyes twinkled, his lips twitched. Andrea peered at the man whose Native American heritage was vividly evident in his bronzed features. She wondered what amusing thought Jim was refusing to share.

Jim reached into the pocket of his denim shirt to extract an airline ticket. "Make an impression on him, demand his attention," Jim requested. "No one in the family wields the kind of power you do over him."

"I have no control whatsoever," Andrea repeated, head downcast, fighting the infuriating tears that had become her constant companion since Hal walked out of her life without a word.

"You're mistaken, Andrea." Those coal-black eyes—so like Hal's—transfixed her, hypnotized her, called to her in some strange, mystical language she couldn't explain. "Prove to Hal that he *is* worthy, that you will be there for him tomorrow and the year after tomorrow. *That's* what he's afraid to believe in. That and the fact that he's sure you're too good for a hard-living cowboy. He's his own worst critic, you know."

Andrea stared at the tickets Jim had placed in her hand. "But my brother's ballgame is tonight in the City. I promised—"

"I know," Jim cut in. "Bernie, Nash, Crista, and I will all be there rooting for Jason. The red-eye to Houston will get you there in plenty of time for this weekend's rodeo.

"If you recall, Hal dropped what he was doing in Montana and came back here when you and Jason needed him." A wide grin spread across Jim's leathery features. "The time has come for you to go to Hal, to let him know how much you care. Go dressed fit to kill," he added with a wink.

"Why?"

"Why not?" he parried. "Is there a better way to get a stubborn, mule-headed man's attention before you sit him down and tell him what's what?"

With that provocative statement, Choctaw Jim started the engine and backed out of the driveway. Andrea stared after him. *Get the man's attention?* She had spent years *avoiding* male attention. And then along came Hal Griffin. He had taught her to trust, to love with all her heart.

Pensively, Andrea wandered into the house, replaying

dozens of conversations she'd had with Hal, remembering his comments.

An impish smile pursed her lips . . . and then she laughed aloud. For the first time in two weeks she felt the whisper of regenerated spirit breathing in her soul.

By damn, she would show Hal Griffin a thing—or three. She would make him sit up and take note, then she'd shake some sense into him.

Afraid Andrea wouldn't be there for him when he needed her? Afraid she wouldn't be there *forever*—if he'd let her? All Andrea Fletcher needed—and wanted—was to be asked!

Hal muttered at the knock at the door of his room at Cloud Nine Motel. He had already shooed away one aggressive female who had stuffed a note in the front pocket of his jeans, after his successful evening go-rounds at the rodeo. He needed time off. No more wild after-hour parties, no more late-night drinking until he couldn't see straight. His bones and muscles ached, and sprawling on the double bed had become his idea of heaven on earth.

For the past two weeks Hal had kept a grueling pace. He'd entered as many events as time permitted, hoping to plot out his haunting memories. He had even entered team roping with Rooster Anderson for the extra money.

From Casper to Omaha and then to Houston, Hal had burned up the roads—and the arenas—with top times and scores. Relentless determination and the luck of the draw had made him number one in the standings—and kept him there.

But his success hadn't stopped the empty gnawing deep

inside him. Without Choctaw Jim and his philosophical hogwash, there wasn't enough enjoyment on the road.

Wearily, Hal ambled to the door. The big, bulky bull-dogger from South Dakota barreled inside without an invitation. Rooster Anderson had a pint of whiskey in one meaty fist and a redhead on his arm. Ace Ketcham sauntered in behind Rooster, toting another pint of liquor and a blank-faced brunette whose bust measurements equaled her IQ.

Hal took one look at the unescorted female who brought up the rear of the procession and swore. His so-called buddies had been fixing him up for two solid weeks. Their latest offering looked as cheap and tacky as the others Hal had rejected that evening.

"Say hello to Heidi," Rooster introduced, hitching his thumb over his bull-wide shoulders. "She saw you ride broncs tonight and wanted to meet you in person."

Hal watched the platinum blonde's face light up with an inviting smile, watched her gaze flood over him until it lingered on the crotch of his jeans. Rooster and Ace—and their brides for the night—made themselves at home on Hal's double bed. Muttering, Hal swallowed a gulp of beer, then plunked down on the nearest chair.

When Heidi Whoever braced her arms on the table and leaned toward Hal, he was granted an unhindered view of her silicon cleavage. He noted the tattoo on her left breast. He didn't bother to ask how many other tattoos were concealed beneath her painted-on clothes.

He didn't really care to know.

"Wanna go over to my place, stud?" Heidi questioned, flashing a provocative smile. "It's kinda crowded here."

When Rooster half-sprawled on top of his date and Ace followed suit, Hal slammed his bottle on the table. Bee erupted in foaming belches. "That's it! Everybody out," he ordered gruffly.

Rooster rolled to his back, gaping at his long-time friend. "What's with you, Griff? You've helped close down the bars for weeks . . . and that's *all* you've done," he added with a meaningful glance.

"A man needs some rest occasionally," Hal scowled, gesturing toward the door, silently ordering his friends to make themselves scarce.

Ace stared at Hal's thunderous frown. "You're serious," he realized and said so.

"Hell yes, I'm serious. Take a hike," Hal demanded. "I'd like to be well rested before I climb on Down and Dirty tomorrow. That bronc has been a holy terror the past month."

"Since when do you need rest?" Rooster smirked, propping himself upright. "You can ride and lasso in your sleep."

"Out!" Hal demanded.

Reluctantly, Rooster and Ace gathered their feet beneath them and swaggered toward the door, leading their lady friends behind them. When Heidi smiled triumphantly, Hal added, "Take her home, Rooster."

The busty blonde's face fell, nearly cracking her thick makeup. "Of all the rude, obnoxious—"

Hal swooped down to whisk her out of her chair and shovel her out the door. Before Heidi could finish venting her irritation, Hal slammed the door. That was as tactful and diplomatic as he intended to get. He wanted privacy—now.

Grumbling at his inability to work up any enthusiasm for a woman, Hal switched off the lights and shed his clothes. What the devil was the matter with him? He had vowed to return to his usual routine on the circuit, riding broncs by day and taking care of his needs when the mood struck at night.

The mood hadn't struck, not even once. Hal wasn't enjoying himself; not the way he had in the old days. Though he had sawed the plaster cast off his arm the previous weekend, and his ribs weren't causing him the least bit of pain, his skin didn't seem to fit him right these days. What could a cowboy possibly want besides high scores, hefty winnings, devoted friends, and an occasional hop in the sack with a well-stacked female?

Pulling the extra pillow over his head, Hal willed himself to sleep. He planned to be rested and focused for the final go-rounds in Houston. When this rodeo was over he would head home for his brother's wedding. Then he'd be back on the road again. California maybe. Or New Mexico, if he felt so inclined.

When he reached Glitter Gulch for National Finals in December he would have the chance to cinch several world titles. Just a few decent rides on good mounts, Hal thought to himself. That was all he wanted and needed.

On that thought, Hal counted a few flocks of sheep in hopes of falling asleep.

He did fall asleep—ten thousand sheep later.

With the roar of the crowd echoing in his ears, Hal strode toward the locker room beneath the grandstands to stow his gear. A decent night's sleep had given him the edge. He was leading the bareback bronc competition, the saddle bronc competition, and he held down second in the calf roping. The bull he had drawn in the last go-round ha provided one helluva ride, launching Hal into first place with a score of eighty-nine.

Rooster Anderson, who obviously hadn't spent his time in bed—sleeping—had scratched with a misthrown loop while heading the calf the twosome had drawn in team roping. Without posting a score, Hal and Rooster were lucky to pick up their meager prize money. If Ace and the Montana Kid hadn't scratched, too, there would have been no purse at all.

Hal was finished for the evening, except for feeding and watering the horses that he and the other cowboys were using for the timed events. Aimlessly, he wandered to the beer stand to wet his whistle. Several cowboys had bellied up to the counter, rating the women as they strutted past in their skin-tight western attire.

"Seven," Rooster crowed, waggling his bushy eyebrows as his gaze followed the pair of tight red jeans and skimpy halter top that wiggled past.

"Here comes an eight if I ever saw one," Ace insisted before swallowing a swig of beer.

Hal cast the approaching groupie a disinterested glance. He could imagine how Andrea Fletcher would have reacted to being rated on the cowboy scoreboard. She made a habit of dressing *down* to discourage men.

"Hot damn," Justin Simms purred when the next contestant approached.

Hal sipped his longneck and studied the Coors sign on the wall behind the bartender.

"Sha-zam!" Rooster squawked. "Here comes a ten. Be still my pounding heart. I think I'm in love at first sight!"

Two rawboned, long-legged Texas cowboys leaning against the counter spun around to scope out the newest contestant. "Ten, hell!" Rocky Fisher hooted. "That's definitely a twelve."

"We don't give twelves," Ace Ketcham reminded the lanky wrangler. Then he turned to see who had drawn so much attention. "Whoa, that sexy walk is worth five points all by itself. That is one fine piece of USDA prime-cut female. Give the little lady a fifteen and you're still underrating her."

Hal tipped the beer bottle to his lips, glancing out of the corner of his eye to study the latest arrival. He choked for breath. Beer dribbled down the front of his striped shirt.

"Judas Priest!" he chirped, spinning to meet the woman who had become the center of attention.

The bottle slid from Hal's paralyzed fingers and plunked on the dirt, gurgling around his boots. He stood there with his lower jaw scraping his chest, his goggle-eyed gaze sweeping from the tiptop of a black Stetson to the toes of shiny red boots.

"Contest over," Rooster clucked, all eyes and a mouth watering grin. "This rodeo angel is all mine. Stand aside and eat your hearts out." With a dramatic flair, Rooster elbowed his way to the head of the crowd. His chest inflated to gigantic proportions as he prepared to strut his stuff. "Ole Rooster will be cock-a-doodle-doing all night."

Hal blinked twice, unsure he could trust his eyes. But there wasn't a damn thing wrong with his vision. That was no mirage sauntering toward the beer stand. It was Andrea Fletcher—in the flesh. She looked like a rodeo fashion plate in her skin-tight western garb. A long braid of auburn hair flowed down over her shoulder and curled over the fullness of her breast. The blouse, cut to a sharp

"V" at the bodice, displayed just enough cleavage to leave men drooling for a closer gander.

And those black denim jeans!

Hal struggled to draw breath—but couldn't.

The denim hugged Andrea's curvaceous hips like a lover's caress. A meticulously applied coat of mascara enhanced her long lashes, calling attention to those extraordinary eyes.

She had every hot-blooded cowboy panting for breath, damn her gorgeous hide! A dozen pairs of hungry eyes devoured her as she paraded toward them, her hips moving in mesmerizing rhythm.

Rooster, who didn't have a timid bone in his brawny body, surged forward to demand Andrea's attention. "Tonight's your lucky night, honey," he cooed in his most seductive tone and flashed his brightest smile. "I'm all yours."

To Hal's utter astonishment, Andrea sashayed up to Rooster and walked her fingertips up the pearl snaps of his shirt. Wolf whistles erupted all around the beer stand. Everyone within seeing distance had focused on Andrea.

Hal gnashed his teeth so hard he practically ground off the enamel.

"You missed your loop in the team roping, cowboy," Andrea reminded Rooster in a soft, sultry voice. "Look me up when you can catch what you aim at."

Laughter overrode the sound of applause from the grandstands above them.

Rooster's chest sagged in disappointment as Andrea sashayed past him, pausing in front of one hopeful cowboy and then another, flashing each man a knock-'em-dead smile. She boldly sized up each cowboy as he devoured her with lusty eyes.

Hal wanted to strangle her. Never in all his years on the circuit had he felt the urge to toss a saddle blanket over a woman and drag her away from the men he considered his closest friends. Possessiveness engulfed him— and jealous outrage wasn't far behind.

"Can I buy you a beer?" The Montana Kid questioned, breaking into a boyish grin that had stolen many a feminine heart.

Andrea turned her head ever so slightly, causing the auburn braid to glide over the tip of her breast, catching every man's attention—again. "I only drink margaritas."

For the first time since she made her spectacular entrance she glanced directly at Hal. "How about you, sugar?" she asked in a honey-coated voice. "Are you a beer or margarita man?"

"Don't waste your time on Griff," Rooster broke in "He's practically turned into a monk the past two weeks No damned fun to be around a-tall. Boring, in fact."

Andrea lifted a perfectly arched brow. "Really? Con verting a would-be monk sounds like my kind of chal lenge."

Another round of howls filled the air. Hal stood ther smoldering in his boots. He was definitely going to stran gle Andrea for flaunting herself in front of this rowd crowd.

When she sauntered closer, her body brushing provoca tively against his, the crowd went wild.

Hal flipped his lid.

"That's enough!" he growled into her grin.

"What's a-matter, sugar?" she purred seductively. "D that big, bad buckin' bronc kick holes in your dispos tion?"

"You're really asking for it," Hal gritted out between clenched teeth.

"But I'm not getting it, am I?" she countered saucily.

Laughter erupted. That did it! Hal snaked his arm around Andrea's waist and half-dragged her toward his pickup. The cowboys hooted in amusement, tossing their usual comments after them.

"What the hell do you think you're doing?" he blared.

"Is this any way to talk to an old friend?" Andrea asked innocently.

"What are you doing in Texas?"

"I came to see you, of course."

"In that get-up?" he scoffed. "Sure you aren't here to incite a riot?"

"You don't like my outfit?" Andrea asked sweetly.

Hal stopped short, staring pointedly at the clinging fabric that cupped itself around her full breasts. He glowered at her tight black jeans, positively certain he could detect the imprint of George Washington's head on the quarter in her front pocket. "You may as well not be wearing a damned thing," he muttered at her. "Everything is pretty clearly defined in that outfit. The cowboys rated you a fifteen, for crissake. Nobody else gets a fifteen!"

Andrea grinned at him. "Yeah? I wonder what I would rate if they got a peek at this underwear?"

"You mean there's room for something else under those painted-on clothes?" Hal snorted, hauling her to his truck.

Andrea's hands went to the top button of her blouse. "Sure is—wanna see?"

"Not here!" Hal snapped. He stilled her hands and glanced around to make sure no one had seen what she was doing.

And who *wasn't* watching! He and Andrea may as well

have been standing on center stage at a Broadway show. The cowboys at the beer stand were monitoring every step of their movement through the parking lot.

Hal whipped open the passenger door and deposited Andrea inside. "I have to pick up my gear," he informed her curtly. "Try to stay out of trouble until I get back."

"I'll come with you—"

"Oh, no, you won't," Hal broke in. "With that walk and in those jeans, you'll have every cowboy at the fairgrounds panting after you. Lock the damned doors." With that terse command, he spun around and stormed off.

In a matter of minutes, Hal returned from the locker room to find a congregation of cowboys clustered around his pickup. He had to bodily remove the Montana Kid in order to slide beneath his own steering wheel. Justin Simms was trying to set up a date for the following evening.

When Hal explicitly—and succinctly—told Justin where he could stash his proposition, Rooster cackled in amusement. "You're getting awfully possessive in your old age, Griff."

"She happens to be—" Hal clammed up and switched on the ignition.

"Hot is what she happens to be," Ace Ketcham supplied. *"Too* hot for you to handle, pal."

Hal thrust the truck into gear, forcing the cluster of cowboys to back off. Without a word, he drove toward the cheap motel four blocks from the outdoor arena.

"Cloud Nine Motel?" Andrea snickered.

Hal whipped into a parking place. Without bothering to assist Andrea from the truck, he stalked to his room. When she sauntered inside, he slammed the door—good and hard.

"What the hell is going on? What was that stunt su

posed to prove?" he demanded, sticking his snarling face in hers.

Andrea struck a pose on the bed that would have done Cleopatra proud. Hal clenched his fists at his sides when a wave of desire hit him like a freight train.

Every protective, possessive instinct had burst to life the instant Andrea paraded toward the beer stand, drawing more eyes than flies around syrup. The discipline Hal had spent two weeks fortifying, the heart-to-heart lectures he'd delivered to himself, crumbled the moment he saw that orchid-eyed siren coming toward him.

He didn't know why Andrea was here, but he ached to peel off those seductive clothes—one garment at a time—and greet every inch of her silky flesh with kisses and caresses. He longed to lose himself in her soft, luscious body until nothing else mattered but the ecstasy he knew awaited him. But Hal refused to drop all restraint until he knew why Andrea was here. If this was some kind of vindictive crusade he'd—

"You can be one bullheaded, difficult man, can't you, Griffin?" Andrea said, effectively cutting through his thoughts.

"You can be one impossibly alluring woman when you set your mind to it, can't you, Fletcher?" he tossed back. "So what the hell was the point of that performance?"

Andrea rose gracefully from the bed and moved toward him. Hal groaned inwardly at her bewitching smile and sparkling eyes. It was all he could do to keep from crushing her to him, but damn it, he wanted answers. Until he got them, he wasn't going to touch her. For if he did, he would be telling himself it didn't matter *why* she had come here, only that she *was* here—and he wanted her like hell blazing.

Twenty-three

Andrea halted in front of Hal, her smile faltering slightly when he made no move toward her. "Didn't you miss me at all?" she asked him flat-out.

Not miss her? Hell, that was like asking him if he would miss breathing! He had worn himself out trying not to think about her all the damned time, trying not to remember the moments of splendor he had found with no one but her.

"You did cross my mind once or twice," he said as impassionately as humanly possible.

"Is that why your friends claimed you've been behaving like a monk?"

Hal refused to answer the question, not until he knew her purpose. "What do you want? Why are you here?"

Her smile evaporated as she looped her arms around his neck. She met his intense gaze, her heart in her eyes. "I'm here because I love you," she whispered softly, sincerely. "I'm here to tell you that what I feel for you never going to change. Although, I must admit, I wanted to shake you until your teeth rattled when Gilmore told me that you paid off my interest payment."

"I wanted to make life easier for you," Hal insisted. "My brother and I went through a financial crunch not too long ago and we know what it's like."

"I don't want your money, Hal Griffin," she insisted. "I never wanted your sympathy, either. I only want *you,* just as you are. All I want is for you to love me half as much as I love you. Now and always and forever."

Hal felt the walls come tumbling down, felt himself reaching out to pull Andrea into his empty, aching arms. With a groan of defeat, his lips came down hard on hers. Never in his life had he wanted to believe a woman the way he wanted to believe Andrea.

"I'm sorry you fell in love with the wrong woman all those years ago. I'm sorry you were hurt badly," she whispered against his lips. "But I'm *not* her, Hal. I want us to grow old together. I want us to make love together, make babies together. I'll still be waiting to hold you in my arms a month from now, a hundred years from now. I'm not going to go away—ever. For me, this is *real.* It's forever. Even when you rejected me and mistrusted what I felt for you, it didn't—*won't*—change what I feel. Nothing can. I've got it bad, cowboy. What's it going to take to make you understand that I love you more than my own life? Don't you realize I risked death when I was taken hostage because I wanted to spare you?"

"God, woman," Hal said huskily. "You better mean every word you've said, because I can't fight you any longer. I've used up all my defense. I want you so bad I swear I'm going crazy!"

When his head dipped down to devour her, Andrea pressed her forefinger to his lips, holding him at bay. Then say the words I need to hear. *Mean* them, Hal Griffin. I didn't come all this way, I didn't stage that outrageous scene at the arena to get your attention for nothing. You know I've never done anything to provoke men because of what I've been through. I did it to prove that I would do *anything* for you. For me, that was like walking barefoot on live coals. It took more nerve than you can possibly imagine. It was my way of proving that I would do anything for you—short of outright murder. And if you keep refusing to believe I'll love you forever, then I just might murder *you,* you bullheaded cowboy!"

Hal tossed his head back and laughed, remembering the wolfish whistles that had him swearing under his breath, remembering that to-die-for walk that had every wrangler sitting up like a trained dog.

"You did put on one helluva show," he said eventually.

"I'm still waiting," Andrea persisted.

Hal stared down into those intriguing eyes that were rimmed with sooty lashes, and he fell all the way to the bottom of his scarred heart. "Okay, Fletcher, you win. The fact is I couldn't bear to be near another woman since the first night I touched you. I was afraid you hadn't been around enough to know what you felt, afraid the turmoil your life had become had clouded your thinking. I was afraid your feelings were only passion-deep, gratitude-deep, desperation-deep. Walking away from you was a that kept me from falling at your feet and taking the risk of making a fool of myself again—"

"Say it," Andrea cut in, grinning impishly at him. "Show a little gumption, you pigheaded, harebrained coward."

Hal mustered the courage to speak the words locked deep in his heart. It felt unnatural, damned near impossible, to bare his emotions after promising himself he would never speak of love again. It took as much gumption for him to express his feelings as it did for Andrea to incite those rowdy cowboys.

Hal rolled the words around on his tongue. "I . . . love . . . you."

"Say it again, and try to sound as if you mean it," she challenged as she pressed full-length against him.

"I love you," he murmured huskily.

"Much better," Andrea encouraged him, her face alight with satisfaction. "Now, why don't you show me, cowboy."

Hal grinned rakishly at that, drawling, *"That* I can do, ma'am . . ."

His hands splayed across her shapely hips, molding her to the hard evidence of his need. He took her parted lips beneath his, savoring the sweet taste that had lingered on his lips for more weeks than he could count. He absorbed the feel of her lush body against him. His hands shook as he reached between them to unfasten the buttons of her blouse.

Hal caught his breath when he spied the lacy, hot-pink bra that emphasized the swell of her breasts.

"Damn, woman, you did go all out, didn't you?"

His thumb brushed over the beaded nipple concealed by the sexy contraption, and she moaned in response. Eager to unveil other tantalizing secrets, his hand glided over her belly to unfasten the snap of her jeans. His eyebrows rose like mountain peaks when his fingertips came in contact with the skimpy elastic band that rode high on her bikini-clad hip. His gaze devoured her body as he pushed the jeans into a pool around her boots. The seductive underwear, designed to cover the necessities, did serve their purpose—barely. The sight was enough to drive a man insane, and make him love every minute of it.

Heat coursed heavily through his body as he knelt to discard her boots. In two shakes, Hal scooped Andrea up in his arms and carried her to bed. When she struck another provocative pose, Hal yanked off his shirt, making the pearl snaps pop like kernels of corn . . . and then he groaned out loud.

"What's wrong?" Andrea question.

"I've been riding broncs and bulls. I need a shower." Muttering, Hall kicked off his boots and undressed on his way to the bathroom, leaving a trail of garments behind him.

Amused, Andrea watched Hal dash buck-naked through the door. Rising, she followed him, peeling off her skimpy garments as she went. When she drew back the shower curtain her gaze traveled over Hal's muscled body, noting the location of each scar, each rippling muscle—and the proud thrust of his sex. The sight of him sent desire rippling through her. She ached to touch every lean, muscled inch of him, to savor each masculine contour, to communicate her love for him in ways words couldn't begin to convey.

Taking the soap from his hand, Andrea lathered him from neck to feet, feeling his flesh quiver beneath her gentle touch. She heard his sharp intake of breath when her soapy hand enfolded him, caressed him. When the shower mist sent bubbles gliding down his torso, Andrea knelt to take him into her mouth, nipping at him, suckling him until he staggered beneath the onslaught.

"Sweet Jesus," Hal hissed through his teeth. "Keep that up and I'll never make it to the bed."

Andrea smiled against his satiny length, her hand stroking from calf to inner thigh—and back again—feeling his legs tremble with each caress.

"Think of this as an eight-second ride, cowboy," she teased. "Just hang on with all your might . . ."

Hal chuckled hoarsely. "I've been hanging on for damned near two weeks. I don't have any resistance left—"

His voice fractured when her tongue encircled him once again. He braced an arm against the tiled wall when she captured him with her mouth. "No more . . ." he gasped, reaching down to hoist her to her feet. "No more . . ."

Andrea grinned, and then tossed back the words he had spoken in his attempt to lure her from her self-imposed isolation. "You're no fun, Griffin. Lighten up."

He dropped a kiss to her lips as he reached behind him to shut off the shower. Grasping her hand, he lead her back to bed. "My idea of fun is drying you off, one drop at a time."

"Sounds interesting."

Turns out, it was. By the time he finished drying her off, the heat of his kisses and caresses had Andrea begging shamelessly for him to end the wild, sweet torture. He came to her like a whirlwind of desire and she welcomed him, reveling in the magic of sharing each breath, each throb of passion that sent them spiraling over rainbows to touch the twinkling stars.

In the aftermath of lovemaking, Hal cuddled Andrea close to his heart, his hands stroking the disheveled auburn braid that flowed over her shoulder. For the first time in two weeks he felt at peace—content, relaxed, utterly satisfied.

When she'd assured him she would be here forever, Hal had made a pact with himself never to take the gift of her love for granted. He had arrived at the conclusion that being in love was a lot like maintaining his circuit standing—an ever-constant challenge. He damn well intended to keep what he had won, to ensure Andrea's happiness—and his own.

"First thing Monday morning, we're getting the blood tests and then the license," Hal announced, his voice still thick with passion.

Andrea propped up on her elbow to gape at him.

"Nash and Crista are having their wedding at Chulosa Ranch next Saturday. The guests are already invited. Would you mind sharing the limelight with them?"

Andrea's mouth dropped open.

"I don't want to wait," Hal told her. "The rodeo camp is scheduled to begin the week after the wedding. National Finals starts the first week in December. I need to focus on the competition, and I need you for inspiration."

"I'll be there, without or without a wedding, Hal. I told you that. I'm not going anywhere—ever."

Hal framed her face with his hands and grinned. "I want you there as my wife, honey. It's the only way I can be sure my rowdy friends won't proposition you when my back is turned. Cowboys can be ornery and outrageous as all get-out, but they are the most loyal group of individuals anywhere. They'll give you information about rodeo rough stock, even if they're your competition. They'll help you when you're down and out, without asking anything in return. And when a cowboy takes a wife, his friends respect that, even if they continue to razz him unmercifully and cast glances at his gorgeous bride.

"That's the code of the cowboy community. No man ignores it, not if he's worth his salt. Even in that getup you wore tonight, I wouldn't worry that one of my friends would try to steal you out from under my nose. And some out-of-towner tried to put a move on you, Rooster

Ace, and Justin would come to your rescue. They may be silently wishing they could change places with me, but they won't break the code. So . . . will you marry me?"

Andrea's eyes misted over as she smiled at him. "I thought you'd never ask."

"If Nash and Crista approve, we'll have a head-and-heel wedding."

Andrea chuckled at the comparison to a roping event. "You've got yourself a deal, cowboy."

Hal pressed a kiss to her lips and cradled her against his shoulder. "How did Jason's game go last night?"

"He played his heart out," Andrea reported. "Crista has been working with him to make sure he was in condition to play. Our team was behind by seven points in the fourth quarter. Jason threw a Hail Mary pass that was probably murder on his mending arm, but the receiver caught it in the end zone. The two-point conversion was a screen pass that hit the receiver squarely in the numbers. We won by one point."

"Sounds like the old Fletcher 'try' paid off," Hal murmured, smiling.

Andrea nodded. "But the most amazing thing of all was when Tony Braden and Friends came over at halftime to apologize. You wouldn't recognize those kids these days. They've really cleaned up their acts—cut their hair and it's western wear all the way nowadays. Brenda says they've taken more interest in school, too."

Hal smiled to himself. Although he hadn't bothered to mention it, he had called Tony once a week, reminding the teenager that he was expected to appear at rodeo camp. Hal wanted that kid to know someone cared enough to keep tabs on him.

Nash had brought all four boys to Chulosa Ranch, paid

them wages, taught them to build fence and operate farm machinery. He and Nash had decided to form their own version of Boys Town, offering guidance to wayward youths in the area.

Hal had also promised four rodeo tickets and travel arrangements for Tony and Company if they proved they were sincere about making a new start. Apparently Hal's form of bribery and long-distance surveillance was paying off.

"Did you ever give your brother permission to attend our rodeo clinic?" Hal questioned. "I'll keep a close eye on the kid, you know."

Andrea nodded. "I'm trying very hard not to be overprotective of Jason."

"Good. I'm sure he appreciates that. For a while there, he thought you planned to smother him."

"I know," Andrea murmured. "He was all I had left and I tried to cling too hard."

Andrea looked away, blinking past the tears that filled her eyes. "Hal, I never had the chance to thank you properly for digging up the truth about my parents' deaths. As difficult as our loss still is, knowing Dad had no intention of abandoning Jason and me makes the grief easier to bear." She muffled a sniff and cuddled closer. "I can't thank you enough for making it possible for me to keep the ranch."

"Justice won't be fully served until Jenna and her suga daddy have been apprehended," Hal amended. "According to Featherstone, the FBI is still trying to track them down. The sheriff is confident they'll turn up sooner o later. I won't be satisfied until Jenna gets her just des serts—served as prison rations."

"If you don't mind, I prefer to forget what's-her-nam

exists," Andrea grumbled before her lips grazed Hal's shoulder. "She's the reason I had such a difficult time convincing you to take another chance on love."

When her hand slipped beneath the sheet, Hal lost all interest in conversation. She was tuning him inside out.

He closed his eyes and mind to everything except the sheer pleasure of her touch, the delicious scent of the woman in his arms. The soul-deep satisfaction of being loved for what he was—checkered past and all—put a lump in his throat.

Only now did Hal fully comprehend the mystical power his uncle referred to. And he understood why Nash had become so hopelessly devoted to Crista. Those invisible emotional tentacles wrapped themselves around Hal until the thought of life without Andrea was inconceivable.

He knew how lost and disoriented Robert Fletcher must have been without Maggie. It must have been worse than having your heart ripped out by the taproot. Hal never wanted to endure such torment and prayed to God that he could hold onto Andrea all the days of their life—and beyond.

"God, how I love you!" Hal groaned as he pressed Andrea to her back and slid between her legs. He came to her with a tenderness that bespoke of the affection he felt in his heart. He became a living, breathing part of her, as she became an integral part of his very being. When Andrea whispered her love to him and shivered around him, Hal held her to him, feeling his body and soul shudder in helpless abandon.

This was what love was, Hal realized with a sense of awe. He wanted to protect this spirited woman from harm, cherish her forever. Because if he ever lost her, he would lose the very best part of himself. What Andrea made of him was all Hal could ever hope to be—whole, alive, and loved unconditionally.

Choctaw Jim glanced sideways, admiring the curly-headed blonde on his left arm. Crista Delaney wore a western-cut wedding gown of white satin. Lacy sleeves and dainty beaded fringe gave the garment the look of country class and style. White lace-up boots and a white straw Stetson, with a trailing veil, completed the stunning ensemble. With those hypnotic cedar-tree green eyes sparkling and a smile of sheer happiness lighting her face, Crista was a breathtakingly lovely bride.

Beaming in delight, Jim glanced at the auburn-haired young lady on his right arm. Andrea Fletcher was dressed identically to Crista, right down to the white boots with an encircling boot bracelet made of silver, heart-shaped conchos. Andrea's radiant smile and twinkling orchid eyes were focused on the other half of the wedding party that waited at the end of the red carpet that had been rolled out on the front lawn at Chulosa Ranch.

Jim smiled wryly as he glanced at the bouquet of red roses Andrea carried. Incredible what a one-way ticket to Houston could accomplish, he thought in amusement.

Jim had purposely refused to travel the circuit with Hal. He had wanted him to experience a deep loneliness before Jim sent Andrea on the flight. The tactic had worked superbly. Now Jim had the distinct pleasure of giving *two* stunning brides away to his nephews.

The wedding congregation resembled the cowboy reunions that had been held at Chulosa since the day Lev Cooper had suffered his accident. At the moment, Lev Cooper—Dogger, as he was affectionately called—sat in his wheelchair on the front lawn, smiling proudly as he served as Nash's best man. Jason Fletcher stood beside Hal, decked out in his western best.

Contentment burgeoned in Choctaw Jim's heart as he strode forward, watching Hal and Nash focus rapt attention on their brides. Both men were dressed in black, western-cut jackets, dress jeans, and black Stetsons. Boutonnières of red roses were pinned to their lapels—at Hal's insistence. He had developed a curious sentimental attachment to red roses of late.

Nash's amber-eyed gaze glowed down on Crista, while Hal's black-diamond eyes sparkled on Andrea. Jim broke into a wide grin, knowing his nephews were suffering severe cases of tunnel vision, so intent was their focus on the approaching brides.

Twice, Choctaw Jim had devised subtle methods of playing Cupid. He wanted to be sure his nephews discovered the kind of love Jim had shared with his wife. If Kathy had lived they would have been celebrating their thirty-fifth wedding anniversary, Jim recalled. The love Jim had discovered—and lost—those long years ago had been revived. He could feel it radiating in the adoring gazes of his nephews. There were unspoken promises of love—the greatest, most rewarding gift ever to be given and shared.

Jim smiled at the memory of Kathy's beguiling young face—a face that time had never erased from his mind. He knew his wife was watching this ceremony with the same sense of satisfaction. Unexplainable warmth swept through Jim's soul, a quiet voice whispered in his heart. *In them, I will always see us. Love without end . . .*

Choctaw Jim felt tears pooling in the corners of his eyes as he offered Crista and Andrea to their grooms. A lump grew in his throat as Jim listened to Nash and Hal voice their vows of love and honor, heard Crista and Andrea return them with the same sincerity.

Love without end, our legacy . . . the silent voice whispered again, and Choctaw Jim smiled that knowing smile that his nephews had never understood . . . until now . . .

Nash drew Hal aside during the reception. To Hal's bemusement, his brother presented him with a package and a spray of flowers. "What the hell is this for?"

"Open it," Nash insisted, grinning wickedly.

Glancing from his brother to the package, Hal set the flower arrangement on the table and opened the box. With a befuddled frown he unveiled the rope that had a hangman's noose fashioned on one end of it.

Nash grinned wryly. "You once said—and I quote—'If I ever start acting as pitifully lovesick as you, get a rope. I plan to hang myself.' " Nash gestured toward the arrangement of flowers and continued quoting his younger brother. " 'The day I admit to love is the same day I'll roll over and die.' "

Hal groaned at his own cynicism. "Thanks for reminding me of my hanging and my funeral," he grumbled. "Nothing like making a man eat his words on his wedding day."

"Crow goes well with cake and punch, don't you think?" Nash teased unmercifully.

Hal set the package aside, his gaze drifting to Andrea. "She's worth all your harassment," he murmured. "She's the very breath I breathe."

Nash's teasing grin faded as his golden-eyed gaze sought out Crista. "I know exactly what you mean."

With shiny gold bands on their fingers, the brothers
Griffin stood aside, watching their brides being passed
down the receiving line of eager cowboys. Rooster Anderson, the ornery rascal, took excessive pleasure in bending both brides over backward, making a dramatic display
of kissing Andrea and Crista squarely on the mouth. Then
he flung Nash and Hal a wickedly mischievous grin.

"You wanna kill that scamp or shall I do it?" Nash
muttered to his brother.

Hal chuckled, then sipped his spiked punch—compliments of Ace Ketcham, he suspected. "Rooster lives to
crow. He's trying to get a rise out of us."

"It's working," Nash replied as he watched Rooster
pass Crista to the next pair of brawny arms.

"What are you whining about, big brother? He gets one
kiss. You've got Curly for the rest of your life . . . What
the hell does Justin think he's doing!"

Nash grabbed Hal's arm when the Montana Kid decided
to outdo Rooster by scooping Andrea up in his arms to
deliver a long smooch.

"Steady, boy," Nash snickered. "Practice what you
preach."

"I don't mind the kissing. It's the tonsillectomy I object
to," Hal grumbled. When Justin grinned in playful glee,
Hal grumbled a curse into his punch glass. His irritation
turned to amusement when both Andrea and Crista sank
down on Levi Cooper's lap. He winked at Nash and Hal
when both brides took turns kissing him a half-dozen
times apiece.

Nash and Hal smiled at the man who was like their
adopted brother. Through the trials and torments that came
with watching Levi cope with his crippling accident, their
sense of loyalty had faltered only once. And in the end,

the friendship that had been established years ago had strengthened into an unbreakable bond.

"I don't see how you're going to concentrate on National Finals with your pretty bride constantly underfoot," Nash murmured.

Hal watched Andrea covetously. "I'll manage." He set his punch glass aside. "Don't know about you, Nash, but I've enjoyed this reception business as long as I can stand."

"I thought maybe I was the only one getting impatient." Nash fell into step beside his brother. "Enjoy your honeymoon, Hal."

"You, too, big brother."

"Don't call me in Fort Worth," Nash warned.

"I don't expect to hear from you while we're in Dallas, either."

The cowboys roared in playful approval when the Griffin brothers scooped up their brides and carried them away.

National Finals was the farthest thing from Hal's mind when he finally got Andrea alone in the swank hotel in Dallas. She noted that it was no Cloud Nine Motel, and she heartily approved of that!

Of course, the five-star hotel that Nash had booked in Fort Worth was nothing to scoff at, either. Hal had the unshakable feeling the other Griffin bride and groom would be enjoying room service more than the sightseeing tours in Texas's sister city.

As for Hal, he was entirely too busy being a model husband to give a Tinker's damn about what was going on in Dallas.

Twenty-four

Andrea sat in the grandstands of Thomas and Mack Arena, her hands clasped around the arms of her box seat. Jason and the four reformed young boys from Hochukbi were seated beside her. Nash, Crista, and Levi Cooper were sitting behind her. Although Andrea was surrounded by family and friends, she found no comfort in their presence. Her total attention was transfixed on chute number four.

Over the past ten days of National Rodeo Finals in Las Vegas, she had been walking on pins and needles, uncaring that Hal had scored high in each event, unconcerned that he had racked up winnings that staggered the mind. Though the title of All-Around Cowboy depended on Hal's last bareback bronc ride, Andrea simply wanted her husband in one piece. She was compelled by the need to protect the happiness they had shared these past few weeks.

Even the gratifying news Andrea had received that morning hadn't eased the apprehension roiling through her. Jenna Randall and an individual named Jim Carlson had been apprehended in California. Carlson, the head of a construction corporation that did business around the country, had been picked up in Los Angeles. According to Sheriff Featherstone, the Feds had raised their eyebrows at Carlson's business ethics twice in the past five years, but they had been unable to pin anything conclusive on him and his private secretary.

After the incident in Kanima County, the FBI had been able to link Carlson to Mafia ties that backed his projects. Carlson's most recent project had been a multi-million-dollar ski resort in the Colorado Rockies. The clientele, it was discovered, was using the remote resort to make illegal business arrangements and contacts. The hunting and fishing hamlet in the wooded hills of Kanima County would have been the third such rendezvous in the States, but thanks to Hal's efforts Carlson had been shut down. So had the swank resorts, and now Jenna Randall was living in the kind of accommodations she deserved—a no-frills jail cell.

Andrea was thankful that grisly business was behind her. Now, if only she could survive this final go-round without suffering a nervous breakdown!

"Hal Griffin will be tearing out of chute number four on Stampede, the saddle bronc named PRCA's Bucking Horse last year," the announcer informed the crowd. "Stampede is one tough bronc, ladies and gents. Let's cheer this cowboy from Oklahoma all the way to the buzzer."

"I can't watch," Andrea muttered, squeezing her eyes shut. "Nine days of holding my breath, hoping Hal doesn't get hurt, has my nerves tangled like a ball of twine."

Powder-blue eyes twinkling, Levi Cooper reached down to pat Andrea on the shoulder. "Relax, Mrs. Griff. Hal has been going gangbusters all week. He won't let Stampede get the best of him."

Andrea wasn't to be consoled. When she heard the chute gate slam open, heard the bronc's whinny and snort she prayed for all she was worth. *God, don't let him get hurt,* she chanted continuously.

When the crowd bounded to its feet, Andrea groped for Levi's comforting hand. "Helluva ride you're missing," Levi chuckled. "Hal is halfway home."

Andrea pried one eye open, watching the bronc bury its head between its front legs and kick with such force that Hal's head snapped backwards. Her heart thudded in rhythm with each high-flying leap. She cringed when denim slammed down hard against the saddle, knowing that angry bundle of bucking fury was wrinkling Hal's spine like an accordion.

She had watched him rise from bed each morning—slowly—trying to conceal his grimaces. She couldn't begin to imagine the fierce pain that was now shooting through his arm while he held onto unleashed fury. Never again would she make the stupid mistake of referring to rodeo as an "entertaining performance." It was an endurance test of sheer strength, a fierce battle of wills.

"Two seconds left!" the announcer called out.

Andrea swallowed an arena full of air. Her heart stalled in her chest, her anxious gaze glued to the bronzed face clenched with determination. When the buzzer sounded, she bounded to her feet. Scrambling down the aisle of cheering spectators, she charged toward ringside, her legs vibrating like tuning forks.

"Ladies and gents, Hal Griffin scores an eighty-four and clinches the saddle bronc crown. You are also looking at professional rodeo's All-Around Cowboy of the Year," he announcer added excitedly. "This fine cowboy sewed t up with one whale of a ride!"

* * *

Hal climbed over the fence and was immediately swallowed up by a crowd of friends converging to offer their congratulations. He glanced over to see Choctaw Jim smiling proudly. All Jim's pointers had paid off. Hal had won the All-Around title and the perks that went with it.

The patter of hurried footsteps caught Hal's attention. He glanced over the sea of cowboy hats to see Andrea dashing down the concrete runway.

She saw the gleam of pride and satisfaction glowing in Hal's eyes as she ran headlong toward him. She was pleased for him, but she wanted to make sure he was safe and sound. That was all that mattered.

"Stand aside, men," Rooster Anderson ordered, grinning in amusement when he saw Andrea. "Mrs. Griff has a full head of steam and she's roaring our way."

As the crowd parted, Andrea flung herself into Hal's waiting arms, showering him with enthusiastic kisses. "I love you," she babbled repeatedly as he hooked his arm beneath her knees and cradled her to his chest.

Laughing eyes twinkled down at her. "You aren't just saying that because I acquired a new title, are you, Mrs. Griff?"

"Don't you dare even think it," Andrea admonished, tears shimmering in her eyes. "Are you okay?"

"Uh-huh," he murmured.

"Sure?"

"Never better, honey."

Andrea wiggled loose, grabbed his gloved hand, and towed him up the runway. "Rooster, you're in charge of gathering this cowboy's gear," she delegated.

"Yes, ma'am," Rooster said with a mock salute. "Anything else, Mrs. Griff?"

"Don't call our room."

Hal's brows shot up. He met each wry smile on every face he passed as Andrea led him away.

"You think they don't know what you've got in mind?" he chuckled as he slid onto the seat of his truck.

"Do you think I care?" Andrea countered. "I've got ten days of anxiety bottled up, ten days of going nuts while you rode and roped, praying you didn't crash land. I'll need valium by the truckload if I have to sit through these ordeals on a regular basis." She heaved a shaky sigh and glanced apologetically at her handsome husband. "I'm sorry to report that I'm turning out to be a lousy rodeo star's wife. My nerves of steel have melted into molasses."

Hal peered into her pallid face, touched by her concern and the depth of her love for him. "If it's all right with you, Mrs. Griff, I'll use my winnings to secure Fletcher Ranch. I'd like to settle into raising beef cattle and training rodeo mounts. Brother Nash seems to have adapted to off-road life easily enough."

Andrea muffled a sniff. "I can't ask you to do that for me. You love rodeo. I'd never forgive myself if I were responsible for depriving you of something that makes you happy."

"You make me happy," Hal assured her. "I'm doing this for us."

When they reached their hotel room, Andrea threw herself into his arms once again, nuzzling her head against his shoulder. He didn't dare tell her he'd pulled a few already-strained muscles that Stampede had aggravated with those jarring bucks and landings.

Hal had claimed the one title he had been chasing for five years, as well as the winnings and endorsements that came with the territory. But more than that, he had Andrea to fill up his days with her vibrant spirit and laughter. And he had her passion to burn down the nights.

When the phone blared, Andrea withdrew from his arms. "If that ornery Rooster is on the phone, I'll take off his head," she promised vindictively.

When she picked up the phone, Hal suddenly recalled the mischievous promise he'd made to her two months earlier. She was about to discover how difficult it was to carry on a phone conversation while distracted by amorous advances.

"Yes, this is Andrea Griffin."

Hal's hand swept down the front of Andrea's colorful western blouse with practiced ease. Grinning in ornery delight, he bent his head to brush his lips against the swell of her breast.

"Thank you." Andrea's breath wobbled when Hal's moist lips skimmed across her responsive skin. "No, as a matter of fact—"

Hal chuckled devilishly when her voice shuddered the instant his hands glided down the zipper of her jeans.

"Could I get back to you later?" Andrea requested as Hal pressed her backwards onto the bed.

When she tried to replace the receiver, his lips skimmed the beaded peak he had exposed while she was trying to talk on the phone. The receiver landed with a muffled clank on the carpet. Andrea moaned softly, her body arching instinctively toward Hal's masterful touch.

"You are a genuine devil," she managed to say.

"I was only returning the favor," he reminded her. His lips moved across her belly to sensitize the silky flesh of her inner thigh. "Who called?"

"Just some hot-shot rodeo sponsor who wanted you

endorse western gear and clothing. He was going to pay you big bucks for ads and commercials, cowboy."

Hal jerked up his head, horrified. Andrea giggled impishly. "Not to worry, All-Around rodeo star. Mr. Allen said he would talk to you at the awards banquet at Caesar's Palace. He wants you—almost as badly as I do."

Hal stared at those captivating orchid eyes and that breathtaking smile. He knew beyond all doubt that he had dared to give his battered heart to the one and only woman who would treasure the gift of his love, who would protect him as he would always protect her. Hal could see eternity in Andrea's adoring gaze, knew that love was not the illusion he once believed it to be.

What Hal felt for Andrea, what she so generously returned, was almost tangible. It shimmered between them like radiant heat.

"I love you with all my heart," Hal whispered reverently.

"I'll love you forever," Andrea promised him.

And then Hal took his beloved wife in his arms and made love to her with every fiber of his being. He gave her all that he was—heart, body, and soul—forever and the eternity beyond . . .

A Note from the Author

I hope you enjoyed the sequel to *River Moon,* which was published in June, 1996. I wish to extend a special thank you to every professional rodeo cowboy who has been an inspiration in the writing of *River Moon* and *Crimson Moon.*

My next book, *Once Upon a Midnight Moon,* will be released in September, 1997. I hope you will join me again for another adventure into romance.

Wishing you love and laughter,

Carol Finch

Carol Finch
http://www.nettrends.com/carolfinch

YOU WON'T WANT TO READ
JUST ONE—KATHERINE STONE

ROOMMATES   (0-8217-5206-5, $6.99/$7 99)
No one could have prepared Carrie for the monumental
changes she would face when she met her new circle of friends
at Stanford University. Once their lives intertwined and became
woven into the tapestry of the times, they would never be the
same.

TWINS   (0-8217-5207-3, $6.99/$7.99)
Brook and Melanie Chandler were so different, it was hard to
believe they were sisters. One was a dark, serious, ambitious
New York attorney; the other, a golden, glamourous, sophisti-
cated supermodel. But they were more than sisters—they were
twins and more alike than even they knew . . .

THE CARLTON CLUB   (0-8217-5204-9, $6.99/$7.99)
It was the place to see and be seen, the only place to be. And
for those who frequented the playground of the very rich, i
was a way of life. Mark, Kathleen, Leslie and Janet—they
worked together, played together, and loved together, all behind
exclusive gates of the *Carlton Club*.

Available wherever paperbacks are sold, or order direct from th
Publisher. Send cover price plus 50¢ per copy for mailing an
handling to Penguin USA, P.O. Box 999, c/o Dept. 1710\$
Bergenfield, NJ 07621. Residents of New York and Tennesse
must include sales tax. DO NOT SEND CASH.